'It could be some instrument to measure tides and currents . . . part of the Russians' oceanographic programme.'

'Could be. But it could also be something completely different. An idea hit me when we were sailing towards the Spanish coast this afternoon. Do you remember what's up beyond that headland towards Cadiz?'

George looked blankly at him.

'Rota,' Joe said triumphantly. 'The United States Navy Polaris sub base at Rota. That's what I think this thing was designed to study—American nuclear submarines, not tides and fish. The mor[illegible] I think about it, th[illegible] make[illegible]'

Ge[illegible]

CLINTON IS ASSIGNED

Malcolm McConnell

Hamlyn Paperbacks

CLINTON IS ASSIGNED

ISBN 0 600 32116 9

First published in Great Britain 1979 by
Hamlyn Paperbacks

Hamlyn Paperbacks are published by
The Hamlyn Publishing Group Ltd,
Astronaut House,
Feltham,
Middlesex, England

Made and printed in Great Britain by
Hazell Watson & Viney Ltd
Aylesbury, Bucks

ELINT (ee'lint) *n.* Acronym, Electronic Intelligence. 1. The acquisition of military information by electronic means, generally involving the use of remote sensing apparatus on an aircraft, ship, or space vehicle.

The job of an operations officer calls for dedication to the point of obsession, if you try to do it well. You have too many secrets; you can't relax with outsiders. It's a very unnatural life, hard on the people who live it. There's a lot of alcoholism and a lot of emotional breakdowns in the C.I.A.

—*Philip Agee, in a*
Playboy *interview,*
August, 1975

* * * * * *

The Soviets' ways are infinitely more sophisticated than the cloak-and-dagger methods of the past, and U.S. experts frankly admit that "they're pretty damn good"—in a minority view, "maybe a little better than we are."

These days, the Russians "are sending over young men who are more American than the Americans," intelligence sources say.

—Newsweek,
August 4, 1975

Prologue

The astronaut awoke before his two companions. He yawned, the pure oxygen tightening his already-dry nose and mouth. The numbers blinking silently on the digital display of elapsed mission time told him there were still four minutes remaining in the first sleep period. The in-flight emergency panel showed only emerald stars. No problems. Behind them, on the service module, a thruster clicked and thumped. He loosened his Dacron sleeping straps and floated nearer the navigation port. His breath no longer fogged the Plexiglas as it had back in the parking orbit.

Earth hung blue and white in the black sky. It was so much smaller now than before they had gone to sleep. His Rolex was set to Greenwich Mean Time: 7:59 P.M., Thur., Jul. 17. At the angle from which he looked, he could not see their goal, the moon.

He gazed at England. Once he had taken his oldest son to the observatory at Greenwich, and he showed him the old brass chronometers inside their primitive vacuum jars. The British Isles were white and gray-green. It was summer twilight there. North America was mostly cloudless, some cumulus in the Rockies, and a series of squall lines in the Gulf, moving north. Houston was clear, hot brown. But he knew those thunder squalls would hit before evening.

There was a lot of cloud in the Amazon basin, all the way up into Colombia. The Pacific was blue and so big, almost half the planet. It would be noon down there. In the Soviet Arctic it was past ten at night. Most of southern Europe and Africa had already slipped over the terminator into night. Spain and Morocco were beige against the blue evening Atlantic. The Straits of Gibraltar were cloudless.

He stretched inside his suit, feeling his toes, far away, remote in zero gravity.

Soon there would be orange juice, calcium tablets, and coffee; then flight-plan updates and guidance calibration would come from Houston. His two comrades slept in the dim cabin. One was upside down, held immobile by his soft Dacron web. Life support hummed beneath their couches. Another thruster thumped. He watched the planet's disc growing slowly smaller.

Eighty-six thousand four hundred nautical miles away, in a soundproof, air-conditioned cubicle, a young man sat at a Fiberglas console, listening to the Greenwich time-signal beep in his miniature earphone. Outside the building it was a humid, south Texas summer morning. In the CAP COMM Booth, the air was chilly dry.

The final, longer beep ended. He pushed a green key bar and touched a yellow button on the console.

"Columbia, Houston here. . . . Good morning, Columbia, Houston here. How copy? Good morning, gentlemen, Houston here. How copy?"

Far to the south, in the Pacific, between Easter and Sala-y-Gomez islands, an American Polaris submarine cruised almost soundlessly eighty feet below the long swell of the Southeast Trades. It was noon, local time. The number two navigation periscope cut the slight chop on the slopes of the swell. Another young man waited in a soundproof, air-conditioned room for the final, longer time beep from the bulkhead speaker. Unlike the CAP COMM or the astronaut, this young man was nervous. He sat in a gimbled navigator's saddle with his eye to the rubber socket of the periscope sextant.

Lieutenant, Junior Grade, Corcoran was not good with the sextant, but he had two more noon sights to do, as well as early morning stars, before Commander Peters would sign off on the lieutenant's conversion exams. It was a pain in the ass, but necessary, even with the Tango

Lima satellite fixes and the computerized inertial guidance.

The Greenwich time beep ended. Lieutenant Corcoran swung the sextant's index arm, sweeping the black disc of the sun down to the heaving horizon in his eyepiece.

"Mark," he said.

"Mark," the quartermaster standing next to the periscope repeated.

Commander Peters looked over the quartermaster's shoulder to read the numbers on the micrometer head. "Not bad, Bob," he said to Lieutenant Corcoran. "At least you got us in the Southern Hemisphere today."

Lieutenant Corcoran smiled. The noon sun shot was no sweat. But what about those early morning stars? He looked at the three million dollars' worth of navigational electronics that took up the full forward bulkhead of the control room.

NAV DISPLAY, PRESENT POSITION read:

23°14′9″ SOUTH LAT
109°46′11″ WEST LON

As Lieutenant Corcoran watched, the seconds of latitude blinked from nine to ten, and the submarine's silent engines drove it south and east, toward Cape Horn, at twenty-eight knots.

The cubicle on the second lower level of the hardened bunker near Varzino was air-conditioned, but not soundproofed. Even with the air-conditioning plant working, however, the combination of Arctic summer thaw above ground and thousands of cubic meters of racked electronics down in the Pit made the atmosphere in which the young man sat uncomfortably humid. The woolen uniform did not help much, either. He was a technical warrant officer, first class, in the naval air arm, a member of Komsomol, and, if he passed his examinations in September and did not get caught "shitting in his sheets," as these air force punks up here all said, he would soon have a regular commission and a chance for eventual Party membership.

The console at which he sat was made of plywood,

steel, and plastic. It would look awkward, antique, if compared to the CAP COMM's in Houston. This entire lower level smelled strongly of hot electronics and tobacco. His earphones were made of thick Bakelite, and they always gave him a headache by the end of his two-hour watch.

He listened to the Greenwich time beep. The final, longer beep ended. On his console screen the scan printing began:

2000
17 JULY 1969
ORBIT 214
COMM/RECONN AUTO STATION VICTOR
ALPHA ROMEO 126

A bell rang softly on his keyboard panel. On the screen, below the identification block, a green star was pulsing:

STATE SECRET OMEGA PRIORITY
STATE SECRET OMEGA PRIORITY

KEY DAILY ACCESS CODE BEFORE PROCEEDING
KEY DAILY ACCESS CODE BEFORE PROCEEDING

He punched out the seven required code digits. Forty meters above his cubicle, on the soggy tundra, a large disc antenna whirred to lock into the satellite as it cleared the earth's horizon to the north and west.

Five hundred eighty kilometers above the North Pole, a three-ton Soviet Military Communications and Reconnaissance satellite, bearing the NATO code name Kingfish, fired thrusters to turn its high-gain antenna and lock onto the signal from the Varzino station.

The satellite's infrared sensors adjusted themselves to the base datum of the polar icecap below. The relatively primitive on-board computer acquired, analyzed, and readied for high-speed telemetric transmission the performance data from the instruments within the titanium pressure sphere. This took .786 seconds.

A program tape stopped, advanced two millimeters slowly, then continued its loop. The primary mission function tape moved one-half millimeter to the transmit head. The satellite was now ready to talk with the technical warrant officer at Varzino.

It was 2000.19 Greenwich Mean Time.

The warrant officer at the console keyed five more buttons. On his screen words appeared:

STATION OPERATION: STANDARD
ORBIT INTEGRITY PREDICTION: STANDARD (POSITIVE)
ORBIT ANOMALY PREDICTIONS (ORBITS 215 THROUGH 218): NEGATIVE
PRIMARY MISSION FUNCTION DATA TRANSMIT:

PROCEEDING
PROCEEDING
PROCEEDING

COMPLETED
COMPLETED

The young man punched the data analysis keys. On his screen two new green stars flashed and pulsed. A buzzer sounded on the left side of the console.

NEGATIVE READING: MARINE RECONN STATION
GEORGE KILO FOXTROT 18

NEGATIVE READING: MARINE RECONN STATION
GEORGE KILO FOXTROT 18

"You sow fucker," the young man whispered. "Why does it have to happen on *my* watch?"

He punched out the data repeat code. A pink bulb lit

atop his console. He could hear Captain Ravankov's muddy boots coming down the concrete stairs.

One thousand eight hundred twenty-six miles to the south and east, at 5°10′3″ West Longitude, a metallic tube, shaped roughly like a one-ended weightlifter's dumbbell, rose on a stainless steel cable from a winch anchored in the ocean mud. The tube arrested its ascent one meter below the choppy surface of the Firth of Clyde. A Teflon-encased whip antenna extended like a wand above the waves.

The sky was rose twilight, cool, with some broken cirrus clouds to the west. A quarter-ton sloop passed the antenna, missing it by thirty yards on the port beam. The man at the tiller was talking to his son and trying to watch the luff of the jib. He did not see the antenna's foam track in the tidal stream.

"Look, Daddy," the little boy said, pointing up, "a shooting star!"

"No, Ian," the man said, "it's only one of those space satellites. See how slowly it moves?"

"But it's like a *star*."

"The sun makes it twinkle so."

Five hundred sixty kilometers over the Firth of Clyde, the Soviet satellite fired its thrusters again. The high-gain antenna turned parallel to the earth's North Magnetic Pole.

From the antenna near the sailboat, a burst of ultra-high-frequency radio energy was transmitted. The two machines spoke to each other in binary, digital language.

001—11—101—0001100—111-01-0111-101011—00. . . .

The total transmission time was 1.8 seconds. In that period, 14,500 bits of data were transmitted and the frequency was changed three times.

The satellite moved south, toward the Iberian peninsula and Africa and its next station, the errant George Kilo Foxtrot 18. The antenna telescoped back into the tube and the anchored winch took up the slackening cable as the tube's ballast tanks were flooded with sea water, and it descended back down into the safe darkness.

Four thousand yards away, in the deeper water of the main shipping channel, a fleet strategic Polaris submarine was moving almost silently south-southwest at a depth of two hundred and thirty feet and a speed of nine knots. On the surface, ahead and behind the submarine, Royal Navy mine sweepers churned along slowly, towing submerged decoy-noise devices. On the polluted mud of the bottom, the metal dumbbell listened to the cacophony. Inside its pressure hull, magnetic tapes moved slowly across recording heads.

In the cockpit of the sloop, the little boy was shivering. "I can't see it anymore," he said to his father. "The shooting star's gone."

In the concrete Pit at Varzino, four officers had gathered around the young warrant officer's console.

"Where *is* Marine Reconn Station George Kilo Foxtrot 18?"

"It's the new buoy at Rota, sir," the captain said somberly to the senior colonel. "They just got it deployed last week, sir. It's the new modification . . . with the Kaleidoscope Frequency Spreader."

The senior colonel glared at the captain. The junior colonel shifted his boots on the concrete, and the warrant officer stared at his own gnawed fingernails.

"Rota, sir," the major said helpfully. "The Polaris base in Spain."

The senior colonel turned to face the major. "Shitmouth!" he swore. "Don't you think I know where *Rota* is? When do we next query the Bird?"

"Twenty-one forty-six," the junior colonel said quickly, getting his information from the console screen.

"Assholes, cocks, and bleeding clap," the senior colonel said to the low ceiling. "I want tide and current patterns for that entire coast. Immediately!"

The warrant officer began punching out keys on his console. He glanced nervously over his shoulder, but the senior colonel was still looking at the ceiling. "There is a file," he said, his voice softer, "a file on that buoy lost last year, the one that came adrift off Subic Bay. I'd like a print-out of that, as soon as possible, please."

The junior colonel exchanged looks with the major. "Please," this *was* serious.

"And get me the Ministry on the scrambler, please. Priority. I'll be in my office."

The four officers came to attention. The senior colonel limped away on his bad leg.

He was a hero of the Soviet Union from the Great Patriotic War, a man who had flown the old Stormovik–3's right into the teeth of the panzers outside Stalingrad. But, now, if that listening buoy at Rota were truly lost, or, worse, had been intercepted by the other side, he was a ruined man.

Five hundred sixty kilometers above the Cadiz harbor, the Soviet satellite, code-named Kingfish, fired its thrusters and re-aligned its high-gain antenna with the earth's North Magnetic Pole. The program tape advanced inside the pressure sphere and the antenna transmitted a micro-burst of U.H.F.

The satellite listened for an answer. There was none. It transmitted once more on an alternate frequency. No reply. The primary mission function tape advanced.

Tumbling slightly in the weak solar wind, the satellite lost its antenna orientation. The secondary mission function tape advanced. In thirty-eight minutes the satellite would transmit again, to a fleet-attack submarine that was tracking an American Polaris vessel near Easter Island, en route from Subic Bay, in the Philippines, to Rota, in Spain.

PART I

Rights of Salvage

1

The Wire Service Man

There was at least one excellent reason why Joe Clinton should not have sailed to Targa alone: he had never singlehandedly taken *Dragonfly* outside the Tangier harbor, and he handled his boat like he did most other things, impulsively, even when sober. Before this, the farthest he had ever gone was across to Gibraltar, and then George Briggs and Harry Rains had been along to help out with the sheets. Now he was alone, sailing a twenty-four-foot sloop through some of the busiest shipping lanes in the world. The course from Tangier Yacht Club to the anchorage beneath the ruined watchtower at Targa was sixty-one miles. It ran northeast into the Straits, rounded Cape Malabata, then cut south past Ceuta. It was a difficult day's sail. If a man did not know his boat, the rules of the road, and have an instinctive feel for tide and current, he could easily get into serious trouble.

Joe was in trouble. At sunset, *Dragonfly* was becalmed, rolling unpleasantly in the residual Atlantic swell fourteen miles from Targa. She was also in the westbound shipping lane, a wooden-masted boat without a radar reflector. Joe Clinton was quite drunk, having finished a good part of the bottle of Teacher's that Renée O'Brien had reluctantly bought him at the embassy commissary in Rabat. Doing the sensible thing, running into Ceuta under power to sober up, was out of the question. It would be a public admission of failure. And failure was a sensitive subject for Joe. Besides, he'd told Renée, George, and Harry that he was sailing to Targa. So, by God, he was going to sail there.

The evening sky above the Rif was that pleasant blue the Japanese always painted on their porcelain, even the cheap crap they used to peddle to the G.I.'s. The breeze, before it died, had been from the port quarter. Now the sails were slack and they flapped annoyingly as the boat rose and dropped with the swell. Joe began sheeting in the mainsail and working jib.

It definitely was time to start the engine. It would be dark soon and there were ships out there in the twilight.

Okay, open the fuel cock. Reach down and flip the injector pump primer. Kind of sick-making, leaning down like that and smelling the bilge. Fuel on, pump primed, advance the throttle. Now the key.

Oh, *shit*. He had forgotten to turn off the ignition key when he'd shut down the engine outside the Tangier breakwater. All this time, since before noon, the battery had been draining into the alternator. He tried to remember the simple formula . . . twelve volts times ten amps equals? . . . Technology was not his big number, never had been, although he'd faked his way through plenty of scientific pieces when he'd had to. But this was not a matter of filing copy for some U.P.I. editor in Paris. This little problem with a dead battery and no wind was what they used to call The Real World.

A dead battery meant no navigation lights; maybe a nasty bump from a freighter in the dark. It also meant having to hand-crank the engine to start it. In the operator's manual this procedure looked easy. But in actuality the operation required two people.

"You screwed up again, Clinton," he said to the empty evening sky.

This was the type of situation the kids at Khe Sahn used to call Flaky-Slash-Nasty. Well, there wasn't anybody shooting at the noncombatant here, and there *were* red and green kerosene lamps some damned place down in that mess in the forepeak. So . . . no sweat, for the moment. At least it wasn't dark yet.

The problem was, he thought, unscrewing the cap of the Teacher's bottle, that he seemed to have this *propensity* for these types of situations. Good word, that. You can still say a word like "propensity"; means you're not so flaky.

Monique had never liked him using "grunt language." She had found it affected. It hadn't been just a language problem, either. She spoke English as well as he did. It was simply that she had always felt that he should have tried to be more of a *journaliste* and less of a reporter.

A light breeze rippled the surface of the water. The sky certainly was pretty tonight. There was the first star, evening summer star, latitude thirty-five North. That would make that baby either Mercury, Venus, or Mars. Lot of help there, if he ever had to use a sextant.

Joe lit one of Renée's PX Kents and looked at the brown Moroccan coast, trying to see from the swelling crests just exactly where it was he was supposed to be going. If he was lucky, the breeze would come up again, onshore, after dark and he would be snugly anchored and buttoned up before midnight . . . at Targa. That nice beach at Targa, where he and Renée had made love, standing up, in the ruins of the Portuguese watchtower. . . . But Renée was still down in Rabat. This was only Thursday.

Joe was going to Targa to be alone, ostensibly to write, for a few days before Renée and the others arrived. He had brought along his Olivetti portable and the manuscript. They were wrapped in plastic in *Dragonfly*'s starboard cabin locker. In Tangier it had been relatively easy to convince his friends and even himself that he would finish the book for Hawks and Spencer. But alone out here on the boat he had to face hard reality. The book was dead. Now he had to make some decisions about his future. For almost ten years, since he was twenty-four years old, his world had been redefined daily, sometimes hourly, as a new story broke and he joined the stampede to the nearest Telex, telephone, or radio transmitter.

A wire service man was not supposed to agonize about the future. He went where the story was and he filed copy, as fast and as accurately as possible. The story had taken Joe to some of the more exotic parts of the planet. He had eaten rice with Chinese farmers on Quemoy and boiled manioc with Congolese soldiers in Stanleyville. He had shared his canteen with Israeli paratroopers at the capture of the Wailing Wall and chewed stale C-ration fruitcake with the marines outside the Citadel in Hué. He had followed the story, in rented trucks, by riverboat, and in the sweaty troop bays of armored personnel carriers. Once, in Indonesia, he had ridden all day on the back of a water buffalo to get an eyewitness view of an erupting volcano. He had arrived in Biafra aboard a limping old Constellation, two engines smoking from the Nigerian flak. Joe Clinton had been on the road since 1960, a long and troubled route.

Along the way he had acquired the ability to write five hundred fast words on a great variety of topics, a Whitney Prize for Distinguished Overseas Journalism, and a fondness for alcohol in most of its known, non-lethal forms. He had also acquired a French wife named Monique, a son named Joseph Clinton, Jr., and a pretty little house among the expatriate villas on Tangier's new mountain road. He still had the Prize citation, which Larry Burroughs had presented him that night at the Overseas Press Club. But his wife had left him, and, lately, he had trouble typing even a letter.

Misfortune had overtaken Joe in the spring of 1968, when, by most measurable standards, he was approaching the zenith of his personal and professional life. The year before, the Wailing Wall story had won him the Whitney Prize. In turn, the Prize had secured him a contract from Hawks and Spencer for a book on the American media in Vietnam. With the advance on the book, he and Monique had made a down payment on the Tangier house. They seemed suddenly to have become lucky. At a Gibraltar auction they purchased, for a bargain price, the effects of a deceased inspector of colonial police: a houseful of Hong Kong teak furniture, a rebuilt Land Rover, and the old sailboat. Monique was pregnant with their second child and Joe was finally off the road, working in his own studio on a real book.

Remembering it now a year later, Joe realized he had brought the trouble on himself. If he hadn't gone back to I Corps for Tet, if he had only stayed in Tangier. . . . But he *had* gone back. And Monique had returned to Paris to have the baby. He had joined her in May. Even then it might not have been too late, but he had insisted on going to the Left Bank to cover the riots, leaving Monique, eight months pregnant, alone with Joey in the suburban Creteuil duplex, without electricity or telephone, in the mounting chaos of the general strike. If only he had stayed where he belonged, working on his book in Tangier, there would not have been the miscarriage and Monique would not now be married to another man.

One year had passed since then. It was summer again, July. Lyndon Johnson was back in Texas; the Russians were in Prague. And Joe Clinton lived alone on the new mountain road.

Alone, Joe realized, was not an accurate adjective to describe his life in Tangier. He lived there without his wife and son, but almost every weekend for the past six months, Renée O'Brien had come up from the embassy in Rabat to be with him. Often, she made the four-hour drive on the muddy coast road after working all day Friday just to have an extra night with him. Most weekends she brought Tommy, her son, and put him to bed in her own small house in the Casbah before driving up the mountain to spend the night with Joe. She always left before dawn, however, in order to be home when Tommy awoke.

Joe understood what the weekend trips cost Renée, in guilt and pride. Renée was a decent, serious woman. That winter they had often lain on the sheepskins in front of Joe's fireplace, talking gently after lovemaking about marriage and divorce and the absolute need to protect the guiltless children who had been born into lives structured around court-ordained visiting rights and parents who lived on separate sides of the planet.

They had also talked about love. They had spoken the word to each other. They had demonstrated the emotion with their lips, fingers, and bodies. And every Sunday night Renée had driven back down that broken coast road to Rabat, to the stultifying respectability of Mrs. O'Brien, secretary in the embassy's Political Section. The Superior Beings in Personnel, who reviewed her performance and efficiency ratings, had found it admirable that Mrs. O'Brien had shown such an active interest in Moorish architecture. The little vacation house she had purchased in the Tangier Medina certainly wasn't suitable for an *officer* or his family, but she put so much energy into restoring it . . . up there almost every weekend. It was an acceptable avocation. And, of course, it kept her from some messy involvement with a *local* in Rabat.

On the bulletin board of Joe's studio in the garden, there was a spread of snapshots showing Renée and the boat. Joe had thumbtacked up a close shot of Renée in her new bikini, sitting in the shade of the mainsail. He would often sit for long periods and look at the texture of the light on her shoulders and thighs. Next to this picture of Renée there was a larger, more formal photograph of Monique and Joey. And next to this, a red map pin held the receipts from the Juárez divorce lawyers. When Joe had made this arrangement of photographs and documents, perhaps he had had in mind some notion of ironic symmetry. But lately he had not liked to look up at them from his desk, even to study the light on Renée's flesh.

In the filing cabinet, next to his writing desk, there were three manila folders thick with worthless manuscript pages he had produced in the past year. There was also a file of increasingly hostile letters from the editors and the general counsel at Hawks and Spencer.

The varnish of Joe's desk was scarred with the interlocking circles from the wet bottoms of whisky glasses and beer cans. If he was drunk enough, they looked like the craters of the moon. If he'd been smoking kif, and was more than normally jittery, the desk top reminded him of the hills behind Khe Sahn.

Joe felt the wind, the onshore evening breeze. The sails filled with a soft thump. He reached down from the cockpit to scoop up some cold salt water and splashed it on his face.

"There's your wind, boy," he said out loud. "Who the hell needs all this crummy *technology?*"

Dragonfly moved well in light wind. Joe played with the sheets until the sails were balanced and he could release the tiller. The boat was sailing itself.

He splashed more water on his face, dried his hands, and lit a cigarette. This was definitely the best time of the day in the Mediterranean. The Rif and the Sierra Bermeja were still catching the sun. Directly overhead the sky was more blue than black, but there were more stars coming out now. The swell kept rolling in from the Atlantic.

Across the Straits he saw the twinkling lighthouses at Gibraltar and Tarifa. Behind him, Ceuta was brightly lit. In a bit, when it was full night, he would be able to see the lights of the fishermen's huts on the beach at Targa. Harry Rains had been adamant about that; there were *always* lights in the summer there, and one could always use them for a safe anchorage bearing.

In a minute, Joe decided, he'd go below and see about that engine and some navigation lights. Now it was pleasant to let the boat sail him along . . . and to unwind inside. There was a lot to think about, to figure out in the next few days. But not tonight.

Joe retrieved the bottle and took another sip of Scotch. Up there, past the forestay and the biggest ridge of the Moroccan Rif, the moon was rising. He smiled. Of course. He ought to get the Zenith out from down below. The astronauts had left orbit now and were on their way. Joe shivered again, but not from the breeze. It *was* exciting, even for an old wire service man like himself. What did the plaque that they had on the Lander say? *We came in peace for all mankind.*

Nice thought, beautiful sentiment. I wonder how *we* look to them. Blue and white and peaceful? Like in *National Geographic*. They're on their way now. Three of them inside that machine, way the hell out there, all warm and cozy, breathing the air they carry along in tanks. *Here men from the Planet Earth first set foot on the Moon.* They had all signed the plaque, even Tricky Dick.

Joe smiled to himself. The single most important news story of the century, and here he was, drinking on a dark sailboat someplace in the Straits of Gibraltar. The reporters would be having a good time in Houston and on the recovery carrier. A better time in Florida. Just phone in the NASA handouts, then get drunk and laid.

Still, the crew was out there, in silent space, on its way. It was really happening. Three men inside a different kind of boat, propelled by different forces than this evening sea breeze. Joe looked up at the moon and his invisible comrades.

The breeze shifted slightly. He let the sails rattle for a moment, then sheeted in once again. On this new heading the mainsail blocked his view of the high Rif and the rising moon.

It was dark now in the Straits. The sea breeze held, but the tide was swinging. Joe stood in the cockpit, bracing against the swell with his left hand above him on the boom. In his right hand he held a hand-bearing compass. He was trying to get a fix. On the cockpit bench at his knee, he had spread out the small-scale admiralty chart of the Straits. Gibraltar and Tarifa lighthouses had given him good targets, but they were closely grouped against the gray Sierra across the Straits. He knew the tide was causing leeway. Ceuta was still on the starboard beam, smaller now, though, less dazzling. He needed another set of lights, something reliable, not an unknown Spanish village. If he were far enough east into the Med, he might be able to get a shot at the radio tower above Cape Trafalgar. . . .

No, Christ, Morocco would be in the way—the whole bloody mountain at Cape Malabata. Joe turned to face the northwest, anyway. He couldn't think of anything else to do just then. He laid the compass down on the cockpit bench. It was *cold*. The breeze whisked condensation drops off the taut mainsail. Joe looked back north, toward Europe.

He saw the satellite, a twinkling star of the first magnitude, coming toward him from above the dark Sierra. For a moment he was confused. This was neither Mercury, Venus, nor Mars.

Oh, yeah, he thought, satellite—Telstar or one of those. He swallowed some whisky. Better check that compass again, just to make sure. No, stay cool. That *is* a satellite, and it *is* going from north to south. That *is* Morocco over there, and all *that*, too, out front. Spain's right where it's supposed to be, behind the stern. Pretty soon there'll be lights on the beach at Targa, just like Harry said.

Things were always a little scary at night. There were huge ships out there in the dark. He could see their navigation lights. They were steaming along through the swell, making twenty, twenty-five knots . . . on autopilot with radar plots and R.D.F. bearings. And here he sat in a wooden sailboat with no lights, not even for the compass.

It was cold in the annex of the code room. Renée O'Brien was glad she'd brought her sweater with her. Outside the embassy there was a pleasant Atlantic breeze blowing among the jasmine and bougainvillaea. But these communications people insisted on keeping their room as chilly as a meat cooler.

Ruth Herbert brought the yellow Priority to the screened window. "Here's your cable, Renée," she said, handing the teleprinter sheet through the opening in the screen.

"It's UNCLASS," Renée said, "and it's *not* an Immediate."

"A garble." Ruth shrugged. "I tried to call your apartment, but you were already on your way over here."

"Thanks," Renée said. She read the yellow sheet. "Why is it Action:Pol, anyway? This should be routine for Admin."

"See," Ruth said, pointing with her pencil, "it's Subject: FSO 3 Robert Young. . . . He's Pol."

Renée rejected the desire to say something nasty to the stupid code clerk. "It's about *furniture,* Ruth. . . . Mr. Young's deep freeze—the one he ordered for the new house. They don't have the model he wanted."

"Oh . . . oh, yeah," Ruth said. "Well, I tried to call you back, but you were gone."

Renée initialed the cable and handed it back through the code room window.

It was after eight already, and she still hadn't packed for the weekend. Tomorrow was going to be a busy day, too. There was that reception after work, and she had not yet sorted out Tommy's clothes for camp next week. At least she wouldn't be duty secretary again for another month. If only she could get out of that reception. She couldn't plead a headache again, not if she wanted to get a decent efficiency report. Mr. Reed was expecting her at the "little get-together." More importantly, *Mrs.* Reed was expecting Renée to be there, looking attractive, but not too sexy, smiling and translating for all those nice Texas A&M professors and their wives while the Moroccan Ministry people yawned, swilled their camouflaged whisky-and-Cokes, and tried to touch her arms and hips.

She left the code room annex and walked along the

mezzanine past the D.C.M.'s office and the Political Section. The filing cabinets and the bar lock all had their red LOCKED tags in place, like a row of cardboard poppies.

Outside it was almost dark. The wind was moving the tops of the eucalyptus trees. She stopped.

No, he was all right. He'd be there by now. George had called to say Joe had gotten away from the yacht club well before noon. He really would be all right. He was stubborn, pigheaded at times, but he wasn't foolhardy. Right now he was probably anchored in the small bay under the watchtower, eating a can of beans in the cabin of the boat. No, drinking a can of beer, more likely. She smiled and resumed walking toward the landing. It was going to be very nice to see that stubborn, crazy Irishman again.

The ship missed *Dragonfly* by about fifty yards. She was the *Olympic Pallas,* a twenty-three-thousand-ton Liberian tanker carrying Libyan crude to Britain.

In the dark Straits her master had taken the precaution of backing up his radar bearings with visual sights and two good R.D.F. fixes. He had then turned the bridge over to his second officer and retired to his sea cabin to watch a World Cup Soccer play-off on British Forces Television from Gibraltar. When the second officer had taken the bridge, he had instructed the helmsman to engage the autopilot, which worked directly from the gyro compass and was more reliable than a man's hand on the wheel. As a further precaution, he had also reduced engine revolutions to two-thirds.

The *Olympic Pallas* was traveling at only eighteen knots when her bow wave knocked the unlit *Dragonfly* on her beam ends. Joe was in the cabin, trying to hand-crank the engine when it happened. The boat rolled sideways into the swell, lay for a moment with the sails in the water, then righted itself on its keel and continued sailing.

Joe hit his head on the wall of the cabin. Oily bilge water splashed up over the floorboards and onto the starboard bunk, and a great jumble of books, clothing, and canned goods rattled and banged in the darkness.

His first thought, after the pain and fear, was that he had gone aground. After a confused moment he heard the ship's engines. Crawling through the mess in the cabin, he looked out through the hatch to see the black sides of the tanker rolling by like the walls of a subway tunnel. The water was illuminated brightly by the ship's green navigation light.

"Son-of-a-*bitch,*" he whispered.

He climbed into the cockpit, prepared for a shambles of broken mast and trailing rigging. But the boat was moving along nicely. Joe looked around. He still seemed to be on course. *Dragonfly* rose and fell evenly, the sails balanced and drawing again. The only indication of the near collision was the salt water dripping off the mainsail. He heard the sound of the tanker's screws, booming through the water like kettle drums.

He licked his lips. His palms were sweating. Ahead, the Rif was outlined crisply against the moon. He watched the ship's stern light rise and fall with the swell.

They had never even slowed down.

2

Targa

Joe stood up to stretch his back. Out to sea the distant hump of Gibraltar and the mountains of the Spanish coast were fading into the haze. *Dragonfly* swung at her anchor in twenty feet of water, inshore from the reef at the end of the tower promontory. The sky was clear and the sea was that soft green that marked the contact zone between the warm water of the Mediterranean and the colder Atlantic currents. It was almost noon.

Joe felt good, a little hungry, perhaps, but the tormenting memory ghosts of the previous afternoon had not returned. Maybe it was all the hard labor. He had been working steadily since six-thirty, sunrise.

Making the anchorage the night before had not been difficult. By eleven the waxing moon was high and there were fishermen's lamps clearly marking the shoal water. That tanker episode had put some extra adrenaline into his system and sobered him enough to work the boat well, close inshore under jib alone, then drop the hook right where he wanted it. He had managed to hand-crank the engine and clean up the mess of spilled provisions and equipment in the cabin. The chaos down below had not been as bad as he had first feared. With the exception of some bilge stains on his sleeping bag and a few broken bottles, there had been no permanent damage. The engine had run all night, too, quietly kicking over at quarter revs in neutral, charging the battery back up to full.

At midnight he had laid his sleeping bag on the foredeck and sat down for a moment to rest. Waking up at dawn he found himself *inside* his sleeping bag, cuddling his empty canteen from the ice chest and an aspirin bottle. The canteen was empty and he had no idea how many aspirin tablets he'd swallowed. Enough, though, because he felt rested, fresh, not at all like he'd drunk a fifth of Teacher's the day before. And the engine was still chugging, so smooth and quiet, a tangible reassurance that there were some difficult problems he *could* solve if he persevered.

He had begun Friday with an unfamiliar feeling of optimistic energy, and it had seen him through the long morning of work, setting up the camp. The most pleasant thing about the morning, discounting the absence of a hangover, was that he had been too busy to think about his problems.

He stretched again, wriggling his toes in the sand. The sun was hot, but not yet overpowering. To his right the beach stretched in a white curve for a mile to the mud-brick fishing village. Behind his beach camp the stubble fields shimmered in the sun all the way back to the foothills of the Rif. There was neither noise nor detectable motion from the village. He was alone on this end of the long beach. If a man wanted solitude to think, Targa was the place.

The camp was set up, the boat cleaned, and the engine battery charged, but the fireplace wasn't finished. As soon as he had the last brick in place—sometime this afternoon—then he would sit down and do some of the serious thinking he had sailed to Targa to do. Joe went into the tent for his first beer of the day.

The tent was roomy, a composite of Renée's Sears beach shade and George's lean-to tarp. There were three comfortable safari beds, another contribution from Renée, and a folding French Army table George had brought back from a trip down to the Casablanca flea market. The sand was covered with reed mats, and Joe himself had made a pair of driftwood benches. Joe looked around and smiled. He was pleased with the tent and the driftwood benches, but this fireplace was going to be his masterpiece. He took a can of beer from the ice chest and went back to work.

Sipping his beer, Joe examined the foundation of granite slabs he had dragged across the sand from the foot of the ruin. He had already shaped the granite sides of the fireplace, using a rusty pick head he had found in the sand. Now it was time for the bricks. From the heap of broken masonry at the foot of the tower, he had collected a stack of loaf-shaped, russet bricks. He used the pick head to trim them for the two fireboxes. The bigger one on the right would hold their bonfires of cedar driftwood. The smaller box would be covered with the cooking grill. Here they would grill their steaks and, hopefully, the fish he and George would spear.

It was an overly elaborate construction for a weekend camping trip, but he liked the feeling of permanence the fireplace acquired as he patiently fitted and stacked the bricks. It was as if by building this fireplace to last for months he was somehow guaranteeing that he would be here in Morocco to enjoy it. He placed a brick on the bed of wet-clay mortar and went back to the tent for another beer. It was hot in the sun and he *was* thirsty. Coming out of the tent, he glanced into the battered shaving mirror hanging on the frame of the lean-to. His nose was beginning to peel.

Monique had bought him that mirror at the French commissary in Saigon during his first contract in Vietnam with A.P. It had once fit into a leather case that had pockets for his toothbrush and razor. She'd always been so thoughtful about things like that, even before they were married. She'd gotten him a pair of canvas legion boots, too, from that French M.A.A.G. captain, way back in 1962, when the few other American reporters in town were still slogging around in leather combat boots on their occasional visits to the bush.

Monique had said those boots and the mirror demonstrated her Norman practicality. She hated mirrors herself, though. They reminded her that she was growing *old*. . . . Christ, at twenty-six she was already worried. She had always been too serious . . . Deputy Assistant French Cultural Attaché (for Antiquities). That had a nice sound in French: Chargé des Affaires Antiquitaires.

Seven years ago; it didn't seem possible. *I wonder what Monique is doing now, right now, at this moment. It's five* A.M. *in Rio. She's in bed with her new husband, Joey's new father*. Come on, don't start that crap all over again, Joe silently reprimanded himself.

Two more bricks slapped into place and he felt his gut begin to relax. It was stupid to dig around in the sick past. He had to think about the future. This Big-Two-Hearted-River routine with the camp was fun, but it wasn't solving his problems. He had faced one unpleasant piece of reality, though. The book was dead, finished. That was one problem out of the way. He still had a few things to worry about, though, like how he was going to get out of debt.

Six thousand dollars to Hawks and Spencer for the advance, five thousand six hundred in mortgages, and a few hundred around town for booze and groceries. More than a couple hundred; the bill at the Parade Bar was one hundred fifty by itself. There were the dues at the yacht club, too. That was less than fifty bucks, but Delambre, the manager, had been hounding him for it, threatening to impound the boat. The club dues would be the first bill he paid when he got some money together.

But, how? A commercial loan was out. He wasn't what you'd call a good credit risk. For most of the past twelve months he'd been drunk more than sober, and he had not written a publishable page. The only security he had to offer on a loan was an already-mortgaged house, a quaintly obsolete sailboat, and a six-year-old Land Rover. That wasn't going to get him out of debt and give him enough to live on for a couple years, or *however* long it took him to write something salable, assuming, naturally, that he ever would write that *something*.

Borrowing money from Renée was impossible. She had already done enough for him. Besides, an embassy secretary didn't make that much, and she had Tommy to raise. Hell, *she* had her own mortgage to pay off on her weekend house in the Tangier Medina. Renée O'Brien was a good woman. She probably even loved him enough to borrow money for him. But he couldn't ask her for money. He wouldn't.

That left George Briggs. There wasn't any mortgage on George's house, not on his Jaguar, either. He did have alimony to pay, but some lawyer handled that with his brokers. George was thirty-three years old and had never cashed a paycheck in his life. He had been finishing his master's in engineering when his own man died, leaving George as sole owner of Briggs Electronics. Three months later the company was snapped up by Cambridge Instruments and George retired. All George knew about money was that he had a lot of it and that his brokers seemed able to invest it for him quite well without his help.

Joe crushed the empty can and chucked it toward the tent. George could sit down and write out a check for six thousand dollars without even considering his bank balance. But, would it really be a *loan,* a debt that would be repaid with reasonable interest in a reasonable period? The answer to that was as obvious as it was distasteful. Without a means to pay it back, taking money from George would be charity, a handout. There was no other word for it. No charity, no handouts. Things weren't that bad yet.

But they weren't good, either. He popped the opening tab of another beer.

"Work," he said. "You need money, you go back to work."

It wouldn't be such a tragedy to give up the cute little expatriate villa in Tangier and get his life squared away by working again. If he stayed away from the booze for a few days, he could sit down at a Telex with the best of them and punch out some pretty good copy. That's what he'd been trained to write, *copy,* not books. Monique had been right about so many things, but she'd been wrong on that. He was simply a good wire service reporter, not a *journaliste.*

He tapped the metal mirror on the tent pole. He had made his decision. There it was.

The answer to his problems was simple when you looked at it. George could *buy* the boat and the car. He loved to tinker with machines and was itching to get his hands on *Dragonfly*'s engine and move that throttle linkage. Joe would let him have them both for six thousand bucks, a fair price. That would get Hawks and Spencer off his back. Now the house. With George guaranteeing the mortgage, Harry Rains at the bank could clear up the financial problems in both New York and Tangier.

So, all Joe had to do was pick up the phone on Monday and call Paul Green at the Southeast Asia desk of A.P. The job was there, waiting for him anytime he wanted it. That's what Paul had said after the last contract. Eighteen-five plus per diem on the road, four R & R's a year. And all Joe had to do was go back to I Corps, back to Vietnam . . . and walk out on Renée, after they'd talk so much about a future together, just like he'd walked out on Monique and Joey when they needed him. To go back *there*. . . .

He looked up at the hot summer sky. His palms were sweating as they had while he watched the tanker's stern light rise and fall with the swell. There were pictures in his head, colored pictures, complete with the wet odors of the tropics. . . .

But there was no place else they would send him. It was a war that needed reporting, and that was what he would have to do.

How the hell am I ever going to tell Renée, when she's already extended her tour of duty in Morocco to be near me?

He would have to find a way.

Joe slapped some more clay onto the top row of bricks and smoothed it with the back of the shovel. There it was, back to Vietnam for A.P. After two more years out there he could come back to Tangier with the house paid off and money in the bank. Besides, if he really was going to write that novel about the marines in Hué, he'd need some fresh material. Hell, a lot of writers *paid* to go out there to have a look around. It wasn't going to be so bad.

Sure, of course. He would wake up one morning on the screened sleeping porch of the bureau house in Da Nang, look in his old tin mirror, and suddenly see Joe Clinton, the *novelist*. Who was he trying to snow this time? Once he packed up that so-called studio at the bottom of his garden in Tangier, he could forget about ever trying to write books again. He was going back on the road . . . a few more years in Vietnam, maybe a short tour in Bangkok, covering Laos and Cambodia. By then, there'd be shooting someplace else . . . Africa or Israel again, probably. *There it is.*

The next beer had no taste, but it was cold and wet

and felt good going down. He leaned across the wooden tent frame and smiled at the bay and the white boat. There were shadows now at the base of the tower. It was well past noon, but he wasn't hungry, just a little sleepy from the beer. Everything was going to be all right. Now he could really enjoy the weekend.

He was sitting on a camp bed putting together the *sebsi* before he consciously knew what he was doing. He stopped and looked down at the little clay bowl full of kif. Hell, one pipe wouldn't kill him.

3

Accounts Payable

There was a loud smack and Joe awoke with a start. He sat up blinking, his head thick with sleep.

"Sorry," George said sheepishly. "I wanted to get this stuff unloaded before I woke you up. You looked really beat." George stood, slightly stooped beneath the roof of the beach tent. A strange, unfamiliar bundle lay on the straw mat at his feet. Joe was groggy and it was difficult for him to focus his eyes against the glare of the late-afternoon sun. His mouth felt dry and his lips tasted sticky.

"Jesus," he said, "did I sleep straight through? What time is it, George?"

George laughed. "It's *Friday,* Joe. I decided to come on over today on sort of a . . . trial run. They've got the road all ripped up past Tetuán and I wanted to make sure about the detour before coming over with the girls in the morning."

Joe ran his hand through his sweat-dampened hair. "Oh," he said dully. His eyes rested on the load at George's feet. "What's all that stuff?" George stooped down and began pulling apart the bundle. Joe saw that there was a British Army surplus pack frame with several oddly shaped sacks lashed to it. *Jesus,* he thought, *that's pure George. He probably carried that damned pack two hundred yards from the car in this heat.*

George wore a faded pair of khaki shorts and scuffed hiking boots. There were red welts on his shoulders where the pack straps had cut.

"Well," George said, "I figured I might as well bring over some more ice as long as I was coming . . . and then I picked up a case of Heineken, and I finally got that extra scuba bottle recharged so that we'd have plenty of air for the weekend." He stooped to open a wet burlap sack, exposing a large plastic bag filled with rapidly melting chunks of ice.

"How much does all that stuff weigh?" Joe asked, getting unsteadily to his feet.

"About a hundred pounds, I guess."

George had the dripping chunks of ice out of their bags and was placing them carefully into the foam chest. He closed the top of the ice chest and used the edge of a burlap sack to wipe the moisture off the squat yellow scuba tank. "It wasn't hard," he said softly. "I needed the exercise, too. Haven't been getting out on the courts as much as I wanted to this summer. I'm getting kind of flabby."

"Yeah," Joe said good-naturedly, "you and Jimmy Stewart. You remind me of a rodeo cowboy I met when I was out West working the wheat harvests. He could eat a pound of steak and a dozen eggs for breakfast and a whole cherry pie. He was about your height and probably weighed a hundred sixty pounds. I don't think you have to sweat getting fat."

"Maybe," George acknowledged. "Anyway, Joe, I had another reason for coming out today."

"Yeah?"

George reached into the pocket of his shorts and removed a folded envelope.

"Registered, special delivery," Joe said, taking the letter in his hand and staring tiredly down at it, "from Hawks and Spencer."

"Ali brought it up to me. And that's not all, Joe." George took another paper from his pocket. "He brought this with it. It's a telegram. It came today after the letter."

Joe read the telegram and then crumpled it into a tight ball. "From Hawks and Spencer, too. . . . They want me to acknowledge the receipt of the registered letter. Sounds like they're getting a little impatient back there."

"The book?"

"Yep," Joe said. "Thanks . . . thanks for coming all the way over here to deliver this stuff."

"How's it coming, Joe? The book, I mean."

"Let's just say that I'm having some minor setbacks." George was about to speak when Joe continued. "Listen, George, I can handle it. I've done some pretty serious thinking. I've decided to cut the book form completely and get it published as a series of articles. I'll probably have to head back to the States for a while, but I haven't been back for almost two years now, and it's probably high time I go."

"You mean you'll be leaving Tangier for good?"

"No, no," Joe lied. "I'll be back in a few weeks. Listen, keep that to yourself, okay? I don't want to get Renée all upset. This weekend is something she was looking forward to, you know what I mean?"

George nodded. He bit a piece of cracked flesh from his lip. "There's something else, Joe," he said. "That guy Delambre came up to your house around eleven and started yelling at Ali, so Ali brought him up the path to my place. He gave me this."

George produced yet another folded piece of paper. "It's a club dues bill for May and June. He said it was overdue and that your check at the Commercial Bank bounced. He said they're having an audit of the club books this weekend and if you didn't pay you wouldn't be allowed to bring the boat back."

Joe looked down at the blue dues bill. "Hey, hang on," he said suddenly. "This is marked 'paid.'"

"I paid him."

Joe stared out the open tent flap at the *Dragonfly*. A slight westerly breeze had come up and the boat was riding prettily at her anchor, the white of her hull and the varnished mast smooth against the deep aquamarine of the Straits. The lean-to fly cut an angle across the softening blue sky. Up in the Rif, the bare ridges gained definition as the sun began to set. Just above the mountain range, the moon rose. The Apollo crew was still out there, Joe thought suddenly, now nearer to its target. The men were preoccupied with lunar orbits and LEM rendezvous instead of fucking bill collectors.

Joe spoke softly, but his strong feelings were clear. "George, I don't want you to go around paying my bills for me."

"It's only forty bucks. You can pay me back when you have it to spare."

"Yeah, when I have it to spare. Don't hold your breath, old buddy."

"That's another thing I wanted to talk to you about this afternoon, Joe. How are you going to keep going with your writing if you're broke? How are you going to get back to the States?"

Joe was silent·

After a moment, George continued. "Joe . . . if a loan would help, I . . ."

"I don't need charity," Joe spat. "I grew up on charity. My old man was the only railroad engineer in America who couldn't even hold a job during the *war*. It really fucks you up, George."

"Look, you're my friend, that's all," George said. "I've got money to spare and you're short. It would be a loan, not charity."

"I know, George, I know. Listen, I've been paying my own way since I was thirteen, and maybe I'm a little sensitive, okay? Let's not worry about it this weekend. This is going to be a vacation. We can sit down and talk about it next week. All right?"

"Fine," George said. His tight expression changed back to his natural smile. "You have anything to eat today?"

"Yeah," Joe lied. "I fried up a bunch of canned sausage for lunch and made a big salad. How about you?"

"I had some brochettes in Tetuán." George was staring down at the empty beer cans in the plastic trash bag next to the ice chest.

'You feel like a drink?" Joe asked casually. "Some gin, a Scotch?"

"No," George said brusquely. "I really ought to head back if I'm going to make Tangier before dark. I hate driving into the setting sun on that narrow road."

"How's the old bucket running?"

"Fine," George said eagerly. "While you were gone I stripped the carb and cleaned it. It's running like a top."

Joe was pouring Scotch into a plastic picnic glass half

filled with chipped ice. "You know," he said, "sometimes I think you like that beat-up old Land Rover better than your Jag."

"It's like comparing apples and oranges, Joe. They're both good machines; they were just built to do different jobs."

"I'll trade you even sometime when you're feeling adventurous, George."

George smiled and turned to leave. "You going to work anymore this afternoon?" He was looking at the level of Scotch in Joe's glass.

"Nah, I'll call it a day· I think I'll get up early and see if I can do some fishing before you get here with the girls. Did Renée call?"

"I called her yesterday. She and Tommy will be up at my place at eight-thirty. She's leaving Rabat at five. She would have come up tonight, but you're out here already and she's got one of those damned embassy receptions."

"Yeah," Joe said. "Well, I hope the weather holds for the weekend and we don't get stuck in this bay with a force-seven sirocco blowing."

They stepped out onto the cooling sand of the beach and, with different emotions, they gazed up at the rising moon.

"It's going to be great on Sunday night," George said enthusiastically. "I finally got my bowtie antenna positioned right to pick up British Forces T.V. in Gib. Then I rigged the F.M. receiver into the set, so I get the audio from U.S. Forces and the picture from Gib. They had half an hour last night on the moon shot. Showed the guys eating, floating around inside the command module. Tonight there's an hour special . . . really a good picture, Joe."

"Yeah," Joe said flatly. He drank some whisky. *Big fucking deal, all that money . . . blown away on toys . . . command modules and bowtie antennae. Everybody has fun, everybody gets rich.* "I'll be back Monday night to watch lift-off from the moon . . . *if* they make it, of course."

"Oh, they'll make it, Joe. I mean, they've got this mission figured out. It's beautiful engineering."

Joe drank more whisky. "Right. Well, you better get a move on, George. It'll be dark in an hour."

George nodded. He walked past Joe and turned at the end of the tent. "You should go a little easy on the Scotch tonight, Joe, if you're going to dive early tomorrow."

"Huh?" Joe said. His mind was a long way off. "Oh, yeah, this'll be the only one. I'm going to be out on that reef at sunrise and get us a big grouper."

George nodded again, uncertainly, then trudged away up the beach.

4

The Catch

It was an easy shot. For a fleeting moment Joe felt an urge not to kill the grouper. It wasn't exactly sporting, running the fish into this pitifully inadequate hole in the reef and sitting outside on the bottom breathing with an aqualung. Free-diving, Joe knew, he could never have gotten down here to forty feet, let alone stayed, quietly inching the tip of the spear closer to the mouth of the hole where the big grouper stared out at him with mournful eyes. They would all enjoy some fresh fish, though. Joe watched the fish's slowly billowing gill plates, seeing the creature not as a living animal, but as a row of juicy fillets sputtering on the grill. There would be lemon butter spiced with fresh dill. It looked like an eight- or nine-kilo fish. It had lived a good life. It was its own bad luck that it had chosen such a small hole for refuge, he thought as his finger tightened slowly, squeezing the slack out of the trigger.

The spear hit the fish just above its nostrils and traveled through the head. It destroyed the brain, then ripped through the stomach to exit just behind the dorsal fin. George's expensive compressed-air gun was a very efficient killing machine. The grouper thrashed once and then settled gently to the bottom of the hole, its gill plates no longer moving. A cloud of brownish blood rose, encompassing the dead fish like incense about a Hindu statue in a temple niche.

Joe slid the fish out of the hole and gazed up at the rippling mirror of the surface forty feet above. The sea was dead calm in the windless early morning. He looked at the big diving watch he had borrowed from George: ten to seven. He'd been smart to work this reef just after dawn. The big fish, like this grouper, were relaxed after the night's hunting and had not yet returned to their sleeping holes. The bottom of the rubber dinghy rippled on the watery ceiling above him, attached to the butt of the spear gun by a nylon tether.

He shivered. He had been in the water almost an hour and, despite the snug comfort of his wet suit, also borrowed from George, the chill was beginning to get through to his bones. He would call it a day. One fish was enough to give all five of them a feast.

Making sure that the fish and gun were resting on the gravel bottom well clear of the reef, he kicked his flippers and rose easily to the surface, emerging into the dazzling sunlight through the glowing bubbles of his own expended breath.

He clung to the side of the dinghy and worked carefully with one hand, unharnessing himself from the aqualung and sliding the heavy air bottle into the rubber boat. Then he treaded water while he reeled in the gun tether and the fish. The grouper was even bigger than he had estimated, and it took a real effort to manhandle it into the dinghy.

He sat back, resting his weight against the thwart while he loosened the tight rubber bindings holding his flippers. It felt good to move his toes again. He unzipped the jacket and pulled off the rubber hood. The morning sunlight was warm on his wet hair and face. The swell of the previous evening had flattened and the gray-blue sea was dead and featureless as far as he could see out into the Straits.

If there were no swells or surface waves, there certainly was a current. Joe squinted against the glare of the rising sun on the water and found that he had drifted more than a mile down the reef from where *Dragonfly* swung on her anchor. It was a good thing he had gone through the trouble of mounting the outboard on the dinghy before starting. He was tired from an hour in the water, and it would have been slow and hard work to paddle all the way back against the current.

The motor started on the first pull. Joe sat comfortably with the sun hot on the black rubber of the wet suit. He took a long pull at the bottle of Spanish brandy and lit a cigarette. The day had begun very well, and in a couple of hours Renée would be here.

The mountains above the coast were fawn-colored in the morning light. He looked for the moon, but it had already set. The astronauts would probably be going into lunar orbit about now, or maybe they already had and were resting, getting in their sleep in preparation for the landing. "Good luck, boys," Joe said to the sky.

Out to sea, just emerging from the foreshortened perspective of the misty horizon, a high-prowed Arab fishing boat headed toward Targa. After a few moments Joe could hear the hollow thumping of its diesel engine. The fishing boat was on a course parallel to him. After several minutes, it looked as if the Arabs were heading for the *Dragonfly* and not for the beach at Targa. *Probably want to sell me a grouper,* he thought, patting the moist flank of the fish. *I'm not in the market. Maybe he'll have some prawns, though. Renée can make some mayonnaise and we'll chill a couple of bottles of rosé. Today we're going to have a real seafood banquet.*

Joe was already standing on the deck of the *Dragonfly* when the old skipper of the fishing boat edged alongside, using the loud, slow-revving diesel expertly in the current. A gangly teen-aged kid in the bow watched over his shoulder until the old man called out in Arabic. The big anchor the kid released looked to Joe like something from a Hollywood pirate movie. Joe secured the rubber dinghy fore and aft to his own rail to act as a fender between the boats and then threw the old man a line to pull himself closer.

The fishing boat looked almost as old as its skipper. Judging by the height of the mast, it had originally been built as a lateen-rigged sailing craft without an auxiliary engine. The dull blue paint of the hull was chipped and peeling, and the deck was littered with coils of frayed line and bits of rusty equipment. Just forward of the tiller there was a rickety, jerry-built doghouse fashioned from old packing cases. Amidships, on either side of the mast, were the big wooden-roller net winches. The worm gears driving the winches were black with old grease and the crank handles looked stiff and rusty.

The old man cut the engine and suddenly the morning seemed very still. He came out from behind the shelter of the doghouse and unleashed a torrent of plaintive Arabic. Joe was able to understand only a few words, but, luckily, Moroccans, like most Mediterranean people, use their hands freely as they speak. From the old man's gestures, Joe gathered that there was something wrong with the boat's starboard net winch. Still in his wet suit, Joe climbed down into the dinghy and up onto the fishing boat.

Coiled on the roller drum of the winch was a dripping, saffron-yellow fish net. The old man shook Joe's hand, and Joe mumbled a mispronounced greeting in Arabic. The fisherman's hand was hard and leathery, like the flipper of a sea turtle. Talking excitedly, he led Joe over to the winch and pointed at the water. The net hung tautly, straight down like a sock full of sand. The old man and the boy had winched it up as high as they could, but whatever was caught in the net was still out of sight at least fifteen feet below the surface.

"Probably a hunk of an old wreck," Joe said in English.

The boy joined them and Joe passed around a package of Winstons. The three of them stood silently smoking as they gazed down into the water. Then the skipper started talking again in a rapid, excited blur of words. *"Jadid, jadid,"* he moaned, patting the Japanese nylon nets. *"Ralli b'zef, b'zef."* The nets were new and very expensive. Joe understood the man's predicament. If he beached the boat as usual, the fouled net would drag on the bottom and be ripped beyond repair. The winch was useless; trying to raise the snarled object to the surface would only rip the net further.

The old man pushed his sailor's hat back on his close-cropped hair. He tried to show Joe with gestures that even if he dove down into the water with a knife, he had no face mask or goggles and would not be able to see the tangled object. And he would not be able to hold his breath long enough to do the work of freeing the fragile net if he could. He ended the charade with a long, high-pitched lamentation, taking Joe's hand and placing it hard against the chest of his patched cotton shirt. The implication was obvious: only Joe, with his magical European diving equipment, could save the old man's net and thus keep the moneylenders away from his door.

Joe was tired. He had been swimming in a strong current for an hour, and he did not look forward to another hour underwater spent delicately separating the strands of the net from the slashing, dangerous weight of the wreckage the old man had snared. He looked back at the fisherman's pleading eyes. There were other things Joe would rather do. He wanted to shave and wash off the salt. Besides, the fisherman had probably snagged the wreckage on one of the badly marked coastal shoals and dragged it all night. The flimsy nylon was probably already so badly damaged that there would be little Joe could do to save it. But the old man, of course, would not want to believe this. He had no doubt borrowed heavily against this summer's profits to pay for the nets and would not want to give in to the unpleasant reality that at least half his investment was a total loss. There were many reasons why he should politely refuse the fisherman's request. But Joe knew that he could not.

The water seemed colder now. It was dark, too. The boats were in the shadow of the Portuguese ruin, and the current, eddying around the watchtower, had disturbed the sand bottom so that Joe's visibility was severely restricted. He hung head down ten feet beneath the surface and let his breathing become regular so that the roaring hiss of the air surging through the regulator quickly settled down to a comforting, rhythmic cycle. Kicking down to the bottom, twenty feet below him, he saw that the speed of the current was greatly increased here against the sloping rock sides of the promontory. He let himself come softly to rest on the sand and looked around, trying to check his position. He could just discern the dark shapes of the two boats swinging side by side on their anchors thirty feet above him. He had been carried out thirty yards by the current in the time it had taken him to reach bottom. It was going to be tricky to hold position beneath the snarled net.

Joe remembered that the boy had dropped the heavy anchor, on a short chain, almost straight to the bottom. That would make things easier. He would simply ride up the anchor chain until he was level with the net. He took a rough bearing on the boats and swam along the bottom until he judged he was near the anchor. Out of the corner of his mask he saw a dark shape in the sand and swam toward it. The rusty flank of the fisherman's anchor stood out red-brown against the sand. He unhitched his underwater flashlight and, shining it into the shadows, gripped the chain lightly with his free hand. Then he let himself rise upward in carefully controlled jerks.

Something dull yellow and then dazzling silver reflected back at him, and he knew that he was level with the snarled net. Curling his legs around the rough links of the chain, he settled down to wait a few minutes. The steady pulses of bubbles rose up around the netting. Then Joe let go with his legs and allowed the current to carry him away from the chain so that he hung parallel to the surface.

The sunlight burst through the murkiness about him like a golden spotlight. He saw the keel fin of the *Dragonfly* and the weedy bottom of the fishing boat. The details of the anchor and chain beneath him were suddenly clear. He rotated slowly, using his flippers to turn his body while he still gripped the chain. He wanted a better look at the net.

Then, suddenly, he froze. His breathing broke and the racing air howled in his ears. Hanging there in the yellow folds of the old man's net was a huge, glistening naval mine. Less than ten feet from him there was enough explosive material to strip his body down to its component molecules and blow him, the Arab fisherman, the boy, and both boats into hell. At any moment the mine could twist lower in the ripped netting and detonate. He saw the first of the morning's wind ripple the surface of the water and clung in terror as the two boats shifted on their anchors in response to the breeze.

The mine was long and shiny, shaped like a one-ended weightlifter's dumbbell. The flat, wheel-like upper end was perhaps two and a half feet in diameter, and the shaft was over six feet long. Trailing from a ring bolt in the bottom end of the shaft were the shredded remains of a steel cable. The greasy, metallic bulk of the mine slithered in the yellow net.

If he filled his lungs with air and then hit the quick

release buckle on the aqualung's harness, Joe could dart away along the bottom, swimming to the beach like a frightened squid. Once his feet touched bottom, he could drop his weight belt and dash up toward the protection of the rocks at the foot of the watchtower. That was the only safe thing to do. The mine might be a dud, but then again, he had heard of too many World War II bombs exploding twenty-five years later in European basements.

The two boats continued swinging with the breeze and the sunlight became more direct, steadily illuminating the water around so that he could now see the slope and details of the bottom. The mine glowed brightly metallic in the brilliant sun. But that was somehow wrong. Suddenly he realized the device hanging there in the net was made of high-quality stainless steel that shone like a burnished laboratory instrument, not what you would expect from a mass-produced weapon that had spent the past twenty-five years in corrosive sea water. No navy during World War II had wasted stainless steel making a mine that could never be retrieved. They had all been made of galvanized and painted iron plate. And now Joe remembered they had been spherical in shape, studded with detonating spikes. The thing in the net was long and streamlined. He felt his tensed gut relax beneath the tight diaphragm of the wet suit.

Well, what the hell is it? he thought. He remembered seeing an article in the *Petit Marocain* about an American oceanographic ship that was paying a courtesy call in Tangier on its way into the Mediterranean. Oceanographic ships carried all kinds of scientific gear. They trailed instruments in the water, testing currents and salinity and temperature and lots of other things. Maybe the object the old man had snagged in the net was a scientific device.

Joe parted the strands of the net and gingerly reached through them to touch the metal surface of the shaft. The skin was made up of long curved plates, riveted smoothly together like the surface of a jet plane's wing. The wheel-like top of the device was tightly enfolded in overlapping layers of netting, but Joe could make out two panels of duller steel that were sealed by rows of Phillips-head screws. Still not completely at ease with the device, he twirled the net slowly so that the shaft rotated toward him. Just beneath the dumbbell top on the far side of the shaft there were two oval panels of some dull, black material that looked similar to the radar domes on the noses of airliners. There was another oval panel lower down. Whatever the device was designed for, there must be sonar or echo-sounding equipment inside it. In his mind he envisioned the device being towed dumbbell end down so that these panels sent out a continual stream of echo-sounding impulses, charting the contours of the bottom. *But if that's the way it works,* he suddenly thought, *why are those sonar panels on both sides of the shaft? If it gets towed by that broken cable, then that would mean one of the echo sounders would be pointing up, toward the surface. That's strange.*

Whatever was inside the tube, Joe realized, it was obviously a very expensive piece of gear, maybe supported by fifty or one hundred thousand bucks' worth of foundation money . . . Ford Foundation, or maybe the Rockefeller Foundation. . . .

The idea hit Joe unexpectedly. *A reward! Of course. There'll be a reward for finding it. How much? Say it's worth fifty thousand. They'll pay ten percent, at least. Christ, five thousand bucks. . . . I could sure as hell use that right now.*

Five thousand dollars. . . . Why not six? That would get Hawks and Spencer off my back, and maybe I'd have time to get a decent contract someplace beside 'Nam. . . . Wait a second, wait one bloody second. That research outfit paid more than fifty thousand dollars for this thing! Look at it. This thing is crammed with specially designed one-of-a-kind experimental instruments, just like a NASA satellite. And a satellite costs hundreds of thousands of dollars. Think about losing a piece of gear like this. Screw the reward. I'm claiming salvage! This thing is probably insured by Lloyds for a couple of hundred thousand bucks! Lloyds will pay to get it back in one piece. They've got to, according to standard maritime law . . . something about first tender or first offer, or whatever, not being able to exceed one-half commercial value of undamaged goods. Christ, one-half value . . . we're talking about a lot of money, friend. Well, now, Mr. Clinton, I think you've just gone into the marine salvage business.

For a moment Joe thought about the Arab fisherman; after all, he had found the damned thing. *Yeah, he found it, and he's about to lose it again.*

The cork-handled diving knife was out of the sheath, poised in Joe's right hand. He tugged at the net, drawing it away from the metal tube. The device twisted and sank deeper. If it had any flotation tanks inside it, it was trimmed for a lower depth. The knife slashed easily through the already-frayed netting. One cut and then another longer one and the gleaming shaft dropped soundlessly away.

Joe watched fascinated as the device twisted onto its side and glided evenly down toward the creamy sand below. This was odd. The tube tilted from a horizontal to a vertical position and stopped sinking. It seemed to stop, cap up, about five feet from the bottom. As Joe watched, the tube, still vertical, was caught by the current and began to move steadily out to sea.

He hung in the sunlit water for a few moments, confused, then dove wildly down after his prize. Gripping it by the ring bolt at the base of the shaft, he was able to reverse the thrust of the current by kicking with hard strokes along the bottom. His arm began to ache dully with the weight. He was making progress toward the shallower water, where *Dragonfly*'s anchor was buried in the sand. He saw the dark line of the chain and followed it for what seemed a long time. At this depth there was no problem maneuvering the device. It was trimmed to float at a deeper level and bounced along the bottom. As he towed it in a half-vertical position, it duplicated the dying spin of a top. Joe removed the coil of the line from his weight belt. Three hitches around the ring on the stock and three through the shackle on the anchor and the tube was secure, out of sight, on the bottom. He tugged one last time at the line to make sure that the anchor was well dug in and then kicked himself up to the surface.

The old fisherman looked stricken. He and the boy had already reeled in the tattered remains of the net. Joe pulled himself up into the dinghy and dropped the aqualung and weight belt before climbing back up on board the Arab's boat. It was hot now that the sun had risen above the watchtower. The old man gazed wordlessly at Joe, his wrinkled face a mask of tragedy.

Joe shook his head sadly. Using gestures, he tried to show that the net had been badly ripped and weighted down with all manner of jagged planks and rusty metal. The old man nodded, mutely staring down at the ruined net.

After a while Joe asked quietly in broken Maghrebi, *"S'hall haddi?"* How much does it cost?

The old man looked up again. *"B'zef,"* he whispered in simple understatement. Very much.

"How much?" Joe repeated.

"Two hundred *reals,*" the fisherman said flatly, examining Joe's face to see if he was suitably impressed.

"How much in *dirhams?*"

"Cent dirhams," he moaned in French. *"B'zef, b'zef."*

Joe stepped down into the dinghy. *"Bla'tib shwia,"* he called to the fisherman. "Wait a moment."

In his wallet on board *Dragonfly* was his last hundred-*dirham* note. He had that and a ten-*dirham* bill and some change. There was thirty dollars still in the bank. But that was all. A hundred *dirham* was only twenty bucks. *What the hell,* he thought, as he took the money back to the old man, *I owe this old guy the price of his net, at least.*

Solemnly, he handed the fisherman the folded one-hundred-*dirham* note. Joe pointed to the net and down to the diving knife on his weight belt in the dinghy. "No good," he said in pidgin English, tapping his chest in emphasis. *"Trop couper,"* he added in French. He reached out and closed the old man's hands around the money. *"Wah'dal jadid,"* he added. Buy a new one.

The fisherman shook his head in wonder at the unexpected turn of his fortune. Timidly, the teen-aged son skirted past Joe and dug down into a hatch just forward of the doghouse. He wrapped several huge handfuls of fresh prawns in a clean cloth and handed them to Joe.

They smoked another of Joe's cigarettes and then the old man cranked his engine into life and the boy struggled with the huge anchor. Joe watched them chug through the breeze-rippled water and around the headland.

It was going to be a beautiful day. Already the haze

out to sea had cleared. The breeze was rising, promising an ideal afternoon for a sail. He had a lot to do and no time for a full breakfast. He reached down into the cabin and took a beer from the ice chest.

If they did sail that afternoon, he would have to do something about moving the tube lashed to his anchor. Dragging it up onto the beach was no good. Every Arab for miles around would show up to see the shiny gadget on the sand, and any chance for an undisputed salvage claim would be shot to hell. He had to keep it underwater. There would be some problems towing it back to Tangier because of the strange flotation system it seemed to have. But that was what he had to do, tow it half-submerged or lashed to the dinghy all the way back to the city. That problem, however, could wait until Sunday. Now he had to find some way to keep it from drifting away if they took up the *Dragonfly*'s anchor that afternoon to sail.

Joe chewed on his cigarette filter as he stared down at the water. "Right!" he said suddenly. "Of course!" He went forward to get the big storm anchor lashed to the foredeck.

Secured to the big anchor, the tube's neutral buoyancy held it just off the bottom. It could ride out any summer squall or swell. Joe looked up at the shimmering surface. He was sure that the tube could not be seen from above. That might be a problem for *Dragonfly*, he realized. The boat's fin keel drew five and a half feet of water, and, from where he hung, a few feet from the storm anchor, he couldn't be sure that there was that much free water between the tube's top and the surface. He'd have to make sure there was no danger of collision. The safest way would be to float up to the top of the tube and then to the surface, using his six-foot body length as a rough measure.

Joe's head was even with the edge of the dumbbell cap when he noticed the identification plaque. It was made of some bronze alloy, yellowish brown, and it was screwed onto the curving side of the dumbbell. He pushed closer to the plaque to read what was written on it. The characters cut into the plaque were deeply chiseled by a machine-cutting tool. The beveled edges of the cuts gleamed brightly, reflecting the diffused sunlight. What caught his eye were the three-inch-high characters CCCP and the date 1969. That was all he could read. The other four lines of smaller characters were in Russian.

5

Rights of Salvage

Renée O'Brien was suddenly awake, lying on the narrow bunk in *Dragonfly*'s cabin. They must have come around, because she felt herself cast to the right now, to starboard. Through the hatch she saw the shadows of the sail on George's and Patricia's bare legs in the cockpit. She could not see Joe or Tommy.

"God*damn* it, Tommy!" She heard Joe's voice through the forehatch. "You gotta stay *behind* the mast when we tack. I told you that ten times; so did your mother. Now, let me see your head. Are you okay?"

"I . . . I'm okay, Joe." Tommy's voice sounded small and frightened.

She sat up on the bunk. The nap had done her good. They must be almost back to the beach. It was a shame Joe had not come down to nap on the other bunk. He was obviously upset about something and irritable. He'd never sworn at Tommy that way before.

She heard their bare feet creaking on the deck above her head.

"Ah, you're okay, buddy," Joe said, his voice soft again. "It'd take more than a thump on the noggin with a shackle to hurt a kid with a name like O'Brien, right?"

She couldn't hear Tommy's answer. It would be all right now, though. Joe would roughhouse a little with Tommy and the boy would end up laughing. But she wondered what *was* eating at Joe.

She steadied herself by the overhead grab rail and swung up into the cockpit. They were close to shore. It was cool again and she could see the orange tent in the shadow of the tower ruin. Forward, she saw Joe staring thoughtfully toward the anchorage and Tommy playing nervously with the anchor chain. The boat cut the still water. A lone gull flew overhead. It was painfully quiet on deck. George looked uncomfortable. Patricia smiled unconvincingly, the way a girl with a proper British education had been taught to. Renée sighed. This was supposed to be a relaxed weekend on the beach. Why was Joe acting like this? He seemed to be preoccupied with something.

Joe turned and braced himself against the rigging. "Look," he said. He cleared his throat. "I . . . well, Tommy, listen now, buddy, I'm sorry I yelled at you. Okay?"

"Okay," Tommy said. He stopped fussing with the chain long enough to smile up at Joe.

"George, Pat," Joe continued, "I've been what is known as a horse's ass for the past hour or so. I'm sorry. No excuse, but will you accept my apology, anyway?"

"Hey, Joe," George said, "it's all right, really."

"No," Joe interrupted, "it's not all right. I was nasty to you and Pat and to Tommy."

Renée tried to lighten the moment. "As I told you, Captain Clinton, 'You're getting too much sun on your head,' I said, but you wouldn't listen to me. . . . Joe, I was asleep through whatever happened, so I'm neutral. I will graciously accept your apology for the assembled ship's company, okay?"

Joe smiled gratefully. He looked at the beach, drawing closer in the cool afternoon. "Fine," he said. "Matter settled. Ah, George, well, everybody, I was, I mean, I *am* a little worried about something, on the boat."

George looked up eagerly from the tiller. Pat seemed relieved.

I knew there was something, Renée thought.

"George, we'll drop the jib in a minute and ghost in on the main. I don't want to use the engine. I think I might have banged the prop shaft Thursday night. We're taking on a little water. Once we're anchored again, would you dive with me to check things out?"

"Of course, Joe. Why didn't you say something before?"

"I didn't want to get everybody worried. There might not be any problem."

You'd been drinking Thursday night, Renée thought, *and banged up the boat and were ashamed to admit it.*

"So," Joe was saying, "Tommy and the ladies can get the fire going and the salad made and all that good stuff. We'll play frogmen for a while, okay?"

"Sounds fair to me," George said.

"Aye, aye, skipper," Renée said. *What a funny guy you are.*

"Mr. O'Brien," Joe said to Tommy, "we shall now stand by to shorten sail on the first mate's order."

Tommy was grinning again.

George bore off to catch the breeze as it died with the sun.

Renée looked at Joe as he ruffled her son's hair. *Joe, I wish all our problems were as simple as this.*

From the cockpit of the anchored boat, they could see the blaze in the fireplace near the tent. There was a glow over the mountains where the moon would soon rise. George and Joe had finished putting on their wet suits. For this shallow dive they wore masks and snorkels, but not their aqualungs.

"I got the big Stillson wrench out of the toolbox," George said. "We might need it."

Joe looked evenly at George across the darkening cockpit. "George, we won't need it. I can guarantee that."

"Maybe the lock nut . . ."

"There's not a damned thing wrong with that shaft, George. And we're not leaking, either."

George frowned. "What's all this about, then?"

"I wish I knew for sure," Joe said. "Look, just trust me, okay? I want you to dive with me. I've got something to show you down there. We can discuss it afterward. But let's get this done while the tide's slack."

Joe snapped the buckle of his weight belt.

George was easing his flippered feet over the rail. "Okay," he said uncertainly, "but whatever you've got down there to show me better be interesting, Captain Clinton, 'cause I'm missing out on Renée's hors d'oeuvres and you're missing cocktail hour."

"Take my word for it, Mr. Briggs," Joe said, "this will be more interesting than smoked oysters and gin." Then he dropped backward into the dark water before George could answer.

Being underwater at night was a new and, initially, frightening experience. The sea felt silky and warmer without the mid-summer sun to create a shocking contrast of temperatures. Snorkeling along the surface, they followed the powerful beam of the flashlight, which Joe played down at the bottom, searching for the metallic cylinder. For a moment he was afraid the tube had drifted free and disappeared out to sea, but then the light's beam hit the shiny cylinder and he signaled George to dive with him.

They descended into the black, velvety pressure with powerful kicks and swam toward the tube, which swung slowly on its shackle just above the bottom. Joe checked his descent and, shifting the light to his left hand, swam over to cling to the cap of the cylinder. He motioned for George to join him. They were both gripping the tube, their fingers and legs slipping down its shiny skin, as they fought to hold their depth.

Joe tapped the bronze identification plate and pushed the flashlight close to it so that they could see the sharply chiseled Cyrillic characters. He waited a moment, studying George's wide-eyed expression. Then Joe touched George's shoulder and they surfaced.

In the *Dragonfly*'s cockpit, they toweled themselves vigorously and passed the whisky bottle. Overhead the stars were bright.

"What the hell's this all about, Joe?"

Joe pulled on his fisherman's sweater and lit a cigarette. He took another swallow of whisky. "I'm not sure," he admitted. "I found the thing this morning. It was caught in an Arab fisherman's net." Speaking slowly, he carefully traced the details of his actions that morning. George, who only smoked to be sociable or when he was preoccupied, accepted a cigarette, lit it, and inhaled deeply.

"Did you get a good look at the plaque?" Joe asked.

George nodded. "It's Russian, all right. One of my roommates at school was a Slavic language major. I used to help him with flash cards for word recognition. I got to be quite familiar with the alphabet myself. What the hell do you think it *is*, Joe?"

"You're the engineer. You tell me."

George drew again on his cigarette, staring past Joe into the star-speckled water. "Well," he said, "it's definitely Russian. I think it's something scientific, too . . . some kind of instrument. I think it's a scientific device to be used underwater."

Joe laughed. "A brilliant deduction, Dr. Briggs. What would I ever do without you?"

"Okay, okay," George said peevishly. "If you've got the whole thing figured out so well, you tell me what it is."

"I wish to hell I could, George," Joe said seriously. "I've been worrying about it all day. I've got some theories, but no proof. I know it's Russian, and I know it's an underwater scientific gadget. . . . I also know what it wasn't designed to do."

"Namely?"

"It wasn't designed to be caught up in some old Arab's fishing net. It was supposed to be anchored to the bottom someplace and float at a certain depth . . . about twenty or twenty-five feet, I think. That means that the Russians weren't exactly eager to have people know where the thing was. At first I thought that it might be some piece of gear off a Russian fishing ship, some kind of oceanographic research experiment. But then I started thinking some more. The Russians don't fish anywhere near here. Their factory ships and trawlers head through the Straits right into the south Atlantic. Whoever anchored that thing around here wasn't interested in fish."

"Could be some instrument to measure tides and currents . . . part of the Russians' oceanographic program."

"Could be. But it could also be something completely different. An idea hit me when we were sailing toward the Spanish coast this afternoon. Do you remember what's up beyond that headland toward Cadiz?"

George looked blankly at him.

"Rota," Joe said triumphantly. "The United States Navy Polaris sub base at Rota. That's what I think this thing was designed to study—American nuclear submarines, not tides and fish. The more I think about it, the more sense it makes."

George nodded his head slowly. "Most anti-submarine work involves hydrophones and sonar, and, from the look I got at that thing, it seems to have both. You notice those black patches?"

"Yeah. I noticed something else, too. What about that bronze plaque? That's been bothering me all day. If this thing really is some kind of secret Russian Navy gizmo, they sure as hell wouldn't put a sign on it saying SECRET RUSSIAN GADGET: HANDS OFF!"

"It was hard to see clearly down there in the dark," George said, "but I *think* that plaque's sort of a warning panel. You notice the lightning flash? That's the international symbol for high voltage. I noticed a couple of other voltage symbols, too. I'd have to look at it again in daylight, but I think I saw thirty-two volts, D.C. . . . Hey, that's funny, isn't it?"

"What's funny?"

"There being both a high-voltage system and a low-power circuit. Why would they need high voltage, anyway? Most of that stuff is probably solid state, unless there is a radio. Yeah, that was an antenna symbol. It's a funny one; looks sort of like a Japanese character."

"You're sure about it?" Joe's voice was getting excited now.

George looked troubled. "Yes, absolutely. And I'm sure about the D.C. low-voltage symbols, too. You know, if that plaque is a high-voltage warning panel—and I'm pretty sure it is—then it *must* be some type of naval instrument. If it were *civilian* equipment, for oceanography in international waters, they'd have written it in English, too. English is the international language for ships and planes. But that plaque is for Russian eyes only. I think it's Navy."

Joe grinned. His luck was holding. Maybe it was even growing. "So, Mr. Briggs, how'd you like to help me on a little . . . ah, *unorthodox* salvage operation?"

George looked troubled in the pale starlight. "What do you mean, *salvage?*"

Joe took a sip of whisky. "I looked the word up in the nautical almanac this afternoon when you had the tiller. The part on 'salvage' wasn't very long, but it refers to some section of international maritime law. The person who finds lost equipment is entitled to Salvage, with a capital S. That's money, George. I'm claiming Rights of Salvage. But I'll need help. This isn't going to be a garden-variety salvage operation."

"I don't follow you," George said warily.

"Just listen a second," Joe said. He was trying to keep the excitement out of his voice. "Do you agree that Rights of Salvage are recognized legal procedures?"

"I guess so, but . . ."

"Wait. Hear me out." Joe leaned forward in his seat. "I need money. You know that. But you don't know how badly I need it. It's time to stop lying about the book. There won't be any goddamned articles out of it. That book is dead. Yesterday I decided to shit-can it for good. I also decided to sell off everything I have around here and head back to Vietnam and A.P."

"You should have told me that, Joe. Hell, *I told* you yesterday that a loan wouldn't be any problem. . . ."

"Fuck your charity," Joe said. The violence of his tone shocked them both. For a few moments they sat in embarrassed silence.

"Sorry," Joe muttered. He took another sip from the bottle. "Okay, let me finish what I was going to say, and then you can tell me what you think."

George nodded.

"From what I read about Salvage, it's a whole hassle—litigation, petitions of ownership, the works. Can you seriously imagine the Russian Navy sending an officer over to the admiralty court in Gibraltar to go through all that? I think they'd want to settle out of court."

"You mean *sell* it back to them?"

"Let me finish. . . . No, not sell it to the Russians. I want the Americans to have it. I've got a hunch this thing is important. The naval attaché in Rabat will be pretty damned pleased to get his mitts on it."

"Yeah," George said eagerly. "They can send one of those crash boats up from the base at Kénitra and load it aboard at night. I could dive for them."

Joe chuckled. "Maybe they'd make you blacken your face just like John Wayne."

"Well," George said defensively, "somebody's got to

dive for it. The naval attaché won't want a bunch of Arabs to see it."

"Right. We can handle the diving side of it. All the attaché has to do is offer a decent out-of-court salvage settlement."

"Joe, we can't charge our own people for it." It was a statement of fact, not opinion.

Joe was tapping his foot compulsively on the cockpit floorboards. "I *want* the Americans to have it. But I wasn't kidding about my financial position. If I don't repay that Hawks and Spencer advance, I can forget about publishing *anything*. And if I don't pay off at least some of the overdue mortgage payments, I lose the house. Yesterday I was willing to go back to I Corps to get out of this bind. Today I have a chance to stay here. Do you see my position?"

"Perfectly. I really do. I just think it's kind of, well, *low life* to sell this thing to our own people."

"Okay," Joe said. "Fine. Sorry I bothered you. I'll find somebody else to help me. I wouldn't want you to get involved with anything *low life*. My word, what would your brokers say?"

George winced. "I didn't mean *low* that way, and you know it. And I don't appreciate that crap about the brokers, either. I meant low life like sneaky, dishonest."

Now Joe sagged from the rebuke. It had been a long, anxious day and he was tired. "Just listen to my side. The honest thing to do would be to notify the Moroccan Coast Guard. This *is* Morocco."

"Right."

"Then they'll confiscate it and sell it to the highest bidder. If you don't believe that, then you haven't had your eyes open around here."

George agreed.

"So," Joe continued, "by claiming a *reasonable* salvage fee, I'm actually saving the American Government a lot of trouble and money. I'm also guaranteeing them that some gang of crooked Arabs hasn't blown the story to the Russians, the French, or Christ knows who."

"But we *could* help them without a *fee*."

"Look, George, I'm only going to claim what's due me, and nothing more—a normal salvage fee, like it says in the books. I'm claiming it from the Americans. You can decide whether or not you want to help me. If you don't, then I'll ask you to keep quiet about this until the deal goes through."

Joe inhaled deeply from a freshly lit cigarette.

"Do you really think they'll pay for it?"

"When I first went overseas for U.P.I., I did my training in Tokyo," Joe replied. "The Americans paid some North Korean second lieutenant twenty thousand dollars in gold for flying over a beat-up old MIG-15. If that thing down there"—he pointed the whisky bottle at the dark water—"is half as important as I think it is, it's worth a lot more than some obsolete MIG."

George took the boat's tiller in his hand and played with it, sculling back and forth so that phosphorescent ripples rolled away from the stern.

"Listen, George," Joe continued, "they've got *billions*. It costs the U.S. Navy a hundred thousand bucks every time a sailor at sea gets an appendicitis attack. Nobody *knows* the C.I.A.'s budget. Believe me, if I weren't in a bind for money now, I'd *give* them the damned thing. The simple truth is that I'm broke and in debt. I cannot and will not take your money, but I sure as hell could use your help. This deal is going to be tricky to pull off without bringing the Moroccan authorities into the act."

George sat stolidly on the damp canvas cushion. Away to the east the sky was beginning to grow pale with the rising moon.

"Well," Joe said, "will you help me, George? Can I count on you to see this thing through with me?"

"Yes, okay, I'll help you," George said finally. "What is it that we have to do?"

"First off," Joe said eagerly, "we have to move it. I tried to keep Tommy from swimming around the boat today, but he's sure as hell going to be out here tomorrow morning with his mask and snorkel. I'd like to keep it a secret from Renée until I work out some sort of salvage deal. We're going to have to move it to Tangier, but we can't do it with the boat. The port's too public. I think that it'll fit in the Land Rover if we take out the front seat on the passenger side. That means leaving it here until the day after tomorrow at the earliest. Tonight we'll have to dive again and drag it farther out to sea. There's a shelf of rock just before the reef begins. I'd like to move it out there and chain the anchor to one of those rocks. That way we're sure it won't get washed away before we come back for it."

George got to his feet and opened the cockpit locker. He dragged out the canvas sack containing the scuba tanks. 'If we're going to be down there fooling around with chains and anchors, we're going to need the tanks," he said.

6

Renée

Renée was happy. The sun was hot on her bare shoulders, but the sea breeze cooled her. *Dragonfly* moved lightly before a steady, following breeze. The boat goosewinged along like a color photo in *Yachting*. Joe was curled up sleeping opposite her in the cockpit. She was glad they were finally alone. Tommy was such a good child; he had cheerfully accepted the suggestion that he drive back to the city with George and Pat while she and Joe returned together on the boat. George had been sweet about this arrangement, too, offering to take Tommy for a late-afternoon horseback ride and let him stay up to watch the moon landing on television. She was pleased that Tommy would remember the landing as the climax to a happy, adventurous weekend. She was happy, too, that he would be watching it with George, who was just as excited about the Apollo missions as Tommy. The two of them could sit for hours, Tommy asking questions and George drawing precise engineer's diagrams on Tommy's school tablet.

Renée looked up at the sails. They were drawing well in this light breeze. Across the Straits, silhouetted against Gibraltar, a big container ship was entering the Mediterranean. Joe slept soundly on the canvas cushions. Relaxed in sleep, his face was free of the tension lines that had been so prominent during the winter and had suddenly reappeared this weekend.

She smiled, secretly, to herself. He had not had much sleep the night before. *Three times,* on the narrow bunk down in the cabin. It had never been quite like that with them before, never quite so purely physical. Often they had lain in bed together, talking for hours, with the actual lovemaking being almost incidental to the close communication, the contact between them. But not last night. Joe had been *hungry* for her, rough with her, but not cruel. Desperate, insatiable—those were flamboyant, embarrassing words, but accurate ones. Privately, Renée recognized that there had been something equally desperate in her own body, something intensely exciting, that had responded to Joe's need. And she had joined him in that wordless quest. They had left Tommy asleep under the stars and rowed quickly out in the dinghy with one thing, urgent and intense, between them. Hours later her nipples were still tender from his lips and fingers, and she still felt the languid flush of so much satisfaction. Maybe it would be like that again, this evening, when they anchored at another quiet beach, just around the next Moroccan headland, in the cove at Ksar-el-Serghir. George was going to call the embassy for her in the morning. An eyebrow or two might be raised among the seersucker ranks in the Political Section. So what? The extra night alone with Joe was more than worth that small annoyance.

And perhaps now, alone together again on the boat, Joe could find a way to open up to her and release his problems, as he had released his body the night before. She knew that he was deeply worried about money, or, more psychologically valid, that he could no longer work and that the book had gone irrevocably sour. Joe was not the type of person who could easily discuss this. There were ways, she knew, in which she could make it easier for him to talk about his problems, but she still had to be careful with him. His emotions, what he insisted on calling his "head," had taken a hard pounding during the past year.

Reflexively, her thoughts jumped back to James, James Hobart Jennings, III, her ex-boss and ex-lover. He had been a man like Joe . . . no, James had not been battered by the world. He was not burnt-out and tired like Joe, with a thirst for whisky and a wild sense of humor. No, James had been *carefully* weak. Everything James had done was the result of well-balanced consideration. He was a true State Department man. Joe, on the other hand, plunged into life and did as he liked. Joe would probably lose more than he would win, but at least he took chances.

Renée felt the boat heel to starboard and pushed the tiller away from her, bringing the bow around so that they were back on a true run. It was easy sailing. There was no compass course to keep. Ahead of them was a jagged cape; all she had to do was keep the southeasterly breeze directly astern and the sails filled and they would clear the headland.

Renée leaned back against the cushion and closed her eyes. No, she thought, James had just been a convenience, the comfortable body of a man to have around without binding complications. Tony, her husband, had been much different. She had loved him unquestioningly for years, as only a young wife can love an older man, a skilled pilot and an unashamedly devoted father to their son. But sometime during that tour, testing the new Phantoms and those four years as an air attaché, he had lost something. He had given up. His spark had gone out and he had drifted back into the safe mediocrity of career air force, the Happy Hour at the officers' club, and the shop talk about compressor blades and landing gears over dinner. And then he started with girls.

The wind was shifting slightly off the headland. She could see it coming in ripples as the late-afternoon sun sliced down across the brown coast to port. Then the Genoa jib lost wind like a pricked balloon and then began to snap loudly against the forestay. The mainsail, sheeted out for a dead run downwind, also began to volley noisily. Joe was awake at once, sitting up blinking on the cockpit seat.

"What should I do?" Renée asked, her voice sounding concerned above the flapping sails. She loved steering the boat once the sails were set and if the wind was steady, but this noisy, uncontrolled flapping scared her, evoking visions of shredded sails hanging from the rigging.

Joe laughed and sank back down on his cushion. He reached across to stroke her knee. "You won't have to do anything," he said, pointing toward the stern. "That was just a little puff off those hills. The real wind's still right behind us. Look, you can see it on the water."

She glanced nervously aft and saw the surface of the swell behind them change to a ripply gray as the following wind returned. The deflated Genoa jib filled with a dull pop and the boat leaped forward. Joe was curled up on the seat again, his crooked arm shading his eyes. Then, after a while, he slipped back into sleep.

The *Dragonfly* bounded along before the breeze. It was only a little past five and they still had an hour of warm, direct sunlight, ample time to make their anchorage. Renée smiled to herself, thinking of her momentary panic when the breeze had shifted. It was silly to worry. Joe knew what he was doing.

He was good at so many things, if he'd only let himself unwind enough to admit it. He had rebuilt this boat, practically on his own, and, although he used to cynically call it "Occupational Therapy 101," he'd been proud when Harry Rains had said it was the prettiest little sloop in the club. Yachts, as Joe loved to point out, were meaningless toys, but the months of hard work he had put into this boat were important. If Joe could learn to pull and refit teak planks and splice thick rigging cable, he could finish his book. That was what she could get him to talk about, if not tonight, then next weekend. He had convinced himself that this book was impossible, that he was broke and could no longer work. But she would make him see that money was not the central issue.

He had let himself go to hell after his divorce. He had soaked his liver in alcohol and muddled his already jangly emotions with too much kif. She knew the symptoms. It was ritualistic self-punishment. Although he would never admit it, Joe was still a smalltown Irish boy beneath all his worldliness and cynicism. The priests and nuns had done their work well on him. He had debased the Holy Sacrament of Marriage. Because of his evil ways, a child had died. These were unrepented mortal sins. A person like Joe did not forget about them. Renée had seen too much of the same thing in her own family.

Her father had been a hard-drinking precinct sergeant and her mother a fanatical religious Québeçoise, tormented by guilty memories of miscarriage and possible visions of the Virgin Mary. With Irish Catholic uncles on one side of the family and French Catholic aunts on the other, Renée had been witness to more than her share of sin, guilt, and self-constructed purgatories-on-earth.

But Joe was different. He was not an old maid like James, and he was not truly self-destructive like Tony, either. One day, she realized, in the next few years, as Tony neared fifty and could no longer function as a vital male animal, he would strap himself into a jet airplane and fly it into the side of a mountain.

She looked up from Joe's face and gazed across the sheet of water toward Spain. The sun was yellow on the mountains above Tarifa. Just on the horizon she could see the bridge and cargo booms of a big, heavily laden freighter riding slowly toward the Atlantic. She would be thirty-one years old in a month. She had one child and would like more. She had tried one marriage and that had not worked. She wanted to try again. There was only so much time in a person's life. The one thing that really mattered was her relationship with a man she loved. The rest of it—money and success, possessions and security—was meaningless in comparison. She wanted Joe. She knew in time he would be stable enough to respond as a man, a companion, a husband, and a father.

Nobody ever said it was easy, she thought, letting her own advice to Joe echo in her head.

The afternoon breeze had died completely. It was cool now that the sun had gone behind the ridge. Joe stood above Renée on the cabin top, stretching, his hands on the wire of the backstay.

"Boy," he said, laughing again, "I really conked out after that wine at lunch. You'd think an old booze hound like me could handle a little rosé better than that."

"It's the sun," she said. "Cold wine doesn't go with hot sun."

"Well," Joe said, "we didn't exactly get in the full eight hours of sleep they recommend to all the guests at Camp Gitchee Gumee, either, did we, my dear?"

Renée blushed. She gathered her jacket modestly around her hips and tucked her bare legs under her. "No, my love, I guess we did not. But we sure had a beautiful time, didn't we?"

Desire and tenderness rushed through his chest again.

Joe swallowed, looking down at her. He remembered once, in May, how he had picked her up at the embassy after work. She had been wearing a crisp linen suit that hid her figure, and her hair had been combed back severely. Mrs. O'Brien, career State Department. But last night all her reserve had disappeared. Her hair tangled moistly with his own, her skin was hot against him, and their separate pulses pumped together in the moonlit cabin. It had never been like that with any other woman, so . . . *full,* so powerfully natural.

Joe sat down next to her in the cockpit. They smoked a cigarette quietly and watched the color leave the sky. The white beach fifty yards away began to stand out against the scrub brush inland. On the western end of the beach a concrete jetty melded with the shadows of the ruined Arab fort, the *ksar* of Ksar-el-Serghir. The twittering swallows had disappeared with the sun, leaving the beach silent.

Joe shivered. He opened the cockpit bench locker and took out his sweater. "Aren't you cold?" he asked Renée.

"Actually, I think I'm kind of broiled," she said, tentatively probing the skin of her thigh with a finger.

"Wash off with fresh water," Joe said. "Get all the salt off and I'll put some vinegar on you."

"Yummy," she said, smiling.

"Come on, now, get going," Joe said playfully.

"Aye, aye, Captain!"

While Renée was busy sponging herself with fresh water, Joe sat on the starboard cabin bunk reading something in the beam of a flashlight.

"What are you doing, Father Clinton," Renée called down, "reading your evening prayers?"

"Tide tables," Joe said flatly. "Just checking the time and depths of the tides on this coast." But in his mind was the metal tube shackled to his storm anchor back at Targa.

The fire had fallen to a mound of red coals. Above them the half moon had cut a vacant disc from the surrounding star field. Joe shifted his spread fingers beneath Renée's hips, lifting her closer and tighter to him.

He had been inside her for so long, but he wasn't tired, nor was she. Making love like this, on a silent beach, after the wine and the three pipes of kif, was so——. He smiled, suddenly happy that Renée was such a straight, respectable embassy lady down in Rabat and that they didn't have to smoke every time just to make it good. It was always good with Renée. With the kif it was different —another kind of good.

Renée's fingers were tangled in his hair, guiding his head down to her stiff nipples. He watched the tan flesh rise toward him in the pale moonlight. She was coming yet another time. On his shoulders and back her hands had gone into tight fists and were pounding out a tattoo, involuntarily, as she trembled with pleasure. Then she was kissing his mouth, languidly, her eyes half open, so near to his. Even in this faint light he could see her look of pure satisfaction.

A breeze crossed the beach and they both felt it play over them. An ember flared in the bed of coals. The shadows of their bodies from the tiny flame seemed gigantic. Wordlessly, they rolled to their sides and Renée shifted her legs so that she was poised above him, their bodies still joined. Her hips were moving again, in a slow circle, then more quickly. His face was in the moist nape of her neck.

Then he felt it all rising up from *below* his hips, from down in the dark sand. When he opened his mouth, no words formed, only a sighing groan. The moon and the dying fire turned in his field of vision and Renée was beneath him again. The throbbing seemed to last so long. Their mouths touched again, lips to wet lips. Joe slid onto his back and lay, watching his chest heave with his slowing breath. The moon hung above, surrounded by its escort of distant stars. He saw Renée's arm against the stars, guiding the fold of the sleeping bag over him. Like a magician's cape, it blotted out the sky.

They lay silently, watching the moon. After a while Joe yawned. "Wonder what time it is," he said. Renée did not answer. She rolled onto her side, her soft hip against the small of his back. A night bird called from somewhere farther down the beach.

Renée shifted over to her back. "Did you say something just now?" she asked, her voice soft and childlike.

"I was wondering what time it was," he said.

"Umm?" Renée murmured.

His voice was mellow and controlled. "If we're going to catch the moon landing, I'd better turn on the radio. It must be almost midnight." His fingers moved across the knobs of George's radio. The Voice of America medium-wave channel was in Arabic. He flipped back to short wave and picked up a strong, static-free signal on the six-megacycle band.

"Listen," he said, touching Renée's warm shoulder, "they're getting ready to land on the moon. Look." Above them the half circle of the moon hung, white and distant.

"Ah, roger, copy that," an astronaut's voice said. The radio signal crackled with distortion.

"They sound like all the pilots I've ever heard," Renée said, giggling suddenly. "One night, oh, it was Tommy's birthday, and we had the project commander over for a barbecue, which was a bit presumptuous for Tony to do, considering he was just a major, but the general had been his wing commander in Korea and they were old drinking buddies. Do you know what they did . . . all those pilots? They left us all alone after dinner and they went to Tony's study, which he'd made out of half the garage, and listened to tapes—tape recordings of Phantom pilots talking to refueling tankers someplace up over Canada in a snowstorm. That was their first big operational refueling exercise, and it snowed. Just a bunch of numbers, really: 'Vector Charlie Echo three-niner.' " Her voice dropped several octaves as she slipped into a giggling but effective mimicking of a pilot's voice.

"You are 'go' at four minutes. You are 'go' to continue powered descent."

"Roger, Houston," the radio intoned.

Renée began to speak again, but Joe reached out to take her hand. He wanted to hear what they were saying on the radio.

"Oh, sure, you listen," Renée said, shrugging. "It just seems to me sort of a waste of time, what with the war and all those things to spend money on here on earth. Why, they could clean up every single slum in America. They could . . ."

But Joe had curled the edge of the sleeping bag into a thick fold supporting his neck and shoulders and was lying flat on his back, gazing at the bright wedge of the moon high above him. Without moving his eyes from the moon, he let his hand crawl across the fire-heated sand to the blanket and return with the cracked leather binocular case. He viewed the steep-sided craters, the glittering, burnished surface of the Maria. The Sea of Tranquility was right there near the grayish-beige terminator line dividing the bright, sunlit face of the moon from the darker area to the west, illuminated by the reflected glow of the earth. Two men just like himself were strapped in front of the flickering lights of instrument panels inside the odd, Erector-set-like machine and dropping through the sunlit vacuum toward the rock and soil of that other celestial body.

"Throttle down better than the simulator." The astronaut's voice traveled a quarter of a million miles through empty space and squawked coolly out of the radio speaker.

"Looking good," someone said in Houston.

Joe's eyes were pressed to the hard plastic of the binoculars. Renée was saying something again, but she seemed a long distance away. The machine was now only a mile above the surface. The palms of Joe's hands were moist. They were up there, they were actually doing it. More numbers were being spoken on the radio.

He heard the words "low gate" and "consumables." Then the calm, emotionless voice of an astronaut flooded over him with sudden strength and clarity.

"Down to two and a half," the voice said. "Forward, forward forty feet. Down two and a half. Picking up some dust. Thirty feet. Two and a half down. Shadow. Four forward, four forward, drifting to the right a little."

Picking up some dust! Joe had seen many strange things in his life. He had witnessed death and birth. He had watched cities being destroyed and nations being born. He had seen the power of hurricanes, tidal waves, and avalanches. Only two years before he had seen the staggering energy of an erupting volcano in the eastern Congo. All of these spectacles had affected him, but none compared to the simple words "picking up some dust."

The rocket breath of a machine made by men, piloted by human beings, was throwing up silent clouds of dust from the surface of an alien world; it was dust that had lain undisturbed for billions of years. He could see the small area of the Sea of Tranquility, where the astronauts were landing. With a sudden, swooping connection, it all clicked into perspective—the gravity of the moon attracting both the astronauts' machine and the infinitesimal dust particles, the earth holding captive the moon, the sun the earth, the galaxy the sun, the numberless galaxies binding and bound by all the others, the entire universal dust cloud held by the primeval forces of gravity and magnetism, expanding, limitless . . . a lifeless mechanism, devoid of compassion, cold, silent, and eternal. His eyes were losing their focus on the silver-gray dust of the moon. His mind was beginning to turn in a lazy, but accelerating, somersault.

"Oh, God." Renée's voice came out of somewhere. "Why don't they hurry up and land?" She was suddenly alert, sitting up next to him. They were not going to make it. Their fuel would burn away and the ungainly machine would fall, tumbling to its side among the treacherous little craters and boulder-strewn slopes beneath it.

"Contact light. Okay. Engine stop."

"We copy you down, Eagle."

"Houston, Tranquility base here. The Eagle has landed."

There were other voices, but they did not hear them. Renée and Joe were laughing wildly, hysterically, hugging each other, their eyes filled with tears.

"Goddamn!" Joe said, shaking his head. "They're actually *up* there. Look." He pointed above them into the moonlit sky. "They're up there! They made it!"

"Oh, this is incredible," Renée sang happily. "They're on the moon. Oh, I'm so glad George is keeping Tommy awake to see it."

"Yeah, twenty years from now Tommy's kids will ask him where he was when these guys landed on the moon. This is really a historic day . . . like Pearl Harbor . . . like the day Kennedy got killed . . ."

"Bigger than that, Joe—this is something that will be remembered for as long as men keep records. It's like, I don't know, like the birth of Christ." Her voice was suddenly filled with acute embarrassment. "You know what I mean. We're lucky to have heard it."

"A couple of minutes ago you were putting the whole thing down as a waste of money."

"That was a couple of minutes ago," Renée said, smiling. She snuggled against him, her breasts cool against the fire-warmed flesh of his chest. He smiled back at her.

"Yeah," he said softly, "I know what you mean. There are probably a lot of better things to spend the money on, but this is really incredible—I mean, that they've actually done it. You know, I was really scared there at the end. It was strange looking through the glasses. Do you want to try? It brings the whole thing much closer, somehow."

Suddenly he was thinking. . . . If the American Government could spend *billions* to put a man up there on the moon, they could spare a few thousand for that buoy.

Joe stood, his shoulders hunched in his windbreaker, holding the mug of coffee with both hands. In the first light of the false dawn, he thought he could see whitecaps out in the Straits. There was a westerly blowing, and they'd be beating into it all the way back to Tangier. It was still too early to realistically gauge the wind's force, and it was bound to puff a bit at sunrise; all winds did. If they got under way soon, they could power out with only the mainsail up and make some real headway before the wind got up again for the day.

He hated to wake Renée. She had buried herself deeply in the double sleeping bag, moving unconsciously in her sleep after Joe had slid out quietly. He watched the sky turn blue again and felt the sting of the wind-whipped sand on his bare legs. There was a good slug of whisky in the coffee. It was warming him now.

"Damn," he said softly. If a freak westerly got up and stayed up for a few days, that bay at Targa would be wide open to it. Even that heavy shackle holding the buoy to the storm anchor would not hold up if the surf line started breaking far enough out. It would be just his rotten luck to get an unseasonal Atlantic storm this far into the Straits in July. "Damn," he said again. "I should have gotten it onshore while I had George there." He began to pace along the beach, kicking up little puffs of sand into the wind.

"I caught you," Renée said suddenly from behind him.

Joe spun around, startled, his coffee spilling over his hands. "Christ, you scared me. I thought you were still asleep."

"I was just faking. Hey, what's with this Hamlet act you were doing? You look like you're rehearsing for a real tragedy."

"I'm just a little upset about the weather," Joe said slowly.

"Is that right?" She sounded skeptical.

The sky was fully blue now. Wave crests were surging out beyond the point. "We ought to get going," Joe said. "You want some of this coffee?"

"Irish I am," she said, "but whisky at four-thirty in the morning is a little too much."

"There's some straight coffee in the Thermos," Joe said casually. His mind was still on the anchor shackle holding the buoy.

"Boy," Renée said, stooping for the Thermos, "you're in a beautiful mood this morning. More nightmares last night?"

Joe shook his head.

"Hung over?"

"Nah," Joe said. "I don't know what the hell's wrong with me."

"I bet *I* do."

Joe drained the last of the coffee from his mug. He was staring at Renée, wondering if she had heard his remark about getting the device onshore.

"You're feeling guilty, Joe. Don't get mad at George, okay? He told me Saturday morning—said you're probably taking off for New York next week. You're feeling guilty. You think you're running out on me just the way you ran out on your wife in Paris."

"Maybe you're right," Joe said quietly. He felt the wave of irritation rush up through his chest and throat. Stiffening, he turned to stare out to sea. "We'd better get this lash-up on the road," he said. "I want to make that point before the goddamned wind gets up again. If we start tacking all over the map, we'll end up in Gibraltar when the tide swings."

He felt Renée's fingers on his neck and the weight of her body pressing lightly against him. "What's become of my passionate early morning lover? Looks like I'm the horny one this morning."

Joe did not answer. He reached over with his left hand to stroke her wrist in a guarded, emotionless gesture of acknowledgment.

"Why the hell do I always get myself tangled up with he-men Irish? You guys are always just as guilt-ridden as wine-drinking altar boys."

"Is that right?" Joe said, still refusing to meet Renée's eyes. "Did it ever occur to you that you don't know what the hell you're talking about?"

Renée released her grip and stepped back. "Yeah, of course . . . you're right, Joe." Her voice was cold and precise. "You didn't go back to Vietnam last year to flesh out that book. You went back because Monique was pregnant and needed you. The whole goddamned Tet Offensive was your fault, too, right? How about Paris—the whole thing in Paris? The riots and the general strike—all that was your fault, too, wasn't it? God, Joe, if you really believe that kind of crap, why don't you just go out and kill yourself? You'll find the real fire-and-brimstone hell much more satisfying."

Joe faced Renée directly. "It's not that easy, Renée." His voice was uneven with a jangly edge. "All I know is that I was down on the Left Bank in bed with some student when Monique was out in Creteuil laying in the mud of our garden with the premature baby dying right in front of her. If you'd seen the blood on the grass, you wouldn't dismiss it all so lightly."

"Answer one question, Joe. Did you go down to the riots to screw girls?"

"Of course not. I was . . . I am . . . a reporter. It was the biggest story to hit France since Liberation. I got stuck down there; the phones were all out. The goddamned C.R.S. had the Left Bank sealed off for three days."

"The whole thing was an unhappy accident."

Joe started to roll up the sleeping bag. "I seem to have a lot of unhappy accidents," he said over his shoulder.

"Well, what are you going to do about that?" Renée sat

next to him on the sand and was nuzzling her face close to his. Joe sighed and stared down at his hands.

"I guess I'll have to work on not having any more."

She kissed him lightly on the face. "I'll help you, Joe, if you let me. I'll help you."

7

George

George Briggs was slightly drunk. That was one of the hazards of associating with Joe, he thought. A person ended up drinking a lot out of self-defense. He felt the can of beer, cold between his gripping thighs, as he shifted into second gear and accelerated the Land Rover up the long incline. Behind them the lights of Tetuán sparkled against the faintly moonlit backdrop of the Rif foothills.

He had done well at that roadblock. Joe had not even woken up. He was still asleep on the pile of sleeping bags and baggage concealing the tarpaulin-wrapped metal tube. It had been sound thinking to pack all the camping gear. The Moroccan gendarmes were used to seeing campers along the coast in summer. They had flashed their light on the Gibraltar license plate and once onto the pile of gear and the sleeping form of Joe and waved them through. George had an opened carton of Marlboros ready with which to distract them, but it had not been necessary. Even if they had poked around inside, they probably would not have found the tube, as it was hidden beneath a carefully constructed, interlocking pile of gear, overlaid with blankets and sleeping bags. Besides, they weren't checking Europeans closely. These late-night roadblocks were set up mainly to deter the kif runners from the Rif.

Joe had wanted to only take the diving gear and the tarpaulin, but George had stood up to him and insisted on carrying all the rest. Now he had been proved right. It would be interesting to see Joe's reaction when he heard about the roadblock.

He wouldn't gloat, though. Joe was naturally nervous,

and the rotten year he had gone through had made him touchy and thin-skinned when it came to criticism. George was content to play the buffoon for a while as long as Joe would finally concede that he would not have been able to pull this deal off without his friend's help, not just the physical lugging and driving the car, but the actual planning necessary to make the endeavor work. Like that business with the extra rope and pulleys—they had been all the way out of Tangier, past the old bull ring, when he had made Joe turn around to drive to the yacht club for the rope and pulleys. Joe had been impatient with the delay, but, once again, George had been right. Even with its ballast tanks drained of sea water, the tube weighed over two hundred fifty pounds. Joe had said they could build a ramp or manhandle it up into the car. But George was an engineer. He knew better. The log tripod George had constructed had been perfect. With the weight spread between the four pulleys, they had actually swung the clumsy, dripping, metal tube up and guided it through the rear door of the Land Rover. If they had set about building a ramp in the dark on the beach, they would still be there.

Joe had had a difficult sail back that morning from Ksar-el-Serghir. Renée and he had not arrived until three-thirty that afternoon, and then at five they had set about loading the car for the secret return trip to Targa. Now it was almost four A.M. Joe would be okay when he got some sleep. The worst part was almost over, anyway. Once they had the tube back in Tangier, all Joe had to do was contact the Americans at the embassy in Rabat and strike his bargain with them.

The night air felt cold as they climbed the last range of hills before dropping down to the coastal plateau outside Tangier. He closed the driver's side window and lit one of the Marlboros, choking on the unfamiliar harshness of the smoke. Ahead, on a dark curve, he could see the winking taillights of a truck; otherwise, the road was deserted. These hills were treeless, grazed out by countless flocks of sheep and goats, and badly eroded. In the moonlight the hills appeared smooth, but beneath the harsh, revealing sun, they were rough with splinters of flint showing through the scrubbrush, which clung to the sparse soil.

With the window closed, George could smell the seaweed odor of the hidden tube. *There must still be a trickle of water coming from the tanks inside,* he thought. *It's a weird kind of ballast system for there to be that much plumbing. Joe's probably right. It's a Russian Navy gadget for spying on the Polaris subs. This whole deal is going to be interesting.*

PART II

A Team of Professionals

8

Inspection and Appraisal

The iodine odor of the sea filled George Briggs's garage. As with most of the villas built into the slope of the mountain, George's garage and servants' quarters were at ground level, a basement to the floors above. With the metal garage doors barred and the overhead trap door to the kitchen pantry shut, they had complete privacy. The cylinder lay like a cadaver on two saw horses, dripping water into sandy puddles beneath it. On the mountain the slightly lower atmospheric pressure had caused the last of the water in the ballast tanks to drain. It was chilly in the garage and the cold light of the fluorescent tubes on George's coveralls heightened Joe's feeling of being in a mortuary.

He sat against the edge of the wood-working lathe, watching George select some wrenches from the racks of tools above the mechanic's bench. Everything was so neatly arranged—the fire extinguishers, the expensive tools. But the equipment was not just for show. George was a skilled mechanic. He had overhauled his Jaguar's engine during the winter and was eager to do the same for the *Dragonfly*'s diesel engine.

"Well," George said, "there she is."

"Yep. It looks so *big* inside the garage, doesn't it?"

George kneaded the muscles of his shoulders. "It looked big last night and heavy, too. We really did need that tackle-and-pulley sling."

"Yeah, of course. Look, you know a lot more about that sort of thing than I do, George. I'm going to have to sort of depend on you for a little while longer, okay?"

"Sure. I knew what I was getting into Saturday night when I first saw this thing. But I'd just like to be kept clear of the financial side of this operation, Joe—you know, the salvage."

"Don't worry." Joe glanced at the electric clock above the lathe bench. It was almost ten o'clock, early morning in New York. Tuesday. "I've got to get cleaned up and head downtown to the P.T.T.," he said. "It'll take me a couple of hours to get a person-to-person call through to Bill Derring at Hawks and Spencer, but I want to talk with him, not some flunky."

George continued selecting socket wrenches from the tool rack. "What are you going to tell him?"

"The truth, for a change—that I'm about to sell some 'property' here in Tangier and that they can expect reimbursement of the advance within two weeks. Then I'm going to call some guys I know on the *Times* and the *Washington Post* and see if there might actually be a feature market for parts of the manuscript."

George looked at his friend. Joe was a bit haggard, scruffy from the two long days and nights, but he looked confident for the first time since George could remember. "That sounds good, Joe. Just one thing . . ."

"Yeah?"

"How are you going to make all those overseas calls if you're dead broke?"

Joe nodded. "Yeah," he repeated. "I forgot about that."

"In the top right-hand drawer of my dresser," George said, "is my black wallet. I've got about two hundred bucks in *dirhams*. Take what you want."

"Only a *loan,* George."

"Okay. Sign an I.O.U. if you want to. I'm going to see if I can open these two bottom panels. There's still sea water inside, and sand, too. This thing wasn't designed to lay on its side like this. I don't want water sloshing around in there and maybe shorting something out."

Joe paused at the foot of the ladder to the overhead trap door. "George, don't misunderstand me now. I really appreciate all your help. But just don't get too carried away. Don't go opening up anything you won't be able to close again."

"Go ahead and make your phone calls and don't

worry about me," George replied. He was holding calipers to measure the size of the recessed bolt heads on the side of the tube. "I just want to drain off any extra water that's still inside."

Joe still looked doubtful. "Fine," he eventually said, then climbed up the ladder.

Joe did not return to George's house until after four that afternoon. It had taken hours to place all his calls from the crowded central post office. But now that job was done. He had gained himself some time. Bill Derring had been decent on the phone, agreeing to "cool it" with the "vultures" in the contract department of Hawks and Spencer. Leo Nitzle at the *Post* had expressed genuine interest in the articles, too. He'd even mentioned an advance. And tomorrow Joe could begin his negotiations for the device with the Americans. Things were looking up for a change.

He rang George's doorbell. No one answered. He could see into the kitchen through the glass terrace doors. Joe slid back the screen door and called. No one answered. He went through the kitchen to the narrow pantry. The trapdoor down to the garage was closed. He tugged the handle, but the door was locked from below.

"That you, Joe?" George's voice was muffled by the heavy wooden door.

A moment later Joe heard the bolt slide free and the trapdoor lifted to admit him. He stared down the ladder at the brightly lit cubicle. Hot anger hit him and he lashed out.

"Just what the hell have you been doing?" he said. He could see the cylinder below him. The previously clean length of the tube was broken in five places, revealing wide, irregular gaps, as if the device had been dropped from the saw horses and the delicate metal skin had been shattered, exposing the electronic clockwork of the interior.

He climbed down the ladder.

"You were gone a long time," George said sheepishly. "Well, I got two of the panels off and I found the others. Maybe I did get a little carried away. But don't worry, Joe, they're inspection panels. They came right off."

"They came right *off,*" Joe said, "but will they go right back *on?*"

"I checked by putting the first one back on before I went ahead with the others. Don't worry, I know what I'm doing."

"I sure hope so," Joe muttered as he peered into the exposed entrails of the cylinder.

The blocks of printed circuits encased in water-tight Plexiglas and the web of color-coded wires reminded him of a communications satellite he'd once seen at a trade fair. He gazed dumbly at the maze of transistors and finger-thick capacitators. There seemed to be acres of printed circuits and miles of wires inside the tube. At the lower end of the cylinder, he stared down at the labyrinth of tanks, rubber hose, and alloy piping.

"That's the sea-water ballasting system," George said, pointing with a long screwdriver. "There are three separate compartments. The bottom one is the ballasting. Here, in the middle, are the batteries and electronic sensors, and the radio gear is up there in the cap. It's a very elegant setup."

Joe looked inside the curved panel at the side of the cap. Then he stood and lit a cigarette.

"What the hell do you make of it?"

"Radio gear looks like it's designed for both short- and long-range communication," George said. "There's a single side band set and a smaller U.H.F. outfit. Here's the loaded whip antenna for both," he continued, talking as he walked down the length of the cylinder, using his screwdriver to point out various details. Joe caught an occasional tidbit like "nickel-cadmium batteries" and "sonar recorders," but most of George's explanation was meaningless technical jargon to him.

"I never would have guessed that the Russians were this proficient in miniaturization," George said, concluding his analysis of the cylinder's equipment.

"That's just great, George. But what does the damned thing do?"

"Why, it's a listening buoy, of course. What did you think it was?"

"A listening buoy," Joe repeated. "Fine. What the hell does a listening buoy *listen* to?"

"Submarines, Joe . . . just like you thought. This buoy's designed to pick up the underwater sounds of the American Polaris subs over at Rota . . . not just the sounds, actually, but the whole spectrum: sonar image, engine heat, magnetic profile, the total output of energy—what they call the 'signature'—that the sub produces as it passes through the water. All of this is probably recorded on those tapes inside there. Look, there they are." He indicated the exposed edge of a black tape cassette, half hidden beneath a block of circuitry in the tube's center section.

Joe made another tour of inspection, stopping now at each open panel to peer more closely at the electronics and plumbing.

"Once the data have been recorded," George continued, "the buoy rises up to the surface and the antenna pops out of the cap to transmit. There must have been some kind of anchored cable reel on the bottom that let the buoy travel up and down when these compressed air bottles blew out the ballast tanks."

Joe ran his hand through his hair and sighed. "I'll have to take your word for most of this, George," he said. "The whole damned thing's too complicated for me. Just tell me one thing. Why would the Russians go to all the trouble of building something like this? It's not a weapon, is it?"

"Not exactly." George paused, searching for the correct words. "While you were out, I looked through some back issues of *Scientific American*. I think I found something interesting. Look at it this way. If you had the problem of keeping tabs on our Polaris subs, how would you go about it? I mean, once they're out at sea, traveling submerged, they put out so much electronic decoy noise and they hide down beneath thermal layers, so they're almost impossible to find. Besides, they cruise out in the open sea, off the shipping lanes. It would be worse than trying to find a needle in a haystack."

"So," Joe said impatiently, "where does this buoy come in?"

"That's the *elegant* side of it. The way the Russians can be sure of hearing a real sub, and not some decoy noise, is when the subs enter and leave their bases. If the buoy picks up the sound of a sub leaving base and sends a message, then they've got that particular sub spotted for the duration of its cruise. They can follow it like a bloodhound."

Joe stared hard at George across the shining surface of the buoy. "I don't follow you at all," he said. "Didn't you just tell me that those subs can't be detected once they're out at sea? Now you're saying the Russians can tail one like a bloodhound."

"That's where the *Scientific American* article comes in. Polaris subs are atomic-powered. Their reactors produce a lot of heat, and the heat shows up as a track on the surface that can be sensed by an infrared detector . . . in a satellite, say, or in one of the Soviet fishing boats that is always hanging around the Straits. If you had a computerized plotting board, you could trace the sub's progress by following its heat track across the surface. But all ships make heat and the whole surface of the ocean is cut by the tracks all the time. That's where this baby comes into play. It signals the exact time a real Polaris sub leaves base. Then the satellites and planes and surface ships take over with their infrared scanners."

"Are you sure about all of this?" Joe asked skeptically.

George seemed flustered for a moment. Then he said, "Hell, Joe, I can't be positive about it, but it makes sense. And I know one thing—this buoy is not just some toy they stamp out on an assembly line. It's a damned sophisticated piece of gear, and they wouldn't have built it so well if it didn't have an important job to do. Our people are going to be very pleased to get their hands on it."

"How pleased? Ten-thousand-bucks'-worth pleased? Twenty? . . . Thirty?"

George looked troubled. "I don't know, Joe," he said, nervously wiping his hands across his coveralls. "I'd rather not get involved in that end of it."

Joe patted the metal skin of the buoy. "Don't worry, George," he said, "with any luck, you won't have to."

Joe's alarm clock rang at seven-thirty. He reached out automatically and cuffed it until the jangling bell went dead. His head dropped back to the pillow, but then he sat bolt upright. He had almost forgotten what he had to do today. It felt strange to be up so early, shaving before the foggy bathroom mirror. It felt stranger still to pull on a freshly ironed shirt and fumble clumsily with the knot of his necktie. It was almost as if he had awakened from a Rip Van Winkle sleep and was on his way down to some wire service office to knock out the morning's copy.

Zorah, his housekeeper, was moving around happily in the kitchen, whipping up an omelet and making toast. Ali, the gardener, came in smiling with a bouquet of frangipangi for the dining room table. They were obviously delighted to see *M'sieu* up early in the morning again, wearing civilized clothes and looking so clean-shaven and businesslike. Ali had even bicycled down to the kiosk on the rue de Belgique and produced a copy of the *Petit Marocain* for Joe to read with his morning coffee. *Shit,* Joe thought, *they must think that I've gotten some kind of a job, that soon Madame and Joey will come home and everyone will live happily ever after.*

He drove down the old mountain road at a quarter to nine, his well-worn leather portfolio sitting next to him on the seat of the Land Rover. Climbing to the opposite slope into the city, he passed wizened old Berber women humped under their loads of firewood. A leather-aproned goatherd was leading his nanny goats up a side lane, ringing his bell wildly to attract the Spanish maids and Arab *fatimas* for their morning liter of blood-warm milk.

As Joe turned off the rue Sidi Amar, he saw veiled and jellabaed Moroccan mothers with their small children waiting at the gate of the whitewashed Spanish school. The summer was half over and they were lining up to register their children for next fall's term. Ali had already broached the subject of little Mohammed. Monique had promised Ali that she would get the child into the Ecole Française. That cost money, not much, but it sure as hell wasn't free. *Well,* he thought, *if all of this works out, it will be okay; there'll be no problem.*

The stressed concrete block of the American consulate general stood solitary and Daliesque against the backdrop of the open valley. A surrealistic cement screen masked the three floors of plate glass with a geometric starkness. It was as if the building was turned in upon itself, that the actions taken within its confines were totally alien to the civilization outside.

He pulled into the parking space between two big American cars. For a long time he sat silently, squinting against the hard white light reflected off the stone monolith in front of him. It was stupid to be so jumpy; this was by far the easiest part of the whole show. His story was perfect. His clothes were impeccable. He fingered the crisp seersucker of his sportcoat and the lightly starched collar of his shirt. They knew him at the consulate. Nobody would raise an eyebrow. Christ, if he couldn't pull this off, what chance would he have dealing with the pros?

Joe opened the notebook in his lap and read the notes he had scribbled there with his felt pen during his second cup of coffee. It was just like blocking out the framework of a story: notes on approach, necessary interviews, travel schedule. At this stage of the game he could simply be writing a four-hundred-word piece for *Newsweek*.

At the top of the page he had written "CONTACT," beneath which he had scrawled "AmConGen, stud book, Emb. Tel. book, etc. Cover: Af trip story, etc."

At the bottom of the page was another block-printed heading: "PAYMENT???" He had underlined the question marks several times. Contacting the embassy C.I.A. men in Rabat would pose no great problem. But devising a foolproof, yet simple, system of payment once the buoy had been handed over to them would not be so easy. Beneath the heading he had noted: "Swiss bank? Am Bank??? Numbered account? Real name, or alias??? SEE: Harry Rains for details."

He read his notes over slowly, then flipped the notebook shut. The details of the money would keep until later. Now the important thing was to make contact with the C.I.A. men in Rabat, who officially did not exist.

"Good morning," Joe said, smiling at the receptionist. "Has Mr. Rose come in yet?"

"Oh, yes, sir," the man answered. "Mr. Rose? Yes, sir. Mr. O'Donald from Rabat, sir?"

Jesus, Joe thought, *this sportcoat's really got him. He thinks I'm an embassy stiff from Rabat.* "No," he answered in a kindly tone, presenting one of his old Associated Press business cards. "It's Mr. Clinton. I'm a friend of Mr. Rose."

The receptionist mumbled an apology and took the card. He punched buttons on his telephone switchboard and spoke in Spanish to Paul Rose's secretary, who said Mr. Clinton should come right in.

Paul Rose was young and athletic, taller than Joe, deeply tanned from hours on the tennis courts. He rose from his chair and shook Joe's hand with painful earnestness. Like Joe, he wore a narrow, regimental striped tie. His close-cropped, balding head of hair belied the fact that he had just celebrated his thirtieth birthday.

"Joe," he sang out, "what a nice surprise. What are you up to? Haven't seen you on the courts for ages."

Joe held up his right hand, still throbbing from Paul's handshake. "Yes, I sprained my wrist on the boat a few weeks ago. Took a long time to heal." *And,* he thought, *that fucking tennis club costs a lot of money in dues, money I haven't got.*

Paul seated him in an imitation-leather easy chair and came out from behind his desk to sit on an angular blue sofa. It was the old diplomat's ploy, keeping the outsiders away from the state "secrets," as if the administrative circulars piled in the "out" basket of his desk were of any value to anyone. *Shit,* Joe thought, *they'd classify the toilet paper as confidential around this place.* On the walls of the office were framed photographs of Paul with various dead animals he had shot on safari in Tanzania.

"So," Paul said, shaking his head, declining Joe's offered cigarette, "what can we do for you, Joe?"

Joe made a show of digging into his leather case to extract a folded piece of paper. He held it up for a moment, then dropped it into his lap. "I've just received this telegram with an assignment for a long *Newsweek* piece on the political situation in the Arab capitals outside the Middle East, kind of a Six-Day-War, two-years-later thing. They want to get the atmosphere in the Maghreb and places like the Sudan and Somalia."

"Great," Paul said. "Sounds like the kind of thing you could do very well."

"I'm going to begin out in Khartoum and work my way back here," Joe continued. "I'll start next week. I'd like to ask a favor of you, though. I know a lot of the P.A.O.'s and political officers at the embassies in the towns I'll be hitting, and I usually like to send them a cable outlining the story I'll be doing in advance, in case they feel like helping out. It's only common courtesy to let them know I'm coming. You know what I mean, don't you?"

Paul was only at the beginning of his second overseas tour. He had no idea what Joe was really talking about, but he was aware that he was dealing with an experienced foreign correspondent and was flattered by a chance to help him. "Sure," Paul said. "What's the favor?"

"Well," Joe continued in an even, unruffled tone, "the way you people keep changing posts, it's hard to keep tabs on who's stationed where. I like to send personal telegrams to the guys I actually know. I was wondering if I could have a look at your *Foreign Service List* and the *Biographic Register*. I've got last year's at home, but I imagine there've been a lot of reassignments since then."

Paul stared at him for a moment, trying to mask his feelings of consternation. He was, after all, a very junior officer. He was quite sure in his own mind that the volumes in question were not classified, but he was wary of making the decision to hand them over to an outsider.

"Right," he answered uncertainly. "I see what you mean." He paused, rubbing his big, muscular hands together and then catching himself and forcing his arms down stiffly against the sides of the sofa. "I'll have to go upstairs and get them from the file room."

He rose awkwardly and slipped out of the office, closing the door quietly behind him. Joe laughed. *Christ, he's got to clear it with somebody. If I had twelve bucks, I could order the two books from the Government Printing Office. And he's afraid to show them to me.*

The door swung open with a bang and Paul was back in the office. "Sorry," he blurted out, "I may as well take these telegrams upstairs while I'm at it." He scooped up his crowded "out" basket and was gone again. This time Joe broke into real laughter. *Close squeak there, old boy,* he thought. *I almost had access to really sensitive stuff. The Reds are dying to know all about the consulate's gas-coupon policy and the schedule for polio shots.*

Joe flipped through a copy of *Hunting World* while he waited. Five minutes later Paul reappeared, visibly more at ease and clutching his "out" basket under one arm and the *Foreign Service List* and *Biographic Register* under the other.

"Here you go, Joe," he said. "You can use that table if you want to make any notes."

Joe accepted the two books: the *Biographic Register,* large and heavy, like a college catalog, and the *Foreign Service List,* magazine-thin. He sat at the coffee table and removed the notebook from his portfolio. He was keenly aware that Paul was watching him over his stylish half-frame assistant secretary's spectacles. Joe got out his own shell-rimmed reading glasses and proceeded to page through the books at a leisurely pace.

The problem was quite simple. He wanted to know the names of the C.I.A. people at the Rabat embassy. Finding out who the spooks were was a basic part of any decent reporter's skills. What made it easy was the fact that the State Department wouldn't let the spooks even claim to be regular Foreign Service Officers, the F.S.O.'s. The spooks always showed up in the lists as F.S.R.'s, Foreign Service Reserves. It was also a well-known fact that the resident C.I.A. people always worked in the Political or Economic sections of an embassy. All you had to do was to separate the F.S.O. State Department officers from the F.S.R. officer ringers in the *Foreign Service List* and then go back and double check against the listing of previous posts and positions in the *Biographic Register* to see if the pattern held true. C.I.A. spooks almost never worked as consular officers or in administration. If a so-called state officer had an F.S.R. label and had always served in Pol or Econ and was language-qualified for a certain area, then you could bet your life he was a spook.

Joe paged methodically through the two books, taking three pages of notes on names and titles of political and public affairs officers from Bjibouti to Algiers. By the time he got to the Rabat embassy, Paul was deeply absorbed in drafting some memo. The Rabat spooks were easy to spot. He truned the page of his notebook and quickly wrote down the names of the two obvious C.I.A. officers. He took a few quickly scrawled notes on their backgrounds, then folded over his pages and stacked the books in front of him on the coffee table.

"Thanks, Paul," he said. "That'll about do it. I'd better get down to the P.T.T. and start sending off my cables."

"You found what you were looking for?" Paul asked.

"Yeah," Joe said, getting to his feet. "There weren't that many transfers. Poor old Nick Richards is still stuck down in Khartoum. Ever run into Nick? He's quite a character."

Joe sat at a corner table on the terrace of the Café de Paris. He had a *café-au-lait* and a brandy chaser in front of him. Toying with the folded copy of the *Petit Marocain,* he glanced surreptitiously down at the notebook, folded inside the newspaper.

Jesus, he thought, smiling suddenly, *what am I hiding my notebook for? I can't start getting paranoid at this stage of the game. There's nobody here who's going to look over my shoulder.*

Just beyond his table the sidewalk was filling up with mid-morning pedestrian traffic. Arab ladies in well-cut jellabas pushed through the crowds, shepherding their miniskirted daughters in front of them. Berber women from the Rif walked along slowly beneath their straw sombreros, clutching a corner of their candy-striped shawls in their teeth as a ritual gesture of veiled modesty. There were many Europeans, as well, mostly German and French tourists. Weaving among the crowds on the sidewalk was a small army of Arab boy street urchins with their pitiful trays of peanuts and wire clips of postcards. The café's resident shoeshine boy kept them away from the clients on the terrace. Out in the Place de France, beneath the gaudy neon tubes of the now-dry fountain, a tall, patiently aloof Moroccan policeman was giving directions to a French tourist. The Frenchman was towing a vacation trailer behind his Citroën, and the traffic on the Boulevard Pasteur had backed up, car horns honking wildly at the bottleneck.

Joe watched the traffic jam for a moment and then turned back to his notes. There were only two obvious spooks at the Rabat embassy. Chances were there were more in the country, under private business cover, in Casablanca, probably. The two in Rabat would be enough for him, though. Barent was forty-six years old and listed as a F.S.R.-2 in the Political Section. MacCormack was only thirty and already a grade four. He was also listed in the Political Section. Barent had a background of European assignments: Paris, Brussels, Marseilles, and Berlin. MacCormack was strictly an Arabist. As a grade-two officer, Barent must be the station chief. There was nothing in Joe's notes that gave any real clue to either man's personality. They were both married. Both had children. In addition to native English, one was fluent in French, the other in Arabic. The brief outlines of their past careers, however, gave the impression of two hard-working, ambitious professionals. Judging from their previous posts and jobs, they were both career C.I.A., Barent having joined the "Company" in the early 1950s. Barent was Joe's choice. He was, after all, the station chief, and the man's almost four years in Berlin must have given him experience in the fine art of buying military secrets.

That was all there was to it. He knew the embassy telephone number. All he had to do now was call to arrange a meeting. He sat back in his chair and sipped the aromatic Spanish cognac. There was no sense in plunging headlong into this thing, though. It was obvious from what George had told him and from his own sketchy knowledge of the nether world of military espionage that the gleaming metal buoy up there in George's garage was worth a lot of money. Again he recalled the story of the North Korean lieutenant who had flown a limping old MIG-15 across to Japan and collected a reward of twenty thousand dollars from the spooks. That had been nine years ago. The maze of secret electronics he had glimpsed through the inspection panels of the buoy was worth a lot more than twenty thousand. How much, though?

Scribbling in the notebook, Joe added up the money he owed to the publishers, the overdue mortgage payments, and the various private debts he had accrued around town. Thirteen thousand dollars would get him off the hook. But then he needed money to live. The Hawks and Spencer book was part of history now. There *might* be money in some *Post* features, but he couldn't count on it. Anyway, it wouldn't be enough to even start paying off his debts. He had to live, and it cost money to live the way he did, with the house and servants, the boat and the car. There were a lot of things he would like to have, as well. The *Dragonfly* was a nice boat, but it was only twenty-four feet long. He sure wouldn't mind something a little bigger, maybe one of those lean, ten-meter Fiberglas "cookie shells," or why not a real yacht, say a teak forty-five-footer, something with a decent engine and a full suit of sails and a lot of comfort below. He could write in the winter and sail in the summer, cruising all the way over to the Aegean. There'd be money to be made with a decent-sized yacht, too. Most of those charter captains in Greece and Italy were getting over a hundred bucks a day during the season. Why not? Why the hell not?

The brandy was warm in his stomach. He signaled the waiter for another. That would be the life—the house all paid for, a fifty-foot sailboat, no more money problems. He could relax then and dig into serious feature writing.

At the bottom of his page of notes he wrote the figure sixty thousand dollars, then underlined it twice. Thirty-five thousand for the fifty-footer; eight thousand in debts, and five to six thousand a year to live on for, say, three years. He drained the second cognac and followed it with a sip of sweet coffee.

An old man was pushing a cart heaped to overflowing with yellow melons up the incline of the rue de la Liberté. A huge, air-conditioned tourist bus wheeled sharply around the Place de France, causing the old man to careen his cart up onto the safety of the opposite sidewalk. Melons cascaded, splitting, to the pavement and were snatched up and spirited away into the crowd by the ever-present urchins. The old man stood still, his face screwed into a grimace as he beseeched God to blacken the face of every *nesrani* tourist. The policeman strolled over, twirling his baton. His proximity dispersed the street boys and the old man bent arthritically to pick up the melons remaining on the sidewalk.

Joe looked down at his notebook. He felt something sag inside. *Christ,* he thought, *who the hell am I trying to kid? Sixty thousand dollars. Sure. Great. They're just going to sit down and write me a check for sixty thousand for that piece of junk up there. And then I'll pay off all my debts and buy a big sailboat and sit down and write Pulitzer Prize features. That sounds like something Ali and Zorah would dream up. I'll be lucky if they give me five for it. Face it. George got a little carried away with all that crap about spy satellites and magnetic signatures. He meant well. It's just that he doesn't know any more about this business than I do. So they build a gadget to listen for American subs, anchor it near the Rota base, and some ship hits it and snaps the cable with its screws. Hell, the Russians aren't stupid. They've thought about the chances of something like that happening. They've probably got fifty of those buoys anchored over there in international waters. They expect to lose a few. That's the way military people think. They figure in their losses in advance.*

Shit, the Americans must already have a whole collection of these babies. The C.I.A.'s probably got their frogmen out there all the time diving around. Sure, they'll buy the thing. They'll want to add it to their collection. But they won't pay any sixty thousand for it.

Joe folded over the bottom of the page and tore it into shreds. He released them slowly in white puffs as a sudden breeze wafted up the bluff from the sea. He felt ridiculous sitting there in the café in a sportcoat and necktie. *What a pipe dream. It sure sounded beautiful, didn't it? Home free with money in the bank and a great big fancy sailboat.* His cigarette tasted bitter after the sweet cognac and coffee. He ground it out and rose to leave the café, shoving a pile of change into the hand of the waiter.

The wider sidewalks along the Boulevard Pasteur were less congested. He strolled with his hands deep in his pockets, his portfolio gripped by his elbow. Stopping at the seaside panorama terrace, he gazed down at the ships in the port and the white caps in the Straits. To the northwest was Cape Trafalgar and Cadiz, with the Polaris base of Rota. *Wonder where he snagged the buoy? Could have been anywhere, of course. Must have definitely been a ship, maybe a tanker like the one that almost zapped me, that hit the buoy and cut its moor-*

ing cable. I'll have to check the chart to see if the currents come down the coast this way. That would make sense; it'd be drifting free with its cable cut and end up on some shoal where the Arabs usually place their nets. Might have been floating free for a long time. Have to get George to see if he can take a reading on the batteries. That'd give some kind of clue as to how long it's been loose. He closed his eyes against the sun's glare and remembered the packed bays of solid-state electronics he had seen through the inspection panels. *All those recorders and that fancy radio gear wasted, down the drain. That buoy is nearly seven feet long and full of goodies. Even has two kinds of radios. What a wasteful business.*

Joe strolled along again, aimlessly. He stopped just at the end of the terrace and stared out to sea again. That was it. Of course. Why didn't he see it before? Two radios. That's what George had said. One long-range and one like an F.M., short-range police-car radio. How simple! All the buoys wouldn't have to be so complex if there were a network of smaller ones listening and transmitting their data to a central station—a recording buoy that taped the transmissions, sorted them out, and stored them to be re-transmitted to the satellite or trawler. The little buoys probably were anchored near the surface and they all came up together—that big baby and all the small fry—probably at night. Once the big buoy had all the data recorded, it probably sorted through the tapes and compared them with some kind of memory bank and then transmitted the best stuff.

That's a whole new ball game, Joe thought as he strode across the boulevard toward the rue de Fes, where he'd parked his car. *If that thing up in George's garage really is some kind of kingpin buoy in a complicated listening system, then I can buy two yachts with the money it'll bring!*

George sipped his coffee and sighed contentedly. His back ached from the hours of stooping over the buoy on the low saw horses. Joe held out the bottle of Martel and George nodded. The brandy mixed with the coffee in the cup sent up a spicy aroma. It was almost ten o'clock at night and neither had eaten since breakfast. Outside the metal garage doors, the east wind, which had been rising all day, was howling up the steep lanes of the mountain.

"That's about it," George said. He accepted a cigarette from Joe and leaned back against the workbench. The bench was littered with wires, alligator clips, and the volt meter. All afternoon and evening he and Joe had worked, forging ahead ignorantly as they sought to decipher the maze of circuits inside the buoy. There were still many gaps, but they had managed to discover the functions of most of the electronic equipment it contained.

"It's a good thing the batteries still had plenty of juice in them," Joe said.

"Well," George answered, "I'd know for certain if I could figure out these instruction plates in the battery bay, but I'm pretty sure they're just about up to full charge. The two that read thirty-two volts are in parallel for the single-side band transmitter, and the twenty-four volts in the other one seem more than enough for the recorders." He looked down at his carefully made notes and diagrams on the ruled pad next to the volt meter. "I think you've hit the nail on the head, Joe. Congratulations."

Joe smiled. "I never told you I had a Ph.D. from M.I.T., did I?"

George smiled back. "Like you said, it's a fantastic system. Makes a lot of sense, too. For the long-range transmissions, it'd be stupid to have all the buoys in the network broadcasting. It'd be too easy to pick them up and get a fix on them. But if the little buoys just transmitted on very low-power V.H.F., say, with a high-speed taped transmission that squeezed everything down to a couple of seconds, then it'd be almost impossible to get a decent fix on them, especially if the frequency was changed at random. I'd still like to dig in there and get those crystals out of the master receiver. The boys out at the R.C.A. station could find out their exact frequency for us."

Joe laughed. "I think that the boys out at the R.C.A. station will have to wait until the boys in Langley, Virginia, have had their turn."

"C.I.A.?"

"That's right—the C.I.A. I've got a hunch that they're going to go wild when they get their hands on this. It really is like some kind of space satellite."

George looked affectionately at the buoy. "It's a beautiful piece of engineering, all right. Like I said, I wouldn't have thought the Russians were up to it."

"I hope the spooks are just as surprised. After what we've figured out today, I kind of think that they will be."

"Are you as hungry as I am?" George asked.

"Hungrier. Listen, lend me another hundred *dirhams,* will you? I'll take you down to the Nautilus and we'll have some steak *au poivre.*"

Harry Rains sat back in his swivel chair and chewed reflectively on the stem of his glasses. The background noise of the morning traffic on the boulevard three stories below was lost against the rumbling of the air conditioner. Harry was on the verge of saying something. He was being very much the British banker and taking his time. Joe looked past his friend to the sailing trophies on the bookcase filled with impressive leather-bound volumes. On the far wall of the office was a framed photograph of a much younger Harry Rains, in the tropical whites of a Royal Navy sub-lieutenant, standing on the bridge of a warship in Singapore harbor.

"Well, Joe," Harry finally said, "I don't see any easy answer. A Swiss bank is out. People think that they'll take on any kind of business with no questions asked, but they just don't operate that way. They will, of course, receive overseas deposits into a regular, established account, but they will *not* take deposits from unknown sources for an unknown account holder. If they would, they'd be catering to every crook and racketeer in the world. You see what I mean?"

Joe nodded. "So, in other words, I'll have to go up there and open my own account?"

"Not necessarily," Harry said, sitting back in his chair. He rested his elbow on his desk. "I appreciate your need to keep this confidential, Joe. The business of ghost-writing books is something I couldn't pretend to understand. But could you at least tell me if the deposits will be made by a check from the publisher or from the 'author'?"

Joe had rehearsed the cover story so many times the previous night that he almost believed it himself. He pursed his lips as if he were consulting his memory for the details of a contract. "I forgot the exact language of the terms, Harry," he said, "but I'm pretty sure they'll be made in two lots, either by cash or certified cashier's check. It's the author's wish that there be no connection between him and me. There's another factor, too. I don't want to pay American taxes on this unless I have to. Technically, the money will be earned in America, but if there's no record of the transaction there, I won't have to pay."

"Quite," Harry said briskly. "I hope you don't mind my saying so, Joe, but this does border on the illegal, you know."

"You can throw me out of your office if you want, Harry," Joe said. "I just thought you could give me a tip or two."

"Mmmm." Harry paused. "I can think of one foolproof way, Joe, and you won't have to go all the way to Switzerland to do it, either. As I say, the old, established Swiss banks are definitely out of the question. But there are other banks operating in Switzerland. There are quite a few Arab banks, for instance, which do a lot of unorthodox financing on oil speculations, that kind of thing. They're bound by the same laws as the big Swiss banks, but let's say they aren't quite as choosy about their clientele.

"But even they won't take money out of the blue and hold it for some unnamed client. They will, of course, deal with another bank. You get on the flight to Gibraltar tomorrow and go over to see the fellows at Barclays Bank. Be honest with them. Explain the whole ghost-writing business. Deposit, say, two thousand dollars. I'll give you the names of two or three foreign banks operating in Switzerland—Lebanese and Kuwaiti banks. You pick one of them and then ask Barclays to effect a telegraphic bank transfer of, say, half your deposit to the bank you choose, explaining that account information will follow by express letter. Then you sit down and write a nice, registered letter to the bank in Switzerland, saying you wish to open a numbered account and that the Barclays transfer is the first small deposit. That'll conform nicely to the Swiss laws. Then all you have to do, when the first of the payments comes through, is give the number of the bank account in Switzerland to your publishers and they can deposit a cashier's check, bank notes, or gold bullion, for that matter. The America tax people will have no legal way to trace that number to you. The Swiss are rather sticky about that kind of thing."

Joe sat silently for a moment. This seemed to be the perfect answer to his banking problems. All he needed now was the capital for the initial deposit, and George would be the source of that. He felt snugly happy inside. It had been only two days since he had had the buoy, and already he had solved his two biggest problems: identifying the American intelligence agents, and planning a foolproof delivery system for his eventual payment. Things were shaking down nicely. It had been a good idea to visit Harry Rains.

"Here you are, Joe," Harry said, handing a piece of office stationery across his desk. "I've listed three banks. You can pick any one you wish. Two are in Geneva and one in Zurich. Personally, I'd recommend the Banque du Moyen Orient. Their home office is in Beirut, but they do the bulk of their operations in Geneva. They're quite used to handling short-term holdings. Mind you, they'll charge an arm and a leg for their commission, something on the order of twelve percent, but they'll also deliver the goods . . . everything strictly confidential, of course."

"Thanks," Joe said, tucking the piece of paper into his portfolio. "Are you still looking for crew for the Málaga race?"

"Yes," Harry said, "as a matter of fact, I am. Are you going to be free on the weekend of the fourteenth?"

"I probably will be," Joe said, rising to leave. "I'll check my calendar and give you a ring."

9

Contact

Joe bought a *Herald Tribune* from the newspaper vendor on the porch of Tangier's main post office. Inside, the marble-topped counters were crowded with Arabs lined up to cash their money orders from relatives abroad and their French Army pension checks. He had arrived from Gibraltar on the old GIB-Air DC-3 at ten o'clock and driven to the post office directly from the airport. George had loaned him the two thousand with no questions asked, and his transactions with Barclays Bank had taken no more than an hour. In a day or two, three at the most, the Banque du Moyen Orient in Geneva would contact Barclays, confirming the deposit and forwarding the bank account number. Then Barclays would telephone Joe with all information necessary to make further deposits. Everything on that side of the operation was ready. Now all he had to do was contact Barent and strike a bargain.

Joc had downed a quick brandy with a beer chaser out at the airport while waiting for his baggage to come in from the plane. He felt good, less nervous than he had two days before when he had visited Paul Rose. Once a person got used to it, there wasn't really that much to this business. The spy-story writers were always jazzing it up, making things seem more complicated than they were. This was just a straightforward business transaction. He had something valuable to sell and now he was going to make contact with a well-known collector.

The wood-paneled telephone booth smelled vaguely of sweat and rose water from the jellabaed Moroccan woman who had just left it. He held the receiver lightly to his ear and listened to the static of the long distance lines as the call went through to Rabat.

"Good morning, American Embassy. May I help you?"

"Good morning," Joe said, forcing himself to speak in slow, measured tones. "I'd like to speak to Mr. Barent in the Political Section, please."

The receptionist did not bother to answer, but Joe heard the connection switch and the buzzing ring of the extension in Barent's office.

"Good morning, Political Section." The girl's voice had a cheerful Midwest twang.

"Is Mr. Barent there, please?"

"May I ask who's calling, please?"

Joe breathed silently in and out, willing his muscles to relax. "This is Mr. Jackson from CBS Television in Madrid. I'm calling from Tangier."

"Mr. Barent's on home leave, I'm afraid. He won't be back until September third."

"Is Mr. MacCormack there, please?"

"I'm sorry, but Mr. MacCormack's on emergency leave. He's in the States, too. His mother died two days ago."

Joe sagged against the wall of the phone booth. He felt suddenly very thirsty. *What rotten luck!*

"Look," he blurted out, "I'm a friend of Mr. Barent. I've got something rather important to talk to him about. It's business—I mean, it's urgent. . . ."

His voice tapered off into silence. What the hell could a secretary tell him? The names of the undercover C.I.A. people in the country? What a rotten break.

"Well," the girl said slowly, "would you like to speak with Mr. Rawlings?"

"Does he . . . ah . . . is he a colleague of Mr. Barent?"

"I'll connect you with Mr. Rawlings," the girl said noncommittally. "It's Mr. Jackson from NBC?"

"CBS," Joe corrected her, "CBS-T.V. in Madrid." His breathing was short now and his voice was beginning to tremble.

"Rawlings here." The voice sounded young, with a strangely familiar quality that Joe could not identify. "This is Rawlings. Who's calling, please?"

"Ah, this is Tony Jackson. I'm a friend of Jim Barent. I had something rather important to discuss with him."

"Uh-huh," Rawlings breathed. The line buzzed tonelessly in the background.

"I was wondering if I could talk to you about it," Joe heard himself continuing. "It's something I'd like to discuss in person, you see, not over the phone."

"Uh-huh," Rawlings repeated. "Oh, could you hang on a second? I've got a call on my other line."

The line clicked onto hold and Joe stood sweating in the phone booth for at least a minute. Then it clicked back to life.

"Sorry," Rawlings said. "What were you saying, again?"

"I've got some rather urgent things to talk about. I'd like to do it in person, you understand?"

"Fine." Rawlings sounded a bit hesitant now. "Why don't you pop in at the embassy and we can sit down and talk?"

"I was hoping you could come to Tangier," Joe said. "Could you come up this afternoon? It really is important, believe me. Check into the Rif Hotel and I'll call you there tonight."

"Who the hell is this?" Rawlings sounded cold and angry.

"Tony Jackson from CBS."

"Look," Rawlings said, "I just checked the file of accredited journalists. CBS doesn't even have a bureau in Madrid. I don't know what your game is, buddy, but you're wasting my time. If you want an appointment, you come to the embassy and ask for one, like anybody else."

The line popped with a painful echo. "Listen," Joe said, "this really is important. I wouldn't be calling if it weren't . . ." Then he realized he was speaking into a dead phone.

Joe sat in the dimly lit bar of the Rabat Hilton. He chewed on one of the machine-made, doughnut-shaped ice cubes from his Scotch. It was nine minutes after midnight, according to the small digital clock on the wall behind the cash register. The bar was reasonably full for a week night, with tourists and visiting U.N. firemen and some fat-cat Moroccan *fonctionnaires* with their mini-skirted girl friends.

Joe rose and sauntered out through the quiet lobby, his footfalls deadened by the rich Berber carpets. Outside in the parking lot the night air was alive and scented after the chill neutrality of the air-conditioned hotel. He caught the eye of a sharp-looking young Arab taxi driver. Even after midnight, out here in the eucalyptus forest suburbs beyond the king's palace, the taxi drivers hung around in anticipation of a big-spending Hilton fare.

The Peugeot was polished, the driver relatively well-dressed. It felt good to sit down in the front seat. His back ached from the long night haul at the wheel of the Land Rover all the way down from Tangier on the vacation-crowded coastal road.

"Tu parles français, toi?" Joe said, smiling at the boy.

The driver accepted Joe's offered cigarette. *"Oui, M'sieu,"* he said, smiling back. *"J'ai fait le lycée militaire, moi,"* the boy said proudly. "I've been through the military school."

"Fine," Joe said. "Listen, I have something important, a message to be delivered. I'm a journalist for American television. I have some photographs to be delivered to the guard of the American Embassy. I can't go myself because I have to telephone New York. I want you to drive to the American Embassy and deliver this envelope to the guard there. He's a marine, a soldier. He's waiting for the envelope. Do you understand?"

The boy was as quick-witted as he appeared. "Oh, *M'sieu,"* he said, "that's impossible. The embassy is closed. I couldn't go there now. They'd stop me, the police would."

Joe was in no mood to undergo a protracted Arab bargaining session. *"Ecoute,"* he said, holding up a crisp hundred-*dirham* bill. He folded the bank note and tore it neatly down the center. The young taxi driver stared at him bug-eyed, as if Joe were some kind of dangerous maniac. Joe handed half the bill over to the driver and tucked the remaining section into the breast pocket of his sportcoat. He wasn't going to argue with this kid about money. "You take this now. When you come back from the embassy, you can get the other half. If you want, I'll give you a new one. Here, take the envelope and get going."

The boy seemed tempted to bargain for more money, but then he saw the expression in Joe's eyes as a passing car illuminated the dark interior of the taxi. *"Oui, M'sieu,"* he said eagerly. "I'll be back in fifteen minutes."

Joe stood on the wide steps of the hotel and watched the taxi speed out of the parking lot and onto the brightly-lit but empty road that bordered the mud-brick walls of the royal palace. It was sixteen minutes past midnight. He went inside to the bar's pay telephone.

The embassy phone rang a long time before it was answered. "Good evening, American Embassy. Corporal Rogers speaking." The marine's voice was young and broke in places into an adolescent squeak.

Joe forced himself to relax. All the way down from Tangier he had rehearsed his story.

"Good evening, Corporal," Joe said mellowly. Out of the corner of his eye he could see a German stewardess signal the waiter for a fresh drink. "This is Tony Jackson. I'm the CBS-T.V. bureau chief in Madrid . . ."

"Yes, sir!" Corporal Rogers interrupted.

"I'm out at the airport. I was going to spend the night in town, but my flight from Lisbon got delayed and my connecting flight leaves in about ten minutes. Look, I've been trying to call Mr. Rawlings for the past half hour, but I think his phone's out or something. He asked me to give him some photographs when I was passing through Rabat. I've sent them in with a Moroccan cab driver. He should be there in a couple of minutes. Do me a favor? Take the pictures and make sure somebody delivers them to Mr. Rawlings first thing in the morning, okay?"

"Yes, sir," the young soldier answered. There was a certain caution in his tone.

"Don't worry," Joe said, injecting a warm camaraderie into his voice, "he's expecting them. They're in a brown Pan Am envelope. . . . Rogers, you said. I knew a Corporal Pete Rogers last year at Khe Sahn. That's not you, is it?"

"Oh, no, sir," the marine answered. "I've only been in the Corps thirteen months."

"Well," Joe said, shifting his tone to a paternal tenor,

"they're calling my flight now. Please make sure Rawlings gets those pictures first thing in the morning. He's been on my back for a couple of weeks for them. Listen, I really appreciate your help, Corporal."

"You're welcome, sir. I mean, no problem, sir. Have a nice trip."

Joe stood in the light of the waxing moon, drunkenly trying to remember which of the curtained windows was Renée's bedroom and which was Tommy's. It has one of her house rules that they never spend the night together in her embassy apartment in case Tommy woke up in the night and discovered them in bed. That had always been a slight bone of contention when she had forced Joe in the middle of the night to drive to a hotel on his occasional visits to Rabat. Now he just wanted a place to sleep, and, besides, he couldn't stay at the Hilton in case that kid marine was sharper than he sounded and had questioned the taxi driver.

He had hung around there long enough as it was, up in the room of Ursula what's-her-name, a Lufthansa stewardess he had met in the bar. Like other German girls he had known, she had been greedy in bed and proficient and cold. He felt a bit used. Now all he wanted was to curl up with Renée and sleep off that goddamned sweet vodka. Once she was off to work and Tommy was at his swimming lesson, he could call Rawlings without the hassle of placing a long-distance call. Anyway, all of that could wait until morning. Now all he wanted was a soft bed. He had mixed his drinks and been awake for twenty goddamned hours. He tried to remember the last time he had been in Renée's apartment in order to envision the layout of the rooms. He was quite sure hers was the last window before the garden wall. That damned embassy doorbell of hers would wake the dead. It was better just to tap on the window.

Joe woke up with the scream still tinny in his ears. It had been a shrill, prolonged burst of terror. The white-helmeted A.R.V.N. security police had caught him changing money with that Chinese restaurateur in Cholon, and they had strapped them both to tables in the basement of the old Institute Technique and had just begun to attach the electrodes to his penis and nipples. In the corner of the concrete room, beneath the hard white light of the fluorescent tubes, a man in a white smock was heating some metal needles over the blue flame of a Bunsen burner.

Under the clean metal table, Joe could see the ashes of his passport and press card. He was finished. They were going to torture him to death.

He was upright in bed with the jasmine-scented air of Renée's garden sucking into his lungs in short gasps. The outside security light lit the corner bedroom. But was it really the bedroom, or the basement interrogation room?

He felt the second scream rising in his chest just as Renée's cool fingers clamped softly around his lips.

He ate oxtail soup with buttered toast and cinnamon tea and then he could look at her and talk about it. But what could he say to her to explain how it had been?

Renée had black circles beneath her eyes. She kept her hand to her brow, shielding her face from the glare of the kitchen lights as she sipped her mug of soup. For two nights she had gotten little sleep. Tommy had fallen sick with tonsillitis only two days before his scheduled departure for summer camp in Spain. She had taken three days off from the office to nurse him back to a reasonable condition so that he could make the navy flight that had left that afternoon with other embassy and service brats bound for a week of water-skiing, hiking, and patriotism. Tired as she was, she had been forced to attend an interminable dinner party that night at the D.C.M.'s and had not arrived home until well after midnight. Once in bed she had rolled around with insomnia, her nerves taut from too many coffees and too many cognacs and the nagging divorced mother's fear that she had acted selfishly in sending her still-sick child away so that she could have one uninterrupted week with her lover. But even this scheme was now untenable. After the three days' leave she had devoted to Tommy, she could not ask for more to spend with Joe in Tangier. She felt sad and angry, and tired.

Now she sat in her embassy-furnished, *Ladies'-Home-*

Journal kitchen, trying to avoid the unsettling eyes of the lover who had come stumbling into her house at three in the morning, stinking of liquor and another woman's perfume. Renée prevented herself from speaking. If she spoke now she would say regrettable things, things she didn't mean. She just wished silently that he would talk himself out and that they could sleep again during what little bit remained of the night. Her alarm was set for six-thirty. In less than two hours she had to be up and washing her hair.

There was a country team meeting at nine the next morning. That meant being at the embassy no later than eight-fifteen to sharpen pencils and lay out note pads and ashtrays in the conference room. There were Xeroxed copies of telegrams and airgrams to be gotten from the code room, as well, and water carafes had to be filled. All this, every piddling detail, had to be letter perfect, or she would suffer the wrath of the waspish D.C.M., the man who, unchallenged, held the title of Biggest Nit-Picker in the State Department. Normally, she would have found the obvious humor in all of this and purposely left at least one water jug half filled and left at least one pencil unsharpened, just to muddle the old fool and thus relieve the tension in the conference room. But this morning she felt fragile and strangely vulnerable to criticism and was determined to act out perfectly her small part in the bureaucratic charade. All she wished was that Joe would stop his boozy rambling and go back to bed. She would even tiredly open her legs to him if that was what he wanted, if that was what it would take to quiet him down so that she could get at least one hour's uninterrupted sleep.

" . . . damnedest thing, really," Joe went on. "I haven't had that baby for a couple of years . . . more than just a nightmare. Damned thing. It's like some kind of hallucination. Know what I mean? Scares the hell out of you, really. . . . It's hard to explain what it's like unless you've had one yourself. . . ." His voice finally trailed off. He sat, like her, hunched up, elbows on the Formica tabletop.

He was searching for some way to confess, to tell Renée that he had just undergone a terrifying bout of delirium tremens and that he was still scared to death; that he had slept with the selfish German girl not two hours before; and that, above all, he found himself being sucked deeper into an involvement with the Russian buoy, which all his suddenly awakened survival instincts told him would somehow end in disaster. He searched for a way to say all this, but he could not.

Renée yawned and gazed levelly across the room to the clock on the kitchen stove. "Yeah," Joe said, "yeah, I guess it's time to hit the sack again." Renée rose without answering, quickly clearing the soup bowls and cups. She dumped them clattering into the sink and shuffled to the door, her bedroom slippers slapping unpleasantly on the rubber-tile floor. To Joe, she became suddenly old and dumpy, with her sleep-matted hair and shapeless robe. He was afraid to return with her to the darkened room.

He made a show of patting the pockets of his trousers. "You haven't a cigarette in here, do you, Renée?" he asked.

She shook her head but did not speak.

"I guess there's still a pack in my sportcoat," he said.

Renée disappeared through the doorway and returned a moment later with his seersucker sportcoat crumpled loosely in her hand. She tried to drape it across the kitchen chair, but the coat fell to the floor and they both stooped to retrieve it. A package of duty-free Marlboros from Gibraltar slid out to rest beneath the chair. Sleepily, Renée lifted the bottom flap of the coat as she rose to her feet. The white envelope of extra Polaroid pictures fell heavily open beneath the chair. In his chair, Joe was paralyzed as Renée sighed and bent again to pick them up. In the white glare of the overhead lights, the vertical and horizontal views of the listening buoy's exposed entrails showed clearly. She scooped up the pictures and held them like a fan of playing cards in her hand as she peered at them, frowning.

"These yours?"

Tell her, his mind screamed. *Tell her the whole story. She'll help. She'll understand. . . .* But he couldn't.

"They're . . . pictures of Tony Littleton's powerboat engine," Joe said quickly. "He wanted me to get them down to the British diesel representative in Casa. He thinks there's something wrong with the fuel injection. . . ."

Renée rubbed the sleep from her eyes and peered more closely at the pictures, turning them, trying to make some sense out of what she saw. Finally she slipped them back into the envelope and handed them to Joe. "Pretty fancy engine," she said.

Joe lit his cigarette, with two hands steadying the jerking matchstick. A new, but weirdly familiar, internal voice began to nag, to harp at him that she knew it all, that she had been part of the thing from the beginning, that her supposed indifference to the pictures was only a part of the elaborate sham. He sucked deeply on the cigarette and tried to think of nothing.

10

Rawlings

In the sunshine everything looked better. Joe sipped his orange juice from the tall, ice-filled tumbler and watched the American girls at the shallow end of the Hilton pool. A terrace umbrella shaded his table from the mid-morning sun and there was a pleasantly chill sea breeze to counteract the heat waves reflected back from the fieldstone terrace and stressed concrete building. The tables around the pool were filling slowly with late breakfasters and early luncheon parties. Beach jackets, bright print towels, and Bermuda shorts mixed with the potted cactus and rose hedges to give the patio around the pool an innocent vacation atmosphere. It was, he thought, a good place for his first meeting with Rawlings.

Joe caught the white-jacketed waiter's eye and signaled for another large orange juice. He would have loved a double shot of vodka in it, or at least a beer, but the memory of the torture nightmare was still too real for him to take a chance. He had to dry out his brain and body. He shifted in the comfortably padded chair. The Valiums he had taken in Renée's bathroom were working fine now, keeping his head on a smooth, almost feathery, plane. All he had to do was sit here at his table and wait. Rawlings had sounded almost eager on the phone. Nothing to worry about, really. If it all didn't work out, then that was the breaks. There were worse things in the world than going back to work. Besides, who said that he had to go back to I Corps and the wire service? He had the Whitney Prize. He had done some pretty damned good feature writing. Even if he was pushing thirty-five, he could probably find a slot with the *Times;* or, if not the *Times,* maybe *Newsweek* or the *Washington Post. Jesus, there are all kinds of possibilities,* Joe thought. *All I have to do is keep a decent grip on myself.*

If this guy Rawlings doesn't want to play ball, then that's all right, too. They can have the buoy free. If there is anything in this deal that could get me seriously screwed up, then it isn't worth it. On the other hand, it might be worth twenty, thirty grand. . . .

"Are you Jackson?"

Joe should not have been so shocked by Rawlings' sudden materialization out of the sun-dazzled complacency of his reverie. After all, the man was a trained intelligence agent. Observing a subject while remaining unobserved was one of the basic skills acquired by every reasonably efficient policeman.

That was Joe's first impression of Rawlings—that he was some kind of policeman, maybe an ex-F.B.I. man. All he could see of Rawlings was his silhouette standing squarely between the shaded oval of Joe's umbrella and the late-morning sun, which had just topped the corner of the massive hotel building, and Rawlings' beautifully polished cordovan wingtips, which shone like the hand-finished fenders of a classic car. Cop shoes, he realized suddenly. The inevitable wash-and-wear suit was of an indeterminate color, giving the impression of crisply pressed, styleless efficiency. There was a hat there, too, lost in the glare surrounding the head and face. Rawlings had positioned himself so that Joe would be blinded by the sun's glare if he attempted to look directly up into his face.

"Yeah," Joe said, "I'm Jackson. Please sit down, won't you?"

Rawlings lowered himself stiffly into the chair opposite Joe so that, even while sitting at the same table, he had an obstacle, the aluminum shaft of the umbrella stanchion, between them.

"That's a pretty goddamned stupid alias, you know," Rawlings said coldly. "It took me all of three minutes to call Madrid to find out that they don't have any CBS guys up there and that nobody's ever heard of Tony Jackson."

Joe rubbed his hand across his eyes, which were still stinging from the sun. Then he scooped up his sunglasses from the table and turned to face his antagonist directly. Rawlings was so light-skinned that the term "Negro" or "Black" seemed inappropriate, but that's what he was. The eyes staring flatly back at Joe's sunglasses were pale blue. The neatly clipped sideburns exposed beneath the straw hat definitely had a reddish tint. He was also young, square-jawed, and stocky, with football player's hands.

"Look," Rawlings continued, "I don't want to waste your time or mine. You may as well come right out with who you are and what kind of game you're playing, because I'm going to find out pretty quick, anyway."

"That is my name, you know," Joe heard himself saying. "I'm not with CBS, but my name is really Jackson."

"Fine, Mr. Jackson," Rawlings said with a triumphant curl to his lip. "I'm sure, then, that you won't mind me doing a fingerprint job on that empty orange juice glass the boy took away a minute ago?"

Joe stared at him without answering.

"Ever been arrested, Mr. Jackson?" Rawlings asked, his mouth a definite smirk now. "Ever serve in the armed forces or get fingerprinted for a government job—mailman, or park ranger, that type of thing? Because, if you did, they've got your fingerprints in Washington, and it'll take me about eighteen hours to find out who the hell you really are."

"Okay," Joe said. He reached into his sportcoat and tossed Rawlings his passport. "You win, Mr. Rawlings."

Rawlings flipped the passport open and scanned the photo and identification data. Then he used his thumb to make a show of casually glancing at canceled visas. When he was satisfied, he closed the passport and dropped it distastefully on the table.

"Issued in Bangkok, Mr. Clinton. Been to Saigon, Vientiane, Phnom Penh, Hong Kong . . . been to Prague a couple of times, too. You're quite a traveler, Mr. Clinton. Ever make it to Moscow or Peking?"

"For Christ's sake," Joe burst out angrily, "what the hell is this, gang busters? If I were some kind of a Communist spy, would I arrange a meeting right here at the Hilton?"

"I really don't know who you are or what you're up to, Mr. Clinton," Rawlings shot back. "All I know is that you called my office trying to get me to Tangier on some kind of wild goose chase, and then, when I wouldn't play your stupid game, you sent me a pile of crazy pictures that are supposed to mean something to me. Now you change your story and say your name is Clinton. I think, perhaps, you've been reading too many James Bond books."

They sat staring at each other for what seemed a long time. Around the table a party of olive-skinned children in brightly colored swimsuits chased and called shrilly in French and Arabic while their wealthy Moroccan mothers sat nearby beneath floppy St. Tropez hats and sipped gin-and-tonics.

Joe pursed his lips and nodded his head in a clean, decisive gesture. He slid his sunglasses off and dropped them clattering onto the surface of the metal table. "Look, Rawlings," he said, letting the caution and reserve he'd felt earlier dissolve, "I know that you're the new boy in the station here and that your bosses have both taken off, leaving you to watch the store. You're probably scared shitless of making a mistake, like any good young bureaucrat." He chopped his hand down to stifle Rawlings' interruption. "But there's no reason in the world why you have to come on so aggressively. So far you've done everything by the book. You've kept me under surveillance, you've got my fingerprints, and, for all I know, a couple of telephoto pictures of me from those slotted doors in the changing cabins over there." Rawlings looked distinctly uncomfortable. "But, Christ," Joe continued, "why the hell this negative attitude? You haven't even given me a chance to explain myself. Believe me, those pictures are very important. I came to see you people in Rabat because the 'thing' itself is still in Morocco, and I figured I'd give you the first shot at it. But I think that I've made a mistake. I've half a mind to get on the next flight to Madrid and see some *real,* experienced agency people up there and dump the whole thing in their laps. And, believe me, when I do, I'll be more than happy to give them the full lowdown on the way you've blown this first meeting. . . ."

Rawlings looked as if he were about to answer angrily, but then he, too, fell silent. An Arab bellhop in scarlet pantaloons wandered among the tables, announcing a telephone call for a Monsieur Benjalloun.

"Okay," Rawlings sighed, "maybe there *is* something to talk about." He glanced sideways across the terrace. "This isn't the best place in the world to do it, though, is it?"

Joe felt a flutter of excitement in his chest. He'd *won* the first round. Rawlings' tough-guy routine had been an act. The *story*, the carefully constructed cover story, would stand. The long hours of ground work were going to pay off.

"I can't think of any better," Joe snapped back, trying to maintain his angry tone. "There isn't a hell of a lot to talk about, really. Here," he said, handing Rawlings a plain white envelope. "I've written up the information you'll need. I'm acting for a friend, a Moroccan Jew living in Tangier. He got the buoy from some Arab fishermen who snagged it in their nets about a week ago. My friend doesn't speak English, and, like most Moroccan Jews, he's scared to death of the authorities. His family emigrated to Canada about a year ago, but he's been sticking around, trying to salvage some of his business interests. When he happened to stumble onto this thing, he figured that he might be able to make some money and get the hell out of here to join his family. He came to me for help. He's a friend and I said I'd try. Besides, from the way he described the buoy to me, it sounds like something the American Government might like to have. He'd turn it over for free if he wasn't in such a bind for money. That's all there is. That's all I know. Everything's written up on that paper there. Take it back to the office and contact your people in the States. It's a straightforward business deal, the kind they're used to. Give me a telephone number where I can call you in a couple of days, someplace where the lines aren't bugged."

Rawlings had hunched down slightly in his chair and was slowly fingering the edge of the envelope. "Just a minute," he said softly. "There're some things I'd like to know before you take off. What's the name of this friend of yours?"

"I'm not at liberty to say," Joe answered. "Christ, figure it out, man. I told you he's a Jew who wants out of this country. Do you think the Moroccans would let him go if they thought he'd just made several thousand bucks on a deal like this? Jesus, they've taken away his passport already just because they think that he's got some of his grandfather's *gold* buried someplace. Look, I can give you my word—this guy is straight. All you have to do is get the go-ahead from Washington, and the deal will go through with no problems."

Rawlings straightened up now. "You make it sound very simple, Clinton," he said, "as if the American Government were in the habit of throwing handfuls of money away to every con man who walked in off the street. Things just don't work that way."

"Look, goddamn it," Joe cut in, "I'm a professional journalist. I've worked in more countries than you could find on the map. I was dealing with people from your outfit when you were back in tenth grade dreaming about a football scholarship. I don't have to sit here and take a lecture from you. Everything I can tell you is in that envelope. You've already got the pictures. I'm going back to Tangier. Send me a telegram at the *poste restante* when you're ready to talk."

Rawlings stood up with Joe and tried to grip his arms, but Joe twisted away and strode off between the umbrellas and chaise longues. He was almost off the terrace when the white-jacketed waiter caught up with him. Angrily, Joe thrust a ten-*dirham* note into the boy's hand and then took the steps two at a time up into the main lobby.

11

The Fair Offer

Joe was asleep when the doorbell at the lower garden gate rang. It rang a long time before Ali heard it. Zorah was in the city, vegetable-shopping, and Ali was out back transplanting roses. It was little Mohammed, their son, who finally opened the gate to stare wide-eyed at the big brown man and the huge embassy car, which blocked most of the narrow lane. It was not yet nine in the morning, twenty-four hours since the confrontation at the Rabat Hilton. Joe awoke now as Ali, poised in the doorway of the shadowy bedroom, announced the arrival of a "Sudani *nesrani,*" a black Christian. Joe slid out of bed and pulled on his bathrobe.

Rawlings was seated on the edge of a patio chair with a silly straw hat held toy-like between his muscular fingers. From the height of the patio, Joe could see the black embassy station wagon and the group of Moroccan neighborhood children thronging around it.

Joe was furious. All day Thursday he had waited nervously for Rawlings' telegram, driving down to the post office twice, standing in line with sweaty hippies at the *poste restante* counter, and there had been nothing, not a word.

And, now, now this stupid clown comes driving up from Rabat in a tank of an embassy station wagon with a goddamned driver, undoubtedly tailed all the way by the Moroccan Sûreté and the Russians and probably the fucking Chinese, as well, and he leads them, the whole gang of them, right to my front door. And now he sits here, with his Rotarian's straw hat, looking so smug and resolute and confident.

For a moment Joe struggled with a wild urge to kick the chair out from under Rawlings and send him crashing down into the hibiscus hedge. But then Ali intervened with traditional Arab hospitality. He came shyly out of the dining room with a tray of drinks and placed them on the wicker table next to Rawlings' chair. There was a chilled bottle of mineral water and a carafe of fresh lemonade. Bottles of Coke and tonic water were arranged neatly beside three cans of PX Budweiser and a bowl of ice cubes with silver serving tongs. Joe stood there, his gut tight, his bathrobe uncomfortably heavy in the morning sun, suddenly remembering the first year in the house with Monique working so patiently and with such success to transform the old Arab veteran from a gardener into a quite passable butler. Ali still preferred to dig in the garden and sprinkle the flowers and shrubs, but he no longer blushed and stammered in the presence of foreign guests. That had been a beautiful year: Monique just pregnant with the second child, Joey crawling around the garden, a new city and a new country to explore. That had been the way a man's life should be, not this—*not dead broke and desperate, half crazy and involved far too deeply with this damned tube in George's garage.*

"Good morning, Clinton," Rawlings finally said.

Joe opened a can of beer. The cold liquid cut through the sleepy staleness of his mouth. He lit a cigarette and stared down at the drying dew patterns on the grass. "I suppose," Joe said coldly after a long silence, "I suppose, Mr. Rawlings, that it never occurred to you that a great big American station wagon with the one remaining C.I.A. man in the embassy might possibly be followed up from Rabat by, say, some of your counterparts in the Soviet Embassy? Or maybe a couple of Moroccan security people who could be curious to see who the C.I.A. knows and works with in Tangier?"

"So what?" Rawlings said flatly. He drank his lemonade and stared up at Joe. "What am I supposed to do, run around in a disguise to please you?"

"Fine," Joe snapped. "Great. I'm sure my Jewish friend will be glad to hear that when the Moroccan screws put two and two together and drag him off for a quiet chat about why he's been seeing so much of old Joe Clinton lately and why Mr. Clinton receives the singular honor of a private visit from the C.I.A.'s man in Morocco."

Rawlings shrugged again. "Okay, think whatever you want. That's your business. But it might interest you to know that I drove up with my wife and children, after having telephoned three or four times on an open line to set up appointments about renting a vacation house here for September. My wife's three streets away right now, talking to some French real estate agent. I'm not exactly new at this game, you know."

"Sorry," Joe said. He meant it. He was getting too jumpy. "I'm a journalist, you know, and the easiest way to ruin your reputation is to become known as a friend of the spies."

"Of course," Rawlings said. "But I wanted to talk to you in person. I didn't want to fool around with all this 007 bullshit . . . *poste restante* telegrams and secret phone numbers."

Ali came out again, this time with a leather cigarette box and table lighter. Joe put aside his half-empty beer can and asked Ali for a cup of coffee. Rawlings sipped his lemonade. Neither spoke for a moment. There were butterflies working up and down the morning glories on the garden wall.

"So?" Joe said. "Let's talk, then."

Rawlings cleared his throat and placed his hat next to the cigarette box. He unbuttoned his sportcoat, then wiped his hand nervously across his face. He saw Joe watching his movements. Their eyes met and they both looked away in unison. *Christ,* Joe thought, *he's scared. He's really uptight about something. Maybe this is the first time he's ever worked on a deal like this and he doesn't know where to begin.*

"You've been in contact with your people in Washington?" Joe asked.

"All day yesterday. I used the . . . we have a safe telephone channel, and I've discussed your proposal at length with them."

"Good, fine. What's the verdict?"

"Well"—Rawlings gripped his fingers tightly together

—"I'm afraid that your friend is going to be a little disappointed. . . ."

"You mean that they don't want it?"

"Oh, they want it, all right. And"—he smiled an odd smile, showing his confidence—"I'm pretty sure they're going to get it, too. It's just that they aren't about to spend sixty thousand dollars! In fact, they aren't going to make *any* money payment at all."

Joe listened dully to the words. Rawlings' pronouncement seemed inevitable, as if part of some traditional ceremony. A crashing wave of *déjà vu* swept over him then and he surrendered to it. He knew. He'd known the second he saw the buoy caught there in the fisherman's net that this scene would be acted out here on this sunlit patio.

Rawlings was still speaking. ". . . not really such a bad deal when you think of it. It'll be a regular, legal immigration visa, not just for your friend, but for his whole family, the ones who are already in Canada. We're willing to pay transportation, as well. My office will also give any assistance needed in smoothing things over here with the Moroccan Government. He'll get his exit visa without any more delay. And I think we'll also be able to convert any Moroccan currency holdings he has here into dollars. In other words, all the headaches he's been having will be over the minute he delivers the goods to us."

Joe stared down at the floor. Ali padded up silently and deposited a steaming cup of *café-au-lait* on the table in front of him. He lit another cigarette, then looked out into the garden again.

"Well?" Rawlings asked.

"Well, what?"

"When do I meet your friend? When do I get a chance to actually see this thing he got from the fisherman?"

Joe was up on his feet, striding purposefully along the edge of the terrace. The *déjà vu* was gone. He was back in reality, morning on the breakfast terrace, with Rawlings giving him some load of double-dealing C.I.A. bullshit about immigration visas for the nonexistent Jewish friend.

"You won't be able to meet him today, I'm afraid,"

Joe said slowly, letting his mind jump ahead of his words and forcing himself to appear sincerely concerned. "He called me last night, saying that he was driving down to Casa this morning. He's got a cousin who knows somebody in the governor's office down there. He was hoping to pay a bit under the table and maybe speed up his passport renewal."

"When does he get back?"

"Not until tomorrow afternoon, he said."

"Okay." Rawlings took out a new leather-bound notebook. "Let's go back a bit. We'll start with his full name."

"Name?"

"Of course. I'll want his full name, home and business addresses, names of friends and acquaintances—as much info as you can give me on him. That way I can get some of my ground work done on the case before he gets back from Casablanca."

Joe stopped his pacing and sat down heavily. "I can't give you his name right now," he said.

Rawlings frowned and slapped the leather-bound notebook impatiently against his leg. His face took on a sarcastic, disbelieving expression. "What's so special about his name? He's going to have to tell us eventually."

Joe let his brain race again, dodging among possible dead ends and skirting pitfalls. "Listen, Rawlings, you're new to Morocco. You can't fully appreciate what it's like for the Jews here, especially the professional classes, doctors and lawyers, engineers—the ones who didn't want to go sweat their asses off in some kibbutz in Israel and opted to stick it out here, the ones who sank every penny they had into this country. No, wait till I explain. Things were pretty good for them until the Sixty-Seven War. Then they started getting leaned on. The level of corruption in the Moroccan Government started going up, too, and the Arabs got heavy-handed. It wasn't just a question of paying off for special favors. The Jews had to come up with regular cash for protection. They're being shaken down by every crummy official, from the postman to the commissioner of police."

"We're going to have to find out his name sooner or later. We can't arrange an immigration visa for a guy without a name."

"I know that," Joe snapped. "Listen, I made a promise to this guy, a solemn, goddamned promise that I wouldn't under any circumstances reveal his name until he was ready to deal with you directly. He figured that thing, whatever it is, was worth a lot of money to the American Navy. This proposal of yours makes everything different. I'll make sure he contacts you directly as soon as he gets back."

"Okay," Rawlings said testily. "Any idea where he keeps this thing hidden while he goes traipsing off to Casablanca?"

"Well, he can't keep it home," was all Joe said.

Rawlings jammed his notebook back into his suit coat. "I'll get my family back to Rabat and be up here again tomorrow night. Call me at the consulate at seven. Ask for Mr. Harris. You got that?"

"Consulate at seven P.M., Mr. Harris."

"We can meet here later to talk business if he's afraid of coming to the embassy. I'll have an unmarked station wagon ready to drive the buoy back down to Rabat. The whole deal shouldn't take more than an hour."

Joe swallowed hard. "You mean you can get it all done tomorrow?"

"Why not? It'd help if I had his name now to start the ball rolling with the Moroccan Interior Ministry people. But there are other ways to do it. We can always get him a Moroccan passport and fly him out on a U.S. Air Force plane. I'll make sure his Moroccan money is withdrawn from the bank and that it gets converted later."

"I . . . I don't know if he'll be ready to leave so fast."

"He wants to get out of this country, doesn't he? Look, this is a bush-league deal. We do this kind of thing every day. Tell him he can be in the States twelve hours after he delivers the goods. That's what he wants, isn't it?"

"Yeah, sure," Joe stammered. "That's what he's been trying to do for a couple of years now. It's been driving him crazy, the thought of his wife and kids over there in Canada all alone."

Rawlings' expression of cynical boredom deepened. "Well," he said, "he can be with the wife and kiddies in less than twenty-four hours after he hands over that buoy.

Tell him that. Tell him that he can trust us . . . that he's *got* to trust us."

Joe nodded dourly. "I'll make sure he understands."

"Do that," Rawlings said. A new, artificially cold tone entered his voice as he continued. "There's something else you can tell him, too. Like I said before, we do want that buoy, and I'm pretty sure we're going to get it. The deal we're offering is more than fair. In the event he doesn't think so and figures he'll shop around a little for a better deal, tell him to forget it. Tell him that this is our one and only offer, and if he tries to pull anything funny he can forget about getting out of this country for a long time."

Joe stared across the breakfast table at Rawlings' pale blue eyes. "I don't get your meaning there," Joe said after a long silence.

"Sure you do," Rawlings said, smiling now. "This kind of a deal is *illegal*. It amounts to an attempt to extort money from a foreign embassy. If your buddy tries to play any fancy games with us, all we have to do is blow the whistle on him to the security boys in the Moroccan Interior Ministry. They'll get the buoy from him, believe me. We might have to pay them a bit for it, but we'll get it either way. That'll leave your friend in a rather embarrassing position." He looked away from Joe. "I may as well tell you the rest. If that ever happened, it would leave you in a pretty bad position, too."

"What the hell are you talking about?"

"I think you get the picture, Clinton. You are involved in this deal, too. I did a little checking up on you. What's the guy offering for your services? Did he promise to pay off your local debts and mortgage with all the Moroccan *dirhams* he can't get out of the country?"

Joe nodded automatically.

"I figured you weren't in this just out of friendship. You took a big chance, you know. This isn't a nice business. I'm sure that it sounded simple in the beginning. Just get the old C.I.A. to come through with piles of fifty-dollar bills like they always do in the movies, heh? Well, the same set of options applies to both of you. If you do your bit in getting our friend to cooperate, then maybe we can offer a little help with your mortgage payments." Rawlings wet his lips and stared hard into Joe's eyes. "On the other hand, if your buddy tries to skip out on us, then he's going to leave you holding the bag. The Moroccan authorities will take a pretty dim view of your part in this. If you were to be deported for criminal activity, they'd be legally able to confiscate all your holdings here—the house, that sailboat, everything—in lieu of the payment of a fine."

"You'd do that?" Joe heard his voice saying. The *déjà vu* crept back into the sunlit garden.

"This is *not* a nice business. The security interests of the United States are involved. Try to see it from our side. This guy happens to get his hands on something valuable, a potentially very interesting piece of hardware. He offers it for sale at a ridiculously high price. What happens if we were to agree to the sixty thousand and then he turns around and says he wants a hundred thousand? Believe me, that kind of thing has happened time and time again in the past. So we cover ourselves; we try to negotiate from a position of strength. Not only is it in your own best interests to accept our offer; it'll be damned unpleasant for both of you if you don't. It's not a gentleman's game."

The morning sun was pouring down now over the tops of the cypress grove. Joe was hot and sweaty and his head had begun to ache. He wanted a drink, something stronger than the fizzy can of beer. He closed his eyes momentarily against the sun's glare. *What a mess, what an impossible mess. They had him. There was no way he could escape. Like Rawlings said, they intended to get the buoy—one way or another. He might as well come clean, own up to the lie about the Jewish friend, and let Rawlings arrange to cart the thing back to Rabat today. Maybe they would still give him some kind of a reward, a little help with the mortgage payments. That would be better than nothing . . . better than getting deported, dead broke with the house and the boat and everything he owned confiscated by some crooked Arab police commissioner.*

He opened his eyes and saw Rawlings watching him. "Like I was saying, it'd speed things up if you'd just give me the guy's name and address so I can get the ball rolling on his passport and exit visa."

Something hot and angry twanged inside Joe's chest. There was still a chance, a chance for money and a clean name. But he needed time. "Jesus Christ," he said, "how many times do I have to tell you that I *promised* him. I don't suppose that means shit to you people, does it? But it does to me. There's . . . well . . . there's something else, too." His voice was calmer now, the initial anger having subsided. "If I tell him that I've signed up for your take-it-or-leave-it package deal and that there's this awful threat of getting turned over to the Moroccan cops, he'll panic. I know this guy; you don't. He's half crazy. That's exactly the kind of thing that'll send him off the deep end. Okay, he was being greedy when he wanted sixty thousand. So was I when I thought I could straighten out my money problems in one fell swoop. I can see that now. I can see, too, that what you're offering is a pretty good deal for both of us. Just let me broach it to him gently. He trusts me. Christ, if he panics, he might even try bolting across to Spain with just the clothes on his back, leaving that tube locked up wherever he's hidden it."

Rawlings nodded grimly, then rose to his feet. "Okay, Clinton," he said, "tomorrow night at seven—Mr. Harris at the consulate. It's the best deal either of you will get out of this, and if you try to jack us around, it'll get bad . . . for both of you."

He was gone, down the terrace stairs and out the gate. Joe could hear the embassy driver cursing the neighborhood kids in Arabic as they chased after the departing station wagon. He poured himself a tall glass of lemonade and vodka. He finished off the drink and refilled the glass a quarter full with straight vodka.

Joe turned the shower on full pressure, hot. Steam condensed on the bathroom tiles and the mirror. He drank the vodka, then set the empty glass on the sink. He was shocked when he wiped away the steam from the mirror. His face was pale. His eyes were sunken, harried looking. He had to get a better grip on himself. For openers, he must stop this goddamned morning drinking every time there was some setback to his plan.

Joe threw aside his robe and got down, full length, on the cool tiles next to the tub. The first push-up was painful. He was panting after five and gasping after ten, but he continued. At twenty, his pulse was hammering dangerously in his ears. He kept on, feeling the liquor percolate out with his own stinking sweat, until he made it to forty-five.

Standing in the hot shower, with the pressure beating on his head, he felt his heart slowing toward a normal beat. He soaped himself, then turned the hot-water pressure even higher. At the end of a long, cold rinse, he felt clear-headed, in control again. Now he was ready to think with something approaching a rational mind.

The idea came to him, full-formed, as he lathered his face with shaving cream. There it was, simple. When he had rinsed his face, he wrapped a towel around his waist, went quickly to the telephone in the entrance hall, and dialed Harry Rains.

12

The Salvage Broker

The faulty air conditioner had been replaced since Joe's last visit to Harry's office. The new machine hummed quietly between the Venetian blinds and the rubber plant. As usual, Harry's cuffs were long and starched, and his summer blazer was freshly pressed. He frowned as Joe concluded his long monologue, seemed about to interrupt, then remained silent, thoughtfully fingering his writing set.

"So, Harry, coming to you for some more advice seemed natural. You're ex-navy. You know everybody over in Gib and you're a friend."

Harry dropped his pen onto the blotter. "I don't believe you, Joe."

Okay, Joe thought, *it was worth a try, and it didn't work. Don't sit here stringing out this line of bullshit and let that buoy wreck a friendship. Tell him the truth.*

But before Joe could say anything, Harry continued. "You didn't come to see me because I'm ex-navy. You came because you believe that rubbish at the club that I'm SIS . . . the bloody *éminence grise,* or however it's pronounced . . . of 'Imperial Interests' here in Tangier. It's *rubbish,* pure and simple. I'm a non-licensed solicitor and a fair-to-middling merchant banker, period. Those retired Colonial Service asses at the club have nothing better to do with their time than to make up malicious gossip. I might add that I *will* help you—give you some advice, that is—but purely on a onetime *non*-professional basis, because you're a friend who's in a bit of a jam. Now . . ."

There was still time to stop him, but Joe remained silent.

". . . my advice is simple, Joe. Leave the salvage of this oceanographic what's-it that your Jewish friend has found to the professionals. I know that sounds like a contradiction of terms, because no licensed maritime lawyers worth their salt would *touch* this transaction. They wouldn't want to deal directly with the Americans or British on this for exactly the same reasons you are reluctant to do it. Lawyers have reputations to protect, just like journalists."

Joe nodded slowly. In the skein of deception, he had lost the point Harry seemed to be moving toward.

"To be brutally frank, Joe, let the Jew find another middleman, someone who can drive a hard bargain with the naval attachés down in Rabat or with the naval intelligence types over in Gib. Can I ask how much the Jew has offered for *your* services?"

"What?" Joe looked up. "Oh, fifty-five."

Harry frowned again. "That ghost-writing payment you came to ask me about?"

"Yeah, Harry, maybe I'd better just . . ."

Harry held up his hand. "I don't want to know the details. You're a friend in a jam and you came for help." He took his note pad and wrote something. "Tell your friend to go see Danzinger, Konrad Danzinger. He has an office in the Quartier Maritime, close to the club, actually."

Joe took the note. He stared down at the neatly printed name and address. "Who's he?"

Harry shrugged his shoulders. "A genuine Tangier type from the International Zone days. Originally Baltic German—Estonian or Latvian national at some point in his life. D.P. after the war. Ended up in Tangier on a refugee I.D. card and stayed. Speaks eleven bloody languages. You know the drill. In any event, Konrad Danzinger is as bent as one of his Baltic pretzels. But he's damned good at what he does, Joe."

Joe felt a thread of confidence returning. "And what's that?"

"Basically, crooked salvage . . . insurance sinkings, too, and warehouse fires—the full spread of the dirty side of shipping operations they never teach the merchant navy cadets. His office here is only a front. Most of his work is done in Spain or out in the Canaries. He does some of his banking here, though, so I can judge how successful he is."

"Would he take this oceanographic device off my friend's hands?"

"It's just his cup of tea, Joe."

Joe stood up. He was feeling a little light-headed. Those push-ups had been too strenuous, or maybe this entire situation was simply getting too complex for him to keep locked up inside his head.

"I'll let you know how it turns out, Harry."

"Please don't, Joe. I don't want to hear any more about it."

"Okay, if that's what you want."

"That *is* what I want, Joe."

Herr Danzinger's office was in a dilapidated, one-story shed within the Quartier Maritime, the customs transit zone of Tangier port. In the International Zone days, before independence and the city's annexation to Morocco, these offices had housed business operations that had been as successful as they were illegal. Shipments of contraband, ranging from cigarettes, hashish, and penicillin to automatic weapons and indentured African labor, had been contracted and financed inside these crumbling, mustard-colored walls. With independence, however, most of Tangier's smugglers and gunrunners had departed for greener pastures in the Far East. The few who remained had invested their capital in near-legitimate operations and had acquired respectability. They owned small villas on the mountain and sent their children to the American school.

Konrad Danzinger seemed to fit the image of a respectable, balding, expatriate businessman. On his desk there was a retouched photograph of his Spanish wife and two daughters. He sat in his swivel chair, quietly tapping his fingers on his blotter as Joe explained the reason for his visit, his smooth features showing no evidence of surprise or interest.

"My friend says he can deliver it today, right here in the port, if you wish," Joe was saying. "His main considerations are quick sale and cash payment—payment for the release of his legitimate salvage claim, that is."

"Of course, Mr. Jackson."

Two Moroccan customs clerks passed the window, chatting softly in Berber. Konrad Danzinger tapped his fingers quietly on the desk.

"Well," Joe said, filling the silence that was growing in the shabby office, "that's about it. I was given to understand that you sometimes take on *unusual* salvage claims and that this proposition would be of interest to you."

Danzinger tapped his fingers. "I am not a salvage agent, Mr. Jackson. If I were, however, I would have to file this claim at the Moroccan Interior Ministry in Rabat and with the governor's office here. It would be months before any realistic discussion of payment could be made."

His English was as precise as Harry Rains', but Joe could not place the accent. It wasn't stereotypical German, though.

Joe tried his most innocent smile. "Mr. Danzinger, I'll be frank. I'm talking about a piece of equipment that is potentially *very* valuable and also rather confidential in nature. I am not talking about a normal salvage claim filed through proper channels in Rabat."

"I understand exactly what you are talking about, Mr. Jackson. Perhaps things are more irregular in Spain these days, but here, in Morocco, a foreign businessman must follow proper channels."

Danzinger stopped tapping his fingers. He looked at his watch. A fat Spanish ship's chandler passed the window and called out a quiet greeting. Danzinger answered in fluent Andalusian.

"Normally, Mr. Jackson, I close my office now for the midday meal. We take the long Spanish siesta, you see."

"I see."

Danzinger closed a file folder on his desk. He opened his drawer and removed a pair of sunglasses with clumsy, 1940s frames.

"Look," Joe said. He was angry and the words came too quickly. "Let's stop fooling around. My friend wants sixty thousand, American. But I'm authorized to make a deal . . . let's say an even fifty thousand, half in front, half on delivery. I . . ."

"Mr. Jackson, really. I do not think you understood me well. I cannot do business with you. This type of transaction is of absolutely no interest to me."

Joe sighed in frustration. "I understand you speak a lot of languages."

"Part of my profession, Mr. Jackson . . ."

"Russian?"

"I beg your pardon."

Joe took the Polaroid photo from his jacket pocket. "If you can read Russian, this might be of interest to you."

Danzinger seemed to glance at the photo of the buoy's high-voltage warning plaque with a mixture of distaste and disinterest. "I am sorry, Mr. Jackson, but Russian is not one of my languages."

Joe snatched up the picture. "I'll call you tomorrow morning at ten sharp. You might have changed your mind by then. Remember, delivery here in Tangier and payment in cash."

Joe slammed the flimsy, louvered door as he left the office. All across the Tangier port men were leaving the sheds and cargo piles and walking toward the gates of the Quartier Maritime toward lunch and siesta.

It was just after three o'clock on a hot, breezeless afternoon. Ali was curled up on his sleeping mat in the shade at the bottom of the garden. Zorah had eventually given up waiting for Joe to come in off the terrace to eat his lunch and had gone down to the servants' room to iron sheets and sing to little Mohammed as he lay on his pallet near the stationary tubs.

Joe sat on the patio, under the split bamboo sunshade, drinking beer and chain-smoking. Next to him, on the patio table, his notebook and several crumpled pages lay, forgotten. His pencil had fallen under the table. It was a shame Rawlings had already left for Rabat. That would just be a wasted trip. He could have taken the buoy back with him today and saved everybody a lot of hassle.

Joe had decided several things in the past two hours out here on his shady patio. At six he would call Renée and have her carry a message to Rawlings. She would be surprised, of course, maybe even shocked by Joe's contact with a known agency officer. But it was safer than trying to call Rawlings at the embassy. Renée's phone certainly wasn't tapped, but the embassy lines would be, by *somebody*, Moroccan Sûreté, probably, and Rawlings' home phone wouldn't be safe, either. It was wiser to dictate a cryptic message over the phone than to try contacting Rawlings directly.

Yeah, that sounded easy. *Fucking fun and games.* Still, it was worth a try, one last effort. Besides, it might even work.

He reached over and gathered up the notebook and his crumpled pages. The last version of the message was probably the best:

> Rabbi Abrahams had to leave the country earlier than expected. He left his equipment behind in Tangier, but will release it for delivery Tuesday on telegraphic confirmation that nine—repeat, nine—thousand dollars has been paid to his local representative.

The message was crudely worded. He was no good at this kind of crap. Rawlings might not even understand what he wanted. What a *silly*, goddamned business.

"I wonder what the hell Renée will think of it. . . ."

He opened the crumpled earlier drafts of the message and burned them one at a time. The black ashes fell straight down to the flagstone patio.

"I wonder what the hell *Rawlings* will think of it. . . ."

Well, getting the message to him tonight would at least give him time to cable Washington for advice. Nine thousand dollars wasn't much money for the bureaucrats in Langley, Virginia, to quibble about. They probably wouldn't risk blowing a deal like this for a crummy nine thousand. And then?

Then he just might have a chance to banish some of the wolves at the door—the publishers and the overdue mortgage payments. And the two thousand he borrowed from George, what the hell about that? Give him the Land Rover for that . . . a fair deal, not charity. And then some money for the overdue yacht club dues. Okay. And a few thousand extra for *Dragonfly*. She was old, clinker-built teak, obsolete, really. A couple thousand for her, operating expenses. . . .

Until he got his first paycheck. Right. The other person he ought to call this afternoon was Paul Green at A.P., because, any way Joe looked at his present situation, going back to work for a living was the only realistic solution he could see. He knew he could forget his day-dreams about a fifty-foot charter boat or a cushy wire service job in Africa. He would be going back where he belonged, in that tin-roofed bureau house in Danang.

"Fucking fun and games," he said aloud.

But it sure was not going to be fun breaking the news to Renée . . . sad . . . about as sad a thought as he could imagine this sunny, windless afternoon.

Konrad Danzinger sat in his nondescript Simca at the top of the mountain, near the Place du Khaddi. A breeze was beginning to move the tall cane surrounding the small holders' plots and the bougainvillaea on the villa walls. Ahmed came puffing up the steep lane on foot. He wore a white summer burnous over the starched khaki uniform of the port police. When he flopped down in the front seat next to Danzinger, the car's suspension creaked dryly.

"I . . . I got it for you," Ahmed said, sucking hard to catch his breath.

"His name? The house? I need it all."

Ahmed wiped the sweat off his face and hands with a graying handkerchief. He regained his regular breathing and smiled at Danzinger. "You mentioned, I believe, *fifty* American dollars."

"I mentioned *thirty*. Here's forty. Now, let's have it, please. I don't have time for long negotiations today, Ahmed."

The Arab policeman took the money, counted it, and slipped the bills inside his burnous. "There are only two Land Rovers with Gibraltar registration that also have Quartier Maritime entry stickers . . ."

"I know all that," Danzinger interrupted. "What's my man's name?"

Ahmed looked at Danzinger with surprise. Normally the German would absorb any scrap of information with silent, but obvious, interest. "Well," Ahmed continued, "the man who came to see you at noon is not the French poultry expert. That one has a Land Rover, the kind . . ."

Danzinger handed across another ten-dollar bill. "Now, you asshole . . . my man's name, his house . . . now!"

Ahmed accepted the extra money with great dignity. "Clinton," he said. "Your name's name is Monsieur Joseph Clinton, American national, Tangier residence permit. His house is only one hundred meters from here. That is why I said we should meet up on the mountain.

"I have the impression, Monsieur Danzinger, that you sometimes think I am stupid. Believe me . . ."

"The house, where is it, exactly?"

"Just there, below the first line of cypress trees. It's one of the small villas, opposite the big house of that European woman who is always inviting young boys to her house *pour faire le pompier*. Do you know the house I mean?"

Danzinger started the Simca's engine. "I know it," he said. "Can we drive past without being obvious?"

Ahmed clicked his tongue. "Ah, no. There the lane is very narrow. There are children playing. Besides, all the Fatimas would see us. They sit in their kitchens and watch all day for strangers . . . this morning for example . . ."

Danzinger reached across and opened the door for Ahmed. "I'm sorry," he said, "but I don't have time today for maids' gossip. You can afford to call youself a taxi. I am in a hurry."

"So I have noticed."

"Perhaps another day we can discuss the traffic on the mountain, but now I must leave you."

The dusty customs office at the Tangier airport was deserted. There wasn't another flight due until six, the Gib-Air DC-3. A charter Britannia had just departed for Gatwick and Birmingham. Konrad Danzinger closed the warped door of the office. Down the hallway a policeman was sleeping through the *chergui* heat on a straight chair, his rifle across his knees at a sloppy angle.

Danzinger dialed the six numbers on the old upright telephone, the direct line to Rabat and Casa.

"Ambassade de l'Union Sovietique," the gruff voice said.

"This is André," he said in quiet Russian. "Can I speak to someone about the spare-tire delivery?"

"The chancery is closed for the afternoon," the voice answered.

"I understand. Would you please tell the ambassador's driver that the spare tires are in Tangier. If he would like to discuss the shipment, he can call me at my workshop."

"In the old town or the new?"

"In the new."

"Understood."

The line clicked dead. Danzinger breathed deeply five times. He spread a grimy customs dossier on the edge of the desk and sat down in a wobbly metal visitor's chair facing it. After a moment, he rose and opened the door to the hall again. The policeman was still sleeping in his chair. The flies were drowsy above the desk, buzzing faintly. Outside the cicadas were shrill.

Twelve minutes later, at exactly three-thirty, the telephone on the desk rang three times. He did not pick up the receiver. He gazed at the minute hand of his watch through two revolutions. The phone rang again. He had the receiver up before one ring was complete.

"André," a man's voice said in Russian, "we haven't seen or heard much of you lately."

"I'm sorry," Danzinger said in Estonian. "André had to go out. Can I take a message?"

"How's the weather up there?" the man asked in choppy, but passable, Estonian.

"It's warm."

"But there may be wind later."

"We can only hope so. . . ."

They let the line buzz between them for a moment.

"I'm listening," the man in Rabat said after the pause.

"I found the missing shipment you've been advertising for."

"Congratulations. That was quick work."

"Your firm spoke of a commission."

"Naturally. Have we ever disappointed you?"

"Never, but this case might be different. The person who has the missing property seems a little unstable. I wonder if you could come up to interview him about the shipment."

"Naturally I *could,* but it might be more convenient if he came to visit me."

"Of course. The only problem I can foresee is that he is asking for an unusually large commission."

"Don't they always?"

"Yes, of course. I think I can arrange an interview with him at your office. How about tomorrow?"

"Yes, that would be splendid. He can speak to my assistant first; that's the normal procedure for this type of interview. Would it be too much to ask your client's name?"

"Now, that would be spoiling *my* chance for a reasonable commission, wouldn't it?"

There was a genuine chuckle on the line. "Certainly. I forgot. We're so *amicable.* But I need his name, *now.*"

"Clinton, Joseph Clinton. Tangier Residence Permit Number 67/803. That's all I have. But he could be working for one of our unscrupulous competitors, and I'd like to keep my connection with him *brief* . . . in the event that he turns out to be, shall we say, *unethical.*"

"I understand your position fully, old friend. Your commission will be paid when this gentleman comes in for his interview."

"With your permission, I will tell him how generous you are in the payment of commissions. That appears to be his overriding consideration."

"Promise him the moon, if that will convince him to come down and discuss the shipment."

"That may not be enough."

"No riddles today, please, old friend." The voice was cold now.

"Sorry. Excuse me. It's just that his possible *parent* company may have already taken possession of the moon . . . on Sunday night."

"Ah, I *see.* . . . well, I look forward to meeting this fellow."

"Also, I need some advice. The sample bill of lading you sent me, the description of the missing shipment, can

I show it to him? If he actually is a free-lance broker, seeing it might convince him to talk to you about it."

Danzinger listened to the dry buzz of the cicadas while the man in Rabat considered his request.

"All right," the man said. "I see your point. If this person were an actual competitor, he already would know the shipment's true port of origin and destination, anyway. If he is free-lance, the bill of lading might sweeten his interest. Show it to him; then destroy it. Anything else?"

"One other thing."

"I am listening."

"I would like to make him aware of how *distressed* your firm will be if this shipment is not delivered on schedule. As I say, this person is unstable, or at least he leaves that impression."

The line squeaked and popped with static. "Tell him this. My firm has the exclusive franchise of that merchandise. Tell him that we must reach a satisfactory agreement. If we do not, I shall use my influence with the local authorities to make sure this person does not do business again for a long time. Do you understand?"

"I understand. So, good-bye, Toivo. . . . The wind might just be coming up now."

"Good-bye, Ilmar. Here the wind is calm."

In the damp sub-basement of the central P.T.T. in Rabat, there was a room with a rusting metal door. On this door there was a sign, written in French and Arabic: *Private Entry Forbidden: Interior Ministry Personnel Only.*

The young lieutenant sat at his worktable, adjusting the volume of the tape recorder. He listened to the conversation in his earphones a second time, then logged the exact duration in minutes and seconds.

"Brahim," Lieutenant Slaoui called to his partner, "come and listen to this. It's a call from the flat on the rue de Meknes, where the Czech consul keeps his girl. But whoever called wasn't speaking Czech. It was Russian, at least at first. I don't know what the rest is."

Lieutenant Ibrahim Marrackchi listened to a minute of the recorded conversation. "In the beginning, it's Russian."

"I *know* that, for God's sake."

Lieutenant Marrackchi shrugged his shoulders. "Where was he calling?"

"Some phone in the Tangier airport building. I couldn't get through to the ministry operator to get an exact trace on the extension."

"Probably all sleeping—a bunch of regular *señors* we have up there."

Lieutenant Slaoui rewound the tape. "What should I do about it?"

Lieutenant Marrackchi put his foot up on a chair and inspected the toes beneath the loose strap of his sandal. "Make a copy for the Americans. Send the original upstairs to Ben Abdesalam. They'll sort it all out."

"But Monsieur Barent is gone from his embassy. So is MacCormack."

"Well, put it in the stack of tapes Omar is saving for them. It can't be anything important. We'd have gotten a special listening watch if it were."

Lieutenant Slaoui had the tape reel off the machine. "Yes," he said, reaching across for the smaller, copying machine.

"Say, did you see the new car the major's going to get?"

Lieutenant Marrackchi laughed. "I hated to look. You know, there is a *lot* of damned money floating around this service."

"I wish some would *float* down here."

They both laughed, but with restraint, covering their gold teeth, as educated boys from good Southern families had been taught was proper.

13

Reappraisal

Joe was sitting down to his lunch at last when the bell rang at the garden gate. He jumped up from his chair, bumping the edge of the table so that water spilled from the carafe onto his plate of cold ham and potato salad.

Rawlings, he thought. Rawlings was back. He'd never left town, but he had been following Joe all morning, to Harry's office and down to see Danzinger in the port. What the hell can I tell him?

Joe was out on the patio, leaning over the edge to watch Ali open the gate. The caller was not Rawlings, but a thin, elderly Arab in the faded brown uniform of an office *chauoushe,* a hall porter, from a bank, perhaps. The old man and Ali exchanged the required formal greetings in Arabic, then conversed briefly in Riffi Berber. Joe stepped back into the shade. If the old Arab was from Harry's bank, then the message was important and confidential, something Harry did not want to discuss on the phone.

"Il vient du port, ce vieux homme," Ali said. He handed up a blue envelope to Joe on the patio.

Joe held the envelope, puzzling for a moment, then ripped it open.

Mr. Clinton:

Please tell Mr. Jackson I have found a generous salvage broker for his friend's cargo. Tell him to come to my office as soon as possible. Time is important in this affair. Do not call. Please initial this letter and return it with my messenger.

My respects,

K. Danzinger

Joe went back inside his house to the telephone table and bent over to initial the message, as he had been requested to. *Wait.* It could be a trick, a clever cop's device to trap him. If Rawlings *did* know about Danzinger, if he'd already grilled the German, put the screws to him . . . Rawlings would need some kind of proof if he really were going to get Joe deported.

How does Danzinger know my real name?

"Pardon, M'sieu." Ali was standing in the doorway with his straw sombrero held shyly in both hands. "The old man says he must hurry back to the port. He has a *petit* taxi waiting up the hill."

"A generous salvage broker," Danzinger had written. What if he had also contacted Rawlings? How else could he have found out Joe's real name so quickly? Joe stooped over the table, the pen gripped tightly in his fingers.

Ali stepped back and spoke with the messenger again. *"M'sieu,"* Ali said, "the old man says that he can ride in your car because you may wish to go with him to see his *nesrani patron.* He says it is a shame to keep the taxi waiting so long because the little clock keeps turning. There is no problem going inside the Quartier Maritime with your car; he says all the police at the gate know it."

The fucking Land Rover, with Gib plates and that big yacht club sticker on it. *How could I have been so flaky?*

Joe initialed the letter. "Tell him to release the taxi. He can wait for me inside the garden. I'll only be a minute, and then we can ride down together."

"Ouah-aa," Ali said. *"M'sieu* is being sensible. It is a waste to take two cars to the same place."

Danzinger had closed the peeling shutters against the direct glare of the sun. The office was shadowy-cool. On the wall a big electric fan creaked through its crescent path, stirring the odors of dust and mildew.

"So, you see, Mr. Jackson, it *would,* after all, be a formally binding salvage agreement. I'm sure the embassy would expect you to sign a legal waiver of any further claim."

Joe smoked, hunched quietly in his chair. Those beers

on an empty stomach had not helped his reasoning ability.

"My name is not Jackson, and you know it."

"At this stage of the affair, Mr. Jackson, names are of little importance. Perhaps my name isn't Danzinger. What does it matter? All my documents state that it is. My children were baptized with that name. The important issue here is not names, but good faith. I have already told you too much, but, remember, the Soviet Government was sincere when they offered that reward. Why, I understand that a delegation from their Ocean Fisheries Service is en route to Rabat right now to inspect this piece of equipment."

"That buoy is not fisheries' equipment, and you know it."

Danzinger looked genuinely surprised. "What do you mean? I was told that it was a remote-sensing station, an underwater device, as you say, to monitor the mackerel and sardine shoals between Mauritania and Gran Canaria Island. It's been missing for weeks. The Russians have been quite embarrassed about this. They thought it might have been picked up by a Spanish or Moroccan patrol vessel. Their trawlers do not always observe the twelve-mile limit, you know."

Joe sat up straighter in his chair. He was being conned, he felt, but he could see the persuasiveness of the German's logic. "Why didn't you want to handle the salvage, then, yourself, today?"

Danzinger smiled for the first time that afternoon. "I had to make some inquiries about you first. You might have been sent by the Moroccan authorities. You have said yourself that this isn't an orthodox salvage problem." Joe stared at him without answering. Danzinger was still smiling. He slipped the flimsy copy of a Telex message out of a folder and handed it across to Joe. "I *do* understand some Russian, after all, Mr. Jackson. Here is the confidential announcement of the loss of this remote-sensing station. This is a copy of the original message sent by the Ocean Fisheries Service and the Oceanographic Institute in Murmansk. I have a friend at the Russian Embassy in Rabat; he's an attaché. He gave this to me last week. He thought my wide business contacts in this area might help in locating it, you see."

Joe examined the flimsy copy of the message. It looked authentic. The teleprinter type was Cyrillic. The weight of the buoy in kilograms and its outside dimensions in meters and centimeters seemed accurate. He could not read the text, but he saw the latitude and longitude corresponding to the coast of Mauritania. There were also some data about radio frequencies and ranges—136.24 Mg. H.T.Z. That was a U.H.F. frequency, just as George had suggested, but it was for communication with trawlers, not with a goddamned spy satellite.

Joe scanned the message again, then dropped it back on the desk. *Shit, I was right the first time, when I saw it caught in that net. It's only an underwater research machine. I got carried away and George followed right along. A goddamned fish catcher!*

"Do you understand the situation better now, Mr. Jackson?"

"Yeah, I think I do." He began to smile, but he caught himself. Mr. Fullback Rawlings and his phony exit visa for the imaginary Jew, all for some fancy fishing gadget. This whole deal was getting to be funny.

"Very well. Now, I spoke with my friend, the attaché, a few hours ago. We discussed the reward. I think, Mr. Jackson, that you'll be pleased. This is confidential, you understand."

"Go ahead," Joe said, regaining his hard exterior. Inside, he was still smiling, but he was also curious, again approaching optimism.

"This device is an important scientific instrument. It was designed by the Oceanographic Institute, it is a prototype. From what I understand, there is nothing else like it yet in service. I am not a scientist, but I *am* a businessman. I know that the Soviet Government will make a very generous salvage settlement if this device is returned to them as soon and as discreetly as possible."

"*Very* generous . . . you mean my original proposal? Sixty thousand dollars?"

"Perhaps not quite that high, but certainly in that range."

"You're not serious."

"I'm dead serious. Mr. Jackson, do you realize what a

huge state enterprise ocean fishing is in the Soviet Union?"

"Yeah, I've heard. I read the newspapers."

"Forty percent of their protein comes from the sea, Mr. Jackson. Now, again, this is confidential, but I further understand that this remote-sensing device could revolutionize shallow-water trawler fishing, especially off the African coast. It uses all the advanced techniques, temperature of water. What is that other business? Sonar, yes sonar . . . hydrophones. The latest techniques, Mr. Jackson. It's a prototype, too. Can you appreciate what it is worth?"

"I'm beginning to." *What idiots George and I were. We're conditioned to think of Russians and weapons. Whoever thinks of Russians and fish?*

"So, Mr. Jackson, I take it that you—I should say you and your friend—are prepared to discuss this salvage deal with the Soviet Embassy."

Joe saw it all clearly. There was nothing crooked about this. It actually was a legitimate salvage operation, after all. George would be relieved. Rawlings would shit a brick. *Rawlings. . . . Christ, he'll be back here tomorrow night.* "When can I talk to your friend, the attaché? Can I see him tonight?"

Danzinger was looking sincerely concerned now. "They would like you—and your friend—to discuss this with them at the embassy tomorrow morning, early. I'm sure all the arrangements can be made in a few hours. I've taken the liberty of arranging a *grand* taxi to pick you up quite early . . . a discreet driver I know. You can be at the embassy by nine. You have more of the same photographs, like the one you showed me?"

"I've got better than *that,*" Joe said, picturing in his mind the bronze plaque itself.

"Good. Now, Mr. Jackson, I must say something that I hope you will understand. Please don't feel it's personal."

Joe frowned. *Now, what the hell is he talking about?*

"There are two ways of looking at this transaction, aren't there? A salvage settlement, shall we say, slightly irregular, but still within the bounds of maritime tradition."

"And?"

"Blackmail, extortion. The potential is there for both—what you call the double cross . . . in other words, collecting the salvage fee, then selling this instrument again, say, to the French or the Moroccan Government or the Japanese, perhaps. They'd love to get their hands on it."

"That had *never* even occurred to me, Mr. Danzinger."

"Of course not. But you must understand the position my attaché friend is in."

"Okay, go on."

"The Russians are not loved by the government of King Hassan, but they do have some friends here. The Russians buy a great deal of this country's phosphates. Russia has important trade links here. There is talk around of an arms purchase . . ."

"What's the point, please?"

"The point, Mr. Jackson, is that extortion is a serious crime. I must caution you."

Joe could almost hear Rawlings' warnings echoing in the back of his head. "I know. I'll get arrested and deported if I try something cute."

"Cute?"

"The double cross."

Danzinger looked relieved. "You understand?"

"I understand that much. What I don't get, though, is why you're being so unselfish about this whole deal."

Danzinger nodded. "I have already been paid for my services—for transmitting your name to the Russian Embassy and for arranging tomorrow's meeting, for passing on my friend's instructions and his warnings, Mr. Clinton."

Joe swallowed. The squeaking fan whirled on the wall. In the code room of the Russian Embassy, somebody is sitting down about now at a Teletype, sending off a long cable to Moscow, *with my name in it.*

"Who do I talk to tomorrow?" Joe asked, looking back up at Danzinger after what seemed a long time.

"So," Danzinger said, taking out another paper from his folder, "these are your instructions."

There was a pleasant sea breeze that night. Up on the mountain the *chergui* heat had broken and it was cool enough for Joe and George to eat dinner inside. Joe had walked up from his own house for the meal at nine and met George, still in his whites after a tennis date with Patricia. Before George showered or Joe made the drinks, they walked around the ground floor of the house to the driveway and solemnly inspected the new padlock George had fitted to the garage door. In the pantry they carried out this same inspection on the trapdoor lock.

George's maid had prepared a buffet and left it in the refrigerator: cold roast *bon* filet, watercress salad, mixed pickles, and gazpacho. "Just leftovers" was the way George had described the meal on the phone when he had called Joe from the tennis club. He had said that he had made an interesting discovery and was eager to discuss it with Joe.

After his second meeting with Danzinger, Joe had some technical matters he was eager to discuss himself. He had returned home at six, excited and confused. For the second time that day he exercised violently and sweated out the alcohol in a hot shower. Then he burned his proposed message to Rawlings and flushed the ashes down the toilet. When he finally did call Renée at seven, they spoke for twenty minutes. It was mundane conversation made tender by their loneliness and the physical distance between them. Joe did not mention Rawlings, and Renée said nothing about Joe's abrupt, drunken appearance in Rabat.

A similar reluctance to discuss important matters at hand prevailed during most of the meal in George's dining room. Finally, unable to continue the small talk about *Dragonfly's* engine, George got up and turned on the bright overhead lights. He cleared away the teak serving bowls and his own placemat to make room on the green marble table. He returned from his den with a pad of drawing paper, a steel straight edge, and some draftsman's pencils.

"Okay," he said, "let me show you what I've found out about that buoy."

George spoke for twenty minutes and Joe listened, drinking chilled Córdoba rosé and smoking. When George had finished, the center of the dining table had been cleared of linen and dishes. The silver Jensen pepper grinder sat in the center, representing the buoy. Smaller demitasse spoons had become auxiliary buoys in the hypothetical surveillance network. At Joe's right elbow there were two rough sketches torn from the drawing pad and a more detailed diagram that George had made with the aid of a straight edge.

"I hope I made myself clear, Joe." George put down the apple he had been holding over the table to symbolize a Soviet reconnaissance satellite. "But when I found the *computer* in there, tucked behind the single-side-band chassis, I just had to dig around some more. You know how I am."

"Yeah, I know. You're sure about that? You're sure it's a computer?"

George tapped the straight edge on the diagram. "I had to *make* sure. That's why I worked for an hour getting those power feeds and antenna cables free so I could unbolt the chassis. It's a computer, all right—what they call a 'mini-computer' now. From the rest of the gear inside the buoy, I was prepared for maybe a block or two of solid-state circuits with analogue capacity. But, Joe, they've got the whole analogue output interfaced to a digital system for recording and transmission. This is *elegant* stuff. I traced the inputs all back to the sensors, through the analogue blocks, and up to the digital encoding and transmission circuits. That's these over here." He tapped the diagram again. "It's fantastic, isn't it?"

Joe drank some wine and refilled his glass. In the silver ashtray in front of him, a smoldering filter sent up rancid smoke.

"You're not angry, are you?" George looked embarrassed again. "Everything's back in place; not a nut or washer is scratched or missing. It took hours."

"I'm not mad, George."

George smiled. "Those black tape cassettes had been bothering me, Joe. I *knew* those damned things weren't just for the sonar recorders and the hydrophones. They're program tapes—codes, radio frequencies, times for surfacing and submerging—the central schedule and control of this entire buoy network. It's just beautiful!" George swept his hand over the display of spoons and the pepper grinder.

Joe pushed aside his wineglass. He stubbed out the

smoldering filter in the ashtray. He had to think straight about this. "Excuse me a second, George." He got up again and went into the bathroom and locked the door.

The cold water from the tap was not truly cold, but it helped. He dried his face and sat down on the edge of the tub. *What if George is right?*

No, that wasn't possible. Rawlings would never have been so casual about this deal if that buoy down there were actually as important as George thought. That thing was complicated, all right. It's got a computer inside of it, fine. But a lot of non-military equipment use computers these days. Look at the Apollo program. And they have automated steel foundries now, whole assembly lines that run on computers around the clock, with nobody doing any operation by hand. No. George has just gotten carried away again. Rawlings would never play this deal so loose and casual if the buoy were that important.

Joe came out and gripped the back of George's chair. "Look," he said harshly, "Let's go down to the garage. I want to see this computer myself. And I've got something I want to ask you."

"Sure," George said. He got up quickly from his chair, obviously uneasy at the cold, urgent tone of Joe's voice, and they unlocked the hatch.

"But the infrared tracks, Joe, on the surface . . . the article says . . . "

Joe threw the magazine across the brightly lit garage. The pages flapped like the wings of a wounded bird. "Fuck *Scientific American.* This is not some seminar in graduate school. I repeat, can you prove that this damned thing is a submarine surveillance buoy and *not* designed for fishery research?"

George stooped to retrieve the magazine. Nervously, he smoothed the crumpled pages into place. "Okay," he said, "I see your point, and it's a good one. I'm not trying to play games, either. But I can't give you a definite answer one way or the other. I'm an engineer, but I've never worked in this specific field. Remote sensing is a whole new area. It's . . . "

"Why don't you tell the real truth, George? You've never *worked,* period. I'm not talking about visiting Daddy's plant on Easter vacation, either. I need some solid, professional advice, not a bunch of jargon about 'analogue input.' "

Joe fell silent and George stared at the floor.

"You can be a real prick sometimes, Clinton," George said, breaking the silence.

"And you can be a pompous Explorer Scout."

The fluorescent tubes buzzed on the ceiling.

"I'm sorry," Joe said. He ran his hand through his hair and automatically looked at his watch. He slapped the metal side of the buoy. "Look, once again, for the record, and then we'll call it a night, is it possible—no, is it *probable*—that this buoy was designed by Russian oceanographers to monitor big schools of fish, sardines and mackerel, in the spawning waters off the African coast? Could the whole layout of little buoys and the various radio setups and that computer inside there *all* be put together to feed information to fisheries scientists on board a big factory trawler? You know what I mean—water temperature, underwater sounds of fish schools, bottom contours."

George fingered the ripped pages of his copy of *Scientific American*. "Yes," he said. "Yeah, it certainly could be exactly what you say it is, a very fancy prototype, even with the dual-factor computer block. But I wonder if they'd go to all that trouble just to catch fish. This thing is worth a lot of money, Joe, hundreds of thousands of bucks."

"Forty percent of the Russians' protein comes out of the sea," Joe said slowly. "That's why fishing is so important to them."

"Oh," George said. "Who told you that, anyway?"

Joe stared at the buoy's shiny metal skin, then looked up at George. "A C.I.A. man named William Rawlings. He's from the embassy in Rabat."

"Oh," George said, in a different, softer tone. "I see now. Well, those guys know a lot more about this business than I do."

"You do okay," Joe said kindly, "for an enlightened amateur."

They both smiled.

"They're interested in paying salvage?"

"Yeah," Joe said. "It's kind of complicated. I can't go

into details now, George. I should have everything worked out in a day or two."

"I hope so, Joe."

George came around from the other side of the buoy. He busied himself, checking the wooden chocks wedged beneath the legs of the supporting saw horses. Joe was absently stroking the buoy's skin again.

"Joe, I don't want to pry into the details of your arrangement with the C.I.A. guys, believe me," George said.

"In a couple of days," Joe repeated, "I can tell you the whole story."

"I'm not that interested, Joe. What I'm worried about is what it's doing to you. You don't look good. Hell, you look *awful.*"

Joe did not answer. He was peering in through the inspection panels in the buoy's side. The blocks of printed circuitry and colored cables made no sense to him. At this level of sophistication, technology became as abstract and meaningless as Chinese ideographs to men like Joe.

His mind's internal eye shifted focus slightly. He could clearly picture the teleprinter in the Soviet Embassy chattering out Cyrillic characters across the message form.

They've got my name; they know exactly who I am.

"Ocean fishing is really important to those people, George," Joe heard himself repeating. "Forty percent of their protein comes from the sea."

14

Dimitry

Joe was escorted up the marble staircase of the former French villa by two gray-suited messengers. He counted two busts of Lenin, one of Marx, and nine blank, closed doors. The corridor was decorated with photographs dealing with Soviet industry and agriculture. Behind one door, he heard a girl's voice laughing sweetly. Behind another, a Teletype machine was tapping out a message. Joe felt uneasy. *Come on. This isn't a movie. They aren't going to kill you in broad daylight.*

The first secretary of the embassy, Mr. Zinchenko, greeted him at the door of his office and dismissed the two messengers with a barely perceptible movement of his bushy eyebrows. Mr. Zinchenko's office was pleasantly bright after the overpowering grayness of the ground-floor reception lobby. Sunlight filled the room from the French doors that gave onto a small balcony. But the sun did not wash out the vivid red and purple of the gladioli that stood in vases on the desk and mantel. Georgian peasant embroideries, shot with yellows and greens, hung in glass frames on the walls. The floor was covered with a rich Kalmuck carpet.

Joe began to relax. Mr. Zinchenko looked harmless. He was a jolly bear of a man, with his mauve suspenders and blue eyes twinkling beneath white eyebrows. His bright office was reassuring, certainly not an interrogation chamber. Joe smiled when they shook hands.

Speaking French with ease but with a rough-edged accent, Zinchenko excused himself for receiving Joe in shirt-sleeves. He motioned toward the open French doors, indicating the heat of the summer morning. *"Il fait trop chaud pour porter le veston,* Monsieur Clinton."

Okay. They're using my real name. Don't let that throw you. Just remember your story. This is a simple business transaction.

Joe was seated in a stiff armchair directly opposite one of the framed embroideries. He had slept well during the taxi ride down from Tangier, and now his initial attack of nerves was receding. This was the procedure Danzinger had told Joe to follow. All he had to do was play the game. These people had their own rules. They were expecting him; they knew exactly who he was, but they still had to be careful.

Joe smiled up appreciatively at the frame on the wall. That was where the camera would be hidden. He may as well give them a full-face shot with a smile. Mr. Zinchenko sat behind his desk, his hands out of sight, undoubtedly adjusting the volume control of his tape recorder as they bantered back and forth cheerfully with introductory small talk.

"Eh, bien, Monsieur Clinton," Zinchenko said. "So, you wish to visit the Soviet Union this autumn?"

"No, Monsieur Zinchenko," Joe said. He noted a slight change in Zinchenko's hospitable smile. "No, actually that isn't the purpose of my visit at all."

"Yes," Zinchenko said. "I believe I recall something about possible information you have that might interest us."

Joe reached slowly down to his briefcase and withdrew the envelope of Polaroid pictures. Zinchenko's face was now showing both interest and some tension. He took the photographs and examined them superficially.

"Could you perhaps explain to me what these are, Monsieur?"

"Didn't Monsieur Danzinger explain everything to you already?"

Zinchenko frowned openly now. "There was some discussion of information, but perhaps you could tell me in your own words."

Joe looked out the open doors at the sunny morning sky. This was some kind of a *screening,* a test. They had to be sure he was really the man Danzinger had sent down. This business took some getting used to. Nothing was straightforward with these people.

"They are photographs taken by a friend of mine, a close friend. He's a Moroccan Jew who lives in Tangier. The pictures are of a Soviet scientific instrument, a very complicated oceanographic device designed by your professors in Murmansk. It was recently put into service as a prototype with your fishing fleet off the coast of West Africa. My friend has now got this device in his possession. He bought it from some Arab fishermen who had snagged it in one of their nets."

"Why didn't your friend come to see us himself?" Zinchenko's voice was still relaxed, friendly.

"He has had some problems with the Moroccan authorities in the past over business dealings. He was afraid to contact you directly. But he sincerely wants the Soviet Government to regain custody of this valuable instrument. He wants to be paid for his services, though—a fair salvage settlement only."

"Yes." Zinchenko was nodding now. "Monsieur Danzinger did mention something about this to a colleague of mine. Hmmm, these photographs, however, Monsieur Clinton, they're not very clear, are they?"

What's he stalling for? "Here," Joe said, checking himself from seeming too anxious. "Perhaps this will make things clearer."

The bronze plaque was heavy in his extended hand.

Zinchenko gingerly unwrapped the brown paper covering it and gazed down at the machine-cut numerals and Cyrillic characters with a satisfied smile. After a long pause he rose, carefully rewrapping the plaque, and excused himself, leaving Joe alone in the room. He was alone for perhaps three seconds before one of the gray-suited messengers entered and began brushing imaginary flecks of dust off the mantelpiece.

Joe watched the man closely. He was middle-aged, but powerfully built, with the straight-shouldered bearing of a military policeman. His iron-gray hair was closely clipped, and there were several crudely stitched scars visible on his scalp. The man finished with the mantel and moved his feather duster to the panes of the French doors.

"Il fait chaud," Joe said cheerfully, pointing out at the sunshine as Zinchenko had. The man smiled back automatically for a moment, and then his face went blank again. *"Parlez-vous français?"* Joe asked.

The man smiled again, but he did not answer. Joe felt suddenly reckless. "Are you a Tartar?" he asked in English. The man smiled silently. "Ghenghis Khan?" Joe asked, pointing at the man. He smiled again, but he would not speak. Joe stood up and walked toward the framed embroidery. The feather duster beat him to the wall. The man's fingers were thickly muscled and shiny with scar tissue. He held the duster's handle like a truncheon. Joe looked appreciatively at the intricate colors of the framed mats.

"Monsieur Clinton? This way, please." Zinchenko led him down the corridor of closed doors to the marble staircase. As they climbed to the third floor, Joe looked back to see the Tartar locking the door of Zinchenko's office.

They entered a comfortably furnished apartment on the street side of the embassy's top floor. A young man with a blond crewcut was seated at a coffee table and studying Joe's Polaroid pictures with a powerful magnifying glass. There was a small transistor radio playing on an end table. The music was orchestra pop from the French service of Radio Rabat. It wasn't quite loud enough to disturb conversation, but it was adequate to foil any electronic bug.

"Clinton?" the man said, glancing up. "Have a seat, please. Would you like a cup of coffee, or maybe something cold to drink—beer, whisky, gin-and-tonic?"

The voice was disconcerting. The man's English was flawlessly Midwestern American. The cut of his sportcoat and slacks and even the well-polished loafers were so purely American that Joe experienced a rush of panic that somehow the C.I.A. and the Russians had banded together to catch him in his double game.

"What'll it be, then?" the man asked. "I think I'll have a beer myself. It's a damned hot day."

"A beer would be fine," Joe stammered.

The man spoke curtly in Russian and Zinchenko replied with unmistakable military deference. He disappeared into the apartment's kitchen and returned with a tray bearing two bottles of East German beer and Pilsner glasses. During Zinchenko's brief absence from the room, the young man continued to methodically study the photographs without speaking to Joe. The beer was poured and Zinchenko was then dismissed with a silent nod, like a lackey. *Zinchenko's a first secretary,* Joe thought, *probably a career civil servant. This guy must be at least a colonel —either with the K.G.B. or G.R.U. Looks too smooth to be military intelligence, though. Must be K.G.B. Probably their senior guy in Morocco, the way he had the old boy chasing after beers.*

From where he sat, Joe could look down on the parking zone in front of the Tour Hassan Hotel. An American Express bus was loading tourists for the morning tour of the city. The young man stacked the photographs neatly on the table and looked up at Joe.

"You can call me Dimitry," he said. "When I was at the U.N., a lot of the press guys used to call me Jimmy, but I got a little sick of that. Cheers." He toasted Joe with his beer glass. "Looks like an auto garage or maybe a carpentry workshop," he said and nodded at the photographs. "I saw the leg of a metal workbench, and in this one"—he selected one of the pictures—"there's the shadow of a big woodworking or metalworker's vise. Can't be sure which, though, because of the angle."

"I don't know where it is," Joe said. "I've got a hunch that it's out in the shed of a farm in Tangier Province."

"They've got electricity out there?" Dimitry asked sharply.

"I . . . I guess they do, yes. I never paid much attention, but I think you see electric lights at some of the farms when you drive out there at night."

"Uh-huh," Dimitry said, obviously not convinced. "So, why don't you start at the beginning?"

While Joe explained, Dimitry fingered the bronze plaque and stared dispassionately out the window. Twice he interrupted Joe for clarification of some minor point, but he remained generally silent while Joe continued.

"Okay," he said simply when Joe had finished. "I guess that makes sense. You said the guy's an engineer?"

"I didn't say."

Dimitry smiled. "Touché. Okay, I'll have to take it at face value, then. He's that scared of contacting us directly?"

"He says that he's been followed day and night for the last six months. He's convinced that the Moroccan Sûreté people think he's got a lot of money stashed away in this country and that they want to get their hands on it before he gets it out to France or Spain."

"Uh-huh," Dimitry said. "Fine. So these Moroccan Sûreté people just let him drive his truck or whatever it was up from the fishermen's village and deposit this big machine in his hideout without bothering to check what it was he was carrying. Do you seriously expect me to believe that kind of B.S.?"

There was a momentary flash of confusion, verging dangerously on panic. *Remember the story. Just think of the story. The Jew is a real person. Think of him; he's real, alive.* Joe nodded tiredly. "Look," he said, "you've got to know this guy to understand the way he thinks. He exaggerates things a bit. I'm sure he is being followed, but not day and night, the way he lets on. He's scared to death of any kind of authority."

"I see. Tell me something, though. What's in it for you?"

Joe paused for effect. "I'm . . . uh . . . I'm broke. I had a bad divorce last year, and it wiped me out financially. I'm in debt. My friend's got a lot of money he can't take out of the country. It's frozen in Moroccan *dirhams.* He'll sign all of it over to me if this salvage deal goes through. I'll be able to pay off my debts and mortgage and then some. It seemed like too good a deal to pass up."

Dimitry sipped his beer from the tall Pilsner glass. He was staring unblinkingly at Joe's face. "You could just be telling the truth," he said casually. "Have you seen this machine that your friend has hidden away?"

Joe shook his head, trying to look earnest and yet not afraid.

"But Danzinger discussed it with you, I understand. He explained why my government is eager to recover it?"

"He even showed me the message from your fisheries service."

Dimitry frowned. "I don't suppose that meant much to you, did it, Mr. Clinton? You don't understand Russian, do you?"

"No, but I know when something looks authentic. And that message looked authentic." Joe paused for effect again. The interview was going much better than he had anticipated. "The message also looked urgent. Danzinger himself seemed quite excited. He told me how eager you people were to get this machine back." Joe smiled now. "I can understand your position. A prototype is *valuable.*"

"My friend," Dimitry said, "you talk too much. Maybe that's why your life is such a mess."

Joe again could clearly picture the Cyrillic type chattering across the teleprinter page at high speed. *Christ, they know all about me.*

"What else did Mr. Danzinger tell you about this machine?"

"Well, he said that it was important, a prototype . . . I, I mean, we already knew that . . . that it was *important. . . .*" He was getting badly flustered now. Dimitry sipped his beer. "What I *mean,*" Joe continued, "is that this device or machine was designed to do important work for your overseas fishing fleet. A lot of research and manpower went into designing and building it. Danzinger confirmed what my friend and I already suspected—that you would pay a generous salvage reward for its recovery."

"Sixty thousand dollars is more than 'generous.' "

"He *needs* at least that much."

Dimitry looked out the window. The transistor droned away on the end table. "I don't care what he needs. We're discussing a salvage settlement."

Joe swallowed hard. "Well, he's in trouble. He said he'll have to pay some big bribes to get his passport and exit visa. He owes money in Canada. His family's been over there for two years and he hasn't been able to send them anything. Also, he needs money to set himself up in business in Toronto. All that comes to sixty thousand."

Dimitry was still staring out the window. "How long has he had this machine? When did he get it from the fishermen?"

"I'm not sure. He's probably had it for three or four days now. He came to me and offered this deal two nights ago."

"I thought you said he came on Sunday morning."

"No, I didn't. I didn't say anything like that. He came to my house about ten-thirty Wednesday night. I was getting ready to go to bed."

"Okay." Dimitry rose and walked to the open window. A breeze had come up and the curtains were billowing attractively. As Dimitry stood by the window, staring into the street, Joe realized that the man was not as young as he had at first appeared to be. The American clothes and the crewcut were deceptive. Although his face was smooth and tanned, there were hard edges around the mouth and eyes. Dimitry's eyes were wide-spaced beneath a blockish forehead, a typically Slavic face, but one that was coldly aloof, lacking any of the open-faced innocence associated with the Russian peasant. Dimitry was an aristocrat, belonging to a class that had nothing to do with bloodlines or ancestry. He was a grand duke of the new Russian aristocracy, a senior officer in the K.G.B., a product of the best schools and training courses, a Party member since his youth.

"Do you know something, Clinton?" Dimitry said. "I think you're lying." He turned and stared at Joe. "I can't swallow this whole song and dance. I'm not sure what your game is, but I don't think you're being square with me."

"Song and dance," Joe thought, *"square." An advanced class for senior officers in American idioms. Not a bad try, but just a little out of date. People don't say things like "song and dance" that much anymore.*

"There's no sure way for me to prove I'm telling the truth," Joe said slowly. "The pictures could have been faked, I suppose, but that plaque looks pretty authentic to me. I don't read Russian, but you do. What does it say?"

"It's real, all right," Dimitry said. "If you'd shown up

here without that and just some bad photographs, we'd have given you the bum's rush, or worse."

Joe smiled. *That wasn't bad; "the bum's rush."* "It's a good thing my friend gave it to me, then."

"So," Dimitry said. He clasped his hands behind him and walked slowly back to his chair. "Sixty thousand American dollars paid into a numbered Swiss account, and then your Hebrew friend flies off to Toronto to buy himself a little shop and live happily ever after."

The transistor was now playing monotonously singsong Arab music. Dimitry sat down heavily on the sofa opposite Joe's chair. "I want to meet this friend of yours, Clinton. I want to meet him and see the machine myself. Then we can talk business. I'm not prepared to deal with third parties."

"That's okay by me," Joe said with conviction. "I'd like nothing better than to get out of this whole business. My job was to make the initial contact. That's what he's paying me for. I think I've pretty well done that. My friend's in Casablanca today. He gets back to Tangier tomorrow afternoon. Do you want to see him then?"

"Can't he come here?" Dimitry's voice was plainly angry.

"I'll ask him," Joe said. "I doubt that he'll want to, though. He's really convinced that he's being followed around by the Moroccan cops. If he won't, will you come up to Tangier?"

"Yes, why not?" Dimitry snapped. "Tell him that I'll be in Tangier tomorrow night. We should be able to settle the whole business then."

"What about the money? He says it'll have to be paid into his Swiss account before he gives up the machine. I hate to say this, but I don't think he trusts you people."

Dimitry swore softly in Russian and Joe caught the word "Zid" in the oath. "He doesn't trust a Soviet official. That's very good, Clinton. That's lovely. He expects us to hand over a small fortune for something we haven't even seen, to pay money into a Swiss account over which we have no control, and then sit back and wait like faithful dogs while he supposedly goes to unlock the door to the treasure house where he's hiding stolen Soviet property. Does he think we're children?" Dimitry's face deepened in color. He was on the verge of losing his temper.

Joe felt the edges of panic he had earlier experienced when walking up to Zinchenko's office. The nasal chanting on the transistor grated. "He's got a plan," Joe blurted out, "a plan that he feels is fair to both sides."

"I'm sure he has plans," Dimitry said scornfully, "plans and pipe dreams. Your friend sounds like a real kosher visionary."

Joe saw Dimitry's angular face puckered in thought. *Don't say any more. Let him do the talking now. He's angry.*

"I have a message for your friend, Clinton," Dimitry said, his voice quietly controlled again. "Tell him that we do not entirely trust him, either. We agree, however, to the general arrangements—the salvage reward and the method of payment. It's going to take us several days to confirm all this with the ministries concerned. I hope your poor, harassed friend will understand."

"Yes, I'm sure he will."

"He'd damned well *better*," Dimitry said. "Now, listen carefully." His face puckered again. He rubbed his square nose thoughtfully. "I will be in Tangier the day after tomorrow to meet your friend—Monday morning at eleven o'clock in the main post office, the P.T.T. After I've talked with him, I will telephone a colleague in Geneva and your friend can then call his bank and confirm that the money has been deposited. Does that sound satisfactory?"

Joe thought through the details. "When will you pick up the machine?"

"We will go directly from the P.T.T. to where he is keeping it. I say 'we.' I want *both* of you there and both of you to come with me when I take possession of the machine. Is that understood?"

Joe could no longer think clearly. "Yes," he answered, "I suppose that sounds okay."

"Don't 'suppose,' Clinton. Answer yes or no."

"Yes . . . yes, that will be fine." Joe was sweating. His shirt was sticking to his back. The palms of his hands itched.

"When I have taken possession of the machine, you will both be free to go on your way. There won't be any problems. At the P.T.T. he can call his bank on the new automatic lines to Europe. Geneva, you said, the Banque du Moyen Orient?"

"Yes, I . . . "

Dimitry turned away and walked to the door. It was obvious that the interview had ended. Joe got up. At the door Dimitry gripped Joe's arm with unpleasant firmness. "Tell your friend something else, Clinton. Tell him that we do have a certain amount of influence in this country, despite that fascist on the throne. Tell him that he will be very sorry if he tries to pull any sharp deals with us. Do you understand?"

Joe nodded grimly.

"Tell him this, too." Dimitry released Joe's arm and moved forward so that their faces were almost touching. "Tell him that his family in Canada and his *friends* here will be the ones who suffer if he thinks he can make fools of us and get away with it."

He's only bluffing. It's a fishing buoy; it's only for catching mackerel and sardines.

Joe licked his lips compulsively. "Okay. Monday, then."

The door opened and the Tartar was there to lead Joe down the stairs, past the busts of Marx and Lenin. Above him, inside the apartment, the Arab music still droned on.

Dimitry stood for a moment at the open window, watching Joe cross the street. No one was following him. "Good," Dimitry said softly. He sat down and finished his beer.

After several minutes of thought, he got up and walked through the apartment's kitchen into the scullery. A metal door, with an electric punch-key lock, hung in the steel frame where there had once been a dumbwaiter. Dimitry tapped out the combination and the door buzzed open. Inside there was a narrow staircase, steep as a ship's ladder. This led down to another steel door, the entrance to the Quiet Room.

The Quiet Room had been a double bedroom when the building was a villa. Now it was the secure conference center of the Soviet Embassy. Only three men in the mission knew the combinations to the electric punch locks that controlled the room's two doors. One was Nikolai, the K.G.B. field services officer, the middle-aged "Tartar" who had kept Joe company in Zinchenko's office. The second man was Zinchenko himself. And the third was the K.G.B. resident, Senior Colonel Dimitry Aladef. Dimitry did not like his surname; it embarrassed him because of its possible Jewish connotations. In the embassy, he was known simply as "Comrade Dimitry."

"It went well, Comrade Dimitry," Zinchenko said. He held aside the double drape of lead foil so that Dimitry could enter without smudging his sportcoat. The room smelled like a refrigerator that had gone unopened for a long time. Lead foil sagged on the ceiling and walls. It crumpled and bunched underfoot. Here there was no need for transistor radios or microwave jamming equipment.

Nikolai stood at the table that occupied the center of the room. He had two case files before him and the restricted-distribution binder that contained all the cable traffic on Marine Reconnaissance Station George Kilo Foxtrot 18.

"I have prepared the surveillance schedule, as you wished."

"Good fellow," Dimitry said. "But we'll wait on that. Now, take some notes, please."

Nikolai sat down. He took the notes on single sheets of stationery and wrote with a simple wooden pencil.

" 'State secret immediate action to Washington embassy. For: Leonard. Supply any possible Defense Intelligence Agency connections. Subject, Clinton. Per Rabat embassy . . .' Add the number there. 'Reply immediate.'

"Now: 'State secret immediate action to the ministry. For: case duty officer, general rank only. . . . Proceeding with retrieval, as per paragraph . . .' "

"Five," Zinchenko added, looking up from the red cable binder.

"Thank you. 'As per paragraph five of Rabat embassy . . .' Add the number there. "Request ministry personnel support soonest. Situation: stable. Prospects: excellent.' "

Nikolai looked up.

"Transmit those immediately by One-Time-Only Pad and bring me back all copies." Dimitry spoke to the older man in a kindly, but commanding, tone.

"At once, Dimitry."

When Nikolai had left for the Code Room, Zinchenko spoke. "You think he may be Defense?"

Dimitry shrugged his shoulders. "I don't know, but he's not an agency regular, at least not according to the ministry."

He paced a moment, rubbing his nose. The lead foil crumpled softly beneath his loafers.

"Look," he said, "on this surveillance we're short-handed. So let's make it a passive observation only: airports, ferryboats, and frontier posts. I've got a feeling he's not going anywhere outside the country, that he will be at the post office Monday morning, right on schedule. If he *is* C.I.A., he'll make his reports via their communications facility at the Kénitra base. That is where we'll put most of our people, at least until this second team arrives from the ministry. As soon as we can get a good field officer to replace Nikolai's team at Kénitra, we'll shift to discreet observation of him in Tangier."

"It's a pity to let him run around unobserved for two days, Comrade Dimitry." Zinchenko's voice seemed more sad than concerned.

Dimitry smiled indulgently at the old diplomat. "Flies go swarming to two things, my friend—shit and honey. They get stuck in both. I am not going to send my entire local organization swarming up to Tangier today to get stuck in a pile of American shit."

"Of course, Colonel. It's just that . . ."

"Have confidence, Alexei Andreiovitch. If he's Competition, he may show himself at Kénitra. If he's straight, he'll be at the P.T.T. Monday morning. Now, one thing we have to work on at once is this Jew. Get me the file on that contract boy in the Jewish community up there."

"At once."

Dimitry held aside the lead drape for the older man. "Oh, yes," he added when Zinchenko was almost out the door, "get a call through to Danzinger. Use the Pole's phone today. Tell him to fly to Madrid to collect his payment, from Peter. Also, tell him to take a vacation, two weeks in Spain. He can drop off his passport with Peter and collect it at the end of his holiday. Tell him to leave his family in Tangier, too. He'll understand."

"Of course, Dimitry."

Dimitry clicked the steel door shut. He resumed his pacing on the dead softness of the lead-foil carpet.

15

The Code Room

Rawlings led the way down the bright, fluorescent-lit hallway. At the door to the vault, he paused, stooping to block the combination lock from Joe's view. After a moment a steel door swung open, revealing another door, this one of thick wire screening. Rawlings produced a key attached to a red paper tag and snapped open the lock of the second door.

The interior of the Tangier consulate code room was also brightly lit. They were in the records section, its walls lined with green filing cabinets, the floor of rubber tiles. Overhead Joe could hear the soft whir of the air conditioning. He stood in the center of the room, embarrassed, like an infidel in a mosque. Still without speaking, Rawlings walked across the long rectangular room to test the lock on the door to the "top secret" alcove, housing the cryptographic machines and teleprinters. He opened the top drawer of a filing cabinet and brought out the inevitable transistor radio. He flipped the dial to Radio Seville and the soft tones of a classical guitar concerto filled the room.

"Sit down, please," he finally said, indicating a swivel chair.

From the chair Joe could look out through the half-opened Venetian blinds and the concrete screening at the sunset colors on the villas and apartment blocks of suburban Tangier. "I didn't want to talk about it over the phone," Joe said. Rawlings stared at him, but he did not answer. "I figured it wouldn't hurt anything if I came here myself."

"Coffee?" Rawlings asked, indicating a chrome coffee machine at the far end of the mail counter. Joe shook his head.

"Well," Rawlings said, a slightly condescending note in his voice, "what's the story now?"

"I met him this morning at the café halfway between Rabat and Casa. At first he was nervous and, well, disappointed about your offer. Then, after he'd thought it over, it seemed better. He drew a complete blank with his contact in the governor's office in Casablanca. He's sure that he's known now among the Moroccan officials and that they'll all hold out for big bribes before he gets anything."

"What's his name, Clinton?" Rawlings' voice was heavy and his thick, young features drawn, as if he had been working too hard and sleeping far too little.

"Wait," Joe said, almost pleading. "Listen to what he wants. He's down in Marrakech tonight. He'll be in Agadir tomorrow and back here on Monday night or Tuesday morning at the latest. He wants to do it like you suggested—a fake passport and a ride out on a U.S. Air Force plane. He's selling off family property in Marrakech and some business interests in Agadir. He'll be coming back with cash, Christ, maybe even gold. Once he makes contact with you, he wants protection. He wants you to keep him in protective custody until he's on the plane. This is important. He's almost run ragged. He's paranoid as hell that if you get his name you'll somehow double-cross him with the Sûreté people in Rabat. He wants a French passport with any Jewish name. You can use any one of these pictures." Joe dug an envelope out of his briefcase. Inside were four different passport-size photographs of a swarthy, balding man of about forty.

Rawlings selected a full-face picture of the man wearing a dark suit and tie. He glanced briefly at the others and returned to the first, staring intently at the man's face, as if the photo would reveal concrete details of the man's identity. He slipped the three others into the envelope and carefully closed the flap. He folded the chosen picture neatly inside a piece of typing paper and sealed it with Scotch tape.

"What does he want for date and place of birth?" Rawlings asked.

"He didn't say." Joe smiled now, letting his tautly held facial muscles relax. He had won. "Make him about thirty-eight or -nine. Better give him someplace in the south of France as a birthplace . . . Marseille or Nice, someplace down there. . . ."

"Thirty-nine years old . . . Marseille," Rawlings droned. "Profession?"

"Well, he *is* a trained engineer. Better call him an engineer, then."

Rawlings jotted a few notes and then snapped his notebook shut. "Listen carefully," he said. "I want you both here at the consulate at exactly four A.M. Tuesday morning. Take a *petit* taxi from the Place de France. It'll be taxi number sixty-seven, and the driver's name is Mustapha. Here." He handed Joe a piece of paper and ball-point pen. "Just write 'Sixty-seven' and 'Mustapha,' so you won't forget."

"I'm a professional journalist, Rawlings," Joe said with sudden pride. "I think I can remember that."

Rawlings shrugged. "Take the taxi to the side entrance of the consulate. The gate will be open and you'll drive right into the motor pool. There'll be an American military ambulance there. We'll pick up the tube with that and then drive down to either the Kénitra or Rabat airfield. Tell your friend to bring everything he'll need for the trip with him because we won't be stopping back in town. Tell him to bring one reasonable suitcase, that's all. We can arrange to have the rest of his stuff sent on after he's out of the country. Do you understand?"

"I do."

"Okay. Any questions?"

"Yes. What about me? You were talking about helping me out with my house mortgage."

Rawlings seemed to relax for the first time, as if some nagging fear had been alleviated. "Yeah, I did say that, didn't I? Well, why don't you ride down to Rabat with me and we can work something out in my office there."

"It's a Tangier bank that's holding the deed."

"Yeah, well, I keep my bag of Moroccan *dirhams* down in Rabat, and if you want any, you'll have to come down there to get them." Rawlings actually smiled now, a warm unaffected grin.

"That sounds reasonable," Joe said, forcing himself to return the smile. "Four A.M. Tuesday. Cab number sixty-seven. Mustapha."

16

The Last Night

The mosquitoes were bad on the terrace. It was the first night all summer that Joe had been bothered by them while sitting outside. He went back into the kitchen and pawed through Zorah's neatly arranged pantry until he found the red cardboard box of mosquito coils. Once the coil was burning under the table, the pungent woodsmoke odor blended nicely with the heaviness of the jasmine, reminding him suddenly of hot summer nights years ago when, as a kid in basic training, he'd burned cattails out on bivouac and the drenching perfume of honeysuckle had almost choked him. Things had been so simple then: two years in the peace-time army and the G.I. bill, a decent degree in journalism, and then off to the wild places of the world to make his name and fortune.

But his life hadn't worked out that way. He smiled, a wry, sarcastic grin. Before him on the table were two miniature bottles of Johnnie Walker. He was drinking slowly tonight, allowing himself four drinks, half a miniature to a drink, with a lot of water and ice cubes. It was ten-thirty and he had one small bottle to drink before going to bed. The house was quiet. The mountain seemed strangely silent, as well, gray-green in the light of the full moon. It had been a hard day, but now everything was done. All the tricky lies and deceptions had been completed. Strangely enough, tricking Rawlings the night before with the pictures had been the easiest part of the whole thing.

Finding those pictures had been a real piece of luck.

The Rabat-Tangier express bus had stopped only once, at a snack bar in a service station in the old Spanish town of Larache. Joe had had a stale sandwich and a tepid Coke and then had wandered up the street, nervously preoccupied with the dangers of that evening's encounter with Rawlings. He had almost walked right past the photography shop, its dirty window crowded with the usual wedding and family pictures and with strips of passport photographs tacked up along both sides.

The sign above the shop door stated that the business belonged to one José Miguel Levy, but inside, in the light of a flickering twenty-watt bulb, Joe was greeted by a sleepy Moroccan kid who spoke only Arabic and a few words of Spanish. Joe's folded ten-*dirham* notes eliminated any communications problem. Five minutes after entering the hole-in-the-wall shop, he was back on the bus with an envelope containing the dusty negatives of passport pictures of long-departed Sephardic Jews.

Joe broke open the foil top of the second miniature whisky bottle and drained the entire contents into his glass. Yeah, that had been the easy part, bullshitting Rawlings with the pictures of a man who did not exist. The hard part had been that morning with Ali and Zorah. It was not as if Joe had asked them to do something unreasonable, difficult, or illegal. All he had proposed was that Ali take his wife and child on the red Estrella de Norte bus up into the Rif to visit his family for a few days, a week's vacation at *M'sieu*'s expense. But Ali had toed his sandals in the dust and stared at the ground with his stubby jaw set in wordless refusal. The flowers would die without Ali's constant attention. Who would water the garden morning and evening? Who would prepare *M'sieu*'s meals and wash his dishes? Who would shop in the market and who would guard the house against thieves when *M'sieu* went out in the evening? It took the better part of an hour to convince the old man that he must obey Joe's orders and take this unexpected vacation. In the end Joe had resorted to yet another dramatic lie. He had gripped Ali's arm and looked sharply down into his eyes. "You will go, Ali. You'll take Zorah and little Mohammed for one week. I'm going to be here with a woman . . . not the *madame* from Rabat, but another woman, and I want to be alone. Can't you understand? I don't want Zorah to know. She's a good friend of the *madame* from Rabat." Ali nodded acceptance, then took the money Joe held out and walked sadly down to the servants' quarters to prepare Zorah for the unexpected trip.

When Joe returned that night from the airline office, the house was dark. In the kitchen there was a chicken *tajine* still warm in the oven. The house was meticulously neat. All the rose beds in the garden were still awash with water.

It had been a hard day. But now the dirty work had all been done. Now the decks were cleared for action. He laughed out loud. *Christ, don't get too bloody dramatic.* If everything kept working so well, there wouldn't be any action. In a few minutes he would go to bed and sleep until the alarm rang at three A.M. Then he would transfer the tube down the mountain to his own garage. George had already been briefed. The Land Rover was all set; the seats had been removed. His bag was already packed. It would be easy in the morning. Meet Dimitry at the post office and explain that the Jew had already gotten out of Morocco, leaving Joe to act as his salvage agent. Confirm the deposit in the Swiss bank and drive Dimitry up here to claim his goods. Then the one o'clock flight to Gibraltar and the three-thirty BEA to London.

Joe found himself pacing along the edge of the patio in jerky, nervous steps. He stopped and filled his lungs deeply with the cool evening air. There was no need to get so worked up. Leaving Morocco for a few weeks was the prudent, self-protective action to take. He had thought over this move carefully.

Rawlings was going to be angry. Worse, he was going to be embarrassed, humiliated. Joe would have "jacked him around," and Rawlings would not take that lightly. He'd be vindictive.

Joe stared out at the gray moonlight on the hedges and jasmine vines. What a situation. In the period of one week, two intelligence officers, one American and one Russian, had threatened him, indirectly, through his "Jewish friend," with nasty reprisals if they did not get what they wanted. Tomorrow morning Dimitry was going to get what he wanted, the prototype fishing buoy. Tuesday morning at the consulate Rawlings was going to find out he'd been double-crossed.

Then the shit would hit the fan.

Joe had no doubt that Rawlings had meant his threats. He had spoken arrogantly of his "bag of Moroccan *dirhams*" down at the embassy. After Tuesday, Rawlings would not use the money to help Joe with his mortgage. Rawlings would spend that money to get Joe into trouble. That was what was known as revenge. It sounded melodramatic, but Joe knew Rawlings was capable of bribing crooked Moroccan police and immigration officials to make things "uncomfortable" for him in Morocco.

But Rawlings won't get the house; he won't get the car or boat, either.

Joe had a plan. From London, he would cable Harry Rains enough money to pay off the mortgage and hire a good French lawyer. Maybe a little money would have to change hands under the table. All right, that was the way a guy had to do business around here. Rawlings would be planning his spiteful reprisal against a scared Jew and a washed-up drunk, not someone with money and good connections like Harry Rains.

It was not going to be easy, but it was going to work. In a few weeks, maybe a month, the dust would have settled and Joe would be free to come home, with no debts and no mortgages hanging over his head . . . and all that money in the bank.

By then Barent and MacCormack would have come back to take charge of the Rabat station, and Rawlings would just have to swallow his hurt pride and resentment.

Tough shit, kid. You said it yourself. This ain't a gentleman's game.

Joe found himself standing in front of the kitchen sink, making a fresh drink from the large bottle of Teacher's. *What the hell? One more for the road won't kill me.*

Back on the terrace he raised his glass and toasted the brightly lit villas lower on the mountain. He drank some whisky and grinned. He would be in London at this time tomorrow, in a good hotel in the West End, with *all* that money safe in his Swiss account.

"Christ, London, with money to spend for a change . . ." He thought he would do some shopping on Bond Street.

An owl winged by, with soft ghost strokes, just overhead in the moonlight. It settled on the roof of the studio at the bottom of the garden. The gecko lizards, which had been chirping in the vine above the terrace, were suddenly quiet.

Joe stopped smiling. *Renée . . . I've forgotten about Renée again, haven't I?*

Eleven o'clock on Sunday night. She would be getting Tommy's clothes ready for camp next week, sewing on the little name tags at the table in her kitchen, that *Ladies'-Home-Journal* kitchen.

He looked up at the bright, full moon. When he closed his eyes, he could see her on the sleeping bag beneath him the night of the moon landing. That seemed like something from a forgotten childhood.

She would be sitting in her kitchen, worried about Tommy's sore throat, disappointed that she and Joe could not have had the weekend together, but looking forward to this next week with him, alone on the boat. *But I won't be here. I'll be in London, doing my high-finance act.*

Joe was pacing again. He finished his drink and made another. From the edge of the terrace he could see the villas below him going dark as the dinner parties ended and the patio lights were shut off. It was late.

Too late to call her tonight. He would write her a letter and leave it with George in the morning. A letter to explain.

Explain what? You're walking out on her.

No, he would call from Gib, call her at the office. She'd understand. He was only going to be gone a few weeks, just until the trouble with Rawlings blew over, until the dust settled. She had some vacation time coming. Maybe she could fly up to London. He would pay for her ticket. She could bring Tommy, after camp. They'd rent a car and go see Stonehenge. That was it. He'd call her from Gib.

He finished the fresh drink in three long gulps. In the kitchen he washed and dried the glass and threw the empty miniature bottles into the trash can.

He brushed his teeth and washed down two Valium

"fives" with a glass of lukewarm tap water. The bed sheets were cool on his chest and legs. He felt better now.

You shouldn't let yourself get so worked up. This isn't an intelligence operation. The buoy is civilian equipment . . . a fancy, expensive, fish catcher.

Just before he fell asleep, he heard the owl call, a brief, lonely note.

17

The Colonel

The hot beam of the flashlight woke him up. Joe had been dreaming, but the dream was cut and forgotten in a micro-second. The glare of the light, forcing him to close his eyes and turn his face into the pillow, was not his only discomfort. It was the stuffiness of the room. He had gone to bed with the French doors to the terrace open. Now the room was sealed tightly, the air dead and heavy. Without opening his eyes, he knew that all the doors and windows were closed and latched and that the thick Berber-weave drapes had been drawn, as well. It was the same suffocating atmosphere that overcame the room when Zorah closed it up against the torrents of a winter rainstorm and the capricious central heating system suddenly came to life.

The fear that coursed along his spine and limbs with the chemical speed of adrenaline was tempered by the alcohol and tranquilizer already at work in his body. Thc only reason the Arab burglars would have awakened him so abruptly was that they had already searched the house and had found no nest egg of jewels or money. What rotten luck. His last night in the house and there was a burglary. At least that was what Joe thought at first.

A piece of furniture, something heavy, scraped along the tile floor.

"Okay, Roy?" a voice said in clear American English. "That's got it. The bottom of the drapes are jammed with the dresser."

"Who are you?" Joe started to say when, suddenly, the

overhead light snapped on and the heat of the flashlight was gone from his face.

"Get up, Clinton." It was Rawlings' voice.

He sat up in bed, blinking. There were four of them in the room, all dressed in dark sport clothes. The drapes were drawn and the bedroom door was closed. An older man with well-groomed gray hair and a navy-blue cardigan was sitting with his back to Monique's dressing table. He smiled at Joe, a kind, fatherly smile.

"Sorry to have to wake you up like this, Joe," he said, "but we have a few things to talk about that won't wait until morning."

"Who are you?" Joe repeated. He felt naked and vulnerable before them in the bed.

"I'm Colonel Richards," the man said, still smiling kindly. He pointed at the stocky man next to the dresser. "That's Larry and this is Roy. I believe you already know Mr. Rawlings." He paused. "I'm sorry it had to be this way, Joe," he continued. "Believe me, we wouldn't have acted like this if it weren't necessary."

"If you hadn't forced us to, Clinton," Rawlings added.

"Perhaps Mr. Clinton would like some coffee," Colonel Richards said.

"Right," Rawlings answered. He walked to the hallway door, flicked off the overhead light, and was gone, carefully closing the door behind him. Joe sat up and dangled his legs wearily over the side of the bed. The light came on again. They were all quietly watching him. He pulled on a pair of trousers and stretched deeply. "What time is it?" he asked, yawning.

"Ten past two," one of the younger ones answered, consulting a big pilot's watch.

"Do you mind if I use the toilet?"

The colonel nodded, and the routine with the door and the overhead light was repeated. Larry, the stocky, younger man, walked with Joe to the open door of the bathroom. The porcelain fixtures were clearly visible in the moonlight.

"No light, please," he said. He handed Joe a plastic penlight. "Use this if you can't see."

"Christ," Joe muttered.

"It's stuffy in here," Joe said. He sat back down on the

edge of the bed with a steaming mug of coffee and a cigarette. He felt much more in control of himself, more awake after washing his face and combing his hair. The coffee tasted strong and sweet. "Can't we open a window?"

They were still watching him.

"I think that we'll wait a bit on that," the colonel said.

"Okay, fine," Joe said. "Pardon me for being so demanding. It's only my house, you know. To what do I owe the honor of this unexpected visit? I thought that everything was worked out for Tuesday morning."

Rawlings strode angrily across the room. Joe cringed back involuntarily. "Yeah, of course, Tuesday morning," Rawlings snarled. He tossed a blue-and-red packet of airline tickets onto the bed. "You were going to fly back from London on a magic carpet, I suppose, to make our meeting."

Joe stared down dumbly at the tickets on the sheet. They had him. That snotty little Gibraltarian girl at the BEA office had double-crossed him. She had promised to hold the tickets for him out at the airport. But they'd gotten to her.

"And there's something else, as well, Joe," the colonel said, sounding like a disappointed schoolmaster. "How can you explain these?"

He rose and placed the phony passport pictures next to the tickets.

"What . . . what about them?" The heat in the room was making Joe dizzy.

"We've got some quite reliable contacts in the Jewish community here, Joe," the colonel said. "We had them take a good look at these photographs. Everyone who saw them is certain that they're pictures of a man named Ben Simone, who emigrated to Israel in 1964. He was a butcher in Larache. He was also a basketball coach for the Youth and Sports summer camps and quite well known in Morocco. There's not much chance of a mistake, I'm afraid." The colonel was standing above him, gray-haired and elegant. The same sad, disapproving expression was on his face again. "Joe, we have a man, a Moroccan policeman, who watches the Soviet Embassy for us on a regular basis. He takes telephoto pictures of all the visitors which we try to identify and keep in our files. What do you make of this?"

He handed Joe an eight-by-ten glossy print, an enlargement of a telephoto shot. The grain was blurred and the focus slightly out, but there was no mistaking his own face as he emerged into the morning sunlight from the door of the old French villa housing the Soviet Embassy.

Joe tried to think of something to say. He was also trying to maintain the facade of indignation, but when he tried to light a fresh cigarette from the butt he held, his fingers were shaking so badly that Larry had to step forward with his lighter to help him.

"Take your time, Joe," Colonel Richards said, his voice kindly again. "I think you want to tell us about it, just take your time."

"The Russians *asked* to see me," Joe began. "When I talked to Danzinger about the buoy, he called their Embassy and set us the appointment." Joe sucked the smoke into his lungs. He was thinking more clearly now. *He didn't have to lie any more.* Hell, he didn't even have to sit here answering their questions at two o'clock in the morning, either, in his own house, as if it were some police interrogation room. But he knew he *should,* that these men were serious professionals and meant business. Rawlings looked angry enough to be violent and that stocky guy, Larry, was obviously nobody to screw around with.

"I went down to see Danzinger and he knew all about the buoy. He had this Russian Telex about it . . . from their fisheries service or ministry—whatever they call it. He showed it to me."

"The buoy?" Rawlings asked.

"No. Listen, ask Danzinger if you don't believe me. He showed me this Russian Telex."

Larry stepped forward and stood directly between Joe and Colonel Richards. "*What* Telex from *what* fisheries service?"

"*You* know," Joe said. He was beginning to get angry again. They were playing with him. "Listen, he's got this Telex describing the lost fishing buoy—dimensions, weight, the whole thing. It's in Russian—a Telex message, for Christ's sake."

"About the Russian *fishing* buoy," Larry said in the same cool tone.

Joe looked up at Larry's face, then looked away. "Yeah, that's right, about the fishing buoy."

Larry's blow seemed to come at him slowly, but the open hand hit Joe with surprising force, striking the side of his jaw and knocking his chin down against his chest. He found himself on his back on the tangled sheets, staring up stupidly at the high ceiling. He blinked. For a moment he thought he was going to vomit.

"Clinton," Larry said slowly, "we do not want to hear any more bullshit about *fishing* buoys tonight. Do you understand now, you lying, *treasonous* son-of-a-bitch?"

Joe sat up. He was still stunned from the blow. His jaw was numb. "You people can't pull this kind of shit in my own house," he finally said.

He stood up unsteadily and turned toward the door. Rawlings and Roy were already there, blocking the way. Larry stood a yard away, relaxed, watching Joe with little apparent interest.

"Where are you going, Joe?" Colonel Richards asked. His voice was concerned, fatherly.

"I'm going to call the police," Joe said. "Breaking and entering is a crime in this country. They've got a constitution, you know. I can visit any damned embassy I want. I can negotiate a simple business deal with *any* diplomat I want, too. I'm going to have you people charged with assault and burglary . . . kidnapping, too, if you don't get the fuck out of my house."

"When you call the police, Joe," the colonel said quietly, "ask for Inspector Drisi. Tell him you're calling in reference to this picture." Colonel Richards held out another eight-by-ten photograph.

Joe hesitated a moment, then crossed the room to take the picture. The photograph was much clearer than the picture taken in front of the Russian Embassy. It was a blown-up snapshot showing George and him unloading a canvas sack from *Dragonfly*'s rubber dinghy. The boat swung at her anchor in the picture's background. Beyond the boat was the familiar silhouette of Tangier as seen from Cape Malabata.

"What the hell is this supposed to mean?" Joe asked,

looking up at the colonel. "This is a snapshot Renée O'Brien took in May. I had the negatives out in my studio, in the garden. Hey, did you bastards already burglarize my *studio*, too?"

"We found the picture on the beach," Larry said.

Joe did not join in the general chuckling that followed Larry's joke.

"That's a picture Renée took in May," he repeated. "It was taken at a picnic out at Cape Malabata."

"Is it?" the colonel said. "Look again. Inspector Drisi thinks it's a picture of you and George Briggs loading hashish aboard your sailboat, Joe. In fact, the inspector has a warrant for your arrest, and several local witnesses will swear in court that they sold you the hashish and saw you load it on the boat. We've done our homework, Joe. There's a police car with two detectives parked just up the street. If you don't want to play ball with us, then you can talk to them."

You bastards, Joe thought.

"Just sit down and listen to what the colonel has to say," Rawlings said.

Joe stared at the picture. "I think you're bluffing. I'm a journalist, for Christ's sake. Nobody's going to believe that I'm a dope smuggler."

"It doesn't matter whether you believe it or I believe it or even whether the inspector believes it, Joe," Colonel Richards said. "A Moroccan magistrate obviously believed the charges, or he wouldn't have signed the arrest warrant, would he? Now, are you going to sit down so that we can continue our conversation, or do you want Rawlings to signal those policemen to come up here and take you away?"

Joe glared silently at the colonel, but eventually he sat down again on the bed. He sighed. "Just what is it you want to talk about, Colonel?"

"Well, Joe," Colonel Richards said, choosing his words carefully, "one thing we do not want to talk about is a Soviet *fishing* buoy."

Joe remained silent.

"I'm sorry Larry got carried away there," the colonel continued, "but you'll understand why when I explain that he's got a brother in the navy, a younger brother, rotting his backside in a P.O.W. camp near Haiphong."

"I don't quite see the connection between that buoy and guys in P.O.W. camps."

"You don't?" Larry said softly.

Joe slipped back farther on the bed. "No, honest to God, I *don't.*"

"Soviet military technology, Joe," the colonel said, filling his pipe. "The Russians build SAM missles to shoot down navy pilots, and they build underwater reconnaissance buoys to shadow and, eventually, help sink American Navy submarines—Polaris submarines. Now do you see the connection?"

Joe blinked. He swallowed and licked his lips. "They told me it was for fishing, a prototype fishing buoy. George and I checked it all out. It's got a computer inside, for underwater sounds and sonar . . . for the trawler fleets . . ." He stopped speaking. They were all looking at him. "Danzinger showed me the Telex," he added weakly.

"We'll talk about Danzinger in a minute, Joe," the colonel said. "I just want you to understand that we really don't have time to waste talking about fishing buoys. That piece of hardware is a late-model ELINT surveillance buoy. It works in connection with a reconnaissance satellite we call Kingfish. It has nothing to do with fish and *everything* to do with submarines. Do you understand now why we came here tonight?"

"Son-of-a-*bitch,*" Joe whispered. "Yes . . . yeah, I do, Colonel."

"Good, Joe. Now that we understand the ground rules, we're going to discuss this business in more detail."

"Okay," Joe said. "Can I have another cigarette?"

"Just one or two more points, Joe, and we can release you from this Spanish Inquisition harness."

Colonel Richards smiled. Joe felt clean and relaxed, despite the sweaty Gaucho shirt clinging to his back and the restricting wires and chest strap of the lie detector. They had been at it for over three hours. Now it was nearly over. He felt better. It was good to get it out, all of it, the lies and deceptions, the anger and frustration. He felt more rested than he had in days. Leaning back in his chair, he stared out of the now-open bedroom window at the sunny rose bed below the terrace. He was only faintly aware of the soft purring of the polygraph as the paper scroll unwound, registering his body's various responses to the questions. Rawlings entered the bedroom with a fresh pot of coffee. It made Joe feel both pleased and ashamed to see the young black relegated to the position of errand boy for these older, more experienced professionals. Joe fished a still-glowing butt out of the ashtray and used it to light a fresh cigarette. He smiled back at the colonel.

"You can keep asking questions as long as you like, Colonel," he said. "Like I said, I've got nothing to hide."

"Fine," the colonel murmured. "Good, Joe, we appreciate your being so frank with us."

Larry accepted his coffee cup and placed it gingerly before him on the dressing table. He was doing something to one of the control knobs of the tape recorder, which sat next to the squat, pigskin carrying case of the polygraph. Throughout the long questioning period, he and Roy had remained silent. They spoke as they tuned their equipment during the initial "talk-up," as the colonel had called it, but not later, during the hours of serious, repetitious interrogation concerning the details of Joe's movements during the previous week. Rawlings had sat, seemingly sulking, at the end of the bed, contenting himself to take an occasional note in his diary.

"I'd like to get back to the meeting Danzinger arranged with the people at the Soviet Embassy, Joe." The colonel's voice was soft and neutral.

Joe nodded. He looked up from the garden, glancing again at the galvanic skin-response electrode pasted to the back of his left hand and the rubber blood-pressure bladder strapped across his right forearm.

"Okay, sure. What would you like to know?"

"Is it true, Joe, that you had had no previous dealing with this man Dimitry prior to the Russian Embassy visit? And you told him nothing of your contacts with Mr. Rawlings?"

"That's right."

"Do you think he believes your story about the Moroccan Jew?"

"I don't think he trusts me. That's why he wants to meet the Jewish guy today."

"Have you ever worked with the Russians before, Joe?"

"No, I have not. Like I told you before, this is the first time I ever had anything to do with them . . . except getting news releases out of their press attachés and regular, normal journalistic contact."

The colonel drank his coffee thoughtfully. He, too, seemed absorbed now with the early morning sunlight in the garden. He slowly filled his pipe and lit it with a intricately made and expensive-looking gas lighter. The chattering of the birds in the bougainvillaea was drowning out the faint whir of the machine.

Joe could see by the alarm clock that it was almost eight o'clock. His stomach rumbled pleasantly in anticipation of breakfast. It was all over. They'd caught up with him in time, before he could get himself into trouble with the Russians. And that was good. That was what he wanted. They could have their goddamned listening buoy. They could have it free. His life had changed now. He might lose this house to the bank, but that was okay, too. It was really Monique's house. He'd go back to work and do his damnedest to keep the booze down. This past week had been the climax of a year of self-destructive craziness. And now it was over. Maybe, maybe he could actually get an African assignment and be near Renée. It wouldn't be every weekend, but they could still see each other fairly regularly. He looked across the room at the colonel's tired, worldly face and at the solid, pragmatic technicians, running their equipment. In an odd way they had saved him. These strangers, whose names surely were not Colonel Richards and Larry and Roy, had come into his life at the last minute and saved him.

The colonel sucked reflectively on his pipe. "Oh, Roy," he said, "has that beta line settled down? You mentioned a while back that it didn't seem to be paralleling the way it should."

"Seems fine now, Colonel," Roy said. "I think it was the ink flow. I guess I didn't get enough solvent through the tubes before I packed for the flight. You know what pressurized planes do to the scribe points."

They were good people, Joe thought suddenly. They were good, uncomplicated technicians doing their job, a messy, lonely job sometimes, but they did it, and, in an ironic way, Joe was proud of them. They had seen through Dimitry's deception. Joe had been a fool to have ever underestimated them, any of them, including Rawlings. The kid had seen right away that he was out of his depth and had sent a message off to Washington asking for reinforcements. Well, there it was. It was all over and he felt good.

"Let's just let the scroll tick over for a minute or so to make sure, Roy," the colonel said. "Joe, try to relax. We're almost finished, but I'd like to let the machine settle down for a couple of minutes before we unhook you."

"Fine, Colonel. Did . . . uh . . . did everything go okay?"

"Perfectly, Joe. It's a pretty wild story, but with the way you were able to explain things, it all makes sense. It seems to jibe perfectly on the machine, too. You've got nothing to worry about. Just relax now so we can get some minimum base values on the heartbeat and the blood pressure."

Joe closed his eyes and thought about breakfast. He smiled suddenly, remembering Dimitry. *There will be nobody to meet him at his eleven o'clock rendezvous. By this time tomorrow I'll probably be in the States,* Joe thought happily, *out on one of the C.I.A.'s country retreats with a bunch of engineers, answering their questions about how the buoy behaved underwater. That would be fine. That would be just fine. They'll give me time to see Renée first, I suppose, to say good-bye for a while. And it is a free ride back. They'll feed me and buy my whisky and probably even give me per diem. This whole crazy part of my life has ended now, and I'll begin again. It's a good feeling.*

He opened his eyes. Roy was standing beside the dressing table, stretching with obvious relish. Larry was glancing through a dog-eared copy of *Time*. The colonel puffed contentedly on his pipe as he sat staring out into the garden. In a minute they'd shut down the softly purring machine and disconnect the wires and straps. Joe closed his eyes again. He was supposed to be relaxing.

"You fuck little Arab kids in the ass, don't you, Clinton?" Rawlings' voice was harsh.

"Huh . . . what?" Joe sat upright in his chair.

"You're a queer, aren't you?"

"What the hell are you talking about?" Joe looked to the colonel for support. "What's he talking about?"

"Answer the question," the colonel said coldly.

"We've got proof that you bring Arab boys up here to your house and keep them all night, Clinton. It's the truth now, isn't it?"

"No!" Joe blurted out. "You're crazy!"

"What about this?" Larry almost shouted. He held up a flimsy brassiere. "We found this in your underwear drawer. You get your kicks by wearing women's clothes, don't you?"

"Answer his question," the colonel droned.

Roy was next to the machine carefully noting the rippling lines left by the scribes across the rolling paper scroll.

They'd tricked him. He'd thought the interview had ended. But they were far from leaving him in peace.

"You're crazy!" Joe said. "You're all nuts!"

"They started blackmailing you years ago when they found out you were a homosexual, didn't they, Joe?"

Colonel Richards' icily phrased accusation was even cruder than the vulgar taunting of the others. "Answer me, Joe. You've been working for them for a long time now, haven't you? More than half the answers you gave me were lies. They're right there in black and white on that paper."

"I'm telling you the truth, Colonel. I never had any contact with the Russians before this week." He could feel his palms sweating and the tight heaving of his chest against the respiration strap. They had purposefully gotten him scared and riled up so that it would show up on the machine. They were trying to frame him, to trap him with their quasi-scientific proof.

"Clinton," Rawlings said with a look of distaste shared by the others, "we've got a file on you already, you know. We're not sure if it was in Hong Kong or Bangkok, but we are sure that you were recruited out in the Far East after they found out how deeply you were involved in the black market. I suppose that they used the queer bit to pressure you, too. You don't have to be ashamed of it. They've gotten a lot of people that way. They play dirty. Why don't you just come clean with us? When did you first start working for them?"

Joe looked back at Colonel Richards for help.

"Answer his question, Joe. Stop lying now."

"I've never worked for the Russians."

"How long have you been a homosexual, Joe?" Roy's voice was less harsh, mellowed by something close to pity.

"I'm not a queer, for Christ's sake! Where did you ever get that from?"

"Joe," the colonel said softly, "what did you do when you found out that your wife had been active in the French Communist student movement? Did you try to talk sense to her at first, or did you go in with them right away?"

"What the hell are you talking about?" Joe was genuinely angry now. "You must be nuts, all of you! Monique's practically a royalist, for Christ's sake. She used to think Eisenhower was a leftist."

Subtly, they had moved from their previous relaxed positions on the chairs and bed and were now standing in a ring around him. Only Larry remained at his post beside the polygraph.

"They paid you to plant this buoy, didn't they, Joe?" Rawlings stood above him, hands on hips like an overweight high-school tackle.

"Answer him."

"No . . . I found it exactly like I said, in a fisherman's net."

"How did you first get in with them, Joe?" the colonel said. "Was it for extra drinking money, gambling debts, or were they blackmailing you? We've had reports of an American free-lance journalist working for them for a long time now. We were pretty sure it was you, but we couldn't be certain until now. You've been lying to us all morning, Joe. Why don't you come clean?"

"Colonel, I swear to God that everything I've said is the truth."

"Where were you last Friday?"

"Friday? Ah, hell, I was at Targa. That's when I found that goddamned buoy in the net."

"George Briggs helped you plant it there, didn't he?"

"No! George never saw it until that weekend. He helped me get it out of the water and drive it back to town."

"How long have you and George had sexual relations?"

"George and I both like *women.* What the hell are you people trying to do?"

"Joe," the colonel said, sitting back down now to puff on his pipe, "we have definite proof that you worked with the Russians when you were doing that economic story in East Africa. I'm sure that it seemed innocent enough at the time and that the money they offered was too good to pass up. I'm not concerned with that now. What I want to know is this: When was the next time you worked for them?"

"I've *never* worked for them."

"Clinton, we went to see George Briggs last night and had a little talk with him. He folded right away and told us the whole story. He's trying to save his own skin." Rawlings paused, letting his words take effect. Larry was staring intently at the moving paper roll in front of him. Joe could feel the colonel's eyes burning into his head. "George admitted that the whole thing was a fraud to trick the American Government, that the buoy never was in the water out at Targa, and that you and Danzinger had it delivered to his garage in a truck when he was out of town. He says that you admitted working for a foreign government, but that you wouldn't say which one. That's the way it really happened, isn't it?"

"No! I found that buoy in an Arab fisherman's net out at Targa last Friday and I contacted Rawlings by phone four days later. Everything I've said this morning is the truth."

"And you still claim that you've never worked for the Communists?" Larry asked.

"I swear to God that I've never worked for them."

"They never tried to blackmail you?" the colonel said, his voice kindly again. "There's nothing to be ashamed of, Joe. We know guys like Danzinger; they prey on homosexuals. Have they ever made overtures to you?"

"No, never!"

Rawlings sat back down heavily on the end of the bed. Roy lit a cigarette. The colonel and Larry were staring at each other, communicating with minute facial expressions.

"Okay, Joe," the colonel said finally, "that's all. I'm sorry. You'll have to excuse this past couple of minutes. We weren't being hard on you personally, you know. It's S.O.P. for this type of interrogation."

Joe sat there blinking while Larry and Roy deftly removed the straps and wires. He was handed a freshly lit cigarette, and, standing up, he kneaded the tightened muscles of his neck.

"Here," Rawlings said. He had come back into the bedroom with a large glass filled with whisky and ice cubes. Joe sat down gratefully with the drink and took a long, cold swallow.

"You're clean, Joe," the colonel said, "at least that's what the machine tells us. It's a pretty good little machine, too. I've never seen it fail in a straightforward guessing game like we've been having here, not with a trained operator like Larry in charge. You came through a hundred percent. We had to get you on several emotional levels, though, you see. That was the reason for this last bit."

"Jesus" Joe sighed, "you had my head spinning. You almost had *me* believing some of that crap."

Larry laughed. "The colonel's done one or two of these jobs before, you know."

Joe shook his head. He felt himself smiling.

"Joe," the colonel said, "it's almost eight-thirty, and you've got an eleven o'clock appointment with our friend Dimitry. I think you'd better get cleaned up and then we'll all get some breakfast."

"You still want me to go through with the meeting?"

"That's a good question, Joe." He was carefully cleaning out his pipe over the overflowing ashtray. "I'd like to talk to you about the future. Later in the day I'm going to ask you to sign some papers. They'll be a special type of contract, highly confidential, of course, but legally binding under the United States Federal Code. Once you've signed those papers, you'll be legally obliged never to discuss or even to refer to this entire business, either verbally or in writing, for the rest of your life. Do you understand me?"

"I think so. Go on."

"This whole business touches upon the vital security interests of the United States. You've stumbled into it, but that doesn't change the fact that you are involved. You may not realize it, but every American citizen has responsibilities, just like paying taxes and serving in the armed forces. You've gotten yourself mixed up in a highly classified and sensitive area of operations. Everything that has happened so far and everything that will happen in the next few days must remain a secret. Actually, you have no choice in this matter. Even if you never sign a paper, you've now been formally warned before witnesses that you'd be breaking several American statutes dealing with classified matters if you ever make known even the smallest details of what's happened this week."

"Okay," Joe said flatly. "I can understand that, all right."

"Fine," the colonel said. The others were sitting silently watching the colonel as he spoke. "Joe, what I've just said is only one side of the coin. You can go to jail if you break this confidence. There's a positive side to this, as well. I can't tell you why, in fact, I can't tell you anything more than the minimum you need to know, but we may want you to work with us, to keep your hand in it for a little while longer. Naturally, we will be willing to pay for your services."

"What kind of work?" Joe was beginning to feel the tension mounting as it had during the interrogation.

"We may want you to string the Russians along on this business. . . . No, wait, let me finish. I know you're not a trained intelligence agent, but for what we have in mind, you won't have to be. To begin with, I want you to go ahead with that meeting with Dimitry at the post office. I want you to tell him that your Jewish friend is stuck down south in Agadir, trying to sell off property, and that he won't be free for a few more days. You'll contact him again in Rabat within forty-eight hours."

"He's not going to like that, Colonel. He's damned suspicious already."

"Well, you'll have to throw him a sop, Joe. I want you to tell him the name of your Jewish friend so that he can do some checking up on his own while he's waiting."

Joe stared at the colonel without speaking. "But the guy doesn't exist," he finally said.

"He does now," Rawlings said.

"Here," Roy said, handing Joe a manila folder from the open briefcase at the end of the dresser.

The folder contained a photostat of a Moroccan Interior Ministry file on one André-Nathan Gessous, Moroccan citizen: age, thirty-seven; profession, civil engineer; residence, Tangier; married, with three children; family emigrated to Canada, 1967. Joe glanced briefly at the rest of the file, noting the various applications for passport and exit visas, the Banque du Maroc foreign-exchange-control transactions, and the references to the Ministry of Commerce and Finance file treating Monsieur Gessous' business interests.

"Christ," Joe said, looking back at the colonel, "it's perfect! How did you people fake this?"

"We didn't, Joe," the colonel said smiling again. "Let's just say that we've had good relations with the Sephardic Jewish community over the years, especially since the June War. When we were trying to hunt down your imaginary Jewish friend, they supplied us with several leads, including Gessous. From everything you'd said, we were sure it was him until the photographs you gave Rawlings didn't fit. Then we discovered that Gessous had slipped out of the country illegally aboout ten days ago. The Moroccans don't know that he's gone yet, and neither do any of his friends or neighbors. They think that he's on vacation. There's enough there to keep the Russians busy for more than a couple of days. Later, when they discover that he's no longer in the country, it will only reinforce your original story—he got out alone on a fishing boat contracted by the Jewish Agency, and even our contact here doesn't know exactly when."

"You guys are amazing," Joe said with genuine respect.

"Christ, he's an engineer. He's got a family in Canada and he's gone underground. When I thought the guy up, I never figured that there really was anyone like that in Tangier."

"The type isn't all that uncommon, Joe," the colonel said. "You did very well when you chose your character. Morocco's full of Jewish professional men running scared and, as far as I can see, about half of them have already gotten their families out to Canada or Australia. Unfortunately, in the case of Gessous, if Dimitry checks too closely, which he probably will, he'll find out that Monsieur Gessous was never arrested and that he *has* been able to send money on a regular basis to his wife and kids in Toronto. We hope that he'll figure the guy gave you a sob story in order to get you to do his dirty work."

"Yeah, but it's still nearly perfect, Colonel. He's an *engineer*." Joe glanced down at the photostat. "Hell, he's even got business dealings in the south. He's in partnership with his brothers in a woodcutting concession and some irrigated grain land."

"It was an accident," the colonel answered, dismissing Joe's enthusiasm, "but a pretty damned lucky coincidence, which we can use to our own advantage. So, when you see Dimitry this morning, play hard to get, but eventually give him Gessous' name and the Tangier address. Make him promise not to check up on him for fear of scaring him off. That's all you have to do this morning. Do you think you can handle it?"

Joe sat back in his chair. He was tired and more than a little scared, but he was also excited. For the first time in more than a year, he felt that he was connected again, that he was part of some bigger, logical pattern and not a lone drifter pissing his life away on booze and the struggle to finish an unwritable book.

"Yeah," he said, "I think that I can handle that, all right."

Joe went to the open bathroom window to dry his hair in the sunlight. He felt fresh and rested after the shower and shave. Whoever was making breakfast must have found that can of Renée's PX Maxwell House, because he could smell the scent of percolating coffee.

Joe was suddenly chilly in the warm sunlight. They were in *his* kitchen, pawing through his cupboards like soldiers occupying the house of a defeated enemy, like *cops* making themselves at home in the apartment of a paid informer. He felt grubby again.

His jaw was still sore and the muscles at the side of his neck ached from the force of Larry's cuffing blow.

"Goddamn it," he said softly. This wasn't the Thursday night movie. It was his *life.* They had no right to *use* him.

This is ridiculous. I'm not some desperate foreign stooge they can strong-arm into cooperation. The hell with this crap. They can get themselves a truck and collect that damned buoy from George's garage. They can have it free.

Joe threw the towel at the laundry hamper and reached for his robe. Leaning past the window, he could see along the side of the house and over the garden wall. A young Moroccan with a close-cropped military haircut leaned against the stucco garage across the lane. Above him, blocking any access to the new mountain road, a black Simca was parked. There were two more young Moroccans in the front seat. Both had moustaches and short haircuts. Both wore dark civilian jackets. And they both had that watchful, but bored, expression common to waiting policemen the world over. They were smooth-faced, southern boys, perhaps from one of the big Glaoui clans, the kind of kids Oufkir favored for sensitive posts in the Sûreté. There was only one noticeable difference between them. The boy in the passenger's seat had gold teeth. They flashed as he spoke into the mouthpiece of the car's radio telephone.

Joe closed the window. He could smell bacon frying now. It was time to dress. It wouldn't do to keep Dimitry waiting.

18

Monsieur Gessous

There was the usual morning crowd at the main Tangier post office. The elderly Arab pensioners were lined up to cash their small *mandats-postaux*. Moroccan ladies, elegant in gabardine jellabas, chattered together through their veils as they waited in front of the wooden telephone counter. An occasional tourist wandered in to buy stamps for a postcard, only to stand bewildered, gazing up at the confusing array of signs in Arabic, Spanish, and French that marked the various *guichets* dividing the marble bulk of the main counter.

It was three minutes to eleven. Joe sat at the far right-hand corner of the main hall, his back to the package counter, as he made a show of slowly filling in the cardboard registry form for an insured package. At exactly eleven o'clock Dimitry entered the post office. He was wearing Bermuda shorts with light blue knee socks and carried a camera and lens cases slung across his chest like bandoliers. In his right hand he held a fan arrangement of colored postcards. Joe joined him in the line in front of the *guichet* where a harassed postal clerk was explaining to a red-faced Swedish matron that the forty-*franc* stamp was for surface mail and that a full *dirham* was needed to send a card to Stockholm by airmail.

"I'm alone," Joe said softly to Dimitry's back.

Dimitry nodded, but he did not leave his place in line. When he had mailed his cards to Denver and St. Louis, he turned past Joe and smiled. "Hi, I didn't see you there. Feel like something cold to drink? There's a nice little café across the street."

They crossed the avenue without speaking and sat down at a table at the far end of the café's shady interior. Dimitry ordered an iced *café frappé* and Joe had a *pastis*. Out on the sunny sidewalk, Joe saw the old gray Tartar, incongruous in pastel sport clothes and with a tourist-type camera, take a seat beneath the canvas awning and sit stiffly, half turned, to watch the open glass doors to the interior.

The waiter brought their drinks and then disappeared back into the kitchen. The bartender, a young red-haired Berber, was absorbed in a Spanish soccer magazine.

"What the *hell* is the story this time?" Dimitry asked wearily.

"He got stuck down south," Joe said, speaking slowly. "He's trying to sell off some timber land and farms he owns with his brothers. He's having a hard time. But he promised to be back within two days. He . . ."

"Two days," Dimitry interrupted. "That's what he said two days ago. Do you think I have nothing better to do than chase after some kike who won't keep appointments?"

"I'm sorry," Joe said. "He sent me a message this morning. He'll be ready within forty-eight hours. He promised."

"I know all about promises, my friend. Governments don't run on promises."

"Look, Dimitry, he'll meet you right at the embassy in Rabat, if that's what you want. He got hung up down there . . . delayed. You can't expect him to just dump the family business before he goes. They've got all their money invested down there."

"Yes," Dimitry said sarcastically. "I'm sure that it's all hard-earned, honest money that they've toiled for with the sweat of their brows. These cry-baby Jews turn my stomach, Clinton. As far as I'm concerned, you've gone back on our agreement. I'm going to have to make other arrangements."

"That buoy can't be very important if you can't wait a couple of days." Joe felt amazingly confident, free of the jumpiness he had experienced during his first meeting with Dimitry. It was good to know that he was no longer alone, that he had strong, professional backing in this game.

"I'll tell you exactly what I think, Clinton. I think that you're a psychopathic liar, that you've probably invented the whole story just to satisfy some twisted inner compulsion."

This time it was Joe who interrupted. "Look, Danzinger was the guy who told me to come see you. I did what he said. I'm trying to be helpful. Hell, did I go out and make that bronze plaque, Dimitry?"

"All right," Dimitry said angrily. "You've got an ace in the hole. I'm just warning you that I smell something that stinks worse than shit. To begin with, I don't believe this 'suffering Jew' story."

"He'll be at your office within two days."

"Will he, now? Then I suppose it doesn't matter if you tell me what his name is, does it?"

"He made me promise not to."

The waiter came back out of the kitchen with a napkin-covered tray of sandwiches and passed close to their table on his way to the sidewalk terrace. Dimitry paused until the man was out of earshot.

"Unless I know his name today, the entire deal is off and I go to work to make things difficult for *you,* Clinton—difficult with the local authorities. This is still a country where money talks. We've got a few friends in the Sûreté. They're stupid, greedy assholes, like most Arabs, but they're tough. I might just give one of them a ring. . . . If I have to spend money to make things hot for you, I'll do it with pleasure."

"He made me promise . . ."

"I really mean what I just said, you know. I'm fed up with this whole ridiculous business."

Joe stalled for effect before he answered. "If I tell you his name, I want you to promise you won't start to make public inquiries about him. He's terrified that somehow the word will get back to the Moroccan police. He's scared to death of them."

"All I want his name for is to check it against our own files to make sure he's not some known reactionary operative. We have to protect ourselves constantly against that kind of people. That's not such an unreasonable request, is it, now?" In fact, Dimitry had transformed himself in a twinkling from an angry bully to a patient, reasonable embassy official.

"Yeah, I guess you're right. Okay. His name is Gessous, André-Nathan Gessous. He's got a combination office-and-apartment on the rue Moussa Ben Noussair, at number thirty-four, on the second floor. Do you want to write it down?"

Dimitry didn't answer. He only smiled, shaking his head. From the pocket of his shorts he produced a money clip and deposited a ten-*dirham* note on the metal table. "Telephone the embassy receptionist the day before he's coming in to see me. Say you've borrowed some films from the cultural center and that they're overdue, and then give the time you'll be delivering them the next day."

"Can you remember his name all right?"

"André-Nathan Gessous, thirty-four, rue Moussa Ben Noussair, second floor," Dimitry recited. "He'd better be there within two days, Clinton."

He was gone then, back out into the bright sun on the avenue.

Joe watched him turn left and stride purposefully away. A moment later the pastel-clad Tartar was up and gone in the opposite direction, walking with the same martial gait.

19

The Mark V

It was hot with all of them crowded into George's basement garage. The two mechanic's lamps on their extension cords cast garish shadows as the six men stood around the metal tube, like so many surgeons poised above a patient.

"I made some notes when I took the panels off," George said. He spoke eagerly, a graduate student demonstrating a research project to a group of professors. "Not notes, exactly, more like diagrams. I wanted to make sure I didn't mix up any of the securing bolts and screws. I've got them all numbered and taped to pieces of cardboard so they'll all go back in the right holes."

"Fine," the colonel said. He yawned and rocked slightly on his heels.

He's dead tired, Joe suddenly realized. All four of them had probably been awake for over twenty-four hours now. It wasn't so bad for the younger ones, but Colonel Richards wasn't any kid. Larry leaned over an open inspection panel and played a powerful flashlight down into the labyrinth of circuits deep inside. "It's definitely a modification of the Four," he said to the colonel. "Outside diameter's about the same, but they've managed to get almost twice as much inside."

"I think we should sit down with that Taiwan file and have a real good look before we shoot off a SITREP," Roy said.

"We'll talk about that later, boys," the colonel said sternly. The technicians' enthusiasm for a new machine disappeared instantly from Roy's and Larry's faces. They straightened up, stock still, but were relaxed, like police guards in a courtroom. Rawlings was leaning against the workbench, studying the Polaroid picture of the bronze plaque.

"This'll probably make more sense to you, Colonel," he said. handing the photo across to the older man. The colonel slipped it into one of the deep pockets of his cardigan.

"All right," he said, "it's almost nine-thirty, and we all need some rest. As I mentioned, George, we're going to have to impose on your hospitality for a day or so. If you could please show Roy where you keep that camp bed, he'll take the first watch down here tonight." He ran his finger around the sweaty collar of his sportshirt. "You mentioned something about a fan, too, I believe."

The bright lights were extinguished and they climbed, one by one, back up the ladder into the pantry between George's kitchen and dining room. The colonel closed the trapdoor and snapped the padlock shut. Then he handed the key to Roy.

"I think, perhaps, a drink and then some dinner might be in order," the colonel said. "I've got a bottle in my overnight bag."

"Oh, I've got loads of booze," George said cheerfully. "Can you show them where the bar is, Joe? I'll get the cot and the fan for Roy. Then I'll see about something to eat. How does steak and French fries sound? That's one thing I know I can cook okay."

"I'll give you a hand," Larry said.

Rawlings walked ahead of them into the living room and pulled the drapes before turning on the table lamps. Joe poured out three generous glasses of Scotch and they settled gratefully into the comfortable Spanish leather armchairs. Very slowly the colonel filled and lit his pipe. After doing so, he looked up at Rawlings and then at Joe. "Perhaps you could make a drink for the boys in the kitchen, Bill," he said to Rawlings. "And they might want a hand getting the food together. See if he's got any decent lettuce in the icebox. I could do with a salad tonight."

When Rawlings had left with the tray of drinks, the colonel got to his feet and walked to George's gleaming stereo set, at the far end of the room. He selected a tape cartridge of the Boston Pops and carefully adjusted the volume. "Well," he said, back in his chair with his pipe and drink, "this has been quite a day, hasn't it? I'm sorry that we had to take off before you got back, but I had a lot of things to discuss with the people in the States, and I obviously couldn't sit down and call them from your phone. You're quite sure you weren't followed back up to your house?"

"Positive. I did exactly as you said. I had lunch at the Parade Bar and then made believe my car wouldn't start. I walked down to the beach and had a drink and a swim and then took a taxi up as far as the governor's mansion and walked back down the side road to my house. It was siesta time and the taxi was the only car on the road. There wasn't a soul on the side road when I came down."

"George seems to be taking our presence here very naturally," the colonel said, glancing appreciatively around the well-appointed living room. "I must say, I've waited out business deals in a lot less pleasant surroundings."

"I think he's kind of enjoying the whole thing, Colonel. He didn't have the vaguest idea about my contacts with Dimitry, and he was expecting you people to show up all along. He . . . well . . . he's a bit of a romantic, you see. Helping out on something like this is the most exciting thing he's ever done."

"And you feel he can be trusted?"

"Completely. He's a good guy and damned honest. He's obviously not in it for the money, you know."

"Fine, Joe. I'm sure you're right. Now, let's just go over your meeting with Dimitry once again. Take your time. I don't want you to leave anything out, anything at all that might be of use to us."

Once more Joe told the colonel the details of the morning's encounter with Dimitry. He carefully described the clothes both Dimitry and the Tartar wore, what Dimitry drank in the café, and, as best he could remember, the exact words Dimitry had used.

"You did well, Joe." The colonel was smiling now. "You did very well. We had a local watching, as well, but it's always good to get two reports. I can see that you're going to be a definite asset to us."

"Thanks." Joe felt sincerely pleased by the older man's praise. "I only did what you told me to do, and it was actually quite simple."

Rawlings reappeared at the door of the living room. "Dinner will be ready in about ten minutes, Colonel," he said.

"You all go ahead and eat, Bill," the colonel said. "Joe and I are going to have another drink and discuss a few things. We'll be along later."

They finished their drinks in silence and Joe went to the bar to refill them.

"Joe," the colonel said, standing up to take the fresh Scotch, "I spent quite a while talking about you with the people back at the home office." He saw the stricken look that came over Joe's face and quickly added, "Don't worry. We've got a very secure voice channel from the base at Kénitra. That's why we were gone so long. Thank God the navy had a regular courier flight coming back up this evening so at least we didn't have to drive both ways in one day."

Joe remained silent, waiting for the colonel to continue.

"You have to realize that you've gotten yourself into a pretty rough business."

Joe nodded. "Yeah, I know. Like I said this morning, I was having a rough time. Everything seemed to be coming apart, and it all boiled down to money. When I found that buoy, it was like manna from heaven. I didn't *want* to get involved with the Russians, you know. But Danzinger made it all sound so simple. I just wanted enough to pay off my debts and give myself a little security for the future."

The colonel sipped his drink. He was staring at Joe with that expression that reminded Joe so much of an elderly scholar listening to the problems of a promising but troubled student.

"Well, that's so much past history. I want to talk about the future. I hope that I'll be able to explain our thoughts clearly. Please feel free to ask any question that comes to mind, all right?"

Joe nodded.

"Joe," the colonel continued, "we need you to work with us on this operation. It's not going to be terribly difficult, but it will require a certain amount of timing and some steady nerves on your part. Hopefully, it'll all be over in three or four days at the outside."

"I'm afraid you've lost me, Colonel. Aren't you just going to pack that thing up and send it back to the States?"

The colonel smiled, his teeth gripping the stem of his pipe. He slowly shook his head. "No. That was what was decided today. Let me just tell you that we already have in our possession a few of these Soviet listening buoys . . . the Mark IV that Larry referred to down in the garage. Some are damaged, and none of them, however, are as advanced or as complicated as that gadget downstairs. It's undoubtedly their newest model, and, what with advances in miniaturization, it probably has triple performance capabilities over the earlier models. The point is, though, that we already know a lot about their basic technology in this field, and, because we do, our military people have come up with ways to circumvent their surveillance systems . . . to render their Mark IV networks harmless on a worldwide basis. Now"—he held up his pipe like a digressing lecturer—"you must realize that technology is a constantly changing process. The Soviets probably know that we've figured out methods of jamming the earlier models. That's why they've gone to the expense and trouble of bringing out this new buoy. . . . Let's call it the Mark V. If they discover that we've figured out a way to render the new Mark V useless, then they'll just plunge ahead and build Mark VI. They're probably hard at work on a new prototype, in any event. But they've just begun to deploy this new model and they're just beginning to set up their networks all over the world. Once they get the system in place, they naturally will want to get their mileage out of it before they have to scrap it and start all over with a new one. Do you follow me?"

Joe let the icy-warm whisky slide down his throat before answering. "Yeah," he said. "Everything you've said so far makes good sense. Please go on."

"So," the colonel said, "it's in the best interests of our country that the Soviets get that buoy back safe and sound and in one piece, and—this is the most important point—that they don't know, that they don't even suspect, that it's been compromised. If they have the smallest suspicion that the top-secret workings of the buoy have been discovered, then they'll scrap the whole system and we're right back on square one. If, on the other hand, they feel that they've got it back intact and they decide to go ahead with the general deployment, and, furthermore, we've figured out enough of the mechanics of this new model, then our Polaris fleet has gained an almost invaluable strategic advantage. Do you begin to see the importance of this operation?"

Again Joe drank a swallow of whisky before answering. As the colonel spoke, Joe's throat had become increasingly dry and an old, familiar tightness had begun to grow in his guts. "Yes . . . yeah," he said hesitantly, "I follow you so far."

"Good. So. Let's try to look at it from Dimitry's point of view." The colonel paused momentarily, rocking back in his chair, staring reflectively up at the ceiling through a cloud of aromatic pipe smoke. "Dimitry would have been alerted recently that the buoy was missing. We know that their people in Spain were alerted, because they've been unusually active along the coast, spending a lot of money and recklessly exposing their local contacts. Now, Dimitry got the same alert, but he's been cooler about the way he reacted. Actually, he didn't have much choice. You may as well know that the K.G.B. has a very small operation in this country. They've been squeezed pretty hard by General Oufkir's security people over the past couple of years and, in fact, they're badly understaffed. In other words, for the moment, at least, he doesn't have the resources to check out your story, and the Jewish community here will not cooperate with any inquiries from the Russians. So he'll have to accept your story. In about three days we'll be finished with the buoy and be ready for you to follow through with the original plan."

"What original plan?" Joe heard the thin edge of irritation in his own voice and tried to check it. "I'm sorry, I mean, whose original plan, yours or mine?"

"Yours, Joe." The colonel smiled warmly now. He shook his head. "By tomorrow afternoon we'll have a team of engineers here from the States. They'll take that buoy apart and thoroughly check out all the new components. Hopefully, within forty-eight hours they'll have the buoy put back together and ready for you to deliver to Dimitry. You'll arrange the pickup, at your house, if you like, or perhaps in your car, parked someplace out in the countryside. We'll work on the details tomorrow. That'll just about do it. You'll get your money in the Swiss bank, and Dimitry will get the listening buoy back, seemingly safe and sound. It may sound like a complicated operation to you, but, believe me, it's relatively simple as these things go."

Now Joe shook his head. He knocked back the rest of the whisky in his glass and took a long filter-tipped cigarette from the ivory box on the end table beside him. "If that's a simple plan, Colonel," he said, "I'd hate to hear a really complicated one."

This time the colonel rose and did the honors at the bar. He handed Joe the fresh drink. "This'll be the last one," he said. "Then we'll have some dinner and call it a night. . . . Well, that's the plan that has been approved at the agency, and that's the plan we're going to follow. Actually, we don't have that much to lose if it doesn't work. If the Soviet naval intelligence figures that their new buoy has been compromised, then they'll have to go to all the trouble of modifying their system and start all over in deploying the modification. We gain time either way. That's what this game is all about, Joe, time—time for the politicians on both sides to come to their senses and figure out some way to control and eventually reduce the number of these damned insane weapons."

"I agree with you there, Colonel," Joe said softly. "It's absolutely crazy to think of all those warheads in all those silos and subs just waiting for somebody to push the button. When I found that buoy, I honestly didn't have any idea that it was this important to the whole nuclear-balance madness. I wish now that I'd never seen the thing. I wish you could just take it back to the States and I could go my own way and forget about the whole business. Hell, I don't even want the money anymore. . . . You're pretty sure that it'll be all over in two or three days?"

Colonel Richards sat back down. "*This* operation will be over in three days, Joe." He paused. "You were frank with me this morning, and now I'll be as frank as I can with you. As I've said right along, you've gotten yourself involved in this business, and your involvement is not going to end when Dimitry accepts the buoy back. There will be a 'controlled de-briefing' and a 'controlled critique' of the entire operation. I'm afraid that's intelligence jargon for a few more hours with the polygraph. It'll probably be done back in the States." Colonel Richards held up his hand. "Wait, Joe, let me finish. Once the critique and the de-briefing have been completed, you'll still be important to the success of this operation. You see, you'll be the only non-professional who will know what happened." The colonel nodded his chin in the direction of the kitchen. "George will only know that we, the Americans, have taken possession of the buoy. You're the one weak point. In theory, at least, there'll be nothing to stop you from going back to the Russians and, for a fee, spilling the beans on the entire business."

"Jesus Christ!" Joe burst out angrily. "You know damned well I wouldn't pull anything like that! All I want is to be left alone."

"Well, Joe, I'm truly sorry to have to tell you that we can't just 'leave you alone.' For the next three or four years . . . for however long the operational life of this new buoy proves to be . . . we have to have some definite *control* over your actions." Colonel Richards relit his pipe and continued on in a coldly precise voice. "I want you to be well aware of this, Joe. Believe me, this is a hard business. There's nothing romantic about it, as George would like to believe. Now, there are several ways we could have control over your actions. We could terminate your services by putting you in jail for five years."

Joe stared through the wisps of blue-gray smoke at the colonel's somber face. He felt the scowl deepening around his lips and chin. The anger burst out like hot pus from a boil. "Oh, bullshit, Colonel!"

Colonel Richards glared at him. Joe sagged inside and looked down at the carpet beneath his sandals. "Listen," he said in a softer tone, "I'm sorry, but you said a minute ago that we were going to be frank with each other. I, well, Christ, Colonel, I'm not some kid grad student on his first trip to the Soviet Union who you can bully with vague threats about 'five years in jail.' I signed your papers this morning, okay. But I'm still a member of the Overseas Press Club. You know that and I know it. Washington's full of young lawyers who'd like nothing better than to latch onto a case like this and blast it all the way up to the Supreme Court. If we're going to talk, then let's talk like the adults."

"I understand your argument perfectly," the colonel said evenly. "But you are forgetting one important item. *American* jurisprudence may not be so easy to manipulate, but we are not in America. This is Morocco. Foreigners, not just teen-aged hippies, but adults, French, English, and American, get arrested here every week on drug-smuggling charges. Normally their respective consulates and embassies do their best to get them light sentences. If that warrant for your arrest, which was duly signed by a respected Moroccan magistrate, were to be acted upon . . . well, I can only say that you'd be lucky to get off with five years. Take it as a threat, if you will. We call it something else—a kind of necessary control where no other form exists. But, believe me, Joe"—the colonel put down his pipe— "if forced to, we'll use that warrant, and you'll get five long years in a Moroccan prison. So, do we understand each other?"

Joe looked up at the colonel's tired face. "Yes," he said. "Please go on with what you were saying."

"Naturally," the colonel said, sitting down, "we all hope that such a termination with prejudice, as it's called, won't prove necessary. By far the best solution will be for you to continue to cooperate with us for the next few years. Believe me, we can use a person like you. No, don't worry, we're not going to try to make a full-time bureaucrat out of you. But we'll want to know that you're available and also that you can reconfirm the initial polygraph debriefing on a periodic basis."

"In other words, you'll sit me down with the lie detector every couple of months to make sure I haven't spilled the beans."

"If you want to put it that way, yes. There's a positive

side to all this, as well, Joe. You seem to have forgotten that the other side plays the game a little rougher than we do. Do you seriously think that the Soviet Government would be content to have you walking around scot-free with the knowledge you have of that listening buoy?"

Joe did not answer. It had never occurred to him that Dimitry would consider him a threat once the buoy had been delivered.

"What we can offer you is protection . . . and freedom. You'll be free to live the way you want. We can arrange a new passport and all the other documents necessary for you to start up a new life anywhere in the world. With your experience as a journalist, we'll probably want you to do some routine assignments for us once or twice a year. And we'll pay you well for your services. Don't worry, the work won't be anywhere near as involved as this operation. The chances are we'll want to put you on the payroll as a part-time employee. We may eventually ask you to run what's called a 'safe house.' You know what that is, I suppose."

Joe nodded.

"So, that's about the size of it, Joe. I wanted you to know the scope of your involvement from the beginning. You're in a difficult position, but you're not in it alone. The money the Russians pay for that buoy will naturally be yours to keep. With that and the controlled protection we can offer in return for your services, you'll be able to start a new life. You'll be a part of a team of professionals, Joe, not hiding, alone and afraid every time the doorbell rings. Think about all this. This morning you told me that you wanted to write, that you wanted to get out of this phony life here in Tangier and buy a boat and just sail and write." The colonel smiled, his gray hair and rugged, intelligent face handsome and confident. "I can't think of a better 'safe house' in the eastern Mediterranean than a sailboat skippered by a competent, experienced man we can really trust."

Joe closed his eyes and suddenly saw the deadly neon glow of the tanker's running lights as the ship bore down to crush the *Dragonfly*. He snapped his head back up and forced himself to smile at the colonel. "I'll have to think about all this, Colonel. I've got a lot of thinking to do."

The colonel stood up again. "Once you've done your thinking, I'm sure you'll see that I've been talking sense, good old-fashioned common sense."

Joe zipped up the side pocket of the Valpac and hefted the bulging suitcase from the bed to the floor. It sat next to the battered two-suiter his father had given him the summer after graduation, when he had landed his first job on the state desk with A.P. in Springfield. He had bought the Valpac that next year when he had gone overseas as a trainee. These two old bags had gone with him to some strange corners of the planet. And now, repacked with clothes, a few books, and several pounds of manuscript, they were about to accompany him once more in an airplane across an ocean on a new assignment.

The colonel had told him to pack up and be ready to go on short notice. He had done as he was told, emptying the Valpac to rearrange the things he had hastily jammed inside two days before, carefully folding his shirts and sportcoats, underwear and neckties. He was going to America, to the offices inside that big white building set back among the trees in Langley, Virginia. There men wore coats and ties and shoes that laced. For a while, at least, he was leaving behind sandals and sun-faded khaki shorts with holes in their pockets. He was going to live in air-conditioned rooms and eat frozen chicken and drink martinis with little machine-made ice cubes. There would be thick newspapers to read and color television to watch and huge cars to drive. And there would be the "controlled de-briefing," the hours in the chair with the wires and straps and the soft whirring of the machine while the questions were patiently repeated. And then . . . and then?

Joe sat down on the edge of the bed. *Yeah, there'd be some training; there's bound to be some kind of a training course they'll put me through before they give me my new name and send me out.* He shook his head. *It's crazy, a real crazy business, the kind of thing that happens to other people, not to me. Three years? Four years, the colonel said. Maybe longer. "Controlled protection." Sort of like being on parole.*

But they'll pay me. They definitely will pay me money and protect me. And in return I'll do what they tell me to when they tell me and not ask questions. There'll be a sailboat and time to write. And, naturally, I'll submit what I write for their approval and I'll sail the boat where they tell me. And if I do all this I'll be safe, and if I don't obey them, they'll lock me up in some Moroccan or Greek jail where the prisoners don't have lawyers. . . .

"Jesus Christ," he said aloud suddenly. "It's crazy, it's just plain crazy."

A week ago he had been broke and strung out, watching his whole world fall apart, but he had been free. Now he belonged to a "team of professionals." Now there would be no more lying awake at night wondering about the future. All he had to do was follow orders and the agency would take care of all the rest. They would supervise his life. He would be free to travel if he told them where and when. He would be free to make friends if he told them in advance who these friends were. If he were sick, they would find a doctor. They'd lend him money. They'd forward his mail. They'd pay his rent.

And when the three or four years were over? Would they let him go? Would they thank him for his loyal service and send him on his way? Or could they convince him that the best course would be to stay on with the agency? Was he in this thing for the rest of his life?

Joe walked slowly to the open French doors. He knew the answer to the last question. No matter where they sent him or where he eventually lived, he knew his bags were packed and he was about to embark on a one-way trip.

Outside in the garden the last of the afternoon sun struck the tops of the cypress trees. Beyond the fieldstone wall of the English villa, the engineers were unpacking their toolboxes in George's garage. By tonight he would be told how long their job would take to complete and when he should be prepared to make his next contact with Dimitry. In three days, four at the most, he would be on an airplane and the one-way journey would have begun.

He heard the toilet flush and the water running in the bathroom. That was Roy. In a moment he would probably pop by the bedroom just to see if he could help Joe with any of the packing and Joe would say "No, thanks. How about a sundowner?" Roy would agree and they'd sit in the living room with their drinks until it was dark enough for Larry to come down the path from George's house to relieve Roy. And after dinner Joe would go to bed, and while he slept the watch would change so that Rawlings would be there until just before dawn, when Roy would return. Joe didn't know if he would ever be able to accustom himself to this feeling of "control."

He looked up. Roy stood in the bedroom doorway, smiling like they'd been buddies for years. "All packed up?" he asked. "It's a hell of a job. I get my wife to do it for me whenever I'm traveling in the states."

"Yeah," Joe said, "all packed up. Were you out in the living room all this time? I didn't hear you."

"Got to reading that pile of old *National Geographics*. I was going to come in and give you a hand, but I got kind of, you know, absorbed."

No, you didn't. You were watching the driveway and garden. It would take more than a magazine to distract you, even during a long, twelve-hour watch. You're ex-F.B.I. You don't get bored.

"Would you like a sundowner?"

"Not a bad idea," Roy said. "I'll get them. You going to stick to your Scotch, or would you like some of Larry's Old Grand-Dad?"

"Scotch with a lot of water, please."

It was crazy. He had roommates again. And he would have roommates for the rest of his life.

20

The Assignment

George's house had been transformed, in less than one day, into a secret electronics laboratory expertly camouflaged behind a metal-pipe and wood scaffolding. By seven-thirty Tuesday morning, a gang of overalled Moroccan workers and two *pied noir* foremen from a Kénitra construction firm had set to work, chipping and repairing the small cracks and defects in the house's stucco walls. By mid-afternoon they were ready to begin spraying liquid stucco and paint. Their air compressor and spray guns were in place, and it was only natural that they hung heavy, paint-spattered tarpaulins to protect the windows and shuttered French doors. On the terrace side of the house, which faced the long, forested slope of the mountain and was exposed to possible telescopic observation, similar tarpaulins had been rigged to protect the woodwork of the windows and doors from the flying sparks made by the two Spanish welders who were installing the new system of galvanized drainpipes. A three-sided tent of tarpaulins had been rigged beneath the bamboo carport to protect the compressor and toolboxes and to offer the workers a shady rest area for their mid-morning tea break and their lunch break. Toward sunset on the first day of work, a closed Peugeot pickup truck from the same Kénitra firm was backed into this enclosure and parked for the night. Sometime after dark the garage door was opened and four American engineers emerged with toolboxes and quickly disappeared inside the garage.

Since construction sites in Morocco were notorious targets for thieves who could make a good profit re-selling stolen tools and equipment, no one questioned the presence of the two turbaned and jellabaed night watchmen who squatted near their fires on either side of the house. They were tough High Atlas Berbers who had the hardened look of French Army veterans. They called back and forth to each other in their mountain dialect and made periodic inspections of their territory, walking together, arm in arm, and swinging polished wooden clubs in their free hands.

At nine that night Joe was summoned by the colonel. He climbed up the path that connected his garden with the back wall of George's villa. On Larry's suggestion he had changed from white tennis shorts to a navy-blue turtleneck and dark trousers. George met him at the open wooden gate at the bottom of the garden. He, too, was dressed in dark shirt and trousers. He seemed happy and excited, and Joe could smell that he had been drinking.

"It's incredible," George said in a quick whisper. "There are four new guys from the States. They're down there right now, in the garage, taking the buoy apart. The colonel didn't say for sure, but I think they plan to get it into pieces and take it out that way when the painters pack up their gear." He shook his head in silent admiration. "These guys are really organized. Look at the house. They've got the whole place draped with canvas so you can't see a thing from the outside."

The waning moon had just risen. In its soft light Joe could see the expression of boyish enthusiasm on George's face. "That thing's not a *fishing* buoy, you know, George."

George grinned. He seemed happy, proud to be part of the operation. "The colonel gave me a briefing," he said, "a full briefing on the buoy. I understand how important it is."

"Did he tell you they were going to take it back to the States, too?" Joe tried to keep his voice neutral.

"No. . . ." George became a bit uncertain now. "We just talked about the technical side of it, about the buoy and the tools I used to open it, you know."

"Yeah," Joe sighed, "I know."

"The colonel's up on the terrace. It's kind of stuffy inside. But he said we can open the tarps after they've stopped work for the night and the lights are out. It's . . . well, it's exciting, don't you think?"

"Yes, it is. It's impressive the way these people come in and take over. They're certainly organized."

A dark, menacing form materialized from behind a hedge of overgrown hibiscus. *"Ah, bonsoir, M'sieu,"* the Berber whispered. Both George and Joe stopped and stared in wonder as the man silently disappeared back into the shadows, his dark goat-hair jellaba blending with the night.

"There are two of those guys," George said, "one in front and one out here in the garden."

"Yeah," Joe answered, "they certainly are organized."

They sat quietly for a moment with their coffee cups and watched the moon climb up over the trees. Joe would have preferred a drink, but the colonel already had the coffee poured when Joe joined him on the terrace. George had mumbled a slightly embarrassed "good night" and retreated into the house when Colonel Richards had made it clear he wanted to speak with Joe alone.

"I think we'll shoot for Friday, in the afternoon," the colonel said, breaking the silence. "That gives us two full days here to disassemble and test the components and put the whole thing back together again for your delivery."

"Okay," Joe said sharply. "Just tell me what I'm supposed to do."

And orange flame billowed for a moment as the colonel went through the ritual of relighting his pipe. In the lighter's flare, Joe could see the colonel inspecting him with slightly raised eyebrows. "That's exactly why I asked you up here, Joe," Colonel Richards said. "I want to go over the next couple of days very carefully. Do you feel up to discussing a detailed plan tonight?"

"Sure. Of course. Why not?"

There was a scraping sound as the colonel shifted his chair on the stone terrace so that he faced Joe more squarely. "I'll tell you why I asked," he said. "Roy reported that you'd been hitting the bottle a bit today, and I have better things to do than go through a detailed operational plan that I'll only have to repeat in the morning."

"Roy *reported*, did he?" Joe said too quickly. The

blood was hot in his ears. "Well, the hell with Roy's report!" He was suddenly on his feet. *"I'm* telling you that I'm ready to listen to your plan. How about trusting *my* word for once?"

"Sit down. Sit down in your chair and keep your voice down, too."

Joe stood for a moment, staring defiantly at the glowing bowl of the pipe.

"Just do what the colonel says, Joe," Roy said softly from the shadows at the far end of the terrace. "It's a lot cooler out here, but if you want, we can always go back inside."

Joe sighed. "Okay," he said. He sat down in his chair. "I'm sorry. I'm a little jumpy tonight."

"You'll recall," the colonel said, "that the success of this operation depends on your ability to follow orders and to muster up something approximating steady nerves. You seem to be lacking in both those departments tonight."

"You're right. I'm sorry. Please go on with what you were going to say."

The colonel's pipe was puffing like a tiny volcano, sending up sparks and rolling clouds of smoke. "You're a long way from being a professional, Joe. It's just possible, though, that if you can function well in the next few days, you'll see that you've got what it takes to face up to some of the harder things in life."

"Okay," Joe said softly. "I'm sorry I blew up. I agree with you that I've gone to hell this last year, but I want to change."

"Well, that's good," the colonel huffed, "because, believe me, buddy, you're working for us now, and we don't have any room for sorry drunks." The colonel cleared his throat. His pipe was burned out and he placed it gently on the split-bamboo table beside his chair. "Now, the plan is simple. Tomorrow afternoon you drive down to Rabat. The next morning you go directly to the Soviet Embassy and tell Dimitry that Gessous has already left the country, that he got out on a fishing boat to Spain, leaving you in charge of the delivery of the buoy. You'll arrange a rendezvous with Dimitry for the next day back in Tangier, at the main post office. Once you've telephoned to confirm the deposit of the money in the Swiss bank, you'll drive with Dimitry out the airport road to some abandoned shed buildings on an old French poultry farm. Dimitry picks up the buoy there and you return directly to your house. You'll be perfectly safe. We'll be watching the house. At nine that night you drive downtown to the Cinema Goya and buy a loge ticket. Once inside the theater you'll be picked up by us and we'll be on our way. Pack an overnight bag for tomorrow. We'll get your suitcases from the house after you leave for Rabat."

Joe nodded.

"Do you have any questions?"

Joe thought for a moment before speaking. "Yes. The buoy's about nine feet long. What's Dimitry going to use to transport it?"

"That's a good question, Joe. Tell him he'll need a closed pickup truck. I'll have a typed operational plan, which Roy'll give you to read in the morning. But let's have some more questions. Even the best plans can be improved upon when they're examined from a fresh point of view."

"Okay. What if he pressures me to find out the location of the delivery spot before we confirm the deposit?"

"Excellent! We've already thought of that, but that's another good question. You'll explain to him that all you know is that the buoy is hidden in some farm buildings out in the province, that there'll be a telegram for you, giving the exact location, which will arrive at the main post office the morning of your meeting with Dimitry. That way, you're both covered. He'll have you as, well, physical security until the buoy's in his hands. Incidentally, we've arranged for a Moroccan *gendarme* roadblock about a hundred meters from the shed buildings; nothing spectacular, just a couple of motorcycle cops on a regular driving license check. But it'll be enough to deter Dimitry from attempting any physical violence against you once the buoy's in his possession. Any other points?"

Joe pursed his lips, thinking. He found, to his surprise, that he was genuinely interested in the complex details of the plan. "If they follow me to the Cinema Goya and don't see me come out, won't they figure that I've given them the slip?" he asked.

"They sure will. They'll be damned put out about it,

too. That's their problem, though. They'll naturally assume that you didn't trust them to leave you alone and that you've gone underground. They'll do their best to try to find you, and this is what we want. They'll be a bit desperate, and it'll offer us an excellent chance to get a look at some of their people in this country. It'll be an added bonus, you could say. Rawlings' office would like to get positive identification of as many of their H.C.N.'s as possible."

"Their what?"

"Sorry," the colonel chuckled. "H.C.N.'s—Host-Country National, *Moroccans* who work for the Soviets. They probably have some other T.C.N.'s, as well, Third-Country Nationals, Frenchmen and Spaniards, men like Danzinger, contract employees. You're going to have to get used to a lot of jargon, Joe. I rail against it all the time myself, but it's a losing battle. I'm sure these young bucks like Roy and Larry could carry on a whole conversation and never use any honest-to-God English."

"By the way," Joe said, "how *do* I get out of the movie house without them spotting me?"

"Don't worry. There's a way up into the apartment house above from inside the theater. You just go to the loge marked on the ticket you buy and you'll be picked up there."

"And then down to Rabat?"

The colonel was filling his pipe again. "Well, let's try to keep to the need-to-know principle for the time being," he said. "There'll be some initial 'controlled de-briefing' at a secure place inside this country. I want to be frank about this, too. It's normal procedure to have one of these de-briefing sessions immediately following any operation that involves uncontrolled, independent contact with the people on the other side. We do trust you. We wouldn't be sending you on this mission if we didn't. It's just standard procedure, that's all. We do it with people who've been working for us for years. After the de-briefing, you'll be leaving the country, probably going directly back to the States, perhaps with a short stop to talk to the boys in Europe. Don't worry, the whole thing will be organized to make it as smooth as possible for you."

"I can believe the organization part," Joe said, glancing up at the scaffolding and tarpaulins.

"I've got a few more details to discuss before we call it a night," the colonel said. "First, I've gotten word from Algeria that three Russian naval intelligence people left the base at Mers-el-Kebir yesterday en route to Paris. It seems that they were issued Soviet diplomatic passports there and took the night flight to Casablanca. They were met by Dimitry's driver and taken up to Rabat. They came in as members of the advance team to a trade delegation. But we're fairly certain they're anti-submarine specialists. Now, listen, Joe. If you have any direct dealings with any of them during this operation, I want you to do your damnedest to remember as much as possible about them—facial characteristics, height, weight, et cetera, whether or not they speak English or French, who seems to be in charge. . . . In short, remember as much as you can to give us the fullest picture of these birds without us actually having to meet them ourselves. Understood?"

"Okay. Fine. I'll try."

"Good. Now, the last point isn't so clear-cut, I'm afraid." The colonel shifted in his chair to face the end of the terrace. "Roy, how about being a nice guy and fetching us a couple of weak Scotches for a nightcap. You can take your time making them, too."

Roy rose and was gone beneath the raised tarpaulin. Joe sat patiently in the half light, waiting for the colonel to continue. At the end of the garden he could see the two long-robed figures of the watchmen bending over a small fire. Higher up the mountain the wind was beginning to moan softly in the cypress trees. Out on the Straits, beyond the gap of the Jew's River, he saw a necklace of white lights, a semicircle of fishing boats, each with a brilliant pressure lamp mounted on its bow to draw the fish into the waiting nets. *Christ,* he thought suddenly, *I love this place, and this is the last night I'll ever have here on the mountain with the Levant wind blowing and with the moon and the smell of jasmine.* A mosquito whined in his ear and he snapped back to attention. The colonel was speaking.

". . . it *is,* Joe. It's a funny business. I've been at it all my adult life, since before Pearl Harbor. I've seen a lot of changes, believe me. One thing I hope I've learned is not to worry too much about the future. Things have a way of working out. I've watched the agency grow from a two-bit operation into what it is today. I know that there's a lot of wild speculation in the press about the sinister nature of the C.I.A., but basically it's just another big federal bureaucracy. The only difference is that we have to remain confidential because of the nature of our work. The agency is a lot more humane and flexible and downright diverse than most people would ever guess. We have been dealing for years with men and women who've found themselves in your position. We understand the problems of leaving one life and setting out on a whole new career. All I want to say tonight is not to worry too much about the future. Trust us. We do look out for our own people."

"That's . . . well, that's good to know, Colonel," Joe said. He could think of nothing else to say.

"So," the colonel went on, "if you feel that you actually have developed a drinking problem, then we have doctors who will be able to help you. If you've got money problems, we can arrange credit, although I think that the sixty thousand dollars the Russians are going to pay you will take care of your financial situation. The only condition we will have to make is that your new life become completely confidential. Do you follow me?"

"Yes, I guess so."

"Fine. When you go back out in the field, it won't be under the name of Joe Clinton. Joe Clinton is going to have to cease to exist. And when that happens, I'm afraid you will have to sever your contacts with all your friends, family, and loved ones. It's a bastard of a condition, Joe, but it's necessary for your own protection."

Joe sighed again. "How am I going to just cease to exist?"

"That's easy," the colonel said. "What if you were to take, for example, an assignment to Vietnam advising a documentary film outfit and you disappeared out in the bush, missing, presumed captured by the Viet Cong. You wouldn't be the first journalist to be lost that way."

"And then?"

"And then you'll be set up in your new job with your new name. It'll be rough for your family."

"Not really," Joe said. "My mother's been dead nine years, and my old man's pretty senile by now. He's retired, living in a nursing home for old railroad men. He was a locomotive engineer on the Chicago-Northwestern."

"I know," the colonel said. "What about your brother?"

"He's a half-brother, actually, from the old man's first marriage. We never were very close. I haven't seen him in about six years."

"And your ex-wife and son?"

Joe sucked in his breath. "Won't I *ever* get to see Joey again? I thought maybe I could convince Monique to let him visit me for a while . . . you know, after I'm settled."

The colonel tapped his toe on the stone of the terrace. "Let's leave that open, Joe. I'm sure we can work something out there. If we can arrange things with the boy's mother, I think we might be able to get him up to your training site in the States."

"I sure as hell would appreciate that, Colonel," Joe said.

"So," the colonel continued, "we'll work something out there. What about the people here in Morocco?"

"George has been a damned good friend. . . ."

"Well, don't worry too much about George. He's in on this operation, too. You'll be able to write to him and to see him personally, eventually. That still leaves the problem of Mrs. O'Brien.

"She's State Department," Joe blurted out. "It'll be okay for *her* to know, won't it? She can sign one of the secrecy agreements. I just can't walk out on her, Colonel. You can't make me simply write her off."

"Take it easy. Try to keep your voice down. Now, we *do* understand your position. But, for the moment, you're going to have to *mislead* her slightly. Tomorrow, when you see her, you will explain this new assignment. . . ."

"*What* new assignment?"

"The documentary film project in Vietnam. You'll explain it, and then you'll say good-bye for a while."

"I have to put Renée through all that crap, through

thinking I've been *killed?* Come on, Colonel, that's too much to ask."

"Let me finish. Between the time you're de-briefed in the States and the time you're routed into a training program, we will have interviewed Mrs. O'Brien and explained the situation. If she wants to see you then, we'll make the proper arrangements. It will only be for a few weeks that you won't be able to contact her."

Joe relaxed again in his chair. It wouldn't be bad, only a couple of weeks. He nodded his head. From nowhere a picture came to him, Tommy and Joey playing together on a green suburban lawn.

They were silent for a moment. As if on cue, Roy appeared with their drinks. "If you don't need me, Colonel," he said, "I'm going to hit the sack. We've got a long day tomorrow."

The good nights were said and Joe sat quietly, relishing the warmth of the whisky. The colonel was again at the task of pipe-filling. "You do like boats, don't you, Joe?"

"Yes, I guess I do. They give you so much freedom."

"And you say that you're not very well known in Greece and Turkey?"

"I've been in Athens about three times, but I wouldn't say I was well known there. Never have been to Turkey."

"Cyprus?"

"Been through the transit lounge of the airport a couple of times."

"How about Lebanon?"

"Once—in Beirut for the weekend. I spent most of the Sixty-seven War in Israel."

"Excellent. Think about this tonight, Joe, when you get to wondering what this new life will be like: a big, well-built motor sailer, something that can sail but has the horsepower in its engines to get you out of trouble; a house someplace in the Aegean islands; and a profitable charter business. You'll have plenty of travel—Greece, Turkey, the Middle East. You'll actually be your own boss most of the year, but you'll know that we're backing you up financially. Not a bad-sounding future, is it?"

"I don't think I'm up to handling a boat like that, Colonel. I've only had the *Dragonfly* in the water this summer, and I've got a lot to learn before I become a professional sailor."

"Well, we'd provide you with a crew, of course, probably a couple of young guys like Roy and Larry who could handle the day-to-day running of the boat and who also could hack the language problem. We've got a fair-sized operation out there, you know. Greece and Turkey form the southern flank of NATO and are important to the U.S. Don't worry, you won't be alone, Joe. We'll be right there with you all the way."

"That . . . that sounds very good, Colonel." His voice sounded flat and brittle in his ears.

"Good. Let's finish up our drinks and call it a night," the colonel said, raising his glass.

21

The Briefing

Joe stretched back on the foam beach cushion. The coffee in his cup was cold, but it tasted sweet and strong with the generous slug of cognac he had added when Roy's back was turned. Sipping it slowly, he gazed out over the garden at the familiar whitewashed smear of the city across the valley. There were whitecaps on the Straits again. Beside him was the two-page operational plan. He had already read it three times, carefully. It was a damned good plan. All his actions in the next thirty-six hours had been anticipated and scheduled. Even the Land Rover had been given a tune-up, grease job, and oil change, and the reserve jerry can had been topped off with gas.

There was nothing more to be done. His bag was packed. Joe had showered and shaved. The clean set of clothes was laid out on his bed, next to the bag. He must now get up and go into the house, hand over the plan to Roy, and change clothes. He scooped up the papers and then strode into the living room.

"You're through with it, Joe?" Roy asked, looking up from his inevitable *National Geographic.*

Placing the papers next to the magazine on the coffee table, Joe nodded. "It's a good plan," he said.

"Well, the old man's had a bit of practice. Listen, he wants to talk to you again before you take off for Rabat. Take the car and drive up to George's. Park it across the street by the Englishman's driveway and just walk right into the house."

"What's up?" Joe asked. It wasn't like the colonel to deviate from a fixed plan at the last minute.

"I don't know, Joe. He just sent word that he wants to see you before you go."

"Okay. It'd be easier to walk up the path, though. Do you figure the house is being watched?"

"I doubt it, personally," Roy said, choosing his words carefully. "On a deal like this, though, you have to plan things as if you were under surveillance. It makes things a little inconvenient sometimes, but it's worth it."

"Okay," Joe repeated. He reached out to shake Roy's hand. "I'll see you when I get back. Wish me luck."

Roy smiled. "Listen," he said, taking Joe's hand, "just don't sweat things, huh? You follow the plan and everything'll be okay. You've got a big organization in back of you."

"Thanks," Joe said.

"I'm down here, Joe," the colonel called up through the open trapdoor to the garage.

Joe climbed warily down into the brightly lit cave of the garage. It hardly seemed like the same room. Thick, multicolored cables entered the garage under the metal door to the street and down through the trapdoor from the pantry. The workbench was covered with a clean white cloth, and banks of electronic test equipment took up most of its surface, their amber, red, and green lights blinking in an intricate sequence. Another table, also covered with a clean cloth, had replaced the wooden saw horses. Crates and cartons had also been pressed into use as tables, holding piled-up technical volumes, tools, and coils of spare wire. Around the big table, two American engineers were working. They wore white coveralls and rubber gloves as they bent over the dissected blocks of the listening buoy's circuitry. Joe recognized the shape of the buoy's empty pressure hull, neatly wrapped in sheeting in the corner of the room. The engineers looked up briefly from their work as Joe climbed down the ladder, but then they returned their attention to the equipment on the table. Overhead, a newly installed dehumidifier and an electric fan cooled the room.

The colonel rose from his folding chair. "Quite a setup, isn't it?" he said.

"It sure is. How are things going?"

"Well," the colonel said, pinching the bridge of his nose, "I'm afraid we've run into one or two problems. That's why I wanted to see you."

The colonel pointed to the test equipment on the workbench. "First," he said, "we kept blowing fuses. Then we had trouble with a couple of broken bolt heads. Now, this morning, we find out that we need some special recording equipment in order to get an accurate transfer of all the data stored on those tapes." He pointed with his pipe stem to the gray-black metallic tape cassettes that lay side by side at the end of the workbench. "In short," he added, "we need at least forty-eight hours more. This is going to complicate things, I'm afraid. What I want you to do is to drive down to Rabat this afternoon, but take your time. Stop for lunch on the way; have a swim if you like. Spend the night at Mrs. O'Brien's and then call the Soviet Embassy in the morning. Say that you're coming to see them later in the morning. When you talk to Dimitry, follow the plan exactly, but tell him you won't be getting the details of the pickup spot from Gessous until Saturday morning. Make your Tangier rendezvous with Dimitry for the same time of day, but twenty-four hours later. That'll give us a full seventy-two hours from right now to play with. We hope to get the new recorders this afternoon, and possibly we'll have them set up and working by morning. Do you think you can handle the changes, Joe?"

"I don't see why not. It seems pretty simple."

"There's one more thing. After you see Dimitry, say your good-byes to Mrs. O'Brien and then get back up here *tout de suite* tomorrow evening. Leave the car at your place and take the path back up here. *If*, and I really hope it won't be necessary, but, if we're still delayed by the recording, we'll have to dream up some way to stall off Dimitry even longer."

"Okay," Joe said. "I'm off, then."

"George'll walk you out to your car. It'll look better that way."

Joe turned back from the ladder. "Do you figure the house is being watched?"

The colonel smiled reassuringly. "Actually I don't. But it's better to be safe than sorry, right? We've got plainclothes Moroccan security people all over the mountain;

they're disguised as gardeners, street repairmen, and delivery men. They've reported absolutely no unusual activity. But, in an operation of this nature, it's always best to keep in mind that the boys on the other side aren't exactly amateurs either."

"Okay," Joe said, "I'll remember that."

22

Emergency Contact

A breeze came in through the open glass doors of Renée's bedroom. Out on the dinner table in the garden, the stub of the candle sputtered once inside a glass bell and then went out. Joe shifted his arm slightly, readjusting the weight of Renée's head and neck. She murmured and turned to snuggle deeper into the pillow. Joe stared up at the geometry of shadows and reflected light on the ceiling. He would have liked to get up, but that would disturb Renée. Awake, she would want to talk, and Joe did not wish to talk anymore that night. More talking would be useless. He could only tell her more lies, which was not the way he wanted to spend their last night together.

From now on it's going to be this way, he suddenly thought. *There'll always be this barrier of lies and cover stories . . . always, even in bed with a woman. I'll always have to stop myself before I speak to make certain that my words conform to the reality of the operational plan. And there'll always be a plan, won't there? The colonel didn't say so, but there will always be one: some new deal in the works; some secret delivery of a thing or a person; some confidential meeting in that dream sailboat or writer's house on the "southern flank of NATO."*

And I'll probably get used to it, too, just like those guys in 'Nam who run the fucking Four O'Clock Follies get used to lying through their teeth so that, even when you get them stoned at night, they still believe their bullshit statistics. I'm going to end up the same way, and there's absolutely nothing I can do about it.

The telephone rang. Its jangling awoke Renée. She sat upright in bed. "What? . . ." she said. "Oh, damn . . . ah, wait." She dashed, naked, clutching her light summer robe, toward the insistent noise of the telephone. Joe got to his feet and pulled on his undershorts and trousers.

"It's for *you,* Joe," she called. "It's the embassy, for God's sake. They want to talk to *you.*" Her face showed a mixture of curiosity and anger at being awakened after midnight by an unexplainable call from the embassy, which, in theory, had no right to concern itself with her late-night visitors.

"Did you tell anybody at the embassy you were here?" she asked, her hand held firmly over the receiver's mouthpiece.

Joe shook his head and took the phone.

"Mr. Clinton?"

"Yes," he said, "this is Mr. Clinton. Who's calling, please?"

"This is the code room at the embassy, sir. We've got a message for you, from Tangier. Do you think you could come up and sign for it?"

"Right away? Tonight?"

"Yes, sir, if you don't mind, sir."

"Okay. I'll be up there right away."

He replaced the receiver and stood looking into Renée's face.

"What is this all about, Joe?" she asked, fully awake now. "How did they know you were here?"

This is not in the goddamned plan. Yes, it is . . . Emergency Contact Procedure. . . . Christ, something's happened in Tangier.

"I gave them your number at the hotel. I said I'd be going to a dinner party and to call your number if there were any urgent messages."

She accepted a cigarette from him and stood back to examine his face more closely. "So, why does the American Embassy have urgent messages for *you?*"

He had begun pacing, but he checked himself in midstride when she spoke. His mind was turning coolly now. "Renée, I'm sorry, but I can't tell you." He reached out to grip her shoulders. "This deal I'm doing with the documentary outfit in Vietnam . . . it . . . well . . . we've got some 'government' sponsorship. Do you understand?"

She nodded. She had been too long in the foreign service to miss the meaning of his words. "I never would have thought that you'd get involved with them, Joe."

"I need the money, and it's a short, easy deal. I'll be back in a couple of months, three at the most."

"You're a big boy," she said. "You do what you think best. Tell me, though, how long have you been planning this?"

"It only came up last week. They sent a guy over from the States to see me. They're getting several people from Europe, as well. That's all I can say about it, Renée."

"And you figure the money's worth all the trouble?"

"You know these people," he said, speaking automatically. "They've got money to burn."

They were walking toward the bedroom. Renée took his arm. "Do you want me to heat up some coffee?"

"No, thanks. I'd better get up to the embassy."

She stopped and reached up to touch his face. "You'll be coming back tonight, won't you?"

He tried to imagine what was so urgent that the colonel risked contacting him in Rabat. It was possible that he would be summoned directly back to Tangier.

"I'm not sure, Renée," he said, speaking slowly. He chose his words carefully. "If I don't make it back tonight, don't worry. I'll call you either tonight or in the morning. They may have something important to go over."

"But, anyway," she said, smiling again, "I'll see you next week in Tangier."

He frowned, puzzled by her words.

"Don't you remember? Tommy gets back from camp. I'm coming up to meet the ferryboat on Saturday."

"Oh, yeah, sure."

"You'll be there, won't you? You're not leaving before then?"

"No. I'll definitely be there."

Joe pushed the starter button lightly and the Land Rover's motor came alive. It seemed to roar in the silence. All the villas and garden apartments were dark. At the bottom of the hill, he signaled for a turn and shifted down into second. The broad Avenue du Chellah was empty, lonely looking, with the dusty palm trees and hanging streetlamps swaying in the summer night breeze. In the winter there would be receptions and formal diplomatic dinners in these walled villas. The streets would be lined with parked embassy sedans and an occasional cabinet minister's Mercedes, their uniformed chauffeurs grouped in the shadows, joking with the extra policemen assigned to direct traffic.

Then, without warning, the car's motor died. Joe swore softly and pushed the starter button again. The starter whined, but the engine would not fire. He braked and pulled over to the side of the road, twenty yards before the intersection. It was ironic. Two days before he had faked a breakdown in front of the Parade Bar, and yesterday the colonel had gone to all the trouble of getting the car tuned up. Now, when he needed the car, the damned thing quit on him. He pushed the starter button again and again, but the motor refused to catch.

Flipping off the headlights, he jerked open the driver's side door. His left leg was already out of the door when the heavy, calloused hand seized his chin, wrenching his head back savagely. He did not have time to cry out before the point of the hypodermic needle jammed through his shirt and into the taut muscles of his neck. There was a sharp, electric rush of pain, followed quickly by a flooding of warmth and blue, wonderfully *blue,* drowsiness. The red generator light on the car's dashboard swelled like a flower. Then slowly the ruby glow faded into the blue of the universe and he was under.

23

The Examination

There had been a wonderful dream, a dream of such complexity and beauty that Joe was content to sit back inside his brain and watch, convinced that he had never known another life, that his whole past and future were part of the dream. There was music too, now, a choir of Moorish warriors on horseback chanting the holy poetry of the Koran as they paraded their stallions before him. And then he was reborn into the world, his birth pangs the stab of the hypodermic containing the reviving stimulant.

His mouth was painfully dry. It was impossible to move his tongue or lips. There was too much light. His head was clear and his eyes could focus, but there was nothing to focus on, only the dazzling wash of light. Slowly, the stimuli of his new world began to register. He was sitting in a padded chair. Someone was holding his left hand in an odd position. The choir of Moorish horsemen became a singsong recording of Arab music playing on a cheap transistor. A sparkling curtain of light was ripping in long, vertical fissures. Through one of the rips he could see the hands and arms of a man. The hands were holding open the fingers of his own left hand and rolling them firmly onto a white card. Someone out there beyond the light was fingerprinting him.

Saliva began to flow again and then the barrier of light dissolved and he could see around him. He was suddenly afraid. His lips drew tightly together. He swallowed, sucking in his breath.

"Don't move your fingers," Dimitry said. "We can just as easily finish up the job when you're dead. But we've started now, so why make things difficult?"

Dimitry was sitting on the edge of a doctor's examination table. Behind Dimitry, Joe could see glass-fronted cabinets containing bottles of drugs and medical instruments. A second man was bending over his hand, finishing with the fingerprint cards and now wiping Joe's fingertips clean with alcohol-soaked cotton. Joe's biceps, thighs, and calves were securely bound to the chair with multiple windings of gauze bandage. Behind him, Joe heard someone move and a deep voice said something in Russian. Dimitry smiled and shook his head, answering with a curt, negative monosyllable.

There were two windows in the room, both hidden behind slotted blinds, which were tightly drawn, admitting no light. No traffic noise penetrated the room. The room was cool, with the unmistakable dryness of air conditioning. It could have been either noon or midnight. Joe had no idea how long he had been unconscious.

"What time is it?" Joe asked.

"A little past two in the morning," Dimitry said. He smiled again. "That's a beautiful drug, Clinton. We had to guess at your body weight, and we wanted you out no more than two hours, so we weren't certain on the exact dosage, but, by God, it worked like a charm."

"You . . . you did something to my car."

Dimitry mimicked Joe's protest in falsetto Russian, and there was an answering splash of laughter from the men behind Joe's chair. "You people never cease to amaze me, Clinton," Dimitry said. He shook his head in genuine wonder and continued. "Voight goes to all the trouble to rig up that elaborate farce up in Tangier with the house painters, but he leaves your control in Rabat in the hands of *Arabs*. That's so typical of you assholes in Operations. You get these Arab flunkies on the payroll, fly them over to Bragg for all that Green Beret nonsense to convince them they're upright, *intelligent* field agents fighting the commie devils, and, Christ . . . you end up believing it yourselves.

"Do you know who he had running your surveillance

from Souk-el-Arba on down? Of course you do. . . . How'd it feel to know you were protected by Moktar M'Barek and his merry band of Sûreté clowns? Ben Rashid shops at the Kénitra PX, for God's sake. Doesn't Voight know these people are *blown?* We've been watching the American girl's apartment for two days. M'Barek's gang has been in and out of there like Western Union boys. But they couldn't even get a decent tap on her phone. Took us about five minutes to bypass it. Ben Rashid's got his *cousin* running the road surveillance. . . ." Dimitry broke into boyish giggles and said something sarcastic to the men in the back of the room. Their laughter was equally scornful. "We led Captain Ben Rashid's young cousin on a little side trip, Joe . . . out to the Casa road for dinner. You and Mrs. O'Brien just got back to her place. He called it in on his *radio* . . . in his beautiful Fort Bragg English. Yes, sir, these Arab boys are pretty sharp cookies; all that time spent training them wasn't a waste of your taxpayers' money." Dimitry giggled again. "He's been following that dummy Land Rover all day. Does Voight *really* think we can rely on Arab scum like M'Barek on an important operation?"

"Who's Voight?"

Dimitry lit a cigarette and stared at Joe for a long time. "Would you like a cigarette?" he finally asked.

Joe wet his lips and nodded.

Dimitry walked around the side of Joe's chair and crushed the glowing tip of the cigarette sharply into Joe's left ear. The pain was incredible. Joe screamed, clawing at the air with his pinioned forearms.

"Listen, my friend!" Dimitry shouted. "You can yell your damned fool head off and nobody'll hear you! We're not here to play Twenty Questions. Colonel Richard Mitchell Voight is your control on this operation. William Rawlings is the field trainee in the Rabat station. Lawrence David Topley is from the Technical Services Division. Leroy Quenton Bush is from the Moroccan desk in Operations. Voight used to be a Plans man, but he screwed up somewhere and they've shunted him off into Operations. George Briggs just got sucked up into this business. But you—you've been one of their 'journalists' for quite a while. . . . Now, do we have to go to work with the doctor's electric needle?" Dimitry pointed toward the cabinet of instruments. "Or are you going to cooperate?"

Joe's ear was throbbing like a drilled tooth. Beyond the pain, his thoughts were racing. He blinked and wet his lips again. As a ten-year-old child, he had once spent a sleepless, nightmare-wracked week following a James Cagney movie rife with explicit Gestapo torture scenes. He could still clearly see the brazier with the heating pokers and the metal-tipped strands of the whips. And then the nightmare of the Saigon torture basement came snapping back in vivid detail. These men were not A.R.V.N. security police, but the same nightmare fate awaited him.

"I didn't know his last name," Joe squeaked. "He called himself Colonel Richards. . . . I didn't know his name was Voight."

"That's a little better," Dimitry said. He pulled up a folding chair and sat facing Joe. "Let's start at the beginning, shall we? When did this operation begin? Who got the buoy in the first place—the agency or the navy?"

"I found it," Joe heard himself admitting. "I found it last Saturday. There never was a Jew, you know."

Dimitry laughed. "No?" he protested in mock disbelief. "Did you think we were going to swallow that crap once we had a name and could do some checking up?"

"Well, it seemed like a good story. There really is a Jewish engineer named Gessous."

"Yes, my friend," Dimitry said, nodding, "and he left the country a week ago, and Voight and his boys were all over the Tangier rabbi's office asking questions and trying to come up with a Jew to pawn off on us. So, *you* found the buoy at Targa. Exactly how and exactly when?"

"It was Saturday morning, early. My boat was anchored in the bay and this old Arab fisherman came by with something stuck in his net. I dove down and cut it free. That's when I saw the Russian writing. I figured it might be from some kind of scientific ship and that maybe there'd be a reward. So I lashed it to my anchor and came back the next night with George to get it in my Land Rover."

"Did the fisherman see it? Was he alone?"

"I'm sure he didn't see it. The water was kind of murky that day. No, he wasn't alone; there was a kid with him, a teen-aged boy."

Dimitry spoke at length in Russian to the men behind Joe.

"All right," Dimitry said, turning back to Joe. "So then what happened?"

"We put it in George's garage and I tried to figure out a way to get some money for it. I'm broke. I'm in debt and I need money badly. I arranged things for a Swiss bank account and then I came down to Rabat to see Rawlings."

"How did you know Rawlings was C.I.A.?" Dimitry asked sharply.

"I looked him up in the foreign service stud book. . . . I mean, I looked for the obvious spooks at the Rabat embassy. It's easy to find them if you know what you're looking for. He wasn't on the list because he's new, but I got the office and his secretary put me on to him."

"Okay. And then?" Dimitry lit another cigarette, smirking openly as Joe cringed back into the padded chair. "Go on, for Christ's sake! I'm not going to burn you again."

Joe spoke quickly, his eyes never leaving the glowing tip of Dimitry's cigarette. It all spilled out in words—Rawlings' plans for the secret departure of the "Jewish friend," Danzinger's role as the salvage broker, and Joe's visit to the Russian Embassy. He slowed down when he reached the arrival of Colonel Richards. This was important. Dimitry had to understand that Joe was not a regular, professional agent. ". . . and they came in and woke me up in the middle of the night—Colonel Richards and Rawlings and Larry and Roy. They had a picture of me coming out of your embassy. They knew the Jew story was a lie. They roughed me up, for Christ's sake. They told me all about the buoy, what it *really* is. I had to tell them the truth. . . ."

"Just like you're doing now," Dimitry said sarcastically.

"Yes!" Joe said, his voice cracking. "Goddamn it, it's

all such a fucking mess. . . ." There were real tears, hot and wet, running onto his parched lips.

"What happened that night when they woke you up?" Dimitry asked.

"They had a lie detector with them. Larry ran it and the colonel asked questions."

"Polygraph," Dimitry said to the men at the other end of the room, accenting the word with foreign inflection.

"Go on, please, Clinton. This is getting interesting."

Joe described in detail his session with the lie detector. Twice Dimitry interrupted Joe with questions as he continued on to discuss the evening session with Colonel Richards in George's house.

"And, so, here you are," Dimitry said. "Do you realize that you've just betrayed some of your country's vital secrets?"

Joe was trembling now, with fear and pain and anger. "I didn't have much choice, did I?"

Dimitry laughed out loud. "Is that all it takes to get you to talk?" He poked his fresh cigarette in Joe's direction. "You're a real credit to your country. The agency can feel very proud of you." Dimitry laughed again.

"Of course, we have our own sources," Dimitry continued, "and we had a real break when Voight and his crew were seen driving into the Kénitra base in that *unmarked* station wagon. I was alerted ten minutes after they got there and had developed pictures of the whole carload an hour later. Then, when the station wagon left the base with only a Moroccan driver and the U.S. Navy Corvair called in to Rabat air-traffic control with a flight plan for Tangier, the rest was a snap. One of my men picked them up at the Tangier airport and followed their taxi right up to George Briggs' house. We really couldn't be sure the buoy was there until the next day, when that house-painting circus showed up. They used that trick before, about two years ago in Tehran. Don't they think we keep records?" Dimitry was swaggering a bit now, but he quickly caught himself. "No, Joe, the painters were the real corker. Maybe we were lucky to have spotted Voight at the Kénitra base, but we did something with our luck, and Voight made it pretty easy for us. They've handled this whole thing like a bunch of college boys planning a panty raid."

"College boys don't go on 'panty raids' anymore . . . and no one still says 'corker' either."

"What? What did you say?" Dimitry's voice was full of menace.

"I said that your English is perfect and your American accent is so good that it's hard to believe. But, well, you use a lot of old-fashioned idioms—like 'corker.' The other day you said 'square' and 'song and dance.' People don't say that much anymore."

"What *do* they say, professor?"

"I really don't know. It's changing all the time. You have to go there and listen."

"Fine. I'll get on the next plane to New York and move right into a beatnik pad to become more enlightened."

"They don't call them 'beatniks' anymore, either. They're called 'hippies.' "

Dimitry was chuckling. "Do you realize that you're spending part of your last night alive trying to improve my knowledge of American idioms?"

Joe went cold to his spine, instantly numb, as if he had been dipped into ice water. Dimitry was serious. They were going to end his life.

"I wasn't going to cheat you!" Joe blurted out. "I promise! I was going to give you the buoy, but they caught me. They've had me guarded ever since. All I wanted was the money. Don't kill me. I'll tell you everything I know. There's no reason to kill me. . . ."

"You'll tell us everything either way, Clinton." Dimitry paused. He reached to massage his neck and then looked directly back into Joe's eyes. "Listen carefully. If you can stop lying and cooperate with me, then it's just possible that we can keep you alive. Do you understand me?"

Joe nodded eagerly.

"First," Dimitry added, "I want you to see something, a little *newsreel*. We don't screw around with obsolete junk like polygraphs. Voight's still operating back in the 1950s, when people actually believed those machines couldn't be outwitted by a trained agent. Even the Jews, the *Israelis,* have got their senior pilots, Sabra apes, trained to withstand both physical abuse and lie detectors." Dimitry looked past Joe's shoulders and spoke in Russian.

"Now, Clinton," he continued, "I want you to watch this and watch it closely. That cigarette was just to wake you up. I'm going to show you a film clip. It was made in '67 in Damascus. The first man you'll see is a Yiddish gentleman, a lieutenant colonel in the Israeli Air Force, a great fighter-pilot ace; he had three MIG-21's to his credit and God knows how many MIG-17's. . . . Anyway, he was a big-shot Arab killer." Dimitry paused.

"One morning he met a real fighter pilot, a twenty-three-year-old boy from Siberia who blasted that Jew out of the sky with three long bursts from his cannons." Dimitry smiled. "The Israeli swore he'd been hit by SAM's. He'd already fired all his Side-Winders at our man and was scooting back for Golan when we got him. Anyway, the man you'll see was a tough, experienced Israeli wing commander. The Arabs used all the old favorites on him—electricity, fingernails, a dentist's drill, the works."

Joe felt his stomach souring and the nausea rise in his throat as Dimitry's words registered.

"So"—Dimitry smiled cheerfully—"the Syrians finally quit and gave him to us. We had the following hard data from him in *nine* hours. Listen . . . squadron offensive tactics, bomb-fuse timing, terrain-avoidance radar characteristics, fuel-ordinance, load-efficiency ratios—everything we wanted to know about F-4 Charlies. And this is how we did it, Clinton, and this is what we're going to do to you in about ten minutes if you don't stop lying to me." Dimitry snapped a curt order in Russian and the lights went out.

A grainy, overexposed black-and-white film danced on the wall next to the medical supply cabinet. It showed a haggard, middle-aged man in a filthy, bloodstained flight suit. Joe caught a glimpse of darkly stained gauze bandages around the pilot's fingers. The Israeli was sitting in a leather armchair in a concrete room, probably an underground bunker. He stared unblinkingly at the bright camera lights.

A pair of clean, delicate hands appeared and rolled

back the pilot's left sleeve. A small plastic hypodermic syringe darted into the flesh of the forearm, and the camera quickly focused on the pilot's face. The dark eyes remained passive for perhaps a second. Then a scream of terror and pain began to soundlessly form on the lips. The lips themselves locked suddenly and remained motionless. The eyes widened in disbelief, but they, too, suddenly froze, open wide in absolute horror, but, yet, still as a waxwork's dummy.

In the corner of the screen, a box appeared with the sharply filmed face of a stopwatch ticking off the seconds. After forty-five elapsed seconds, the pilot's frozen face had still not thawed; the scream was still unuttered on the paralyzed lips. A full minute passed, then ninety seconds. At ninety-eight elapsed seconds, the same delicate hands appeared and administered a second shot into the pilot's right arm. Twenty seconds later the Israeli was slouched in his chair, sobbing, his mouth spewing bloody spittle. At two minutes on the watch, he was upright in his chair, drinking a glass of water. At four minutes he was speaking slowly into the camera.

The whirring projector stopped and Joe blinked up at the bright fluorescent lights.

"That drug," Dimitry said, "has never failed. It blocks the nerve synapses' functions in the *entire* body—the autonomous first, then the voluntary. The heart stops, the lungs stop . . . all feeling leaves the body, sounds and smell cease . . . only vision and conscious thought remain for about one hundred seconds. The brain's oxygen-rich, you know, especially under stress.

"So, the subject can sit back and watch himself die . . . well, not watch, he can *feel* himself already dead. The antidote brings him back, both physically and emotionally, from death. It took only one shot to get this pilot babbling like a baby, but then we'd already let him sit through a couple of sessions with a big Sabra Charles Atlas-type tank commander who didn't want to discuss radio frequencies. The tanker finally sang his filthy ass off, but we gave him an overdose just to soften up the pilot. And that's how you're going to die tonight, Mr. C.I.A. -flunky Clinton . . . unless you can stop the double-dealing bullshit and answer every—and I mean *every*—question I ask with the exact truth, not that pack of horse crap you were trying to peddle me before."

"You're worse than the Nazis!" Joe blurted out. His head sank automatically, waiting for a blow or cigarette burn.

Dimitry laughed. "Not bad, Joe, not bad. Actually, we're much better. We don't have some half-baked beer-hall-Wagner-Druid superstition to fall back on. We have history, and history is never wrong. Now, shall we talk, or do you want your first shot?"

"I'll tell you anything."

"Let's go back to your talk with Voight. When did he dream up this plan to have you go through with the delivery of the buoy to me?"

"It was when he was at the navy base in Kénitra. He talked with Washington by radio. He called it a 'secure voice channel.' He arranged to have the engineers come over from the States to take the buoy apart and test it up in George's garage."

"And that's what they're doing now, testing it?"

"Yes. The colonel told me that they already have an earlier model of the buoy, so they know how it works, basically. They wanted you to get the new buoy back as if it hadn't been compromised. He said that if the Americans could figure out ways to jam the buoy and that if the Russians deployed the whole new system, then our Polaris subs would be safe for a few more years."

"He said that, did he? He certainly has delusions of grandeur, your colonel. Well, what about the testing? What have they come up with?"

"They set up a lot of equipment to measure the circuits and the radios, but the colonel told me they were having trouble with the data on the tapes. He showed me the tapes. They're big gray-black casettes. He said they need some special recorders. He was hoping to get them set up by tomorrow morning and finish recording by the end of the day. Then it would take another day to put the buoy back together again. The delivery was supposed to be on Saturday."

"And then, I suppose, you were just going to live

happily ever after on my government's ransom money?"

Joe let all the pent-up bitterness spill out in his words. "Hell, no. They were going to take me back to the States. They said that there'd have to be a 'controlled debriefing,' with the lie detector again. They said that they'd protect me from your people. I'd have to stay where they could keep an eye on me. They want me to come in for lie-detector sessions a couple of times each year. They're going to set me up with a sailboat in Greece and make me work for them."

"And you agreed to all that?"

"What choice did I have? He said they'd put me in a Moroccan jail to keep me quiet if they had to. That was the choice Colonel Richards gave me—either work for them, or go to jail for five years."

Dimitry looked away from Joe. He spoke a long time in Russian. A door opened behind the chair and Joe could feel a draft of humid night air on his neck. Dimitry gave some orders and there was a movement of feet. The door closed.

"Here," Dimitry said. He took a surgical knife from the counter next to the storage cabinets and cut Joe's bindings. "There's tea there if you want some," he said, pointing toward a low wooden table at the opposite end of the room, "cigarettes, too, if you still feel like smoking. Relax. I'll be back in a little while."

Joe sat in the chair, rubbing the numbness out of his legs. Dimitry went out the door. The lock snapped shut. Warily, he got to his feet and looked around the room. He was alone. On the table a tulip-shaped glass of steaming pink tea sat on a saucer with two neatly stacked sugar cubes and a tiny spoon. There was a package of Salems with a box of matches next to the tea. The transistor was silent. He pulled back the Venetian blind and stared blankly at the metal shutter a few inches outside the window glass. His ear was throbbing. In the second supply cabinet he found a jar of medicated petroleum jelly and carefully rubbed some onto the blistered flesh. He began to pace the room. There was a thickness in his brain from the drugs. He knew that this might be the end of his life, but somehow he could not bring himself to care.

Without thinking, Joe stirred the sugar into the tea and drank down the hot, sweet liquid in two big swallows. Replacing the glass in the saucer, it occurred to him that the tea could have been poisoned, that it represented a logical execution device. But he didn't care. The Salem tasted cool and minty. He sat down in the chair and waited. After several minutes passed, he stood, lit another cigarette, and began to pace again. He felt like a whipped animal. There was no need to care or hope or struggle. He had absolutely no control over his eventual fate. He paced and smoked, lighting each cigarette from the butt of the last.

He spent a long time alone in the examination room. His mouth became dry again from the smoke, and his throat was sore and constricted. In the medical cabinet he found a two-liter bottle of distilled water and drank a good part of it in quick, sucking gulps. A key snapped in a lock and Dimitry came into the room. He was carrying Joe's sportcoat, wallet, and watch.

"There's a taxi outside," he said. "It will take you to the Avenue du Chellah. Drive your car back to the O'Brien woman's apartment and go to sleep. In the morning you'll call the Russian Embassy at five past nine. Ask when you should return the films you've borrowed from the cultural center. You'll be told to bring them right in. Park your car in front of the Tour Hassan Hotel and come directly into the embassy. I'll have more instructions for you then. Here." He handed over Joe's things.

"You're letting me *go?*"

"Of course not," Dimitry snapped. "We've got the woman's apartment watched and two men are in the building. If you try to leave or phone for help, they'll come in and kill you both. They'll use the drug you saw in the film."

"But what are you going to do with me?"

"I'll explain that in the morning. Let's just say that I've got some work for you. If you do it well, we shall be prepared to help you. Go on, now, and try to get some sleep."

"How can you help me?" Joe still had his sportcoat and wallet in his hands.

Dimitry looked at him quizzically. "You said that you don't want to go to jail or have to work for the Americans, right?"

"That's right, I don't."

"Well, maybe it's possible for us to help you. You're obviously not cut out for this kind of operation, but my ministry could use a man like you in some other field. You know a lot about Western press media. What would you think about teaching a course at the University of Havana? I was there recently. Cuba gets a bad press because the government's closed down all the Mafia whorehouses. But, believe me, life can be very pleasant there if you know the right people. Think about that, Joe. Think about that."

Life, Joe thought, *a very pleasant life.* He followed Dimitry out of the examination room and down a dark corridor. It appeared that they were in a pre-independence villa that had been converted into a private clinic. A man unlocked the front door for them. Outside on the concrete front porch of the clinic, Dimitry stopped Joe by placing his hand on Joe's shoulder.

"This is one of the strangest cases I've ever worked on," Dimitry said in a friendly, conversational tone. "What you told me tonight answers a lot of questions, but it's still strange. I'm fairly sure that you were telling me the truth." Joe was about to speak when Dimitry continued. "If you are able to follow instructions tomorrow and help me bring this ridiculous game to a proper conclusion, then I'll be willing to go to bat for you. . . . Is that too old-fashioned, 'go to bat'?"

"No," Joe said. "People say that all the time."

"Good. What I mean is, if you make an effort to help us, we'll do the same for you. Just remember that."

Joe clenched his teeth, nodded solemnly, and stepped down off the porch.

The beat-up *petit* taxi stank from the driver's black tobacco. Joe sat back against the broken springs and closed his eyes. They had turned out of the villa's grounds and onto a red dirt lane bordered by the inevitable eucalyptus trees. A Peugeot sedan was following them at a discreet distance. Just before Joe closed his eyes, he saw the green and white lights of the airport beacon ghosting through the tops of the shaggy trees. They were somewhere out in the countryside, near the Rabat-Salé airport; exactly where did not interest him. His eyes closed. He leaned back deeper into the seat.

PART III

Payment of Salvage

24

The New Plan

"Are you positive a truck can make that turn?" Dimitry asked. They sat with their elbows up on the round table. The blinds of Dimitry's apartment were half closed against the morning sun. Joe looked at the detailed surveyor's map of the old-mountain section of Tangier.

"You say it's a small truck?" Joe asked.

"One of those glorified *deux chevaux* the electrical workers use when they repair the power lines. You've seen them, haven't you?"

Joe nodded and looked back at the map. He was confused. They hadn't told him much so far. All they seemed interested in was the best access route to George's garage and the sketch of its interior. He looked up at Dimitry and then at the other man at the table, noting again the bad complexion and the curly, yellow-gray hair. "Well," he answered, "the Kénitra truck couldn't make it, but I make that turn all the time with the Land Rover. The Citroën truck can't be any longer than my car."

Dimitry spoke in Russian and the older man nodded his agreement. "Good," Dimitry said, closing the map, folding it neatly. He pushed the large artist's pad closer to Joe and tapped the sketch with the tip of his pencil. "Here's the canvas shelter they've put up to cover the entrance." He carefully drew a line from the edge of the street, through the doors, and onto the penciled rectangle that represented the workbench holding the testing equipment. "Now, how far . . . how many meters would you say it is from the roadway, here, to the table where they put up the recording equipment?"

Joe bit the end of his own pencil. He closed his eyes and tried to visualize the scene. "Between six and eight meters," he said, "certainly no more than eight. . . . That's around twenty-seven or twenty-eight feet, isn't it?"

Dimitry nodded curtly and spoke to the other man in Russian. The transistor on the coffee table across the room was playing American show tunes. The two Russians were absorbed in conversation now, staring down at the sketch and occasionally indicating some detail or measurement with their pencils. At one point the curly-haired man put on a pair of plastic-framed reading glasses and did a short calculation on a slide rule, noting down his figures in a cheap notebook in front of him. While he did his calculations, Dimitry stared neutrally past Joe's face. Finally, the older man spoke and Dimitry smiled. The other man rose. Taking the sketch pad and notebook with him, he left the room.

Dimitry picked up the folded map and smoothed out the tablecloth. "Care for some more coffee?" he asked Joe pleasantly.

Joe held out his cup while Dimitry poured. They got up and moved to the more comfortable chairs grouped around the coffee table. Dimitry adjusted the volume of the transistor so that they could speak in normal tones.

"It's almost half past ten," Dimitry said. "I want you back in Tangier no later than two-thirty. Can you manage that?"

"I think so," Joe said. "I could be there by one-thirty."

"Good. Now, listen carefully. You'll drive to your house, as Voight told you. Then walk up the path and report in. There will have been some phone calls for you today, but I doubt if the man who's guarding your house would have taken them. The phone will be ringing off and on all morning if nobody answers it. At around noon, a messenger will bring up a note asking you to call the yacht club manager as soon as possible. Do you follow me so far?"

"Yes, I guess so."

"Good. Now here's the important part. I want you to get into that garage. I don't care how you do it, but I want you to get a look down there. Maybe the colonel will be with his engineers and he'll be stupid enough to invite you down like he did yesterday. Your job will be to find out if they've finished recording yet. If they're still at it, try to get out of there as soon as you can and make the phone call."

"What phone call?" Joe was truly puzzled.

"The call to the club manager," Dimitry said impatiently. "If the recording work is still in process, I want you to make that call. Even if they've finished recording, but the tapes—ours and the ones they've used for the copies—are still out on the workbench and exposed, make the call, as well. The thing we have to know is whether those tapes' reels are exposed, not packed inside any protective boxes or casing. Do you understand me?"

"Yes," Joe said. "You're not going to try to bust in there and steal the tapes, are you?"

Dimitry laughed. "That's the kind of asshole trick your friend Voight would try."

"Well, what are you going to do?"

"Let's just say that those tapes are sensitive to magnetic influences and to intense radiation . . . such as X rays. Do you get the picture?"

"The electrical repair truck?"

Dimitry avoided the question. "Just get up there as soon as you can, check out the garage, and make the phone call. Then your side of the bargain has been kept."

"And the delivery goes through as planned for Saturday?"

"Exactly as planned. You follow all of Voight's instructions. We meet at the main post office at the appointed time. I go with you out to the farm and we pick up the buoy in a truck and you return to your house. You leave for the Cinema Goya, just as the colonel has planned, but you'll never make it to the cinema. We'll pick you up on the way, and then you'll be under our protection. Let's not make any changes. The plan is simple enough the way it is."

"There's one thing," Joe said. "I forgot to mention it when we were talking at the table. What if the colonel wants to give me another lie-detector test tonight or tomorrow or sometime before Saturday just to make sure I haven't compromised anything to you?"

Dimitry looked evenly into Joe's eyes. "Then, my dear friend, I'd say they'll take you to that Moroccan jail and lock you up . . . if you're lucky . . . or they may decide that a car accident up in the mountains is the best solution."

Joe thought of Roy and the colonel. Dimitry's suggestion seemed absurd. These men were trained, professional bureaucrats, not cold-blooded killers.

"I can see that you don't believe me," Dimitry said, smiling. "Let me tell you a little story.

"Once there was an American Air Force sergant who retired in Turkey with his Turkish wife and found that his pension didn't go far enough. So he began working for your friends, just routine safe-house and mail-drop work. Occasionally he'd dress up in his old uniform and drive a mobile radio unit that picked up traffic from their people in Rumania. They paid him well and he was happy.

"But then he had a falling out with his wife and started drinking heavily. He was gambling, too—poker with his old buddies at the base. He needed money. He came to us and we paid him for some information. Then the C.I.A. caught him. His case was similar to yours, you see. He was a private citizen. He hadn't broken any American laws. The agency didn't quite have the Turks in their pocket, as they do the Moroccans, so it would have been messy to try him openly in the Turkish courts—too much publicity. The other method was safer. Poor Sergeant Dixon had a nasty car accident one night. He'd been drinking, of course, and nobody was too surprised. The car went right off a bridge, fell about sixty meters. There wasn't much left of the sergeant to bury."

"It could actually have been an accident."

"He was drugged and force-fed whisky," Dimitry said crisply. "Our men were watching. The agency people loaded him into his car and drove him up to the bridge. They propped him behind the wheel and sent the car accelerating right for the guardrail.

"Can't you see that you're in exactly the same position as Sergeant Dixon? If they think you've screwed up on this deal and are untrustworthy, then you're worth more to them dead than alive. Don't kid yourself about them, Joe. They can be cold-blooded and ruthless."

"But the K.G.B. does the same thing." Joe had spoken without thinking. He sat in silent fear as his words echoed in his head.

Dimitry did not hesitate. "When we have to, we act with equal determination," he said. "The point is, we don't hide behind any screen of moral superiority. There's a lot of talk about 'détente.' But in reality we're at war with a decadent, imperialist enemy. And war is a nasty business. . . ."

"I've noticed," Joe said sarcastically.

"The difference is," Dimitry continued, "and this difference is important in your case, that you will be worth more to *us* alive than dead. We get occasional native-born American defectors, but they're usually pretty mediocre material, army deserters, undisciplined young fools who call themselves Communists . . . clowns like Oswald. You're a professional journalist. Besides your native English, you're fluent in French, and your Spanish is good. Our overseas information program could use a man like you. *They* can offer you a choice of jail, if you're lucky, or maybe a flunky job running a yacht as a courier boat. *We* can set you up with your own office and apartment and a decent salary. The work will be interesting and honorable; no more sneaking around and lying. The job could involve the press magazines, even cinema. There'd be a lot of travel, too . . . not just Cuba—Berlin, Bucharest, Prague. . . . Doesn't that appeal to you?"

"It sounds better than being dead or in jail," Joe said.

"It's a hell of a lot better. In a socialist country, men with demanding, responsible positions are rewarded for their work. It makes me laugh every time I read in *Time* about the harsh living conditions in Cuba and Eastern Europe."

Dimitry silently mused for a moment, as if savoring the memory of some pleasant encounter in Warsaw or Havana. Then he got up quickly and looked at his watch. "It's almost a quarter to eleven. You'd better get going. Remember this one thing: if the tape reels are still out in the open, make that telephone call. We'll take care of the rest. And I'll see you back at the Tangier post office the day after tomorrow. Good luck."

His handshake was firm. He smiled warmly and Joe smiled back. Joe was halfway to the door of Dimitry's apartment. "Oh, Joe," Dimitry called. Joe stopped and turned to face him. "There's one small point I'd like to emphasize." All the friendly warmth left Dimitry's face. "You still seem a bit confused and bothered by this business. A person in that state of mind is often tempted to run for cover, to bug out of the whole thing. I wouldn't advise you to try that, Joe. You're not in this alone, you know."

Joe frowned.

"My government considers this a vitally important military matter, Joe," Dimitry said slowly in the same cold tones. "*I* consider it important, as well. I like my job, and I don't want to lose it. I wasn't just talking last night when I said we were watching Mrs. O'Brien very closely. If you break down and talk to Colonel Voight, *she* will be the one who pays for your weakness. And don't get any bright ideas about getting her inside the embassy for protection. Her son, Thomas, is in Spain at that military vacation camp. *We* have people in Spain, too, Joe. If we couldn't get to her, we could get to her child."

Joe unlocked the front door and stepped cautiously into the entrance hall. He threw his dusty sunglasses on the telephone table and dropped his overnight bag to the floor. With the shutters closed, it was hard for his eyes to adjust to the dimness, especially after three hours on the sun-blasted highway. He needed a cold drink, a beer.

"Hi," Roy said, stepping through the doorway to the living room.

"Who's that?" Joe asked, squinting.

"It's me," Roy said. "You're back early. How'd it go?"

Now the whole business begins, Joe thought dully. *Now I follow the new plan. If I don't, Dimitry kills Renée and Tommy. Think, listen to each question before answering.*

"Just like you said, no sweat. I finished up sooner than I expected, so I came right back, the way the colonel wanted. Any beer in the fridge?"

"Yeah, tons."

"Well, I need a beer and a shower and a change of clothes. They've got the road all torn up north of Larache. I've been eating dust for an hour."

"Fine," Roy said. "Kind of shake a leg, though, would you? The colonel will want to see you right away."

Joe walked through to the kitchen and took a can of beer from the refrigerator. In the bathroom he threw his dusty clothes in a heap and was about to enter the shower when Roy called through the half-open door.

"Oh, yeah, I almost forgot—the phone's been ringing all morning. It stopped around noon and then an Arab kid on a bike came up and stuck this note under the door. It's in a yacht club envelope."

Joe tore open the envelope and read the note. "It's about the goddamned boat regatta this weekend. I was supposed to take part in it. They want me to call them to confirm my place."

"You'd better call them, then, Joe. No sense in having people wondering where you are."

Joe let the panic run through him as he stood naked before the hissing shower stall. "Yeah, you're right," he said. "I'll call when I'm dressed."

His hair combed back and still dripping from the shower, he stood at the telephone table, holding the receiver and the note in his left hand as he dialed with his right. Roy stood watching him from inside the living room. Glancing down at the note, he dialed five of the telephone number's six digits and quickly put the receiver to his ear. There was a popping buzz and then silence. He shifted his weight on his feet and tried to stare blankly at the wall. After what seemed a suitable pause, he put the receiver down. "No answer," he said. "They must still be at lunch. I'll call them later."

"All right," Roy said. "You'd better go up and see the colonel now."

Joe walked slowly out through the kitchen and down the terrace steps into the garden. His palms were sweating badly, but he suppressed the urge to wipe them dry.

"That sounds fine, Joe. That sounds very good." The

colonel was smiling. He sat in a folding chair against the garage wall and smiled up at him.

Willing his fingers not to tremble, Joe lit a cigarette and smiled back at the colonel. The report on his Rabat trip had gone much better than he had hoped.

"Say"—the colonel pointed with his pipe—"what happened to your ear?"

Joe felt the blood drain from his face. Dimitry hadn't briefed him on this. He stammered, holding up his cigarette. "I hit a bump on the way down and my cigarette came flying back in the wind right into my ear. Gave me a nasty burn."

The colonel seemed to be staring at him for a long time, but Joe convinced himself that it was only his imagination.

"Excuse me a second, would you, Colonel?" The shorter of the two engineers in the garage stepped past them and called up the ladder through the trapdoor. "We've got miles of extra cable down at this end, Don," he said, holding a bright yellow cable in his hand. "You get branched yet?"

"Just about," a voice floated down. "Hang on a sec, okay?"

"George's fuse box will never be the same again," the colonel chuckled. "We'd better go upstairs, Joe, and give them some room. It's kind of crowded when all four of them are in here."

Joe glanced around the room, taking in the new recorders and the snaking cables. The two gray-black data reels had been mounted on what looked like the front plate of a computer chassis. Different colored wires fed from the device to a similar machine on the workbench. The other engineer in the garage was soldering a jack plug to a wire.

"How's it going?" Joe asked, nodding toward the recorders.

"Pretty well," the colonel grunted. "I'm glad our friend in Rabat agreed to delay, though. It's taken us the better part of a day to get this stuff set up and tested. The actual recording shouldn't take all that long. Hopefully, we'll have it all back in one piece by this time tomorrow."

He rose and pulled himself up the ladder. Joe followed, looking back over his shoulder for one last confirmation that the four tape reels were actually unprotected.

In George's kitchen Joe turned to the colonel and spoke. "I wanted to ask you about this phone call, colonel. Roy says that they've been calling all morning and that they finally sent a kid up with this note." He handed the envelope over to the colonel. "Is it okay to call them? What shall I say? They want me to take part in this boat regatta over the weekend."

The colonel chewed reflectively on his pipe, slowly reading the note. "Go ahead and call them, Joe. Just say that you're sorry, but you won't be able to make the regatta. Say you're being called away on business."

Joe plopped down into an armchair. "No sweat, Colonel," he said. "The regular club secretary wasn't there, so some French guy took the call. He said I'd have to forfeit the entrance fee, but that's okay. I never paid the fee, anyway."

It was strange being inside the tarpaulin-darkened room with the lights all lit when just outside the window the mid-summer sun was blinding white. The colonel looked tired again, a bit older, and crotchety, like an ornery night-court judge.

"I'm really surprised that Dimitry agreed so easily to the delay," he said.

Joe had spent three hours alone in the car rehearsing his answer. If he did not pass this first test, Renée and her son would die. He breathed easily before he spoke. "Well," he answered as coolly as he could, "he didn't actually say so, but I got the feeling that they still think Gessous is in the country and that maybe they could use the extra time to track him down and deal with him directly."

"Maybe," the colonel answered. "How's your ear feeling?"

Joe reached up involuntarily to touch the blister. "Much better, actually. I have some antibiotic salve in my bathroom. It took the sting right out."

They were silent for a moment. Outside, the house painters' air compressor was chugging. They looked at each other across the ten feet of carpeted living room. Neither spoke. Larry crossed the doorway, carrying the pigskin suitcase that held the main unit of the polygraph. He passed by the living room and entered the guest bedroom, where the cots had been set up. Joe felt his mouth go dry and the sweat begin to pool in his armpits.

It was then that he made his decision. He was getting out of this rotten business, all of it. The colonel could keep his sailboat in Greece, and Dimitry could go stuff all his luxury apartments in Havana and Prague. That was no way to live. It was simple. If they caught him, he would die. But if he got away, he would be free again.

Like a clairvoyant, the colonel nodded his head, almost in agreement with Joe's thoughts. "I'll have to ask you for your passport, Joe . . . your passport and your health card and all your other I.D. material. You'll get them back in a couple of days, after de-briefing. It's S.O.P., you know. We just don't have time right now for another interim de-briefing. You understand, don't you?"

"Is there anything wrong?" Joe asked with concern. It was suddenly so much easier to lie. Once the decision had been made, the lying became an automatic, reflexive action.

"No," the colonel said, yawning. "It's just that we're a little understaffed on this job, with Barent still gone. We don't have all the control we would like. Don't worry. I'll give you back all your papers in a couple of days. . . ." He stopped speaking and stared evenly into Joe's eyes. Joe handed over his Moroccan billfold and the colonel glanced briefly at its contents.

"I might need my driver's license on Saturday."

The colonel frowned and then yawned again. "Of course you will," he said, straightening in his chair. "Here," He handed back the billfold. "Take your license and your Moroccan I.D. card. Go on back home and get some rest. Tomorrow I'd like you to type up some notes on that curly-haired Russian. He's definitely one of their anti-sub boys from Mers-el-Kebir. That's all you'll have to do tomorrow. The rest of the day I want you to relax. Saturday's going to be pretty busy for all of us."

"Fine," Joe said. "That sounds good to me."

"Maybe I'll see you tonight," the colonel said. "Anyway, I'll send George down to keep you company. You can go out if you like. Where do you usually eat when you go out?"

"The Parade Bar."

"That's a good idea. You and George go downtown tonight and have a nice dinner. We don't want people to start asking questions about why you've dropped out of circulation."

25

Travaux Publics

Colonel Voight and Joe were both stretched out on their beds, both unsuccessfully trying to steal an afternoon's sleep, when the cocoa-brown Citroën pickup truck rounded the curve at the top of George's lane and rolled down toward the canvas shelter hiding the garage. Jammed into the front seat of the truck were three Arab workmen, dressed in blue workers' smocks and plastic hard hats. When the truck was opposite George's garage, it stopped and one of the workers got out to direct the backing up. The truck was backed off the pavement and over the edge of the short parking apron.

From the shadow of the scaffolding, one of the *pied noir* foremen strode out and began to berate the electrical workers in Maghrebi Arabic. "*Yah,* Mohammed!" he yelled. "You can't park that thing there! How are my supply trucks supposed to unload?"

The driver smiled sheepishly and tugged at his moustache. "*Yah, sidi,*" he answered, waving a paper. "We won't be long at all, I promise. In ten minutes, *Inshallah,* we'll be gone."

The foreman examined the work authorization from the Tangier office of Travaux Publics. It was stamped across with the word URGENT in red ink. There was no sense in arguing with the electrical workers. They would only go back downtown and complain to their boss and, the next thing, he would have some pompous Arab *monsieur* from the main office asking all kinds of questions.

"What kind of job do you have that's so urgent and

will only take ten minutes?" the foreman asked, smiling now. "I know you T.P. boys. The first thing you'll do is set up your teapot and lay out your sleeping mats. You'll be parked in my driveway through next Ramadan."

The workers laughed. "Up there, *sidi,*" the driver said, pointing at the wooden utility pole half set into the stone wall of the English villa. "There's a cracked insulator. That whore of a French countess up the hill isn't getting enough current. She's a great friend of the caliph, and she complained directly. The boss said we should change the part *tout de suite* and bring the old one right back to the *chantier* to prove that we've done the job. He doesn't trust us."

Again they all laughed. *"Ouahah,"* the foreman conceded. "Do you want my boys to give you a hand?"

"La, schugran," the driver answered. "We've done this before, you know."

The foreman frowned. "Are you Algerian?" he asked the driver.

"Me?" the driver answered, smiing again. "I was born in Fès, *sidi.*"

The foreman nodded, dismissing the electrical workers. He stood watching as they unloaded their ladders and equipment from the truck's roof rack. *Goddamned Algerians,* he thought. *They lie and steal their way to independence and then, when they've got it and can't find any work in their socialist paradise, they come sneaking across the border to bribe their way into jobs here. Travaux Publics, too. Well, they always say that the commies stick together.*

The foreman turned back to supervise his own men. He never noticed that the truck sagged heavily in the rear, despite the obviously reinforced leaf springs. He would never have guessed that inside there were hundreds of kilos of nickel-cadmium aircraft batteries and the heavy bulk of a portable X-ray unit.

"So, when do you think you'll be back?" George asked. He spooned some fresh cream onto his slice of apple pie and looked across the table at Joe.

It was quiet here at the rear of the Parade Bar garden. About half the candle-lit tables were filled with late diners and there was a boisterously happy drinking crowd inside the bar itself.

Joe had worked out this new deception carefully as he lay on his bed that afternoon. If his escape plan was going to work, George was the first one to convince. He sipped his coffee, shrugging his shoulders. "In about a month, I guess," he said. "I'll go with them to the States and help them with their reports. I'll probably spend some time in New York with my literary agent and then I'll head on back here."

"Maybe I'll see you in the States," George said.

"Really?"

"Yeah. The colonel suggested I take a little vacation when this deal is all over. He didn't actually promise anything, but he hinted that they might be able to find a position for me."

Joe looked down at the pooling wax of the candle. He watched his hand pour the remainder of his brandy into his coffee. "Is that so? Well, how does that appeal to you?"

"Depends on the job, of course," George said. He seemed to have developed a surprising new sense of confidence and directness since the colonel had come into his life. "These last few days have been good for me. I like the way I've been able to work with them."

"It hasn't been too much of a drag, ripping your house up that way and invading your privacy?"

"I've enjoyed it. There're a lot of things going on that I don't follow, but that's understandable. That colonel explained the need-to-know principle to me, and it makes good sense. Maybe on the next deal *I* will be on the inside and actually know what's going on."

Joe began to sigh, but he forced himself to yawn, instead. "I've got to get some sleep," he said. "Let's get the bill and go home."

"You don't mind my sleeping up at your place?" George asked for the third time. "I can take one of the sleeping bags."

"I don't mind at all. Besides, that's what the colonel wants, so we're better off going along with him, aren't we?"

The waiter arrived at the table and George paid the

bill. He left his billfold conspicuously on the table. "Funny, Colonel Richards hasn't paid you anything yet."

"Only expense money, and not much of that. I'm just about flat-broke again."

"Listen," George said, "I went to the bank this morning. I've got pretty near fifteen hundred bucks in French *francs*. Would you like another thousand? That'll make it an even three, and you can pay me back when they pay you."

"That'd help a lot. I want to leave some money for Ali, and I'd like to arrange to have the boat slipped if I don't make it back before the end of the season. I hate to have to ask the colonel."

"No, don't do that. Take the extra thousand and pay me back in the States. I'm sure I'll be seeing you there."

They rose and walked out to the car, nodding to the Parade regulars who called out greetings from their tables.

George signaled for a left turn at the Place de France.

There's no sense in stalling, Joe thought. *I've got the money now. I've got to get the boat ready sometime. . . . It may as well be now.* "Hey," he said suddenly, "I almost forgot. How about going down to the yacht club for a minute? I want to ask Delambre to move the boat to a better mooring. He's hard to get on the phone, and I'll be kind of busy in the morning."

"Okay. We can have a nightcap there."

Joe looked down at the heavy Frenchman, trying to mask his contempt. Getting Delambre to stock the boat would be the easiest part of the escape plan. That man would sell his mother for the right price.

"Oui, Monsieur." Delambre glanced down at the crisp French bank notes on his desk. "I've made a note. I'll have everything ready in the morning."

"Make sure to strain the diesel fuel," Joe said softly. The door of Delambre's office was ajar. Out in the barroom there was a wave of laughter. Several tipsy French voices were crooning some raunchy lyrics. Joe glanced over his shoulder and saw George seated at the rattan bar with a glass of whisky. He was beaming down at a pretty, suntanned girl from Gibraltar. The regatta gang had already begun to arrive in Tangier and were making the most of the club's hospitality.

"Have Mohammed buy some new plastic jerry cans for the extra water, too," Joe added. "I'm not fussy about the provisions. Just tell Madame Dangy that you want canned food for two people for twelve days. She'll know what we need. She's done boat-provisioning before. . . . Oh, yes, when Mohammed's in town picking up the food, he can buy a new chamois to strain the fuel. He should drain and clean the injector pump, as well. Make a note of that, please."

Delambre scratched another note on his pad. "Will there be anything else?"

Joe stood for a moment, looking down at the pudgy Frenchman. "Yes." He peeled off two more hundred-*franc* notes from the stack inside his sportcoat pocket. "I'd like to ask for your discretion. The lady I'll be sailing with is *married*. You understand? It would be rather embarrassing if our cruise together became common knowledge." He slipped the two bank notes under the edge of Delambre's blotter.

Delambre smiled. "Of course," he whispered, "*bien sûr.*"

Joe continued, "I'm being so frank because there is a divorce pending and she might be followed. There is a question about custody of the children. However, I will be marrying this lady once her divorce is final, and she comes from a very good New England family. She's in a position to be very generous, you see."

Delambre nodded.

"Could I ask you," Joe said softly, "to make sure that Mohammed uses equal discretion when he loads the boat? As for any inquiries by Americans about my plans for the boat, I think I can trust your discretion."

"There will be absolutely no problem, Monsieur Clinton. Mohammed will be quite busy for the next two days loading supplies aboard the regatta boats. I'll have him put the *Dragonfly* on an end mooring and only load it after dark. Anyone watching will think that he is carrying supplies for the other boats. You have my word that I will handle any other inquiries with complete discretion."

Delambre scooped up the money from his desk. "Would you like receipts for the fuel and provisions? There'll be some change, as well, although it will probably be in Moroccan *dirhams*."

"No," Joe said. "Give Mohammed a tip and keep the rest yourself. You've been very helpful to me, and I haven't been in a position recently to show my gratitude."

"You're very generous, Monsieur."

26

The Course South

Joe awoke suddenly. There had been a noise outside his bedroom door. From the angle of the sun on the wall, he knew that it was late. He had drunk enough the night before to make him sleep. The Valium had helped, too. It had been a long, restful sleep, with no dreams, until now. . . . He had been dreaming of Renée when the noise woke him up.

In the illogical simplicity of the dream, Renée and he had been making love in the comfortable cabin of an eighteen-meter ketch, moored in Nice. But the cabin had actually been low and cramped, smelling of bilge and diesel fuel, *Dragonfly*'s cabin, and the bunk had been sand, a beach. Renée had been smiling up at him. "How *wonderful* for us, Joe . . . what a wonderful new job."

That was all he could remember. He closed his eyes tightly. He had to sleep again to recapture the dream and discover Renée's wonderful secret. There had been a job, something good, a chance for them to have a life together.

"Come on," George said, shaking Joe's shoulder gently. "It's past eleven."

Joe sat up in bed and took the cup of coffee George offered him. George was dressed and shaved and seemed excited.

"Take a look," he said, pulling back the drapes. "They're gone—scaffolds, tarps, everything."

Joe put on his robe and went to the window. Past the line of cypress trees he could see the newly painted white expanse of George's back wall. There was no trace of the equipment or workmen.

The dream drained away from his thoughts, irreversibly. There would be no life with Renée. They would never make love in that tangled bed again, or on an empty beach with the moon reflecting on the sand. He swallowed.

"They must have started at dawn," George added. "I went up a little while ago. Everything's back in its place. They even laid my tools back out on the workbench just where I'd left them. All the new wires are gone. It's weird, Joe. You'd never guess that they'd been here. Those guys are incredible."

Joe nodded in agreement. "They're all gone, huh? Silently folded their tents and stole away?" This was an unexpected, interesting change. "Did they leave word where I can reach them?"

"Not a word," George said. "I'm sure Roy knows, though."

Joe sucked in his breath. "Roy?"

"He's in the kitchen, making breakfast. He asked me to find out if scrambled eggs are okay with you."

"Yeah," Joe sighed, "scrambled eggs are fine."

Roy was stretched out on the living room sofa, reading a paperback copy of Churchill's war memoirs. George had left an hour before to keep a tennis date. From the bookcase at the end of the room, Joe slipped out a bulky folder of Atlantic Ocean coastal charts and laid it silently against the wall of the entrance hall outside the door. Roy was deeply engrossed in his book and did not look up. Joe walked to the middle of the room and stopped to take a cigarette from the coffee table. He tugged at the belt of his robe.

"Christ," he said, "it's going on five o'clock and I'm not even dressed yet. The colonel told me to relax today, but this is carrying things too far."

Roy looked up, smiling. "Did you finish up those notes he wanted?"

"They're in the bedroom. I took out the typewriter ribbon like you said, too. They're all together, the notes and the ribbon, inside a manila envelope next to the bed."

Roy nodded and looked at his watch. "Fine. The cab'll be here in an hour. Why don't you start to get cleaned up?"

"Yeah. I think I'll soak in the bathtub for a while. Give me a shout if I fall asleep."

Joe was halfway to the door when Roy called him.

"Hey, do me a favor, okay? Flip the tape over."

Joe went to the machine and removed the thick, eight-track tape cartridge. Turning it to side one, he re-inserted it into the maw of the machine. For almost four days the same monotonous Tijuana Brass band had been playing over and over.

He locked the bathroom door and turned on the hot and cold taps of the bathtub, then sat down on the edge of the tub and spread the charts out before him on the tile floor. Using one of Renée's forgotten eyebrow pencils, he made some quick calculations on a scrap of legal pad. *Food and water for two people eating for twelve days . . . so, actual food and water for one person for almost a month. Forty gallons of fuel at half a gallon an hour . . . eighty hours of powering, enough to clear the Straits and be well out to sea, even if the wind and tide are against me. . . . And then what? Where do I go once I'm clear of the coast and out to sea?*

He dug into the bundle and removed the small-scale chart showing the African coast from Cape Spartel to Cape Verde and Dakar.

Over a thousand miles down there—Morocco, Spanish Sahara, Mauritania, Senegal . . . thirty days' sailing, minimum of thirty days, with no safe ports between here and Dakar. I'd stick out like a sore thumb in Spanish Sahara or Mauritania, but at least there are yachts in Senegal. I could run a French flag and slip into some cove. They'd never be looking for me that far south. They'll think that I've headed north or into the Med. But what the hell do I do once I'm ashore in Senegal? I'll be a white man with no passport. That's not as bad as it sounds, really. I'll have the boat registration, at least. And I'd be surprised if I couldn't find some Lebanese merchant who'd fix me up with a new passport for a couple hundred bucks. And then what? I can dump the boat for a thousand or so down in Dakar. Hell, the engine alone's worth more than that. . . .

Joe sat back, drumming his fingers against his thigh. He stared down at the huge chunk of the African continent etched onto the paper of the chart. It was a crazy scheme, but he did not have any alternative. All he had to do was sail down that long, desert coast until his food and water gave out and then come ashore. There were books on board. There was the radio, as well. The weather was no problem at this time of year. It would be hot, but there would be rain once he was south of Mauritania. That should help to stretch the drinking water. He just might be able to pull it off.

But it was a long trip, more than a thousand miles of ocean to sail alone. His only knowledge of offshore seamanship came from the charts and cruising books he had acquired when he bought *Dragonfly* at the auction. The old Englishman had been a competent sailor and an avid collector of charts and manuals. They were all he had to work with. They would have to suffice.

After carefully folding the charts back into their waterproof wrapper, he placed them next to the bathroom door. In ten minutes he was bathed and shaved. On his way back to the living room, he slipped the charts back against the bookcase. Roy was still absorbed in his book.

27

The El Minzah

Taxi number sixty-seven was a reasonably new and well-maintained Seat four-door, driven by Mustapha, a smiling, older man wearing a soft felt *tarboosh.* He had declined with a *"No, muchas gracias, señor"* to Joe's offered cigarette. Depsite Mustapha's graciousness, Joe knew that the man's assignment was to deliver him from the house to the El Minzah Hotel, just as a prison warder escorts a defendant from his cell to the courtroom.

The rue de la Liberté was filling with evening strollers as they stopped before the Moorish-modern front of the El Minzah. One of the bellhops, in brocade jacket and Thousand-and-One-Nights trousers, leaped to open Joe's door. Larry was standing in the entrance of the expensive souvenir gallery to the right of the hotel's entrance. He was decked out in tourist uniform and dark, wrap-around sunglasses. He seemed absorbed in examining the cut-alabaster ashtrays displayed in the window. Mustapha had not yet moved his taxi, but sat double-parked with his motor running, making a show of replacing coins in the change dispenser. Joe had no choice but to enter the hotel. He walked through the crowd in the lobby and down the stairs to the beautifully tiled courtyard. A fountain was splashing in the center. It was shadowy and cool. It would have been pleasant to sit there for a moment and not think about anything. But the colonel's orders had been specific.

Joe sat alone at one of the white metal tables on the edge of the terrace and watched the young people around the swimming pool. An English girl was lying on a mat at the extreme end of the garden, where the last of the afternoon sun had cut out a yellow rectangle in the shade. She reached behind her back to re-snap her bikini halter and then rose and dove into the pool in one smooth movement. An Arab waiter in the same kind of Thousand-and-One-Nights costume worn by the bellhop brought Joe his gin-and-tonic, and then, just as he left, Joe noticed Larry come out onto the terrace. He was opening a fresh pack of cigarettes. As he pulled out the foil covering paper from inside the pack, it slipped from his fingers and settled next to Joe's chair. Larry bent to pick it up.

"Finish your drink," he whispered, almost without moving his lips. "Three-twenty-eight. Take the elevator to the fourth floor and then walk down one flight."

Larry rose and wandered down to the end of the garden to take a picture of the sunlight against the stucco walls and tile roof of the hotel.

The elevator door closed behind Joe. He was alone in the softly lit corridor on the fourth floor. Far away, to his right, at the end of the corridor, he saw the glowing red fire lamp marking the staircase down. The rubber matting under his feet deadened his footsteps. It would have been good to stay there, perhaps to find a maid's linen closet and just curl up on a pile of freshly pressed sheets and wake up in the morning and it would be all over. He did not want to face the colonel.

All afternoon the dread he now felt choking off his breath had been building up. If the colonel had changed his mind and decided to hold one last session with the polygraph, then Joe was dead. Even without the lie detector, his nerves were so frayed that his façade of calmness could easily flake away and he would break down and confess the entire sordid business. But he had no choice. Down in the lobby, Rawlings or Larry would be blocking the way. Mustapha was sure to be waiting on the sidewalk. He hated it, but there was no other way. He must see the colonel.

"Come in, Joe," the colonel said. He was smiling. His silk pajamas and well-cut dressing gown gave him an even greater paternal aura than usual. The hastily made bed and the tiny fleck of shaving cream just behind the colonel's ear suggested a relaxed afternoon nap and a leisurely pre-dinner bath.

They were alone in the room. There was no sign of the leather polygraph case. Joe smiled back.

"Help yourself to a drink," the colonel said, walking across to the night table to switch on the transistor radio. Nasal yeh-yeh rock filled the room unpleasantly. It was quickly replaced by the sad lament of a Portuguese *fado*. "How are you doing? Did you get any rest?"

"I'm okay, I guess . . . a little jumpy, but I suppose that's natural. George and I had a nice dinner last night and then went down to the yacht club for a couple of drinks. We got back after midnight and I slept until eleven this morning."

"Good." The colonel nodded. "Were you able to type up that report?"

"Roy's got it back at the house."

"Fine. Is there enough ice? I can always call down for some more."

"No, there's plenty."

The *fado* singer held their attention for a moment. Through the room's open window, they could hear laughter and splashing rising up from the pool, three floors below.

"How jumpy is 'a little jumpy'?" The Colonel's words were soft-spoken, concerned.

Tell him, tell him the whole thing. There's still time. They can get Renée out to the embassy . . . but what about Tommy? No, just follow the plan. . . . What plan? Whose plan? Try to relax. He doesn't know anything. Smile.

Joe smiled. "I'll be okay. It's just that this last week has been crazy. I'll be happy when it's all over . . . but, at the same time, I'm afraid to face Dimitry tomorrow."

Working slowly, the colonel began his pipe-filling exercise. "Do you have any particular reason to be afraid of Dimitry?"

"No." Joe had spoken too quickly. He caught himself and forced his speech to continue at a slower, almost halting, pace. "It's just that, well . . . we're pulling a pretty nasty trick on him, aren't we? If . . . if he ever got wind of it, he'd be furious. He'd want to get even. Don't get me wrong when I say this, but both you and Dimitry are in the same business. I know the agency doesn't run labor camps and fake insane asylums, the way the K.G.B. does, but, face it, you and Dimitry are both colonels. . . ."

"How do you happen to know Dimitry's rank, Joe?"

"I don't . . . not really. I only guessed. Call it an educated guess. But the way he had old Zinchenko hopping around, I figured he must be the equivalent of their station chief, at least a lieutenant colonel."

"Please continue," Colonel Voight said coldly.

"Okay." Joe sat up straight and spoke rapidly. "The guy's like a machine. I've seen him twice, three times, now, and I still can't get used to his English, his *American* English. It's too perfect. I keep getting the feeling that he's some kind of an American defector—that he was raised in the States and then went over to the Russians. He couldn't have learned all that in some fancy intelligence school."

Colonel Voight smiled wryly. He seemed to relax a bit. "You'd be surprised what a smart, well-motivated officer can be taught," he said. "When you're back in the States I'll give you Dimitry's file. I'll ask you to write up a bio-critique as a training exercise. I think that file will answer a lot of questions. He is not any kind of superman or science-fiction machine. He's a thirty-eight-year-old colonel in the K.G.B. and has twenty-two years' training and experience behind him. When he was sixteen he had the equivalent of a B.A. in European languages and political economics. Then he had to pass an exam, a very special exam. For the next *seven* years he did nothing but study English, French, and Arabic. Do you realize that he spent two years in Chevy Chase High School? They pawned him off as the stepson of one of their military attachés in Washington. He's always looked young for his age, and at eighteen he could pass for a kid two years younger. He used to drive around the suburbs in a Nash Rambler convertible, watching Frankenstein movies at the drive-in movies and eating hamburgers and French fries.

"A couple of years later, he showed up under another name as the visiting nephew of the Soviet first secretary in Paris. It took him three years to complete the five-year Arabic language *licence* at the Sorbonne. After all that, he served in the military, an airborne reconnaissance battalion—like our Rangers. Don't get me wrong—he's good, damned good, but there's been a lot of time and money invested in making him that good."

Joe nodded. He was remembering the face of the Israeli pilot on the clinic wall.

"In training," the colonel said mellowly, "you'll meet agency officers who are every bit as competent as Dimitry, men who have driven all over Eastern Europe, speaking German with such good *Hungarian* accents that they used to get put up in the guest quarters of the Hungarian embassies in Berlin and Bucharest. There's a black gal who learned her Congolese languages so well that she even fooled the old, blind chief of her supposed native village. I could go on all night. The point is, Dimitry is not that special. There's no reason to be afraid of him—wary, yes, cautious, naturally, but not afraid. Do you understand?"

"Yes," Joe said. "I understand a lot better now."

The colonel smiled. "You meet Dimitry at four tomorrow afternoon. The time couldn't be better for surveillance. It's the middle of siesta and the streets will be empty. We'll have you under observation all the way out to the farm."

The colonel shook his head in answer to Joe's unspoken question. "No, don't worry. We won't actually be following you. We'll have men posted along the route. The two gendarmes who'll be at the roadblock are both dependable, well-trained men. They're officers in Moroccan military intelligence. They have radios on their motorcycles, and there'll be two fast cars, with equally dependable men, waiting no more than three minutes away. I'm sure that Dimitry will not want to drive back into the city once he's got the buoy. He'll probably cut over to the side road and join the main route south to Rabat. All you have to do is drive back into town. The gendarmes will be watching for you. If you feel you're in any danger, pull over and get out and check one of your tires. If they see that, they'll call in an alert and we'll put a tail on you. Can you remember that?"

Joe nodded. "Thanks," he said. "You seem to have everything figured out pretty well."

"That's not all, Joe," the colonel said. He lit his pipe and sat back in his chair. "We won't actually have a car following you unless you've called for help through the gendarmes. But we will have people watching for you on the route in. Let's go over that route now, shall we?"

The colonel spread out a tourist map of Tangier on the bedspread and they both squatted down next to the bed to look at it. A red felt pen had been used to draw Joe's route back into the city.

"You come right back in on the airport road to Avenue San Francisco, all right?"

Joe nodded.

"Okay." The colonel made a flourish with his pipe stem. "You turn left on Sidi Bouhari and head out toward the mountain. By the time you get to the bottom of the valley, you'll have gone through three of our checkpoints. If you've been followed, we'll know it by then. Just to be on the safe side, I want you to turn *left* here"—he pointed again with his pipe—"and go up past the Christian cemetery. Keep going all the way up, past the small mosque at the top of the new mountain. Stop for a paper at the *baccal* just past the Place du Khaddi. You know the one I mean?"

"It belongs to the Soussi with the son who's blind."

"That's right. If there's anything wrong and you shouldn't continue, we'll get word to you at the *baccal*. From there"—the colonel tapped the map again—"you turn right and come straight down this long lane, stop for a minute at George's house, then drive right to your own front door. It's an easy setup. Your house is in an excellent position. There are only two routes to it. We can observe all the traffic coming from either below or above without being observed ourselves. Once you're home, you'll be completely safe. My guess is that Dimitry won't try anything until late at night. By then we'll have picked you up and we'll be on our way."

Joe lit a cigarette and stared down at the red line on the map. "It looks pretty foolproof," he said, trying to put some enthusiasm into his voice.

"Do you have any questions, Joe?"

Joe shook his head. "No. Frankly, this whole plan is kind of . . . well . . . unreal feeling. Do you know what I mean? You read about things like this in spy stories and they always seem logical, but doing this myself seems weird, unreal. . . ."

"Take my word for it," the colonel said mellowly, "I've used this system more times than I care to remember, and it's never let me down. If I thought that you were going to be in any danger tomorrow, I'd call the whole thing off. I'm convinced that we've built up the most effective shield we can and have kept ourselves completely covered at the same time. Believe me, I'm not very enamored with the James Bond foolishness we went through this evening—the taxi down and getting my room number from Larry out by the pool—but there are times when these techniques are necessary. I've been careful on this operation, and I think it's paid off."

Joe returned the colonel's confident smile.

"There's one more small detail," the colonel said, becoming crisply serious again.

Joe felt his gut tighten. "Yes?" he asked softly.

The colonel rose and walked to the carved door of the closet. The sweat began to run down Joe's chest. *The polygraph will be inside the closet.* He felt sick inside.

The colonel opened the closet and removed a pastel lime sportcoat and a rust-orange straw hat. "I assume that Dimitry will stick to his American tourist costume tomorrow, so I want you to wear these. Carry a camera case over your shoulder, too. To any observer, you'll look like a couple of guys off a cruise ship. Here, try them on for size."

Joe slipped into the jacket and placed the hat on his head. It felt ridiculous to wear a hat again after so many years.

"Perfect. You look just like an appliance salesman from Cincinnati."

Joe joined in the laughter as he looked at his reflection in the full-length mirror.

"There's another reason for the coat and hat," the colonel added. "By the time you complete your phone call to the Swiss bank, get the telegram from Gessous, and drive out to the farm, it may be getting dark. It could be around six-thirty when you drive back. The green coat and orange hat will show up well in the twilight. Our men watching for you are going to be off the road, and we want to give them an easily recognizable subject, don't we?"

Joe nodded.

"Take a look down there," the colonel said, pointing out the open window. "Do you see the way the browns and blues all blend into gray in the twilight? But look at that girl with the yellow beach wrapper. See how the brighter colors stand out?"

"Yeah," Joe said, "I see what you mean."

The colonel reached for his drink. "It's a beautiful place, Tangier. I was here years ago, the winter after Pearl Harbor, actually." He held out his glass without speaking and Joe took it for a refill. "It was much more of an Arab-Spanish town then. I was a young-buck first lieutenant in the O.S.S. . . ." He accepted his fresh drink with a smile. "You know, I sometimes wish I could write a book of memoirs. I might try it when I retire. It would have to be classified, of course, but perhaps in a few years they could release it for publication."

Joe listened, with a respectful smile fixed on his face. Inside he was wary, tense. The colonel had relaxed with almost identical mellowness on the morning of the lie-detector test, just before they had all turned on him. He would not let himself be caught that way again.

"I've seen this business change a lot," the colonel went on. "In those days *people,* agents, were the important thing. Now it's all *machines,* like that listening buoy. Do you know what my job was here that spring in Tangier? I had to make contact with a certain Vichy artillery captain in Algeria and bribe him to delay the shipment of some anti-aircraft guns from Constantine to Casablanca. That was all. It took me damned near three months to get the job done, too. We were getting tooled up for the north African landings, you see, and those flak guns were considered pivotal to our plans." He shook his head. "What a circus this place was then. I worked out of the old legation building down in the Medina. There were about ten of us young studs, all with vice-consul titles. But everybody knew we were O.S.S. The Germans and the Italians had even more people. We used to sit at adjoining tables in the Socco Chicco cafés and glare at each other. There were more spies in this town than there were prostitutes, and there were quite a few of them, although I'd guess half the girls were agents for somebody. . . ."

They laughed again. The *fado* music had ended and was followed by a Beethoven symphony.

"All that's changed now. The machines have taken over. Until you started this business with the buoy, there wasn't a single agent in Tangier. Did you know that?"

Joe shook his head.

"That's right," the colonel said. "Who needs people when you've got satellites and computers and hardware like that buoy to play with? It's ironic, actually. I started my career here, and I'll be ending it up here, as well. This'll probably be my last overseas job. I doubt if the doctors will check me out for another one. They seem to think that there's something wrong with the way my heart beats." He tapped his chest. "Feels fine to me, but you can't fight city hall."

Joe tried to think of an appropriate reply, but he could only nod his head with polite deference.

"They've got me slotted for a training assignment, and, quite frankly, I'm pleased. It'll mean regular hours for the first time in years. I'll even have weekends off to spend with my wife and grandchildren. The only thing I wonder about is my own ability to prepare youngsters for the kind of work they'll be expected to do in the field. They're different, the kids we recruit these days. We used to get a lot of young service officers who were fed up with the military. Then for a while we got quite a few fellows with law degrees. These days, it seems they're all engineers. They practically have to be. I was on a selection board a little while back, and we had one boy who was actually proud of the fact that he'd made almost fifty thousand tax-free dollars engaging in industrial espionage for a large and supposedly respectable corporation. The agency hired him, practically over my dead body, but they did hire him."

Again, Joe could think of nothing to say in reply. The swimming noises from the pool had gradually given way to the subdued, but unmistakable, murmur of cocktail-hour conversation.

"The agency's a big organization, Joe," the colonel said. "I do hope, though, that they'll let me have the time to work with you and George during your training period—at least the part of it in the States. . . ."

"So, George really is coming in, as well?"

"You don't seem too surprised."

"Well, he implied as much last night. He told me that you had approached him about it."

"He's a good man—stable and dependable. Between you and me, I don't think he has the same flair or imagination that you have, but he's got a sound technical education and he's highly motivated. He *wants* to work with us."

"I suppose it'll be good for George, too. His life's been empty here. He's been at loose ends since his marriage broke up."

The colonel had his pipe set firmly in the corner of his mouth. He stared at Joe with his expression of paternal amusement, his gray-white eyebrows slightly raised. "You know, Joe, you sound like you might be describing your own experience. You've been at loose ends here. You've led an empty life, haven't you?"

The anger snapped hot and sharp inside Joe like a broken spring. With great determination he checked himself from speaking. *You old hypocrite,* he thought, *don't come on now with this concern about my welfare. I'm just a goddamned pawn to you. If I function well, I get a pat on the head. If I don't, then you'll slap me in jail and throw away the key.*

"I'm serious," the colonel said. "George'll be okay. He's stable, but a bit dull; let's face it. You are another person altogether. I'll be honest with you. You've gone through some shaky times these past couple of years. You've got scars. Well, in this business, that type of thing can almost be called an occupational hazard. Believe me, we've got some damned fine doctors working for us—not pansy, fifty-dollar-an-hour head-shrinkers, but serious, well-motivated men who specialize in cases very much like your own. You've already said that you're drinking far too much, that you've come to depend on marijuana and tranquilizers. I can guarantee you that three months from now you'll be over all that. You're not the only one who's had this happen to him. That's the main reason I'd like to be in on your training in the States, Joe. I'd like to see you get yourself squared away, get your self-confidence back. I may be wrong, but I think you need something more serious in your life than half-baked dreams about writing 'fiction.' You're a doer, an action man who needs to get himself involved."

Joe rose to refill their glasses. He really had nothing that was not sarcastic to say.

The colonel took his drink from Joe and held up the glass. "Here's to tomorrow, Joe. I have total confidence in your ability to complete this operation. As an indication of that confidence, you'll find that Roy has packed up and left when you get back home. You're on your own from now until tomorrow night in the movie house. Just try to relax. You know the plan inside out. You've got nothing to worry about. Dimitry won't try anything until late tomorrow night at the earliest. Most likely, he intends to invite you down to Rabat or Casa for a little chat in a day or so. Make no mistake, he'll be watching you closely, and we've got our people on alert."

"So what do you want me to do tonight?" Joe asked flatly.

"What do you feel like doing? What would you normally do?"

Joe made a face, as if he were actually thinking over the question. "Well," he said, after a suitable pause, "there's a dance at the yacht club tonight. Most of the regatta boats have arrived from Spain and Gibraltar. I suppose George and I would probably wander down there after dinner and just hang out."

"What does that mean, exactly?" The colonel's voice was suddenly professional again.

"We'd probably go down and see if there were any stray BEA stewardesses who've hitched rides over on Gib boats. The moon's just past full, and we might want to take them out for a sail. You know what I mean."

"No," the colonel said emphatically. "I'd rather you left the boat alone, Joe. You're under surveillance by Dimitry's people; they might get the wrong idea if they see you taking off in your sailboat. Go down there. Have a good time. That's excellent. But don't go off in your boat. What time do you think you might go to the club?"

"After dinner. The dance starts at nine, and we wouldn't want to show up too early."

"Why not?"

"Well . . ." Joe shrugged his shoulders, as if he were obliged to reveal some embarrassing truth about himself. "These British girls are a bit put off by all the married frogs who'll come on strong as soon as the dance begins. If we waltz in an hour or so later, our chances are a lot better. They'll have had something to compare us with."

There were sparks flying out of the colonel's pipe again. "And how does Mrs. O'Brien figure in all this?"

Joe frowned, genuinely confused by the colonel's words.

"What I mean, Joe, is . . . you did spend the night with her the day before yesterday, didn't you?"

"Yes, I did," Joe answered in the same flat voice.

"And tonight you'd just go and pick up another girl and sleep with her, too?"

"I suppose so."

There were more sparks and sweet, billowing clouds of smoke.

"Well," Joe said, "you did tell me to say my good-byes to Renée, didn't you?"

"If there are any girls tonight, you make damned good and sure that they're English and that you have them out of the house by nine tomorrow morning. Do you understand?"

Joe nodded. "Short and sweet," he said.

The colonel went to the dresser and glanced at his leather-bound travel alarm. It was obvious their interview had ended.

"Well," Joe said, placing his empty glass on the edge of the dresser, "I'll be off, then. Tomorrow I'll just hang around the house until it's time to go down and meet Dimitry. When will I see you again, colonel?"

"Tomorrow night," the colonel said, his voice professionally neutral again. "I'll see you about ten, after we pick you up in the cinema."

They shook hands and for a moment the colonel stared hard at Joe. Surprisingly, Joe found it easy to return the older's man's questioning gaze.

"Well," he allowed himself to say, "wish me luck . . . sir."

"Good luck, Joe. Try to relax tomorrow, and, remember, we're backing you up. Follow your plan and everything will be easy."

The door clicked shut behind him and Joe was padding down the rubber-carpeted corridor. He felt fresh and springy. He could almost taste his freedom. By this time the next day he would be on his way. Everything was going to be all right.

28

The Club

"Jesus Christ," George whispered. He shook his head again. They sat on the dew-wet cushions in *Dragonfly*'s cockpit. The colored bulbs and Japanese lanterns sparkled on the greasy water of the club moorings. Fifty yards away, on the clubhouse patio, the last round of a dancing competition was just winding up. Monsieur Delambre had done a good job of organization for the regatta.

He had also done very well for Joe. The *Dragonfly* was the first boat on the long line of moored yachts that stretched rail-to-rail to the inner end of the mooring basin. Leaving would present absolutely no problem. All Joe would have to do was slip his mooring warps and sail.

"Everything makes a lot more sense now, doesn't it?" Joe said.

George spoke with genuine admiration in his voice. "Those guys are amazing. What a fantastic trick. Jesus. And they got the whole thing set up and organized in just a couple of days. How did you, well, how did you react when they said that they wanted you to contact the Russians?"

Make it good. It's important that he believe this. If George starts acting funny now, Voight will notice.

There was no one aboard the big Spanish cutter moored next to them, but Joe still chose to answer in a barely audible whisper. "Well, I was scared at first, but then when I saw how professional the colonel was, I relaxed and began to enjoy it."

"And that's what you were doing down in Rabat, contacting the Russians?"

Joe nodded, trying to produce a confident smile.

"Fantastic," George said.

"I meet this guy Dimitry at four tomorrow and we call the Swiss bank. Afterward, we drive out to the farm and he gets the buoy. I've got a rendezvous with the colonel later that night. I'll probably be back in the States in forty-eight hours. It's a pretty wild deal, isn't it?"

"It sure as hell is," George said. "What a beautiful double cross."

"What do you mean?" Joe asked coldly.

"On the Russians," George said. "They pay for the buoy, but the colonel's people have already gotten everything they need from it. It's beautiful."

Joe relaxed in the semi-darkness. He toyed with his can of beer. "George," he said, after a suitable pause, "the colonel will probably tell you himself about all this after the operation's over. So just keep it to yourself until he does, okay?"

"Of course."

"I wanted you to know, though," Joe added, "because you were in on it from the beginning, and you went out on a limb to help me. I figured you had a right to know the real story."

"Thanks, Joe. I appreciate that."

Once again Joe felt mild amazement at his ability to lie so naturally to someone he considered a close friend. His life would be so different when this insanity was over. Much more of this and he would begin believing the lies himself.

"You see now why the colonel asked you to stand by at your house tomorrow and watch for me?"

George nodded.

"Well, I've got a big favor to ask, George," Joe said, allowing his voice to rise above a whisper. "Ali and Zorah were back when I came up from my meeting with the colonel. It looks now like I probably won't be coming back to Morocco for a hell of a long time. I don't know what's going to happen to the house, or to them. I just don't have the heart to face them tomorrow afternoon. What I'd like to do is stop at your house and stay there until it's time for me to go down to the cinema. I'd like you to go down to my place and talk to Ali and Zorah. I'll have some money for them. Just tell them that I've suddenly been called away on business and that they should take care of the house . . . that I'll be sending them some more money. Will you do that for me, George?"

"Sure, I guess so. It doesn't quite square with the colonel's instructions, though."

"I know it doesn't," Joe said, adding the proper amount of anxiety to his tone. "I can't see any way around it, though. I'm worn out by all the tension I've been under the past few days. I'm just about living on Valium. Believe me, walking right into the Russian Embassy on orders from the C.I.A. took more guts that I thought I had. I'd feel a lot better about tomorrow if I knew that I didn't have a heavy emotional scene to face with Ali and Zorah when the whole thing is over. You've never let me down in the past, George; that's why I felt I could ask you. It doesn't screw up the colonel's plans. I wouldn't want to do it if it did. I'll still make my rendezvous with him down at the cinema."

George had obviously made his decision. "Don't worry. I understand exactly how you feel. I'll be glad to help you out."

Joe smiled in the half light. "Thanks, buddy," he said. "I appreciate that. Do you want another drink?"

"No," George said, looking at his watch. "We'd better head back home. It's late."

"You're right. Anyway, it looks like the frogs have all the decent-looking girls monopolized."

He took George's empty glass and ducked down into *Dragonfly*'s cabin to put it in the galley sink. With only the small battery lamp lit over the chart table, it was difficult to see the shapes lashed securely into the open lockers above the two bunks. He reached out and patted the bulging canvas bags of provisions and the cool sides of the extra plastic water cans. He snapped off the lamp and joined his friend in the cockpit. After carefully inserting the companionway boards, he pulled the hatch and locked it. The key felt secure in the pocket of his jeans.

29

Course Lines

Joe filled his plate with a second helping from the clay bowl of fish *tajine*. Zorah had risen early on her first full day back and had been at the fish market before seven o'clock. She had cooked the hefty chunk of turbot, marinated with lemons and coriander, slowly, until it was juicy and the flesh fell away from the bones. There was fresh bread, as well, the dark whole wheat that she knew Joe liked so much. Sometime during the morning of floor-washing, dusting, and cooking, she had also managed to make a chilled watercress salad dressed with capers and her own garlic-flavored vinegar. She had no way of knowing it, but she had prepared one of Joe's favorite lunches for his last meal in Morocco.

Joe allowed himself one more glass of rosé before replacing the cork in the bottle. There wasn't time for a leisurely, relaxing meal, nor was there time to sit here in his chair, chasing Renée's smiling dream-face through his consciousness, trying to freeze yesterday's dream, then let it roll forward so that he could learn the details of their new life. There would be no life with Renée. He must now try to forget her, like he had tried to forget Monique.

It was almost two o'clock, and in less than two hours he had to be down at the main post office to face Dimitry for their final meeting. Outside, bees were humming in the morning glories that had remained open, protected from the sun by the shadow of the house. *Christ,* he thought, *it's not easy to leave this place.*

But he *was* leaving. In about five hours he'd be at sea,

heading through the Straits and into the open Atlantic, alone in a small boat with over a thousand miles of water ahead of him before landfall.

In the living room he placed his wineglass on the edge of the coffee table and again opened the stiff chart folder. That old Englishman had been so thorough. He had outfitted *Dragonfly* with a set of charts covering every conceivable cruising ground he could reach from his retirement flat in Gibraltar. Joe picked up the admiralty hydrographic chart for the Atlantic from Gibraltar to Cape Verde, everything he needed to know about prevailing winds and currents for the month of August.

He ran his finger lazily down the line of his intended course. It couldn't have been better. The Canary current flowed with such dependability and the prevailing northerly winds seemed so reliable that the boat could practically *drift* down the African coast. With a fresh breeze behind him, *Dragonfly* would average over a hundred miles for a twenty-four-hour run. Even when he slept, with the sails furled and the bow held into the wind on a sea anchor, he would be moving steadily along in the desired southerly direction. With any luck, he should make the coast of Senegal in less than twenty days.

Joe carefully folded the chart into three vertical pleats and, using Monique's small sewing scissors, cut the paper along the folds. He folded the three separate sections once again so that the stiff, water-resistant paper nestled easily into the bottom of his camera case.

From the loose-leaf binder labeled Admiralty Lists–Radio Beacons, Joe removed the six-page section covering the coasts from Lisbon to Dakar. The pages fit easily on top of the chart sections in his camera case. He replaced the binder, still thick with other lists and updates, back on the bookshelf.

Joe looked down, satisfied. That's all he would need. He had already cut and folded the detailed chart for the coast of Senegal. There was a sextant on board, tucked away somewhere in the lockers with a Royal Navy manual on its use and a navigator's workbook. But Joe hoped, with these charts, he would not have to resort to celestial navigation. There were two good compasses on board, and the radio direction-finder was dependable and simple to use. The radio beacons from the lighthouses along the Sahara coast would carry far out to sea, especially during the hours of darkness. All he would have to do was to stay out in the Canary current, steer south-southeast, and try to get a nightly fix from the beacons. The hydrographic chart had noted that gale-force winds and seas were almost never encountered along his route in August.

He smiled. Two days before, the escape by sea alone in such a small boat had seemed a wild folly. Now he knew that it could be done. *Dragonfly* was a strong, light keelboat. Only a full ocean storm could capsize it, and even then it would right itself. He placed a specially cut rectangle of paper over the chart sections in the bottom of his case and laid the spare lenses of the Pentax on top of the paper. He laughed now, softly to himself. The colonel had been the one who had suggested he carry a camera when he met Dimitry.

So, Joe thought, *this part of it is over. Now for my little present for the good colonel and my dear friend Dimitry.* Joe opened the chart folder once more and removed four small-scale charts covering the western and central Mediterranean. Using a sanded piece of wood from the garden trellis as a straight edge, he began plotting out a strange zigzag course, east out of the Straits, then north toward the empty water below the Balearic Islands.

On the first chart he also scribbled a number of penciled notes, referring to compass courses and distances reduced to hours under way. Working steadily, with occasional nervous glances at his watch, he completed all four charts with course line and notes in less than forty minutes. Twice he had to sharpen the soft-leaded artist's pencil he was using. When he had finished, he laid the four charts side by side on the living room floor and gazed down at the crazy, dog-legged pencil line of the route, which stretched northeast from Tangier, then cut east and south again below Sardinia, gave Sicily a wide berth, and cut north again into the Adriatic. The line ended on the coast of Albania. He laughed again. It was beautiful. There was only one safe place in the whole Mediterranean for a man being chased by both the C.I.A. and the K.G.B. That was Albania.

He looked at his watch again. It was after three. He'd

have to hurry now. "Zorah!" he called. A moment later she emerged from the kitchen, wiping her hands on the tucked-in billows of her skirt. *"Kauwa,"* he said, *"s'il te plaît."*

She stood a moment, plump and fresh-faced, and then smiled. It was obviously a good sign when Monsieur wanted coffee instead of more wine. For a moment she glanced down at the confusing array of charts covered with the strange lines. Then she frowned. Ali had so often scolded her for telling little Mohammed that the world was flat. He had angrily reminded his young, city-bred wife that he, Ali, had traveled almost completely around the planet's sphere as a soldier in the French Army, and he could attest to the fact that the world was, indeed, round. But, now, here was Monsieur, who had traveled much more than Ali, and Monsieur was squatting, studying maps of an obviously flat world.

When Zorah came back from the kitchen with a mug of hot Nescafé, she frowned again. Now Monsieur was using a white rubber eraser, like the one Madame had once given Mohammed to play with. He was rubbing the eraser hard over the maps to remove all the lines he had just written on them. *Safi,* she thought, *the* ensara *are a strange people.*

Joe finished erasing the last chart and looked down once more at his handiwork. To the naked eye it was difficult to follow the tracing of the lines and notes. But the colonel or Dimitry, whoever got the charts first, would not be using instruments as primitive as the naked eye.

It was time to go. He must now put on the lime pastel sportcoat and silly orange straw hat, shoulder his camera case, and drive off to meet Dimitry. It was strange how calm he felt inside. There was nothing for him to worry about. Both Dimitry and the colonel wanted the delivery of the buoy to go off with set-piece smoothness. There was no way for things to go wrong. What Joe thought about as he strode across the fieldstone terrace was the sea. He could look down the side of the mountain, through the gap of the Jew's River Valley, and see the blue water of the Straits, flecked with an occasional whitecap. The wind was fair from the east. It was going to be a beautiful night for a sail.

30

The Delivery

The colonel had been right about the delay in calling Switzerland. Like so many other technical services in Morocco, the automatic-dialing lines from Tangier to the Continent were once more *en panne.*

"Well," said Dimitry, smiling at Joe, "we just have to wait a little while. You're in no hurry, are you?"

The barn-like marble hall of the main post office was echoing emptily at the height of the afternoon siesta. The colonel had been right about that, as well.

"We could just skip the call," Joe said softly. "Just go through the motions, in case they've got somebody watching."

"They do have somebody watching," Dimitry said in the same low tones, "and listening in to the phone lines, too. No, we wait for the call."

Dimitry walked back to the sleepy telephone clerk behind the varnished wooden counter. "You can do us a great service, my friend," he said in faultlessly accented French. He produced several folded ten-*dirham* notes. "Our call must go through in fifteen minutes; otherwise, it will be too late. Why don't you see if you can't find a free line for us."

The clerk snapped out of his lethargy. Expertly, he cuffed the money in his fist and slipped his hand unobtrusively into the pocket of his smock. *"Oui, M'sieu,"* he said, smiling, "I think I'll be able to help you."

Dimitry and Joe went to the worn benches near the main entrance. For the first time that afternoon, Joe was beginning to feel uneasy. Dimitry sat calmly on the bench and stared off at the chipped plaster of the mural map on the wall behind the main counters. They were alone in the hall with the telephone clerk.

"I could go around to the *poste restante* window and pick up the telegram," Joe said. He was pacing now in front of the bench.

"Sit down and try to relax," Dimitry answered calmly. "The plan calls for the telephone confirmation first and then the telegram. Relax. We've got plenty of time."

They sat side by side for several minutes, neither one speaking. It was painfully quiet in the big hall. Outside, the Avenue Mohammed V was equally empty and silent.

"That's a beautiful sportcoat," Dimitry said finally, with mock seriousness. "Was that one of your friend's brainstorms?"

Joe nodded.

"And the hat, too?" Dimitry asked, pointing down at the rust-orange straw hat in Joe's lap.

Joe found himself smiling with Dimitry. "Yeah," he said. "Voight thought that the green and the orange would be easier to see if I got delayed until dark. He figured that you'd be dressed up as an American tourist, too, so we'd look natural together."

Dimitry glanced down at his own fishnet shirt, dove-gray slacks, and, finally, at his sandals. He had also worn rimless, lightly tinted glasses for the meeting. With his suntan and close-cropped hair, he could easily pass for a French tourist, or even a *pied noir*. Again, Joe was impressed by the effectiveness of Dimitry's deceptively simple disguises. But it was not only the clothes—it was also the way Dimitry wore them, the manner in which he let the Gitane dangle from the corner of his mouth. He had *become* French, perhaps an engineer of the Assistance Technique, or a small businessman on vacation from Casablanca.

"One of the things people learn early in this line of work," Dimitry said, "is not to repeat successful gimmicks, not to fall into a pattern that can be predicted or traced. *Some* people learn the lesson; others never do. That was typical of your colonel—to guess that I'd dress like an American tourist. It's just like his using that shopworn house-painting business to cover up George Briggs' villa. I wish the Central Intelligence Agency had more people like Colonel Voight. It would make my work a lot easier."

Joe nodded solemnly, as if he were absorbing an important axiom.

"You say he's got your route back from the farm completely covered?"

"Yes. That's why he wanted me to wear clothes that showed up easily at dusk."

"Does he actually think I'd try any strong-arm business right here in Tangier?" Dimitry seemed slightly offended.

"Yes . . . " Joe hesitated. "He . . . he said that you'd try to 'get' me tonight."

Dimitry chuckled merrily, then sighed. "I see that he belongs to the dirty-commie-bastards school of thought," he said. "What amazes me is that he thinks I'd risk the diplomatic cover of my whole office by pulling something as risky as a kidnapping in broad daylight."

Joe remembered the midnight hypodermic in his "stalled" Land Rover. "No," he said, "he figured you'd wait until the middle of the night to try it."

"Well, that's more likely," Dimitry said, again smiling disarmingly. "Actually, if this were a normal operation, we would have recruited you for further work early in the game, so kidnapping wouldn't enter into the picture. Later on, you'll be given a number of case histories to read. You'll see that these operations are flexible, but they tend to follow some fairly rigid ground rules."

Dimitry stopped. A midde-aged Arab wearing a European suit and *tarboosh* had entered the post office. He carried a cardboard package under one arm. Without looking in their direction, he walked to the parcel counter and rang the bell to wake up the dozing clerk.

"Je vais voir combien de temps encore il faut attendre," Dimitry said, his cigarette bounding from his curled lip as he spoke. He rose and spoke to the telephone clerk. "How much longer?"

"Allons," he said, returning to the bench. *"Prenons un pôt au café en face. Toutes les lignes sont prises jusqu'a cinq heures-quart."* No free telephone lines until five-fifteen.

They walked out onto the broad concrete stairs of the post office, then across the empty avenue, where they took seats beneath the awning of the café. Dimitry brought the drowsy waiter quickly to his feet with a gruff burst of Maghrebi Arabic. A moment later the boy reappeared from inside the café with a bottle of Pernod, glasses, and a bowl of ice cubes. Dimitry poured the drinks and sat back comfortably in his chair with a fresh Gitane.

"How many languages do you speak?" Joe asked softly in English.

"Seven," Dimitry said, flicking the ash from his cigarette, "eight, actually, if you count Russian."

Several doors away down the street, a merchant rolled up the metal shutters of his tourist shop. A taxi sped by, leaving a trail of greasy smoke. Tangier's siesta was coming to an end.

"Ali! Ali!" Zorah called. "There's a *man* here. Come here right away!"

True to form, Zorah was standing half hidden in the doorway to the terrace, a kitchen towel held across her face as a makeshift veil. Ali shook his head. City women were more superstitious than country women, who worked side by side with their men in the fields and soon learned to forget this veiling nonsense. The holy Koran enjoined women to be modest, but there was nothing said in the book about veils. He'd seen hundreds of blatant whores flashing their eyes lasciviously from behind their transparent veils. This trip to the village had done him good. He had seen that he must take Zorah in hand and make a real wife out of her.

"Ali, Ali!" she called.

"God's mercy, woman!" he yelled. "I'm not deaf yet. God still graces me with good hearing. What is all this noise about?"

"There's a man at the gate. He wants to come in."

Ali straightened his turban and hitched up his trousers. He rounded the bottom of the terrace and went to the gate. A deliveryman in dirty white coveralls was leaning against the stone gatepost, looking bored and sleepy. A crumpled paper dangled from his hand. Just behind him on the edge of the paved lane, a three-wheeled delivery scooter was parked.

"Salem al-likuum," Ali said cheerfully. "How can I help you, brother?"

"Yah," the man said sullenly in response to Ali's formal greeting. "Is this the house of the Englishman, Clinton?" He quinted down at the paper.

"M'sieu is not English," Ali said proudly. "He is an American."

"English, American," the man said coldly, "what's the difference? Is his name Clinton?"

Ali nodded, with reciprocal coldness. *"Aiwah,"* he said. "This is Monsieur Clinton's house. Why do you ask?"

"I ask, old man, because I've been driving all over this dog's nest of a mountain for hours trying to find it. I have some new gas *bonbons* for this house." He nodded back over his shoulder toward the scooter. Ali could see the yellow tops of two propane gas bottles over the edge of the scooter's rusty carrying box.

"The Monsieur is not here," he said. "He had to go into the city in his car."

"That doesn't matter," the man said, "all I know is that he's been telephoning the store for days, asking for new *bonbons,* and that Jew-whore of a secretary has been tormenting me to get them up here. It seems that the water heater hasn't been working properly; there wasn't enough pressure. The *patron* had to order some new kind of *bonbons* from Casa. They came today." He flourished the paper. "They came by special truck. He must be rich, your Monsieur."

Ali frowned. *M'sieu* had said nothing about new gas bottles.

"You can help me carry them," the man said. "They are joined together with the new regulator. It's difficult for one man to carry, and I'll not break my guts so that some *nesrani* can have a hot bath."

Together they manhandled the squat, clumsy cylinders from the scooter and through the gate.

"Allah," the old gardener said, panting. "These must be forty kilos each. They're much heavier than the old ones."

"Where do they go?" the man grunted.

Ali indicated the small wooden door at the base of the terrace wall. They struggled through the door and into the low-ceilinged storeroom. Up against the damp concrete wall stood the two normal gas bottles, their copper connecting tubes snaking up through a hole in the ceiling to reach the kitchen and bathroom.

"I'll get my tools and change the hoses," the man said, breathing hard, sweat running down his face.

"Would you like some cold buttermilk?" Ali asked. "We have spring water, too. It's cold, from the electric refrigerator."

"You don't have any wine, do you?" the man asked, tugging at his moustache. "I would sell my first son as a dancing boy for a glass of wine."

Ali nodded sadly. "I'll get you some." He watched the man swagger back out to the scooter for his tools. *It was typical of these Algerians,* Ali thought, shaking his head. *They curse the* ensara *who give them work, and then they refuse good Arab hospitality for a taste of* nasrani *wine.* Al-lah, *they were an unpleasant people.*

31

The Farm

Joe was whistling, slightly drunk from the Pernod. He drove fast, but casually, on the asphalt road leading toward the Tangier airport. On either side of the narrow highway, the fields were sere-brown, sun-baked with forlorn clumps of wheat stubble among the clods. He flicked on his parking lights in the rising gloom of the evening. Behind him, the driver of the brown pickup truck also switched on his lights.

Dimitry sat slouched against the passenger door. He held up the telegram to the dying light. "That's not bad, actually," he said, tapping the telegram form.

"Hmmm?" Joe asked.

Dimitry lowered the volume of the crackling transistor that rested between them on the seat.

"I mean the garbles in the telegram," he said. "Voight's got a nice flair for details. The telegram wasn't sent from France, of course. It was probably printed right out there in the back room of the post office. But he put in a couple of transmission garbles so that it would look authentic. That's not bad."

"We turn up here by the crossroads," Joe said. He couldn't have cared less about the fine points of Colonel Voight's professional technique. "Should I signal for the turn?"

"Sure," Dimitry said. "Why not?"

He seemed a little drunk, as well. Joe wondered if it was just an act or if the four glasses of Pernod at the café had actually penetrated Dimitry's shell.

They made the left turn and continued on, without speaking, past a stand of dusty eucalyptus trees. A shepherd boy in a ragged jellaba waved his stick cheerfully at them, and Dimitry waved back, calling out a greeting in Arabic. Ahead of them on the flat horizon, they could see the airport beacon guiding in the late-afternoon flight from Gibraltar.

Dimitry lit another Gitane. "He didn't say where they were going to try to play back those tapes, did he?"

Joe snapped back from his thoughts of tide and wind. "No, he didn't say anything about that. All I know is that they're gone—the tapes and all the gear they set up in the garage."

"He probably sent them over to the base in Rota," Dimitry mused. "But, then again, he might have sent them straight back to Langley. I don't think that the C.I.A. boys are too close to the naval intelligence people. That's better, actually. They'll have to build a computer unit to run the tapes through. That'll take them a while. I'd like to see their faces when they find out the tapes are useless."

He laughed out aloud. "You know, Joe," he continued, "this has actually been a lot of fun. It's like a well-played game of chess. Do you play chess yourself?"

"No," Joe said. "My wife used to play, but I could never get into it. I guess you have to have more patience than I have."

"You should try it sometime. It's the best mental exercise I know."

Joe slowed the car and signaled for another turn. Ahead of them to the right, they could see the half-ruined concrete sheds of the abandoned chicken farm. Two Moroccan gendarmes, looking sinister in their leather helmets and jackets, had parked their motorcycles on the road a hundred yards past the faint track of the turn-off leading to the farm buildings. A Volkswagen with Madrid license plates was stopped at the low barrier while the two officers examined the driver's papers.

"I'll drive out through their *contrôle* when I leave," Dimitry said, smiling. "I'd like to get a good look at those two flunkies."

The Land Rover jolted up over the dried mud of the track and crawled ahead in first gear toward the sheds.

"I hope that truck's got good springs," Joe said. "The buoy weighs a hell of a lot, you know."

"I know it does," Dimitry said coldly. "That truck's been modified to carry about two thousand kilos."

"Where should I park?"

Dimitry squinted at the telegram in the light of the dashboard instrumentts. "It says the last shed, so that must mean the one on the end. Park there. Turn around so that your headlights can shine in through the door."

Joe followed Dimitry's instructions. It was still not quite dark. The long summer dusk seemed to hang in the sky without any sign of fading into night. There was a scraping of tires beside them. The Citroën truck squealed to a stop next to the shed, and the old Tartar, dressed in oversized mechanic's coveralls, got out and walked around to open the rear door. Joe saw the curly-haired man with glasses emerge from the back of the truck. Dimitry lit another cigarette.

"Wait here," he said to Joe. "When I wave to you, turn the headlights on the high beams. When I wave again, turn them off."

The three Russians filed into the shed through the empty doorframe. Joe could see the beam of a powerful flashlight slice among the rubble and old straw on the floor and come to rest on a heap of crumbled masonry. A cloud of pink dust rose in the flashlight's beam as the Tartar bent to tug at a canvas tarpaulin buried beneath the pile of broken plaster and tiles. Dimitry waved to Joe, and he flicked his headlights onto the high beams. The three Russians were working together now, pulling away the rubble and exposing more of the canvas until the unmistakable shape of the tarpaulin-wrapped tube could be seen.

It was dirty, back-breaking work. The Tartar was taken by a sneezing fit from the dust and had to come outside briefly to get some fresh air. Using a broken shovel he had found on the floor, the curly-haired engineer cleared away the rest of the debris around the buoy and then bent to unwrap the canvas. The Tartar was making trips back and forth from the truck to the shed, carrying armloads of tools and equipment. Joe saw the tubular pipe sections of a portable mechanic's hoist go past on one trip and a heavy chain lift on another.

From inside the garage, Dimitry waved again and Joe killed the lights. The engineer was working now with a flashlight as he knelt to unbolt one of the inspection panels. Once the panel was off, he bent even lower to peer inside the buoy, shining his light slowly back and forth. After a moment he looked up at Dimitry and nodded. Dimitry walked back out to the Land Rover.

He leaned in through the open window and turned on the transistor radio lying on the seat. "Another nice little detail," he said to Joe. "The colonel went to all the trouble of soaking the canvas in sea water so that there'd be a coating of salt on the buoy. Not bad. He's better than I gave him credit for. If he hadn't screwed up with that navy plane and the house painters, he might have gotten away with it."

Dimitry opened the door and swung into the car. He turned up the volume of the radio. "Here," he said, "have a little of this." He took a pull on a flat bottle of clear liquid and handed it over to Joe. "Vodka. You look like you could use some. Not still feeling nervous, are you?" Dimitry laughed. "Who's going to come along and catch us, Joe? Those two security stooges out there are *guarding* us. There are probably guys hidden in the bushes across the road, as well. We're well protected. The last thing in the world the colonel would want would be for me to get nervous and take off without the buoy."

Joe sighed. "Yeah," he admitted, "I guess you're right." Inside the shed the engineer and the Tartar were rigging the tripods of the chain lift.

Joe took another swallow of the vodka.

"Finish it up, Joe," Dimitry said. "It will calm your nerves."

Joe shook his head, handing the bottle back. "I've got to drive this car back. I'll have a drink when I get home."

"Okay, suit yourself. . . . Well, I guess you're free to go. We'll be out of here ourselves in about five minutes."

They were silent for a moment, watching the moving flashlight inside the shed. "You haven't told me about tonight, yet," Joe said, breaking the uneasy silence.

"I know that," Dimitry answered. "Why should I have given away anything more than I had to until I knew that the buoy would actually be here? Okay, listen carefully. I don't want any slip-ups."

"I'm listening," Joe said.

"You leave your house at a quarter to nine, just like they told you to. Drive down to the cinema and park your car in the lot up the street where the buses park when they bring tourists to the Koutoubia Palace to see the belly dancers. Don't worry. There'll be a parking place for you at the back of the lot. When you get out of the car, use this door." He patted the doorframe on the passenger's side. "It'll be dark on that side. There'll be a tour bus with its motor running next to you. You get in the rear door and lie down on the floor. The bus'll pull out of the lot as soon as you're inside. The whole thing will take about thirty seconds. If they're watching for you in front of the cinema, they'll never notice."

"Where will the bus take me?" Joe asked. His voice sounded lost and afraid.

Dimitry smiled. "You're lucky, Joe," he said. "The timing couldn't be better. There's an East German liner in port. It sails tonight at midnight, when the passengers get back from their tour. The bus will drive right down to the port to pick up a load of ship's officers. On the pier you get out and walk up the crew's gangplank. You'll be met inside and shown to your cabin. How does that sound?"

Make it convincing. Think of some question. He's still testing me, probing.

"What if somebody asks for my passport? I haven't got one."

"You won't need one. I've planned the whole thing. You'd better be on your way now." Dimitry held out his hand and Joe shook it with a sensation of dream-like unreality creeping over him.

"I'll see you in a couple of weeks, when the ship docks. Have a good time on board. I'm sure you will. I understand that there are a couple of French-speaking stewardesses . . . and those German girls are really hot stuff, believe me." The dry hand squeezed Joe's once more and then Dimitry turned away. Inside the shed Joe could see the buoy rising in the half light as the old Tartar heaved on the unseen chain lift.

He started the car's engine, shifted into reverse, and

began backing away from the farm shed when Dimitry waved and called out. Joe killed the engine and waited, the tension snapping through his gut while Dimitry ambled slowly over to the driver's side window. Dimitry looked at Joe steadily while he spoke. "It slipped my mind with all these other details this afternoon, Joe," he said. "I got a cable from our consulate general in Rio this morning."

"Rio?" Joe whispered, his voice an irritating squeak.

"Yes," Dimitry said, "Rio de Janeiro. My friends there report that your son—Joey, you call him, don't you?—is a very good student. He goes to the French *école primaire* now. He takes a school bus every morning and comes home late each afternoon with a big leather satchel of books. It's a shame the way the French work these little children in school, isn't it?"

"What the hell are you talking about?" Joe asked, blind rage choking him.

"Your *son,* Joe, your one living child—that's what I'm talking about. I'd like you to remember little Joey on your way to that parking lot tonight. I'd like you to keep him in mind as you drive back to your house. Do you get my meaning?"

"Yes," Joe heard himself saying, "yes, I get your meaning. Christ, Dimitry, I haven't done anything to screw you up. Honest to God, I haven't, I . . ."

"Not *yet,* you haven't," Dimitry interrupted. "Let's just keep it that way, shall we?"

Colonel Voight sat in an easy chair next to the open window of his hotel room. He sipped his coffee and stared down through the open curtains at the candles on the poolside tables. On a nightstand beside his chair were a telephone and a note pad and pencil. A numbered list had been carefully printed on the pad in block letters. Items one and two—"post office" and "farm"—had been crossed out. Items three, four, and five were "route back," "*baccal,*" and "villa."

The telephone rang.

"Señor Anderson?" a voice asked.

"*Sí?*" Colonel Voight said.

"Doctor Rodriguez asked me to tell you that his nurse

has left the hospital for the office and that he will be leaving shortly himself."

"*Muy bien,*" Colonel Voight said. "*Muchas gracias.*"

He hung up the phone and bent over the pad. With a precise stroke of the pencil, he crossed out the words "route back." Then he settled in his chair and proceeded slowly to fill his pipe.

32

Baccal

Joe was at the stage of intoxication in which his thoughts were bounding away rapidly in strange directions, but his physical reflexes were still nearly normal. He let one part of his mind concentrate on driving the Land Rover down the long incline from the city into the valley below the mountain. With the rest of his brain, he tried to plan out his actions for the hours, days, and months ahead.

It was almost ended, the whole crazy business. In a few minutes Joe would find a way to convince George to put on the green sportcoat and the ridiculous straw hat and drive the Land Rover the rest of the way down to his house. That was easy. George had already agreed to intercede with Ali and Zorah. The actual escape would be easy, as well, down through George's garden and over the wall to the high grass field surrounding the unfinished villa of that Moroccan businessman who had gone bankrupt. It would be full night in a few minutes and no one would see him moving down the goat path, which cut diagonally from the field to join the paved lane just behind the shabby Camping Hotel, facing the Dradeb. There was a café across from the hotel where one could always find a taxi driver relaxing over tea and a pipe of kef. In less than half an hour he would be aboard *Dragonfly*.

There were only two routes to Joe's house by car, but there were dozens of ways on and off the mountain for a person on *foot*, something the colonel had not considered. The suburb was a warren of cane windbreaks, stone walls, and a hodgepodge of European villas interspersed with small Moroccan truck farms. Beneath the gaudy sportcoat, Joe wore a dark shirt and navy-blue slacks. Once he left George's garden, they would never find him.

And then? Then he would have a hell of a long boat ride on his hands. If he were reasonably lucky, the engine would get him nicely out of the Straits and into the long open swell of the Atlantic, out of sight of the Moroccan coast, before dawn. There would be a lot of work to do that night, and Joe now regretted the Pernod and the vodka. But he could make coffee once he was under way, and there was some Benzedrine in the medical kit if he really needed it. By this time tomorrow night he would be in the current and on his way south.

Joe signaled for a left turn and slowed the car. Ahead of him was a T-shaped intersection, the right-hand fork cutting up to the old mountain, the left to the new mountain. He turned left.

He felt reasonably confident that he would be ashore someplace in West Africa before the end of August and that, with luck, he would be back in Europe on a false passport sometime in September. But, then, what? He'd be broke, a fugitive wanted by the two most powerful intelligence services in the world. With a sudden, sagging feeling inside his chest, he saw that the long boat ride south was only a temporary respite. If they wanted to find him—and they most certainly would give the task top priority—then it would be a matter of weeks or months, at most, before they caught him.

The car slowed to less than ten miles an hour, the motor chugging hard against the steep incline. Joe shifted down into first gear. *Shit*, he thought, *all of this planning will be meaningless. They'll get me in the end. They have to get me. I know too much. They have to make sure that nobody else finds out my secrets, that no word is leaked to inquisitive reporters, that* Time *and* Newsweek *don't have a field day with the story.*

It was then that the idea struck him. Of course! It was so obvious. Once the story was out—once every lousy detail of Colonel Voight's threats and duplicity and Dimitry's elaborate double cross had become public scandal, editorialized to death and kicked around on television news shows, meat for congressional investigations and distorted, variously, by the left- and right-wing press—once that had all happened, then Joe would be free again, purged of any secrets that could make him valuable to the C.I.A. and K.G.B. They would be furious, obviously, but he would have become too hot to touch. It was so easy. All he had to do was tell his story, to tell it honestly, without whitewashing his own weaknesses and sordid role in the affair. That was one thing he was well equipped to do, to tell the story. He was a professional journalist, or at least he had been one before this rotten business had taken hold of him. He would pull himself together and tell the story the way it had really happened, naming names, dates, and places.

It would ruin them, of course—Dimitry, the colonel, Rawlings, Larry, and Roy. There would be denials and counter-accusations and smokescreens to brand him a drunken, has-been paranoid. He needed proof before any decent paper or magazine, even something like *Ramparts*, would touch the story. But he had proof. There actually was sixty thousand dollars in that Swiss bank account. The money would remain there until he personally ordered it transferred. Dimitry had been quite emphatic about that. Even the K.G.B. couldn't find a way around the rigid Swiss banking laws. Dimitry's plan, of course, had been to get Joe to transfer the money back into Eastern Europe once he was safely on their payroll. But until he did, it would remain safe in that numbered account, proof that his whole fantastic story was not just a pipe dream.

It would take a while to write the story. And he would need a secure and quiet place to do it. He would need "protection," not the false security offered by the colonel or Dimitry, but real cover. He must make contact with somebody powerful, some respected columnist with an ax to grind, or perhaps a senator or congressman who could pick up the story and run with it to his own political advantage.

He slowed the car again, just before the somber walls of the abandoned palace of that quisling sultan whom the French had installed before independence. He lit a cigarette, his fingers shaking. There would be more than enough time to work out the details when he was safely aboard the boat. Now he must concentrate on getting himself out of Tangier.

Again the Land Rover engine chugged, violently. Joe raised his left foot to engage the clutch before shifting to a lower gear. His leg remained posed, his right foot weightless on the accelerator. The motor whined loudly and died. He sat numbly in the driver's seat, staring ahead into the cone of yellow light cast by the headlights. *Joey*, he thought with coldness slicing through the alcoholic shield, *they will catch little Joey and kill him on his way home from school.*

The cigarette burned into his knuckle and he dropped it reflexively to the floor. He sat a long time staring out into the night. Then he swallowed hard and started the car motor again. His mind had played a strange trick on him, he suddenly realized. He had to watch himself more closely. A moment before, he had let the car stall and had wasted an indeterminate number of important minutes staring out through the windshield like an idiot. He shook his head sharply back and forth. Something had scared him badly a minute before, but now he could no longer remember what the fear had been.

The blue-painted wall of the *baccal* general store showed up in the wash of his headlights. He parked directly in front of the store and went in, carrying his camera case. The interior was lit by a flaring acetylene torch that cast stark shadows against the rows of canned goods, boxes, and bottles. The bent old Soussi grocer looked up from his account book and greeted him with a nervous smile. The man's son stared straight ahead, his blind eyes emotionless as Joe asked for a copy of the *Petit Marocain* and a fresh pack of Winstons.

The grocer dug beneath the counter and rose with the paper and cigarettes. *"Des allumettes, aussi, M'sieu?"* he asked, holding up a package of matches.

Well, Joe thought, *that's not a bad idea. They may not have packed enough matches with the boat's provisions. And batteries, Christ, I'll need flashlight batteries for the radio.*

If the Soussi was surprised by Joe's purchase of twelve flashlight batteries and two ten-pack cartons of matches, he showed no trace of astonishment. He accepted Joe's hundred-*dirham* note and made change with mincing, Oriental politeness. The matches and batteries took careful packing to fit into the camera case, but after several minutes' concentrated effort, Joe hoisted the now-heavy case and said a polite *"Bonsoir, M'sieu"* to the Susian.

Outside, the waning moon was just visible over the foothills of the Rif. The white minaret of the mosque on the Place du Khaddi appeared to glow against the blue of the evening. He could smell jasmine somewhere close by, jasmine and cooking smoke from some farmer's evening fire, and there were goat bells tinkling pleasantly in the darkness.

He laid the camera case on the floor, below the front seat, and started the engine. Now the tricky part was coming, and he had to keep his wits about him. Using his low-beam lights, he swung the car into the steep and narrow lane, went past the *baccal* and rolled down between the rustling cane fences that overhung the road and brushed against the luggage rack on the Land Rover's roof. He caught himself biting his lip and clenching his fingers, bloodless white, on the steering wheel. *This won't do, this sure as hell will not do.* Forcing his muscles to relax, he took deep breaths and tried to clear his mind of all conscious thought. The lane seemed to twist and dip interminably. Finally, he turned the sharp corner between two whitewashed garages and saw George's villa. He pulled up and parked at a right angle to the rear of George's sports car.

He was halfway through the gate when he remembered his camera case, still inside the Land Rover. Cursing silently, he dashed to the car for it, but he forced himself to walk back through the gate at a normal pace.

"Up here, Joe," George called down softly from the terrace.

"Hi," Joe said, slapping George lightly on the shoulder. "How are you doing?"

"How are *you* doing?" George asked. He had a Scotch-and-water already mixed. Joe took it gratefully. From the melted ice cubes, Joe guessed that George had been a long time waiting for him.

This is the last lie. Make it good. Relax.

"I'm okay," Joe said, letting the whisky soak into his

fluttering stomach. "Everything went off perfectly. Are you ready to go down there now?" Joe nodded toward his own house, below them on the mountain.

George seemed hesitant. Finally he answered. "It won't just be Ali and Zorah I'll have to talk to, Joe," he said.

Joe felt his gut contract sharply. "What do you mean?"

"Take a look," George said, holding out his pair of binoculars. Joe took the glasses and turned the focusing knob. On the wall of his terrace was a lamp that cast a semicircle of yellow light. He could see Renée sitting on a patio chair, and Tommy and little Mohammed were at her feet, playing with a model airplane. Renée had a drink and a cigarette and appeared through the glasses to be calmly awaiting Joe's return. Her dark hair was brushed back neatly, and she wore a fresh-looking sundress.

"She called me about an hour ago from her house," George said. "She said she'd just picked up Tommy from the Algeciras car ferry and was trying to find you. I tried to discourage her, Joe, but she insisted on coming up here to wait."

"Shit," Joe muttered. He looked at his watch. It was almost seven-forty. "George, please come inside a second."

They went through the French doors into the living room.

Just get rid of her. Have George send her home.

"No," Joe said, "leave the lights off. I want you to help me. Take this coat and hat." He handed them over to George, who stood holding them with a quizzical smile on his face. "This is serious," Joe said coldly. "I want you to put them on and take my car down there. Park it where I always do. Tell Renée to leave. Tell her I'll see her at her place at about nine o'clock. Tell her that I'm still downtown on the documentary film business." George frowned. "She'll understand," Joe added. "When they've gone, you can take Ali aside and give him the money. When you finish, leave the coat and hat inside and come back up here on the garden path. Have you got all that?"

George stood still, holding the sportcoat and hat. "Are

you sure all this is okay with the colonel's plan?" he asked.

"It is, George," Joe said, thinking quickly again. "Listen, I'll explain it all when you're back up here, but let's not waste time now. The Russians probably have people watching the house. They have to see that I came back home. Believe me, there are reasons why I don't want to face Renée or Ali right now. Go on, now. It'll only take you five minutes." George hadn't moved yet. "Go on, George. Please, don't let me down now. I was counting on you."

"If you're sure that it's okay," George said, slipping into the coat.

"I promise you it's okay," Joe said, taking George's elbow to guide him to the door. "I'll be here when you get back. Just try not to waste any time."

The sportcoat was short in the sleeves, and the straw hat looked schoolboyish on George. But his face was tensely apprehensive, belying any comical appearance produced by the clothes. "Okay," he said, "I'll be back up in a couple of minutes."

33

Control

Colonel Voight replaced the telephone receiver. With his pencil he cut a sharp line through item number four on his list, *"baccal."*

"Sorry, Larry," he said, looking up over the smoking bowl of his pipe. "What were you saying?"

"That I checked out that phone call; I listened to the tape myself down at Major Ben Abdesalam's office. It sounded straight to me. Ben Abdesalam said it was solid, too. The maid called at about nine-thirty to ask for two propane-gas bottles to be sent up. She chattered away in Arabic with the clerk like she knew the guy, talked about her trip to the mountains, the works. She was on the line for over three minutes.

"But then," Larry continued, "I got to thinking. I ran that last house tape of the maid, Zorah, talking to her husband and compared it with the phone tape. My Arabic's zilch, so I called Ben Abdesalam back, and had him listen. Well, Colonel, I hate to say this, but whoever called for those gas bottles wasn't Clinton's maid. The major said it was Tangier Arab dialect, and a good voice imitation, but it was definitely not the same woman on the two tapes. Dimitry must have gotten a branch trunk on Clinton's line. . . ."

"And what time were the gas bottles actually delivered?" the colonel asked. There were sparks coming now from his pipe.

"Four-thirty-three," Larry said softly, glancing down at his note pad.

"Four-thirty-three," the colonel said coldly. "And it is now seven-thirty-eight, and this is the first I hear about it? Correct me if I'm wrong, Larry, but am I, or am I not, 'control' on this operation?"

"I'm sorry," Larry mumbled. "I didn't get the report myself until after six. The Moroccan plainclothes guy didn't tell Ben Abdesalam until he came off duty."

"We should have stopped him at the *baccal,*" the colonel said flatly.

"Do you actually think it was Dimitry?"

The colonel was silent. He rose and paced to the bathroom door. Turning sharply, his hands tightly clenched behind his back, he strode to the open bedroom window and stared down at the tables on the pool terrace. "Christ, I hate these sloppy foul-ups when something's all wrapped up."

Larry looked at his watch. "He should be in the house by now," he said quickly. "We could call him and have him clear the hell out of there."

"And show our hand to every spotter Dimitry's got covering the house and the phone? No, it's too late for that now."

"We could get somebody up through the garden to warn him," Larry said, "somebody he knows. I could call Bill or Roy. They could get in there without being spotted."

"Maybe you didn't hear me correctly," the colonel said with sudden harshness. "I said that it was *too* late. He's on his own up there. We will make absolutely no attempt to contact him until he sits down tonight inside that movie theater. Do you understand what I'm saying?"

"But, Colonel," Larry protested, "those propane bottles . . . Jesus, that's one of their standard techniques. Dimitry'll have had his boys mix enough real propane and naphtha and kerosene in with the *plastique* to burn off any traces of deliberate explosion that the gendarme lab people could pick up for court evidence. We've got to do *something*. The gardener and his wife and kid are there; it's not just Clinton."

The colonel spun sharply to face Larry. "You'd better check into Medical when we get back, Larry," he said coldly. "Your so-called perfect hearing seems to be giving you trouble—either that, or you've developed a new habit of ignoring direct orders. But that's not like you, son. It must be your hearing. I'd hate to have to write a case report mentioning obvious insubordination on the part of a T.S.D. technician to his case officer. Once more, for the record, Larry—we don't go near Clinton until he's inside the Cinema Goya. Is that clearly understood?"

"Yes, sir," Larry said. "Yeah, I understand."

34

Payment of Salvage

Joe heard the Land Rover back away from the house and drive down the lane. He turned off the light on George's terrace. Shouldering his camera case, he slipped down off the steps and trotted across the garden.

The garden wall was still sun-warm to the touch. He hoisted himself easily onto the wall and sat for a moment, straddling the wall. From his perch, Joe could easily see the terrace of his own house, less than fifty yards away. It was stupid to sit there, silhouetted against the afterglow of the sunset so that anyone watching his house could see him. But he remained there on the top, breathing heavily, watching Renée and the two children. She was a good woman, solid and dependable, and she loved him. She loved him and trusted him, and now he was running out on her, like he had run out on everything before. He could smell the black tobacco of Dimitry's Gitanes and the sweetness of the whisky on his breath. He had to calm down. He would just sit there a moment and get his wind back. There was plenty of time. He must try to relax now before going on.

He saw George, tall and gawky in the stupid hat and sportcoat, taking the terrace stairs two at a time. Renée rose to greet him. They talked briefly, Renée reaching up to smooth her hair as she always did when she was confused or nervous.

Jesus, Joe thought, *I love her, too. And George, he's my friend. He's down there now where I should be. He'll come back up to the house and I'll be gone. I'll have run out on him. What a rotten business this all is, what a rotten, fucking business. I may never see them again. I may damned well never have a chance to explain.*

Renée was gathering up her handbag and sweater, bending down to speak to Tommy. The boy rose hesitantly, whining, tired from his long day of traveling. And there was Ali, with his baggy old army trousers. He had cut a bunch of roses to give Renée. He always gave her flowers. One of these days he would have to go down to her Casbah house to get those window boxes started. Joe had promised to send him down with some flower cuttings and fertilizer after the first rains. He had promised. There were many people he had *promised.*

The bomb exploded as Joe was drawing his left leg up to the flat top of the garden wall. The shock wave of super-heated air crossed the fifty yards that separated the terrace and the wall in less than a second. It was this shock wave that saved his life, sending him ahead of the cloud of glass and razor-sharp fragments. He was gone, backward, legs above him, screaming in the darkness, the image of that incandescent flash and the blast of burning air forcing aside all thought or comprehension. He lay in a crumpled ball in the brown grass. He lay there for what seemed a long time, feeling the blood flow, hot and salty, from his nose, as the big hunks of stone and brick fell heavily into the dark field around him. Something hard smashed into his legs. He sat up, howling in pain and fear. The night was suddenly brown, dusty-tan from the tons of pulverized stone and masonry. From across the valley the echo of the blast rolled back like summer thunder.

Joe got to his feet. His left shoe and sock were gone, ripped cleanly away by the shock wave. Stumbling through the dust cloud, he hit into the wall. There was a fire inside the shell that had been his house. Squinting against the dust, he could see that only three solid stone walls remained of what had been a two-story villa. The roofs were gone. He was staring at a broken-toothed volcanic ruin, a frame from a newsreel of the London Blitz.

He began to run. Twice he stumbled on shattered hunks of brick and stone. He fell headlong into the darkness. Then he was up again, running hard. Squirming out through a thorn hedge at the bottom of the field, he continued to run down the darkened lane. The street-lights were out; so were the electric lights in the villas on either side of the lane. Shards of broken window glass glittered in the light of some kerosene lanterns. Other people were running in the dust cloud. They swept past, panting and coughing up the hill toward the site of the blast.

Then he was out of the dust. He slowed to a lopsided walk. His dark shirt was tan with dust and dotted with spattered blood. He stopped. It was all wrong! He had forgotten his camera bag and the batteries. He had only one shoe. It was all wrong! From across the valley he could hear the clanging of the fire trucks. He sat down.

Joe got to his feet again. He had to get away. To his right was the gate of a European-style villa. A small twig fire burned at the gatepost. There was a bicycle and a threadbare jellaba folded as a backrest against the gate. The night watchman must have been one of the dark forms he had seen running past him in the dust. Without hesitating, he pulled on the sour-smelling jellaba and, hoisting the skirts, climbed onto the bicycle. At the bottom of the lane, where it intersected with the old mountain road, there was a communal water tap. He stopped there to wash the blood from his hands and face. He mounted the bicycle again, with the musty hood of the jellaba over his head. As he coasted down the slope of the mountain road, he could hear the sirens climbing above him. The fire engine had taken the other turn and was now bottlenecked in the narrow lanes below the Place du Khaddi. Above and to his right, half the mountain was in darkness. He could clearly see the dome of tan dust, illuminated by the flames at its core. He crossed the valley and began pumping hard up the opposite slope into the city.

Joe's hand went up again to his face. He forced it away. He must not pick at the cotton plug in his left nostril or the bleeding would begin again. His right hand moved back down to join his left on the varnished tiller. The boat was sailing well on this tack, with Genoa filled and the mainsail taut and white above his head in the weak moonlight. Another half an hour and he could come about. Then he would start the engine and force his way west against the current under mainsail and power until he was well clear of the Straits and into the Atlantic.

Behind him and to the right, Tangier cast a city glow bright enough to wash out the moonlight. Joe released the tiller and felt the bow swing to windward. Reaching behind him, he eased the mainsheet until the boat was steering itself, riding nicely on the starboard tack, up and down the swell. If the wind increased there would be a real chop, wind across tide and current. But now he was all right. Holding the whisky bottle between his knees, he unscrewed the cap and threw it over the side into the hissing wash.

The bastards, he thought. But his thought lacked any conviction. He was tired. He was exhausted by it all, and he could not find the energy for real anger. "Look at it," he said aloud. "Go on, *look* at it."

Turning slowly on the cockpit bench, he glanced back at the city, his eyes automatically searching out the darkened half of the mountain. Like faraway rubies twinkling in the moonlight, he saw the red lights of the police cars and fire trucks. The flames were gone and the dust cloud had dissipated. He was hungry, the whisky burning unpleasantly in his gut. He took another hard pull from the bottle. In a minute he would go down below for a sweater. The boat rose and glided back down the swell. It was a good, passage-making tack. He would keep on it for a while. He watched the Tarifa lighthouse for a moment. There were some fishing boats across the way on the Spanish coast. In a minute he would get out the flashlight and the chart of the Straits. There was a current running and he'd better get some bearings. At least the log was working. That was something. It would help him to judge the speed of the current.

What he ought to do was go down below and heat up some coffee and a pot of soup before the wind got up and it became too rough to cook.

He laughed suddenly, remembering the face of that skinny customs guard at the port entrance. The jellaba and the one shoe had really freaked him out. But the handful of ten-*dirham* bills and the drunken banter of an

English yachtsman had snowed the poor bastard. *He must have seen even stranger types than me with this regatta going on . . . and those fucking frogs with their blackboards and diagrams and slides, of course. The whole clubhouse had been packed. You'd think they were planning a Murmansk convoy instead of a three-day yacht regatta.*

"What a lucky son-of-a-bitch I am," he said.

He tried to laugh again, but his lips continued curling, beyond a smile to a wail, an open-mouthed howl.

"You, *bastards* . . . you fucking bastards."

Warm tears ran down his face, falling in heavy drops on the varnished wood. He tried to scream again. But what he felt, clenching hot in his chest and throat, was far beyond anger or outrage. He was sobbing, a rhythmic, uncontrolled spasm coming from his groin to his throat.

They're dead, they're all dead.

Salty tears continued to fall on his hands and on the whisky bottle. The boat rose and dropped with the swell. The spasms of pain and grief subsided slowly. When he looked up again, the moon was brighter, the city glow of Tangier less distinct.

He rose, steadying himself on the boom. Behind him in the Straits, he saw the running lights of a big ship. Squinting, he could distinguish a red and a green and one very bright masthead light.

"Tanker," he said. "Big bastard, too."

Both a red and a green. . . . That means bow on. If that bearing holds steady, the tanker is on a collision course. But it's back there, east of the cape.

Is it? . . . Sure.

He's westbound. The westbound lane's all the way over on the Spanish side. I can't start panicking every time I see a ship.

Joe swung down into the cabin and groped for the overhead light. The tanker was coming up fast, still red and green, bow on.

What's he doing, changing lanes, for Christ's sake? No, don't panic. He's westbound for the Atlantic. He's actually north of me. Angles just look weird at night.

Joe looked around him. He had come down here for some reason, but he couldn't remember it. Coffee . . .

he would make some coffee now and fill the Thermos. It was going to be a long night. He swallowed some more whisky and rested the bottle in the galley sink. The amber liquid sloshed with the roll of the boat.

Westbound ships do take the northern lane, don't they? Or is it the other way around?

Joe stood braced against the swell, staring stupidly at the cabin floorboards. He shouldn't leave the whisky bottle open, not with the boat rolling so much.

What's that noise? . . . It sounds like a drum, a drum thumping in the water.

There was plenty of time to check the chart. Now he must close the whisky bottle and make some coffee.

But he could not remember where he had put the cap. And it was hard to think with that twanging sound coming through the water . . . an odd sound, like a kettle drum.

—Lindos,
February, 1977